P9-DCL-828

## More praise for *Strange Fire*

"A smart, crisp, political page-turner . . . this book is a stunner."

—*Booklist*, Editors' Choice 2001

"A master of the sardonic, Bukiet plays the story for both political intrigue and guilty laughter, like the black humorists he admires: Joseph Heller and Thomas Pynchon, and he has a better ear for the punch line than either."

—*Buffalo News*

"Witty, engrossing."

—*Publishers Weekly*

"Bukiet's imagination is extraordinary and he brings it to every part of this novel."

—*Baltimore Sun*

"A fantastic trip through the subterranean fields of Israeli paranoia. . . . Bukiet's bold, mocking shtick and antic imagination nail the read till the last page."

—*The Forward*

"Bukiet's prose is, in fact, so beautiful that it often overshadows the complicated plot of international intrigue. . . . And for all of the suspense, the politics and the darkness lurking in the eaves, the wisdom of this novel comes from the fact that our (lame, blind, jaded, earless) guide is endowed with such wit, intelligence and humanity."

—*Salon*

"*Strange Fire* generates a continuous sense of suspense, particularly through its unpredictable twists . . . a fast and exciting read."

—*Hadassah*

ALSO BY MELVIN JULES BUKIET

*Signs and Wonders*

*After*

*While the Messiah Tarries*

*Stories of an Imaginary Childhood*

*Sandman's Dust*

*Nothing Makes You Free: Writings by Descendants of Jewish Holocaust Survivors* (Editor)

*Neurotica: Jewish Writers on Sex* (Editor)

# STRANGE FIRE

*Melvin Jules Bukiet*

W · W · NORTON & COMPANY
NEW YORK · LONDON

Printed in the United States of America

First published as a Norton paperback 2002



The text of this book is composed in Filosofia Regular
with the display set in Filosofia Unicase
Composition by Alice Bennett Dates, A. W. Bennett, Inc.
Manufacturing by The Haddon Craftsmen, Inc.
Book design by Rubina Yeh
Title page photo: Gary Powell/Photonica
Production manager: Andrew Marasia

Library of Congress Cataloging-in-Publication Data

Bukiet, Melvin Jules.
Strange fire / Melvin Jules Bukiet.
p. cm.
ISBN 0-393-04938-8
1. Attempted assassination—Fiction. 2. Russians—Israel—Fiction. 3. Speechwriters—Fiction. 4. Gay men—Fiction. 5. Israel—Fiction. 6. Blind—Fiction. I. Title.
PS3552.U398 S77 2001
813'.54—dc21　　　　00-053306

**ISBN 0-393-32359-5 pbk.**

W. W. Norton & Company, Inc., 500 Fifth Avenue, New York, N.Y. 10110
www.wwnorton.com

W. W. Norton & Company Ltd., Castle House, 75/76 Wells Street, London W1T 3QT

1 2 3 4 5 6 7 8 9 0

TO JILL LAURIE GOODMAN

# STRANGE FIRE

# CHAPTER 1

Here's Simon in public: "Of course the Palestinians are people. Of course they have mothers and grandmothers whose food they love, whose kitchens they remember. Of course they want homes and schools . . ."

It's nicely composed if I do say so myself, the alliteration, the parallel structures, but it's Simon who puts it over. No other mouth, from Jerusalem to Tel Aviv, from Eilat to the Golan—or beyond, make no mistake, Simon's as comfortable in the U.N. as the Knesset—has the same potent bass that hardly requires a microphone to fill a fund-raising parlor or a vast public hall or a nation. In transit from the elaborate sequence of raised bumps on the scroll that emerges from my special Braille typewriter to the growling caress he imparts to them, the words are transformed. Now, rolling over the multitude, they convey a deep, humanitarian feeling of sorrowful regret at the pass we've come to. "Homes and schools," he repeats. "Homes and schools and hospitals. . . ." He takes the next step as if one component of civilized life after another is occurring to him as he speaks.

Is that a tear welling at the inside corner of Simon's eye? The glittering emerald orb can fix the object of its contemplation with any emotion he desires on a scale from compassionate understanding to enraged rectitude like a hammer fixes a nail. You can torque to the left or right, but there's no escape.

"Homes and schools and hospitals and police stations of their own," he echoes himself, moving inexorably to the conclusion that I alone, of all present here today, anticipate. Author! Author!

"Homes and schools and hospitals and police stations of their own . . ." Simon repeats the theme one last time, adds, "and . . ." and then concludes, "armies."

Even before that last word slams the cymbals loud enough to raise the dead, the meaning is clear.

Part of the trick is language. The man knows his syntax. Note that "the Palestinians" he commences with turns to "they" and in the motion from proper noun to pronoun two things occur. First, *we're* at a tinier remove once a name is withheld. No longer specific, *they* become a category, easier to displace or remove than a named entity.

And then, think, who are they? They're the ones *with* mothers and grandmothers. But in reality, some of them *are* mothers and grandmothers. *They* have sons and grandsons. But the only Palestinians Simon has evoked are youthful, rock-strong in short pants and T-shirts with violent slogans spray-painted across their scrawny chests, smelling of the smoke of burning rubber. Just imagine *them* in uniform.

Thus slyly in his most ostensibly humanistic speech of the year, delivered to a skeptical audience at Rabin Square—and ah, to hear him how Simon misses Yitzhak, the fond tales he tells about the "old soldier's" great courage and smoking habits—he's entirely disarmed the crowd and prepositionally rearmed them with the single word there was no need to mention: "but."

Simon's a genius.

I watch as well as I can. Simon is only a shadow to me. Yet in a more profound way, I perceive him more clearly than the rest of the audience. He appears full-bodied to them, even robust with his volleyball muscles and semi-public, semi-private sexual appetites, whereas my flawed vision detects his secret. Even if Simon literally has a body, that body is missing a heart. He is hollow. Just because I can't see him does not mean that I can't know him.

Question: What does Simon know about me?

Answer: That I'm smart, that I despise him and everything he stands for, and that I am, despite my evident inadequacies, dangerous.

Second question: Why does he keep me around?

Second answer: Because I'm useful.

"What he means"—I am already composing my own speech to the assembled gentlefolk of the fourth estate—"is that in a perfect world, armies would not be necessary."

Needless to say, Israel exists in an imperfect world. Therefore we must work and strive and struggle—maybe I'll leave the oratory out of my own press conference and let Simon, my master and puppet, mouth those nice phrases himself on a later occasion. Oh, hell, the fountain is broken, the pump spouts and spouts, replenishing its basin endlessly. Words flow from me in lieu of impressions.

"Work and strive and struggle to attain that," I say to the journalists who have gathered in the municipal auditorium lobby as the rally outside breaks up and people straggle off to find their cars and go to the beach. It's a warm Sunday in the pre-Utopian era.

I continue to gloss Simon's words—they ceased to be my words the moment he spoke them—leaving implicit the idea that until the new millennium, the big three with three zeros, arrives nearly a thousand years from now, we must maintain certain stringent controls on other people's powers. To do this, we must keep our army and inhibit theirs. We must also continue to build settlements and protect territories, and above all, we must keep in mind the one major goal that all lesser goals must serve: Elect Simon.

"How are the polls?" A smooth tenor from the back of the room cuts through the babble like a sailboat slicing the waves on Lake Kinneret. Outside, the crowd is dispersing, but here the second part of the show is just commencing.

In the military terms Simon loves to use, every press conference is a "debriefing," because indeed every speech is a "maneuver." Amid the inner circle, we are constantly "reconnoitering" for information or "outflanking" the perennial Labor opponent, Weiner, at least when we succeed, as apparently we have so splendidly today. Simon loves the double meaning of the word "campaign."

But now, with a voice like melted butter, an unexpected emissary from the enemy camp has infiltrated our domain. A silence fills the room, not merely because of the question that's on everyone's mind and no one's lips, but because of the identity of the questioner. No one is attending me on the platform anymore. Even Goldie's ears are perked from her spot on the floor next to my left foot. Pencils are poised, the scratching sound that usually accompanies my deliveries held in abeyance. We have a visitor and he wants to know about the polls.

"Holding up nicely, Gabriel," I respond.

"We can always hope," he replies, leaving—deliberately?—uncertain whether he hopes the polls will hold up or collapse.

"You'll stick around for photographs," I say, "I hope."

"Only if you take them."

Photographs, me!

My whole world is vagueness and blur, my only reality auditory. Stunned by the cruelty of the comment, I am at a loss to respond. Just two people can shiver my heart like this, Simon ben Levi and Gabriel ben Simon ben Levi. The first knows this and uses his power when he wishes; the latter has only learned it this minute as he must perceive the pain I cannot conceal on my misshapen face. Though Gabriel may be the only person in Israel who hates Simon more than I do, they are made of the same stuff.

Then I hear the shame in his voice. "I'm sorry. That was uncalled-for."

It's as if an oak tree has dropped a seed and given birth to an olive tree. Gabriel is as strong as Simon, but he is different. I must keep him talking, so that I can keep listening to the voice that comes from the blurred face. I know he is beautiful, because I am told so. Everyone in Israel has seen his image on the front page of *Ha-Aretz*, posing for the camera in front of some ancient ruin he has uncovered, while I have had to remain satisfied with the extract of the text offered in the bumpy edition for the blind. It's the idea of Gabriel ben Levi's beauty rather than the thing itself that must satisfy me.

Simon enters the room in a bustle of advance men and flacks and the perfume of Serena Jacobi on a current from the open door, all flushed with the success of his performance. In a second, he detects the atmosphere, glances around to discover its cause, and, unscripted, says, "Gabi."

"Father."

Immediately Gabriel forgets that I am alive. If he gives me any thought at all later on tonight, it may be to wonder how a creature as disfigured as his father's lead writer is capable of the appearance of pain. Damn your eyes.

As the two approach each other, the photographers' fingers tense, as avid to record this handshake as they were for the old soldier's clasp of Arafat's stubby, nicotine-stained fingers on the White House lawn years ago.

Simon steps forward, out from his claque, his mind a whir of machination. Simon needs Gabi's support. Despite my evasive reply to Gabi's question, Simon is wavering in the polls. One moment of reconciliation, one photograph of a handshake—or better yet, a bear hug—will go further toward overcoming Weiner than any number of speeches. Simon is charging now; he will have this moment whether the ambivalent son wishes to give it to him or not.

And another figure emerges from the crowd. He's a dark and writhing coil of compressed energy. A long coat, frayed at the edges, a hat tipped askew even before he's knocked to the floor, as if the frenzy of thought has burst through his scalp.

We've seen this before, not a hundred yards from here.

Time speeds up for everyone in the room, but it slows down for me. I can feel the second hand of a clock sweeping as slowly as the oar of a rowboat through the water. I can pull an imaginary trigger twice before the real one goes off.

From then on it's pandemonium. I spin around like a top in a spray of red, Simon's bodyguards pounce on the would-be assassin, and the photographers are beside themselves. One lucky political paparazzo's image will be chosen for the front page of the *New York Times* and the cover of *Time* magazine and *Der Spiegel* and *Le Monde* and the royalties will gush. That's part of the joy of the Israel beat. In the marketplace of news, Israel is always in demand.

For a second, I believe that my head has blown off as I lay in a puddle of blood that smears my preimpaired vision. Simon is already out of the room, hustled by a phalanx of guards, just in case there's a second gun. He's out of the building, in a helicopter tearing the sky back to Jerusalem—above the chaos, I can hear the rotors—where he will address an even larger convocation of journalists. Here it was the political beat followers; there it will be A.P., UPI, the international corps ripping their hair out because they chose to cover Weiner's peace conference rather than Simon's event—with words not written by me. If I'm dead, it's the opportunity of a lifetime for some young speechwriter. Simon may never have the benefit of my words again. What a loss.

Nobody is allowed to leave the room. Shin Bet has cordoned off the premises, while Shin Bet's version of Nathan Kazakov is already writing the tortured explanation of how they allowed this to happen again. I don't envy that task. They should have known: lightning does strike twice. Heads will roll.

Finally, somebody notices me. I can smell the dust of countless ages—it's in his pores after a decade in the desert—mingled with the sweat of today. Only one person smells like that. He lifts my head, and immediately his fingers are covered with my blood. "Hey," he whispers. At least it sounds like he's whispering, because all the sounds in the room are suddenly so far away. "Are you okay?"

"I've been better," I answer, lying once again. Lying with my head on his lap, I've never felt better in my life.

"Hold on. An ambulance is on the way."

I'm sure of that. One thing we're good at is rapid response. A space is cleared around me, but then again, I'm used to a space around me. No one likes to stand next to me at parties.

"You'll be all right," Gabriel ben Levi reassures me.

"Yeah," I answer. "Just like Lebanon."

The next thing I know I'm on a stretcher, harsh woven canvas like sandpaper underneath me, padded straps keeping me from bouncing off the damn thing as the attendants rush us to the curb, blood in my nose, and the bulbs keep flashing. After Simon's exit and the shooter's apprehension, I'm the best image they've got. Now if they can only capture the drama while avoiding the ugly, twisted lines of the victim's face, they've done their job. Not an easy job; it's a delicate balance between sympathy and disgust.

# CHAPTER 2

I hate hospitals. Maybe more than synagogues.

I used to think that these rooms and corridors that I know as well as I once knew my mother's home and kitchen smell of death, but now they don't smell at all. If Hadassah's trustees decided to market their secret disinfectant formula, they'd wipe the floor with Mr. Clean. Maybe that's what the researchers in the basement, funded with millions of American tax-deductible dollars, have been working on instead of, just for example, new eyes.

No, that's not true. This place is full of whiz-bang professionals, and when they can fabricate and insert an effective model of that great little optical mechanism I'll be the first to know, and the first to see. Forget about some kid who's been blind since birth. Forget about the opera singer with the tragic disease, or the scholar whose parsing of crumbling manuscripts has led to retinal deterioration, or even the construction magnate who was in a motorcycle accident and has since decided to magnanimously endow a fellowship in the eye/ear/nose division on the Hadassah campus. Forget about *them*;

I'm the most most famous blind person in Israel. The problem is not that the scientists aren't working; it's that they're failing.

In the meantime, the very lack of discernible odor nowadays feels more like death than the rancid decay I vividly recall from Lebanon. At the time, alive, alone, among the scattered bodies of the men of Squadron 306, the aroma of flesh and pulp seemed loathsome, but I didn't realize then that every sense must be treasured. I didn't even notice the pink and green thistles poking up from between cracks in the ancient beige mortar of Tel Arnon.

Lebanon was a godsend that I failed to appreciate. Even the Hezbollah Hilton, its awful room service and putrid hole-in-the-floor unsanitary facilities, reeked with a clarity I miss.

To discern the walls around you is still the best way to know you're human. I recall the broken masonry of Tel Arnon like yesterday. A heap of foundation, support, and parapet stones that broke irregularly through the surface of the hill like a newborn's teeth through gum, a few mosaicked patios, it lured Squadron 306 off the road with a promise of history and shade. But not safety. Tel Arnon made no such claims, and sure enough its clay curtain protected six modern soldiers as well as it had some forgotten civilization.

Squadron 306, cruising along a road as bumpy as Braille, stopping for a picnic. Yes, a picnic, how adolescent, how benign! But then again, we weren't much more than adolescents who had just worked up a mighty hunger benignly razing a dozen Arab hovels—half mud, half corrugated metal—before we chose to relax rather than heading for base. We were hungry for the egg salad sandwiches and pickles and little plastic containers of coleslaw and potato salad packed by the mess in case the operation took longer than expected. It didn't take any longer than expected. The de-engineering corps did its job well. But afterward we were hungry, and I traded my side dishes to Akiva Nussbaum for his chocolate pudding—because cabbage and potatoes reminded me of a previous life—just before a teenage Arab hero with a machine gun emerged from somewhere.

He must have fled his family's shanty before we arrived and hid in the ruins that must once have ruled this neck of the woods, when indeed woods flourished in this now parched and blasted landscape. The cedars used to build Jerusalem's Holy Temple had grown here—together with the people who harvested the cedars, now buried under several thousand years of dust.

Last winter, I attended a lecture by Gabriel ben Levi at the university. He stood, a tall gray blur by the lectern in front of a screen which he commanded to change from one image to another with a click of a button. Lord knows what that screen revealed, but each click sent a jolt of electricity through me as he described the growth and abandonment of early cities. In those days, there was no particular pride in or allegiance to particular places. When the water ran out or the crops died or the location was deemed indefensible, the population simply left. So what if the townsfolk had invested in some built-in cabinets or a sunken living room; the time had come and the city was over.

Then, over the centuries, dust accrued. The winds brought layer after layer of desert. Unswept, the layers gathered, filling the corners and then the centers of the empty rooms. At first bandits may have inhabited the premises, but they, too, needed the water or the crops or the farmers to pillage, and they, too, split. Eventually the layers built up and coated the windows and the roofs, which collapsed under the weight, until finally the entire town disappeared beneath the sands of time. Come the advent of the archaeological sciences, of which Gabriel is an expert, all that remained was an enormous, incongruous hummock in the earth. Dig, and ye shall find.

To look into the eyes of the person about to shoot you, to catch the glint of Lebanese sun off the sight of his Kalashnikov—and oh, how I remember those babies from the old country—to witness the spark of light that seemed to jump out of the barrel and propel Akiva, strands of half-chewed coleslaw spraying from his mouth, over the ancient stones, that was living.

I dove into the wreckage just before a stream of bullets bit away at the column behind me like Michelangelo's chisel smacking chips of marble from the block destined to become David.

Hunched over, I dashed between waist-high walls, with the boy with the gun in pursuit. I turned left then right then right again, in search of denser terrain where I might escape him, but my lethal, local child hunter obviously knew every twist of this particular maze and was able to take shortcuts to head off his human prey. Once, when I briefly thought I had lost him, he leaped out from between two pillars with that evil Soviet instrument that had slaughtered my friends cradled in his skinny arms. But if the man who couldn't have hit me in the municipal auditorium if he tried did, so the boy who couldn't have missed me at point-blank range did. The bullets obliterated an ancient fresco, and I fled back into the alleys.

That's how the chase went until, panting, stumbling, exhausted, I took refuge in a forgotten structure dense with shattered statuary that may have served its original residents as a place of worship. I thought I had spied an exit on the far side of the ruin, but my impression was a trick of the eye, one of the last tricks my eyes were ever able to play on me. Those jokers.

Hearing footsteps, I ran for the apparent exit only to discover that it was an illusion created by the shadows. Desperate, I crawled beneath a wide, shallow bowl-shaped extrusion jutting out from the wall, where I quivered in a fetal ball while my stalker's dark, sandal-clad feet entered into the last slice of vision left to me. All he had to do to find me was squat, but he walked past, and I pressed against the protective hollow in a futile attempt to reduce my own body until I felt the bricks behind my spine give way, and I tumbled backward, down a sandy incline.

Suddenly I was in a cavern. Though it was utterly dark except for a chink of light from up top, I could feel the immensity of the space. This was the first time I had to rely on the intuitive sense of volume that most people have, yet are privileged enough to be allowed to leave vestigial. I reached out to touch . . . nothing, but inched forward through a stillness that hadn't been disturbed in ages, and found a rough stone wall and followed it until an opening. Thinking back on those first tentative baby steps, I wonder what I was afraid of. Bumping my forehead, probably, but worse things have happened in human history.

I felt my way along a narrow tunnel into an underground labyrinth. Clever as Hansel in the Black Forest, I marked my every turn with a medal unpinned from my khaki shirt, and when I ran out of medals I used buttons. I traced branch after branch off the trunk corridor, but I needn't have worried about getting lost; every path led to an inexplicable dead end beneath the ruined city. Only later did I learn from Gabriel ben Levi's lecture that such tunnels were secret in their own time, too. Priests used them to sneak behind containers such as the bowl that saved me to retrieve the offerings deposited there for the gods.

Ignorant of ancient history, but certain that where there was an exit there must be an entrance, I redoubled my efforts and delved farther into the tunnels, with no luck. The only thing I found that I had missed on my first go-around was a storage alcove that contained ranks of broken clay tablets, some no larger than a pocket notebook, while others were as substantial as tombstones. I ran my fingers over their indented surfaces, feeling the wedge-shaped cuts that must once have meant something to someone.

Discarding the tablets as neither comprehensible nor edible, I ventured forth a third time. I suppose that one of the dead ends was actually a silted-up stairwell that led back to the outside world, but, scratch at the blank walls where the corridors ended till my fingers were raw, there was no way I could escape. I had to return to the incline, from which I peeked out at my nemesis, or at least his feet, joined now by the similarly sandaled feet of one of his friends, and another pair of feet that I recognized immediately. Splayed out in front of the opening to my underground kingdom lay Akiva's size-twelve boots.

Maybe there had been one precious moment of opportunity during my explorations, when the first Palestinian youth went for reinforcements, when I could have escaped, but now it was too late. Even if he couldn't find me, he knew I was nearby. And though he was surely baffled, he must have been so secure in his knowledge that he dragged the bodies of my former friends to the area beside my cubbyhole to taunt me. He did everything but sing, "Come out, come out, wherever you are."

I think I inhabited the subterranean world for several days, but it's difficult to know. Between intervals of sleep that might have been naps or comas, and moments of terror that might have lasted seconds or hours, and my initial, temporary experience with loss of vision and, especially, with hunger, the passage of time remained as mystifying as the physical passages in which I was either saved or trapped. Again and again, I toured my domain until I was convinced that it was truly sealed off. If there had only been food, I would have stayed indefinitely, but all I could find to eat were a few spiders where the wall met the floor, minuscule balls of vile nourishment whose webs stuck to my teeth like floss.

The stalemate lasted until, finally, like a starved kitten hiding behind a refrigerator and tempted by a bowl of milk, I made the only decision I could. If I remained underground I would die and the priests' quarters would become my tomb. Already I was weakened and surely slower than I had been during the initial chase, but luck and adrenaline might save me yet. If I snuck out at night, I could run for it—maybe—hurdling the half walls, hugging the hills, and making my way to the border.

I planned to wait until it was as dark ahead of me as it was behind, but a flickering light from my hunter's campfire refused to quit, so I summoned every last bit of resolve I had once there was silence beyond the crackling of flames and the sandaled feet were as motionless as Akiva's boots. Also, the feet were alone; my hunter's companions had probably gone for reinforcements. In the half-light, I scrutinized his feet with the care of a podiatrist. They were narrow, pinker in the instep than the arch, with a bony ridge and thick nails, but their most distinctive characteristic was a scar that ran horizontally from the left foot's big toe nearly to the ankle. It looked like the seam on a sneaker this boy would never wear. No matter that he was the hunter and I was the quarry, the vulnerability the scar revealed gave me the confidence to crawl up the incline to the exit, where I immediately revived as the first breeze I had felt since I entered the dark, airless chamber caressed my face.

Pause, and pardon my vanity, but what a face it was: slim, dark, and dangerously lupine, with large soulful eyes that hypnotized the young girls of Peredelkin the way Simon's do any registered voter's.

My face still had all of those qualities at Tel Arnon, and presumably still does, though my slimness has contracted into gauntness, my dark complexion prematurely cracked and wrinkled as a desiccated riverbed. The waves of black hair that once framed that face are now gray and shorn to a quarter-inch crew. As for my eyes . . .

I pressed a palm to the underside of the basin and rose silently, poised on the balls of my feet like a sprinter at the chalk line in the Maccabeah Games. Waiting for an imaginary starter's pistol—"Ready! Set!"—I was about to "Go!" when two flashlights aimed from different directions pinned me as perfectly as a dead butterfly to a matte, and a distinctly Arabic voice said, "Shalom."

"Shalom." The doctor breaks my little reverie into the archaeological past.

He's big, I can feel his bulk hovering, and he speaks Hebrew with a gruff Russian accent. A landsman. Of course, his language skills are not as developed as my own, but he manages a decent bedside manner, chuckling amiably and giving forth the aroma of breakfast as his thick fingers peel away the bandage from the side of my face. "Nice. Very nice," he says, admiring his work.

Indeed, the sutures feel neat and smooth to my own touch as I reach up to stroke my half-shaven head and probe the surprisingly small hole that tunnels toward my brain. It's so perfect, one might think I never had an ear.

So maybe blindness is a blessing, the dark cloud's sweet silver lining adults describe to delude children. If I could see my own face in the bathroom mirror or reflected off the glass that protects the artfully framed, pastel-colored, peaceable kingdom landscapes that surely decorate the walls of my room, I'd really be depressed. If I could see the perpetual wince on the nurse who tiptoes behind the enormous doctor, that would be worse.

But the lack of smell that permeates—or fails to permeate—the atmosphere is worst of all, so I am grateful for Ivan's morning visits, though he seldom does more than riffle the pages of my chart and comment with a glib, professional demeanor he probably learned in medical school. I can do without his patronizing, but the smoky and goatish scent he carries is always welcome. I am tempted to say, "Please, never bathe, I live for this," when he asks, "Feeling well?"

"Eggs with cheese," I reply.

He's missed the point and thinks I'm complaining. "Yes, hospital food leaves something to be desired."

"I was referring to the eggs and cheese you had for breakfast."

Although I can't say for sure, I know that his eyes underneath brows like caterpillars shift from the chart to the loose tie that peeks up from his billowing hospital smock. "Hmm," he says after he's had a chance to examine the tie for spots. "What kind?"

"Cheddar."

"No, Jarlsberg."

"No, that was yesterday." His menu varies only slightly from day to day, but I can tell the difference, and he knows that I'm right. Just to rub it in, I flip through an index of citrus scents in my head and conclude, "Grapefruit juice."

Like the sense of volume, that of smell is dormant in most people. Given the gift of sight, they simply have no need for other, lesser senses. Bothering to smell has thus become as primitive a notion as using a number two pencil instead of a computer. But a writer whose computer crashes may pick up a pencil with gratitude. And like a pencil, the nose can, with proper training, work just fine. That's what I have, a nose as sharp as a pencil. Moreover, as Simon appreciates, I wield the sharpest pencil in town.

In fact, when one sense fades, others naturally become keener. Unfortunately, most blind people don't know what to do with their newfound abilities. Me, I've used my enhanced olfactory apparatus to develop a parlor trick that compels people who can see to look for something that's not visible, although in this case there may actually be congealed bits of egg in the doctor's beard.

He's really quite a mess, this man who's the only one around here whose human smell rises out of the antiseptic void, unlike, for example, the crisp, invisible nurse aflutter at my display of psychic powers. I wonder if she whisks off her uniform and replaces it with a fresh one from a nifty plastic zip-lock bag whenever she drops a bead of sweat. The emptiness in the spot where I know she's standing, eavesdropping on my performance, must be disorienting for the staff, though it's even worse for those of us who are already, as the folks in my support group like to say, sensorially challenged.

See no evil, smell no evil, feel no evil.

Yes, I can't feel, either, because I'm pumped full of morphine via the delightfully semi-self-regulated drip attached to my left arm. One might even say I was "etherized upon a table." Another trick of the trade: memory.

Fairly soon after my return from the front, I realized the true extent of my loss. The face of Doc Ahmed—as I secretly christened my captor—and my dungeon I could do without. My rescuers' faces I could do without. Hadassah Hospital, with its semi-self-regulated drips and stained-glass windows, I could do without. Even my mother, sitting by the bedside when I regained consciousness, I could do without; besides, her image was imprinted on my brain. "Nathan," she said, and I swear I might just as well have seen her lips move. But the first small request that came out of my mouth before I had a chance to think it through made too grossly obvious the one thing I could not—but would have to—forgo. "Tolstoy," I said.

"Tolstoy?" she replied with bovine incomprehension.

"Bring me Tolstoy," I demanded. "*Anna,*" I specified.

"But Nathan—"

"Do as I say," I nearly screamed as and because the futility of my desire came dawning.

Nevertheless, a mother will do anything for a son—especially an only, injured son—so, two hours' round trip to our flat later, she sorrowfully handed me the leather volume that sat over my bed in the home I hadn't seen for two years, but knew as well as I knew a series of Palestinian homes until the Israeli Army retrieved me. Only then, when my fingers touched the familiar calfskin—it was a fine edition I had saved for weeks to purchase at the rarities room in the House of Books on Kalinin Street—and opened its pages to . . . nothing, did I break down. Only then, for the first time since my ordeal began, and the last time since, did I cry, because I knew that from that moment on this unhappy family was going be different.

Yes, I learned Braille in record time, but most of the books available at the Lighthouse Library near the American Embassy were moronic Yankee best-sellers.

Q: "What can you say about a twenty-five-year-old girl who died?"

A: "There are songs that come from the blue-eyed grass."

Okay, so I amused myself by pressing flat and illegible the dots of the *g* and the *r*, but juvenile humor could hardly satisfy an earnest émigré poet who had published—if you can use that word to describe five hundred offset copies of a thirty-two-page chapbook distributed in the coffeehouses along the Arbat—his own contribution to the Slavic canon, and I yearned for Babel, Bely, Mayakovsky, Mandelstam, and Count Leo, whom, miraculously, I discovered buried in the crevices of my own brain. The less I could find that I could bear to read on the metal shelves of the library for the blind, the more delighted I was to find out that none of my previous reading had disappeared. Rather, it may have literally disappeared, but literarily it remained as vivid as ever. At first traces and then phrases and then stanzas came back to me, until I realized that cantos and entire epic poems from my youth were lodged securely inside my damaged skull. As the door to the external world closed for me, another door that I didn't know existed until then swung wide.

I was a walking library. Moreover, I could recall any episode from my past with absolute fidelity. Take, say, the sun-dappled afternoon when I handed a complimentary copy of my chapbook to Boris Anchypolovski, the critic from *Izvestia*, who happened to be eating herring and guzzling schnapps at the Marlboro Café as I distributed my opus. The queasy look on his face is as clear to me today as it was then. Poor man, it was probably the herring.

Some scientists claim that memory is a function of chemistry, because tracks of amino acids etch patterns onto the byways of the mind—imagine a garden of forking paths with the one path actually taken, whether randomly or deliberately makes no difference, outlined forever on an internal map—but I think it's more like alchemy wherein the leaden dross of facts is transmuted into golden ideas. Who says that abstractions can't be more real than bygone reality?

Why shouldn't an ancient kiss linger in the brain for longer than it lasted upon a pair of lips? As a formerly promising poet, I ought to have realized that life is just a premonition of memory. Unfortunately, it's also a precondition, so, though I recalled my entire past in infinitesimal detail—from the typographical error in the introduction to my Lermontov to my Lermontov to the hair of the girl I read Lermontov to in the gardens by the Tretyakov Gallery to the guard who glared at us with a combination of suspicion and envy to the tarnish on the button of the guard's overcoat to a similar tarnish I had once seen on the brass bannister in the Sadowa Ring metro station—I had no present and therefore no future.

Released from the hospital with a full pension, I could quote *Eugene Onegin* chapter and verse, but when I tried to write, I couldn't. Not a stanza, not a canto, not a line, and surely not the kind of thing I had been callowly scribbling from my youth into my soldierhood: naive sonnets about Russian summers and dreadful paeans to the promised land that took me in with its false promises. Bang my head against my shiny new Braille typewriter with helpless frustration, the page in the platen remained as blank as my mind. Yes, memory is always a miracle, but every miracle exacts its price. As my mnemonic capacities exploded, my poetic facilities atrophied. Somehow, poetry had been burned out of my head along with my eyes.

What can you say about a young poet whose soul is dead?

On the other hand, a Russian/Hebrew dictionary's worth of vocabulary was seething inside me like a volcano's magma beneath the earth's crust. I had to release some of it somehow or I'd burst; so, for lack of better occupation, I started editing the newsletter for the blind. In short order, I became so valuable that the director whose grammatical errors I turned into smoothly articulated prose allowed me to take my "work" home to the third-floor flat I shared with my mother. There, I sat in my bathrobe at the kitchen table, gnashing my teeth at the idiocy in front of me.

"What's that you're saying, dear?" my mother asked as she brought my tea in a tall glass with two cubes of sugar on the side.

"Nothing."

"You're muttering again, Nathan."

"Just because they can't see doesn't mean they shouldn't be able to write a coherent sentence."

Nonetheless, I've got to thank the guild. If my first noble calling as a poet had not been overly well rewarded, and my second as a soldier entailed its own disagreeable results, my experience with the newsletter provided me with a marketable skill which I soon decided to sell to the highest bidder. I briefly wrote covers for paperback novels and considered advertising, but if I was going to write shit, I wanted it to have more effect than moving an extra can of cherry-flavored soda. If I was going to sell shit, I wanted it to smell. Then I heard about a speechwriter's opening with a new political party. Enter Simon ben Levi.

At first Simon was reluctant to hire me. Who wouldn't be? The Knesset could enact a million "Disabled Persons' Rights" laws, but the acknowledged legislators of the world could not define beauty. Shelley may have been right, but Keats was a jerk.

I had already grown expert at differentiating the degrees of disgust my appearance caused—call it an ascending order from reflexive aversion to moral abhorrence to personal loathing to outright nausea—but Simon's reaction was different. Usually voices came at me sideways, because my companions' own, less marred faces angled away from mine—"Isn't that a pretty wall?"—but Simon's strong bass rejected me straight on. Rather than avoid this deformed beast, he stared at me with frank and heedless directness. That was why I decided to work for him, but he still had to decide to hire me. If I sincerely wanted the job, I had to prove that I deserved it. He faced me, so I faced the challenge. "What's your number one priority issue?" I asked.

"What do you think?"

Challenge accepted. Fine.

"The term 'settlement' sounds so warm and cozy," I extemporized glibly on the only subject I knew anything about: words. "We think of a fire burning in a bright hearth in front of a happy family, with laughing children. . . ." I thought of my mother's frigid Moscow apartment, and lied. "We think of health and prosperity."

Et cetera, et cetera, until I turned the coin. "But think again of how the cinders settle into the underbelly of that fire. Think of the smoldering residue that forms the necessary aftermath of any fire. . . ."

Shameless, I evoked the Holocaust out of which the Israeli citizenry—settlers all, from the First Aliyah to the literal survivors of the Shoah to the Russians like myself to the Ethiopians—emerged. Already, I was staking out my corner of the political stage. Others, like Serena Jacobi, yet to enter the picture, still a graduate student of international affairs at Hebrew U., might know more about policy and its enactment and repercussions, but I had an intuitive sense of the raw, human dimension that had nothing to do with administration on the ground, yet everything to do with how decisions made by government leaders are perceived by the electorate.

I hardly knew what Simon's politics were, but that didn't make a difference. My spontaneous prose sample had caught the essence of the settlers' position and thus gone an inch toward justifying it and creating the atmosphere in which, five years later, one of those heroes was to put a bullet in my head. At the time, however, I walked a subtle line between empathy and rigor that might have led either a hawk or a dove to vote for whoever delivered my words in a speech. Those words were like atomic energy, useful for electricity or war.

I knew I had done well, but Simon still stared at me. I couldn't see him, but I could feel the heat of his vision. He was thinking.

What he was thinking was that, besides my obvious skill, there might be a secondary benefit to my employment. Years ago, speechwriters were relegated to the back room, but roles had changed. Whether modernity's lack of shame meant that public figures no longer had to pretend to pen their own words, or whether it was part of a contemporary fetish for "teamwork," speechwriters had become part of a candidate's image. In such a climate, in this nation, a wounded soldier was a political asset. After all, Israel has more disabled vets per capita than any other country. Though Simon himself hadn't been lucky enough to lose a limb in a war, I was objective proof of his patriotism.

We were a perfect match—my words, his mouth, unbeatable.

For three years, Simon and I, joined eventually by Serena and a slew of consultants, hit the hustings. Every night, in motels from

Haifa to Eilat, I knocked off a variation of the same basic speech on a special word processor that punched out bumpy copy for my fingers to revise while it transmitted my words into the campaign computer for the others to read. Then, as now, on the road or at home in the palace, I was just doing what I always did: thinking about words.

Take the word "drip": it makes me think of coffee, real coffee from Abdullah's Café, which abuts the Old City ramparts less than a kilometer and a universe away from here. Abdullah serves a heavenly brew with inch-thick sludge in the bottom of eggshell cups that couldn't be more different from the Styrofoam containers of tepid brown ink the Hadassah volunteer ladies bring in a cart along with stale pastries at four o'clock every afternoon.

"Coffee break," they chirp, then cringe as I reply, "Break from what?"

Usually they scoot away before I can follow up with further comment. No loss: the stuff they serve is not only deodorized but decaffeinated. I hate hospitals. But not quite so much as I hate the Prime Minister's office.

Until I get out of here, I have just one drip, semi-self-regulated. Note the caveat: "semi." Full self-regulation is denied just in case you're tempted to overdo it.

Sometimes, to busy and entertain myself, I ponder the history of the technology on which I rely. Surely the morphine drip itself came before the self-regulation, but it must have required an army of nurses to calibrate and dispense the mix for each patient until the breakthrough that allowed individuals to exercise control of their own anesthesia. Maybe there was some debate in medical journals about the wisdom of ceding prerogative to laymen, but the experiment worked better than anyone expected. Self-regulation lowered hospital overhead and freed doctors from maintenance to engage in more expensive procedures. Also, rather than abuse the privilege, most people actually took less of the drug when they were given the option. Maybe self-dosing called forth some sort of atavistic stoicism that I for one have long transcended.

Q: But why then was self-regulation further regulated? Why the "semi"?

A: The danger.

Theoretically, patients would fall asleep and stop pressing the magic button—which is sort of like the device Gabriel ben Levi used to show his slides—before they were likely to overdose, but maybe some cleverly depressed fellow rigged his drip to a weight and managed to do himself in. Goodbye, cruel world.

As a result, the next generation of drip was both heat- and pressure-sensitive, but doctors still underestimated the motivated suicide's ingenuity. Perhaps an unhappy Rube Goldberg circumvented the machine's second line of defense by weighing the button down with a frying pan attached to a hot plate set to body temperature.

Back to the drawing board until, behold, the semi-self-regulated drip, state-of-the-art, the Puritan valve that won't permit more than five minutes of bliss at a time. I take all it offers and think of other methods of semi-self-destruction. For example: enlistment.

Again, this brings me back to Tel Arnon. "Shalom," Doc Ahmed greeted me.

My ears were not so well attuned then, so, for a second, I thought the cavalry had come. Wrong. When the flashlights angled away from my eyes, I saw the boys who found me and another figure, the one who spoke, a middle-aged man with a stubbled face under a striped gray burnoose—Jericho chic.

"I surrender," I cried, and prepared myself for a blast from the machine gun aimed at me. I couldn't see the weapon very well because of the flashlight that temporarily blinded me after my days underground.

"I know," the voice replied calmly. Moments later, I was trussed and tossed into the back of a pickup truck—off on a two-year jaunt that only ended when Israeli paratroopers crashed in the doors of the latest "safe" house to contain me—yet another ramshackle dwelling that might have fit in well at the nearest settlement—and this time a familiar accent said, "Shalom."

Smoke from the IDF grenade which announced my liberation seared my nostrils, and my ears rang with the rattle of a dozen Uzis. Both senses had had plenty of time to develop since Ahmed's initial procedures.

Poor Ahmed, he lay on the floor, his last gasps drowned out by the burbling of blood from his punctured throat. Over the two years we spent together, the Arab doctor and I had come to understand each other. Oh, we had our spats, and I still think he overreacted by painting my lips with Drāno and pinning my eyes open to the Lebanese sun, but he could have done worse.

An Israeli soldier snipped my shackles with a heavy-duty bolt cutter and sensation gradually returned to my fingertips. Then he took my hand and started leading me outside until I cried, "Wait!"

"What?"

"I . . . I . . ." I wasn't used to asking for anything anymore. "I have to do something."

"You can pee later."

"No. Not that." The soldiers were in hurry, and the helicopter that had dropped them out of the sky had alit and was waiting outside with a tremendous roar, but I wasn't to be denied. Determined but discreet, I whispered my request.

"Are you fucking cr . . ." The soldier looked at me. "Sure."

Holding my elbow, he escorted me throughout the rooms of the house, halting several times and saying, "Here."

At each spot, I knelt down to touch the feet of my captors, ignoring those with shoes—even the by-now-expired Ahmed—until I finally reached the foot I sought, the one recalled from my underground hideout back in Tel Arnon. The dead boy had grown considerably since our first encounter, but I recognized him immediately by the scar. It felt as though a rope were inserted under the surface of his skin.

As much as I missed sight, I also missed feeling, and somehow the Israeli commando's professional hand was not the touch I required. I stroked the dead boy's alternately smooth and torn and lovely and still-warm flesh.

I heard another soldier muttering to the commander, but he said, "Leave him alone."

Fucking Jews. If they weren't so sensitive, they wouldn't be in this mess.

The kid might as well have shot himself two years earlier in Tel Arnon or two minutes earlier, or his parents might as well have shot him the moment he emerged from the womb twenty years ago, for all the good he did in the world. Nonetheless, he died for his beliefs, even if the only enduring effect he accomplished was to bring about one former poet's blindness.

"Shalom," I said.

"Shalom," the doctor repeats.

"Oh, it's you, Ivan."

On my first day in the hospital, the doctor introduced himself as Dmitri Tatarsky, but I've decided to rename him after my favorite Karamazov. I can hear his pen scratch the clipboard as he jots down a note, probably something about delusional fantasies. "And what is your name?"

Reality check.

"Call me Smerdyakov."

"What?"

"Or, like Melville and the Arabs, Ishmael."

I'm feeling the drip now and associating wildly. Ahmed and Ivan, two of a kind, maybe they studied together at Moscow University. Maybe they both developed an appetite for sliced and fried pig flesh prohibited by both their traditions in the medical school cafeteria. I continue my display of nasal prowess where I left off before my day-dream. "And bacon."

"Yes, bacon," Ivan murmurs sheepishly, but I don't care if he keeps kosher.

"Oh, yes. And cinnamon raisin toast." I'm rolling now. I can probably tell him what he ate for dinner two weeks ago.

Finally Ivan catches on to my game, stops writing, and becomes more sociable than usual. "You're lucky," he says.

"Lucky," I repeat, mustering sarcasm out of my narcotic daze.

"An inch to the left and you'd be a goner."

"What about an inch to the right?"

"I didn't think you could get any farther right."

Touché! The doctor has really surprised me. Instinctively I turn toward him the same way I made him turn toward his tie. This guy has a sense of humor, but he stops as if he has violated unspoken hospital etiquette. One shouldn't rile the guests here in the Hadassah Hilton by discussing politics.

Of course, everyone else in Israel discusses politics endlessly. It's how we know we're alive. Without argument we'd be a boring island of hedonism like Majorca or Mykonos. How often do those folks get their names in the newspapers? Luckily we have fertile grounds for dissension. *Vive la differénce.* You've got Jews vs. Arabs, Ashkenazi vs. Sephardi Jews, First Aliyahniks vs. newcomers, haredim vs. secular Jews, a whole array of spectrums of identity politics at its most divisive.

And where does Ivan fit along these multiple bandwidths? He's a Jew, a Russian Jew, a liberal Russian Jew, probably wears a Weiner button on his lapel. He sounds older, established, probably arrived here a wave or two of emigrants before myself. I imagine Ivan outside of the hospital, eating his breakfast on a terrace overlooking the Dome of the Rock, or sitting in Abdullah's, smoking his nasty cheroot and talking politics, pounding his fists on the table before setting off to meet the invisible nurse for a postoperation romp, make her sweat.

I wonder what it would be like to bed this jolly trick, but he's not my type. Ivan's probably got a hairy ass. My tastes are more refined, more, shall we say, academic, not that I ever get to satisfy them. The smell of Gabriel cradling my head in Tel Aviv comes to mind, Gabriel the beautiful, Gabriel the unobtainable. On the other hand, I've been told that doctors are acquainted with manifold physical acts foreign to the laity. Despite the drugs, I am distinctly aroused under the thin bedsheet.

Perhaps Ivan has X-ray vision, or maybe he can read my mind, so, back to business, he says, "We'll have you out of here in no time."

No, you don't. I'm enjoying this interplay—call it conversation or call it flirtation—too much to let it end. "That's just what we say to the Arabs."

Unfortunately, the rules of this little game are that the doctor gets the last word and, perhaps disturbed by my overt interest tenting the sheet, he intends to take it now. "Well, one thing is true. Jews always mean what we say. Bye-bye."

I listen as he lumbers down the hall to the elevator lobby. "You wouldn't leave me, would you, Goldie?" I speak to a sweetly snoring shepherd at the foot of my bed.

A few moments later, the elevator arrives with a hydraulic whoosh. Like smell, sound keeps me sane. Thank the Lord for sound.

They haven't told me the bad news yet, which is that in addition to the ear itself—or rather, subtraction—I've lost all hearing in the sinister half of my countenance, but I guess that things will be fine as long as I've got one ear left, my right. It's not like sight, where losing one eye deprives you of three-dimensional perspective. One less ear, more or less, is no big deal if the other one's okay.

But now I've got to protect that precious flap, since, like the only nose I have, it connects me to the physical world. How's that for a title: My Right Ear.

With one cartilaginous appendage, I can hear the squeak of patients' IV poles wheeling down the hall to the television nook that must be set to a twenty-four-hour soap opera channel. Sandra is thinking of leaving Jason, who is having an affair with Sandra's illegitimate daughter, Noel—where do they get these names?—but Noel is really in love with Brian, who is obsessed with . . . oh, someone with some problem. A disease, a tragic past, the usual.

Even without one ear, I keep in touch with whatever passes for life in this eight-story, billion-dollar anteroom to death. I relish the gossip of nurses whispering in the passage about which doctor is cute and eligible and which patient has diarrhea again and who's got to clean her now. It's better than TV.

My ear is also able to pick up every wheeze from the bed across the hall, and that, too, links me to life. Room 404's nasal passages are clogged and he moans, "Daddy," continuously.

I've got a lot of bad news for Room 404 if he's got the ears to hear. First bulletin for the damned: he's going to meet his Daddy real soon, and I hope I'm not here when it happens, but that's probably a needless worry. Whenever he enters a terminal stage, they will shift him off this floor, "down the chute" as the nurses privately refer to the back elevator to the second floor, just above the lobby, closest to the disposal facilities.

"Daddy," he calls again.

Second bulletin for the doomed: given your age, which I'd place in the mid-eighties, Daddy has to have been dead since the Yom Kippur War.

That's how we date things here. If it's old, it's the Yom Kippur War; if it's ancient, it's the Six-Day War; if it's paleozoic it's Suez; and In the Beginning was the War of Independence, otherwise known simply as '48. Where that places places like Tel Arnon is up for debate. I guess they represent cosmic time. That's the era that Gabriel ben Levi occupies, though his father starts the clock in '48. For all the votes the religious parties give him and all the debt he owes them, Simon is an entirely secular being. Oh, he goes to synagogues the way the American politicians he emulates go to church, but his thoughts are elsewhere. In his mind, Simon prays to pollsters.

Simon refers to '48 a lot, is delighted when I concoct some dubious justification to insert Ben-Gurion and Latrun into his speeches. He likes to say that he was born with the nation, but conveniently avoids the chronological corollary. If Commander-in-Chief ben Levi was a squawling infant in '48, then he must have been in grammar school during Suez and, most problematically, of army age during the Six-Day War, when, instead of fighting in Gaza, Golan, or the Old City he now loves so well, he was matriculated in the uncontested territories of Cambridge, Massachusetts. Instead of a submarine, Simon served Harvard crew, though maybe his time on the Charles provided excellent training for chairing a cabinet meeting, "Stroke, two, three. Stroke!"

Granted, by the time the Arabs sneak-attacked on Yom Kippur '73, Simon knew that his future lay on this side of the Mediterranean, so he served in a tank battalion in Sinai. I'll give him that. He can have that. I'm not a military man myself, not anymore.

Me, I'm just a patient, an impatient but otherwise ideal patient. I ask for nothing and offer my arm up to authority whenever it's requested. Take my blood, please. I may rage inside, but here in Ward Six—maybe I'll change the doctor's name to Anton—I'm a good boy. No screams, no yells, no trouble, and excellent ink to boot.

Press releases on my condition are issued daily, though they haven't appeared on the front page of *Ha-Aretz* since I stabilized. Still, every mention of my housing brings credit to this fine, odorless institution. I'm the best p.r. the Hadassah administrators could ask for. They should be paying me. Instead, my insurance policy will buy Ivan a new pool for his villa in Mevaserrat.

Then, maybe it's health returning, or maybe she's just the only one besides Ivan who's stronger than the local disinfectant, I smell Serena in the hallway, her distinctive odor of civet and sex, even before I can hear her two-inch heels clicking with military precision. Now she's standing in the doorway, contemplating me and steeling herself for the task ahead.

Serena is beautiful. Whenever she enters the Knesset, I hear the breathing patterns of the men, whether bodyguards or black-hatted legislators, change into the short panting intakes of dogs.

"Hello, bitch."

She's always disconcerted when I recognize her. Maybe she thinks that I'm only pretending to be blind for my own devious purposes but let down my guard when her glorious self appears. Then, however, she must confront a paradox: if I really can see her, how can I remain aloof? I guess we all have our little secrets, and mine is that you're not my type, Miss Milk and Honey. Add, say, a five o'clock shadow and six inches below the belt and we'll talk. This irks her. Serena distrusts anyone who is immune to her natural charms. Smart women can be quite stupid.

"Wonderful to see that nothing's changed, Nathan." She deliberately uses the *s* word as she strides in and bends down, her nostrils flared so that twin streams of hot air jet onto the unshaven cheek her narrow, dry lips peck. Unlike the few other women who are infrequently called upon to place their faces next to mine, she kisses my left cheek. Everyone else veers to the unmarred side of my nose, but Serena's tough; she'd fuck a corpse if there was any benefit. Consider her relationship with Simon.

Serena has a mission and she will follow orders. Simon says, "Visit," so visiting she is. "They're treating you all right?" she half declares, half asks.

"The only one they'd treat better would be the boss."

She snorts.

"How is he?" I say.

"The question is, how are you? He was so worried."

That's bullshit and she knows it. "Maybe I should write his condolence note to my mother in case I croak."

"Oh, Nathan, you're too mellifluous to croak."

"*Et tu,* Serena."

"Cynicism does not become you."

Even more ridiculous. It's the one manner that does become me. "What do they know?"

I don't intend to make this visit easier for her, but we're beyond games. As much as Ms. Jacobi wants to get out of here, I want to know what's happening outside. Nobody has told me anything. Nurses would rather chat with 404.

In pure Israeli fashion, the truth is both utterly familiar and more uncanny than expected.

It wasn't an Arab.

Remember, we were in a pressroom off Rabin Square, and when I thought, It's happening again, I was more correct than I knew.

Logic said "Arab," but intuition told me that the timing was off. An Arab would have started blasting immediately or, more likely, set off a few sticks of dynamite strapped to his belly along with a box of tenpenny nails. Even then, as the clock ticked, I must have known that terrorists don't disguise themselves as Hasidim. The only ones who dress in seventeenth century Polish costume are those who act as if they inhabit seventeenth century Poland. Arabs don't dress up as Hasidim; their tailors can't make the cut. Besides, the Orientalist mind may be diabolical, but it's never ironic.

Of course, the would-be killer was a true believer in a faith so all-encompassing that it can embrace its own hypocrisy. It's 1680, these Jews announce with their clothing and their customs. They eschew movies and everything modern, yet somehow forget that the first followers of the Baal Shem Tov did not pack revolvers under their gabardines.

But before we ponder the shooter's motives, we have other, more immediate questions to ask. What does this slight inconvenience mean, other than the return of the prodigal son to his hospital home away from home?

Together, Serena and I go through the same calculations she and Simon surely did as they lay together postcoitus. The night after my wounding must have been wild, indeed. Whenever a bomb goes off in a bus, Simon does, too. Politics and danger are the only things bound to arouse him. But Simon only sees the practical aspects of any given situation, whereas I prefer the abstract. That's what the vixen and I have in common. We dig into analysis the way a starving man does into a plate of spaghetti, the way Gabriel ben Levi does into dirt. No Arabic reticence and no Hasidic hypocrisy here.

So what are the effects of the event in Tel Aviv? Foremost, one bullet in the speechwriter's ear virtually guarantees four more years of the speechwriter's job. The assassination attempt is unbearably splendid for votes. Gets the wavering guilt-ridden left, because if the right wants Simon dead, maybe he's okay, and of course the right has no alternative.

I thought the best move was Gabi's handshake, but this is infinitely better. Simon has spiked in the polls. "Up fourteen percent," Serena says with giddy sensual delight, and she might as well be saying his cock is now fourteen percent larger. And no cavities.

But this is treacherous territory. The polls could shrink as swiftly as they tumescently rose. A lot depends on how sympathetic the shooter is. "What's his story?" I ask.

"The name is Isaiah Rubinstein and he came from—"

"Brooklyn," I interrupt. Already I know the rest.

"How—"

"They always come from Brooklyn. Probably Borough Park, but possibly Crown Heights. Let's say he's thirty-two."

"Three."

"Made Aliyah four years ago."

"Closer to five."

"Lives in a settlement near Hebron."

"Why not Jerusalem?" she catechizes.

"The locals wouldn't be caught dead in Tel Aviv. They prefer to make a mess in their own back yard."

"Good, what else?"

"Attends yeshiva and has between four and seven brats."

"You're hedging."

"Say six."

"Bingo."

Okay, so Serena and I do share certain personal pleasures. She's the keenest political thinker I know, because she's the most amoral person I know. Maybe that's why I can stand her. Unlike Simon.

I continue with the story as if I've read the late city edition and the op-ed column by Zev Schechter: "Lives a quiet life in the hills with his bald wife and six brats. But then he makes the mistake of getting involved in politics. Discovers that he likes to carry a gun as much as he likes to carry a Torah around the one-room shul they built before they installed indoor plumbing. His wife knows absolutely nothing. His rabbi knows nothing, either, though the rabbi carries a gun, too. Nobody knows anything other than that Mr. Rubinstein's been out late recently. He has new friends, and nobody seems to know very much about them, unless he's squealed, which he hasn't."

"He can't."

"Can't?"

"You know a lot, Mr. Kazakov, but you don't know everything," Serena purrs with satisfaction. She has information that she might have withheld, but we're all classified here. Besides, she respects my opinions too much, or needs my input. She drops another bomb. "Reb Rubinstein is dead."

Until this moment, I assumed that I was the victim of a lunatic, but now I'm impressed with the seriousness of the situation. Possibilities rattle around inside me like pinballs. Viz: Tommy.

The man with the gun was not killed in medias res à la Baruch Goldstein, and surely his questioners from Shin Bet were not over-enthusiastic. After all, the same bunch managed to cart Yigal Amir to jail in one piece.

Ohmygod, there's another analog, and it's not ours. This one belongs to Israel's ally across the ocean. Think of the scenario: the lone killer killed before he can spill the beans. It's our own little Dallas. "When?" I demand, scenting a whiff of conspiracy.

"On the way to the jail," Serena says.

"How?"

"Heart attack."

I am reminded of a young man on the fifth floor who killed himself by stealing a discarded syringe and injecting himself with another patient's urine. I only heard this through the whispers of the nurses, because the death was hushed up. At the time, I didn't concern myself and just wondered why the suicidal young man didn't use his own urine. Now I think about the official death designation: cardiac arrest.

What an absurdly convenient coincidence. A heart attack avoids a messy inquiry and trial, and by now Rubinstein is six feet under the holy ground according to Orthodox burial law. We all have hearts and they all break.

I need to hear about this. I need to mull it over, consider it, solve the puzzle.

I play over the events in my head. The Jew with a gun had time; that clock swept slowly. Depending on how much target practice he had had back on the West Bank, he might have missed, but not by so much. Maybe the gun had been deflected; maybe a quick-thinking reporter slapped Rubinstein on the wrist with a spiral notebook just before he pulled the trigger. No, surely Serena would have known that. What a scoop, the snoop who saved the P.M.'s life. I was talking to Gabriel ben Levi. We were a few feet apart in the front of the room when Simon strode toward us, from the left, from the plaza entrance. Add several degrees for B.P.'s error, but there were still no less than thirty degrees of arc between the presumed and actual victims of the shot. The problem is that the late Reb Rubinstein was not stupid. He picked his time, and he also picked his target. Yes, he missed that target, but not by much. The truth strikes like a bullet. Rubinstein was aiming for me.

"What are you thinking?"

"Nothing," I lie. My mind is awhir. First, I know fear. It's an emotion that doesn't come naturally to me, and is not entirely unpleasant. Just call it another way to know you're alive. The sheer tingling awareness of the presence of danger, retrospective and ongoing, is comparable only to the exercise of power. Affecting the world and being affected by it operate on the same node in the brain. Despite the molasses time in the pressroom, I didn't use what ought to have been my last precious partial seconds on earth to fear, and thus discover whether I'd respond nobly or basely, with panic or composure, because I was too dull to hear the mental alarm bells that started ringing as soon as Rubinstein appeared. It's a mistake I won't make again. Now that I know better, I relish the sensation.

Roller coasters, horror movies, and front-page photos from the scene of the crime are for amateurs. The vicarious doesn't interest me. Maybe that's why, after Lebanon, I can't write poetry. Triumph over adversity, real adversity, the threat of imminent bodily extinction, will do that. In comparison, the thrill of turning a phrase pales. Oddly, I never felt fear in Lebanon. Pain, fury, sorrow, and regret, yes, but never fear. The temperature of the hospital seems to have dipped. Under the sheet, I'm shivering, and—hark, the truest sign of terror—my erection is gone. That's a trade I can live with, at least in Serena's company. If Gabriel was in the room, I might reconsider. In the meantime, I'm doing the same thing I'd be doing if Gabriel was here. Above the sheet, I'm thinking.

If I claim that I was the target for an assassin, I can request armed guards, and, of course, I will receive them, paid for out of the P.M.'s discretionary budget. Even if I'm perceived or diagnosed as paranoid, I'll be protected from imaginary demons, if for no other reason than to keep me quiet, because Simon will not want my anxieties revealed. If there's even a rumor that I was the real target, there goes the sympathy vote, unless I run for office. Just kidding. Simon needn't worry; I run *from* office. This does, though, whether proved, unproved, or disproved, tuck a nice chit in my wallet. But this is a small practical matter, and there are larger, more interesting questions that really excite me.

Mostly, I'm curious, so I start with the basics. Who, where, and when have been answered by a hundred eyewitnesses, great term. Rubinstein, in the pressroom, at 11:12. The what remains my private ken. How, however, is more interesting. Yes, yes, we know it was an army-issue pistol, but that's not what I mean by how. Weapons are about as rare as accelerator pedals in Israel, and the latter take far more Israeli lives each year. Still, every time a fertilizer-filled truck blows up an embassy, people always ask how the vehicle got so close. So how did Rubinstein get past security? Unfortunately, this is not a question that can be puzzled out; it requires sources or video data. This leaves why. Above all, why? Why did Mr. Rubinstein want me dead?

Maybe his younger brother was the *faygele* with *payes* I seduced in a bathhouse in Ramat Gan last year, and the big boy with the tzitzis only got the news yesterday, and felt he had to defend the family honor. Nonsense.

Likewise, any form of personal revenge is out. No one can hate me, because no one knows me. Yet I am a public figure, and maybe that's significant. Maybe Rubinstein was a failure of a poet himself, envious of my renown. No, poets take out their frustrations at home, on their loved ones. Besides, envy me? Ludicrous.

Next category: publicity-seekers who would do anything for an inch or a second of media. Like Simon. But that kind of killer wouldn't have the grace to suffer a heart attack, assuming Rubinstein's pump really cracked en route to police HQ on Allenby Street, which I don't believe for a second. Anyway, either way, that scenario doesn't pan. A publicity hound wouldn't have a heart attack, because he couldn't bear to miss the attention; he'd want to read his clippings. Besides, who would bother to arrange a heart attack for a loser? Let's leave pending other questions that the good rabbi's fortuitous finale brings up, because that brings in another who. For now, I must face the front man.

So if there's no rational reason for Rubinstein's actions, what about irrational? Maybe he was a six-for-a-shekel psycho, a guy with a grudge against the world, aiming for sheer body count. My bad luck, wrong place, wrong time, etc. Surely, once a year a chunk of asteroid bonks someone. You're going to pick up a newspaper in Saskatchewan, you're tilling a field in Argentina, about to hack off your neighbor's head in Rwanda, taking a nap in the outback, or a crap in an outhouse in Glasgow. Shit happens. Sorry, chum. No, a random nutcase would have done better in the square. How did he get past security?

None of this adds up, but two facts remain. One: the gun was aimed at me. Two: we don't have lone assassins in Israel. Oh, maybe they act independently like Goldstein and Amir, and surely they get blamed independently, like Goldstein and Amir, but Israel is not America. The Oswalds, the Chapmans, those guys, the ones who sleep in motels and walk the streets, they come out of a lack of social context; their crimes are those of disconnection. Our murderers come from too great a connection, first with their peers in the cheder, and then with the voice beyond their classrooms. Our killers come from God.

They also come in waves. Like Arab bus bombers. They are produced on an assembly line, and it doesn't make a difference if the factories are Palestinian propaganda shacks or Talmud Torahs. God's soldiers receive their marching orders from Holy Writ. Each bomb is a text, each bullet a commentary.

# CHAPTER 3

Here's Simon in private. "There's this politician . . ."

All of his jokes involve politicians. He collects these gems, saves them, trades them with colleagues. Whenever he comes up with a good joke that doesn't feature a politician, but a rabbi and a priest or a Pole or a butcher, baker or casket-maker, he substitutes a politician if feasible. Sometimes the fit is awkward, but he knows what he likes. Sort of the way I use salt, on the eggs, in the soup, sprinkled liberally prior to tasting. In the wounds, because it is good.

I'm lying in bed, ready and waiting to be released, when he finally makes the appearance I've been anticipating. Security arrives first to clear the corridors of possible danger, and I hear grumbling from the nurses who will have to scramble for the rest of the day to make up for missed rounds and from the old folks banished from the television nook lest they harbor grenades in the colostomy bags under their pee-stained smocks. Just because they're excited by the P.M.'s visit doesn't mean they're willing to miss the latest installment of *One Life to Live*. Nelly's abortion went badly and Brian is claiming that the baby wasn't his anyhow.

"Daddy!" Room 404 moans.

Noam Abravanel is next, ensuring that everything is more than safe, but cozy and copacetic. There's nothing a duly elected head of state enjoys less than surprise, so it's Noam's job to deflect the unexpected, to drown surprises at birth, like unwanted kittens, or better yet keep them from being born, like Nelly's fetus. Officious twerp, he probably took the heat from the last appearance which turned into such a debacle. As if it's my fault, or because he has a weak stomach, Noam hardly looks at me. I can tell from his drift to the corner of the room and his fiddling with the window blinds. There's a gentle rattle and a shift in the light.

"'More light,'" I quote, but Noam doesn't catch the reference and slams the blinds nervously.

What does Noam think when he sees Mount Zion? Or, to turn the question around: what do I see when I think Mt. Zion? Both Noam and I are immigrants, but his parents arrived here from Yemen a few years before my mother arranged our transit from Russia, so he's old guard, and resents the attention our little Slavic pilgrimage received. He also resents the government jobs, subsidized housing, food allowances, language and swimming lessons, and psychiatric care for the feeble bestowed upon the refugees from the Pale.

Like us, the Yemenites must have felt the difference between freedom and repression, but the landscape that met their eyes upon stepping off the airlift at Lod was the same one they left twenty-five hundred kilometers south of here—sere desert and tired, inconsequential mountains. Even though Jerusalem is roughly equidistant between Yemen and Moscow, the Sephardim from the Arabian Peninsula as well as those from Iran and North Africa feel at home in Israel in ways we never will, maybe because the physical surroundings are normative rather than the extraordinary—or extraordinarily disappointing—act of the imagination that this dinky little sliver is to the mind of the steppes.

Comfortable they may be, in control they're not, however, because the Pale mentality dominates local discourse and politics. God may have created this place, but Yids from Russia shaped the human landscape in their own image. Behold.

The Sephardim have learned to vote in recent years, but they haven't developed their own politicians and must make do with Ashkenazim like Simon with whom they have made a temporary, mutually dissatisfying peace. They may be Jews, but they're also, well, Arabs.

Noam, despite his patriotic name, is small and dark, though I don't know precisely what he looks like because I've never run my fingers over his face as I usually do with most people I meet. It's an interesting process, through which I can determine as much about character as countenance. I can feel a grimace in the tension of the jaw, detect sorrow in the depth of an eye socket, regret in the relationship of cheek to cheekbone. Every sexual secret is evident in an earlobe. Whatever Noam's lobes are like, he has a new girl on his arm every time the occasion allows. He's partial to Scandinavian tourists he picks up at the big hotels on the west side, a business he refers to as "lobbying." Whether he has some innate, ferretlike charm or woos his blond broads with tales out of school, I'm not sure, but I've never trusted Noam. Simon brought him in to represent the Sephardi constituency, and I'll admit that he does his job well. Still, something about him grates. He speaks in a high-pitched voice an inch from a wail and instead of boiled meat and onions, Noam gives off a rich, Eastern effusion of unidentifiable spice.

Someday, Noam wants to enter a room the way Simon does, grandly, with a courtier, preferably European, unrolling the virgin red carpet before his feet, making sure that things are cozy and copacetic. Noam is smart or he wouldn't have the executive assistant job, but until he acquires a little Slavic confidence to complement his Oriental slyness, he'll remain the carpet rather than the feet.

Speaking of feet, I finally hear Simon's brisk pace down the corridor. It's the same sound that I heard in Rabin Square, along with the same attendant regiment. Today, his escort consists of a half dozen Hadassah administrators who see this as an opportunity to push funding for some fabulous technological toy they've been coveting, but the boss brushes them off with a quick, "Noam, take a note," which really means, "Noam, take a note and flush it down the toilet."

The regular entourage brings up the rear: first Serena Jacobi, then, Guildenstern to Noam's Rosencrantz, shuffling Willy Weitzman, no relation to Israel's first P.M. though he pretends otherwise, and last and least, a handful of gofers. They mill around while Doc Ivan bustles into the room. I'd heard him summoned via the hospital PA system under the nom de scrub of Dmitri. Clearly harried and smelling of blood as well as cheddar—he's a man of habit—he probably dashed out of the op room to perform this more important little ritual. While the assembled multitude, more people in here than Babi Yar, watches as if the world's first brain transplant is occurring, he takes my pulse, notices that it's racing, and ignores it. Instead, he pinches me affectionately with a tiny painful twist, the way I like it. I guess this means we've established a bond. Hell, we're the only ones who belong in the room; everyone else is an interloper.

Of course, the press comes, too, and snaps pictures of Simon by my bedside, right profile only, please, hand extended toward me, his prop, as if drawn by Leonardo. I can't see the beringed handshaking machine, but I can feel it snaking through the odorless hospital air and feel its strong grasp for the cameras.

Click.

Mission fulfilled, most of the cameras leave, but a few remain. They know that from now on this is off the record, but they love that even better than the rotogravure. The scent of proximity to power is intoxicating (note root word: "toxic"). Press conferences are for stringers unless there's advance notice of an assassination attempt. Now we have the real players with their shirts untucked, pants unzipped, cocks waving metaphorically.

There's Zev Schechter from *Ha-Aretz* and Michael Burg from *Ma'ariv* and Chester Llewellyn, the new bureau chief from the *Times*, who simply must be allowed into this company by virtue of the status of his affiliation. Simon's especially aware of him and cautious.

"Enjoying yourself?"

"It's bettah than Washington." Llewellyn speaks with an accent that Henry Higgins could place within two blocks on Mt. Auburn Street. The man was probably conceived in a Ha-vad biology lab, graduated into the State Department, and then—what a rebel!—entered the crass world of journalism. He smells like wool despite the ninety-degree weather and will acclimate only to the extent that he'll exchange his herringbone tweed for a cardigan when the thermometer hits one hundred. What Llewellyn thinks of Israel has yet to be determined, but his first dispatches have been models of measured neutrality. Unfortunately, neutrality does not go over well here. The Palestinian "entity" he calls our neighbor, so already we hate him. "Neutrality" is a synonym for "enmity." Whether you call it perception or actuality makes no difference; perception *is* actuality in the Middle East. Except, of course, when it's not.

Anyway, we'll see when the disdain becomes mutual; it's only a matter of time. The only thing that may stop Chess, as Llewellyn tells us to call him, from hating us back may be a greater detestation for our neighbors.

"Bettah than Damascus, too," Zev Schechter comments. Schechter is the dean of the Israeli press. Ever since he filed his first story as a high school kid in *Ma'alot*, an eyewitness account of the bombing of the nursery, he's been hooked on newsprint. A paratrooper during military service, he found time to edit the IDF paper *For Freedom*, in which he broke a story about corruption in the quartermaster's corps which led to the resignation of two generals. His sources are the best in the country, and still the subject of envy and mystery. For all we know, some of them may be in this room. Schechter's literary voice is the opposite of Llewellyn's; he only writes from the inside, whether it's the inside of a bomb-making factory on the West Bank or the mourner's Kaddish for the latest victim of the bomb factory. He leaves others to parse the map of the territories from the bar of the International Hotel; he knows every rut in the road to Jericho.

So here we are, just us chickens. Whether Simon likes this company or not, it's his self-created world, and at this point he'll be himself. Might as well let the Ha-vad lad know the truth; he'll discover it sooner or later.

Llewellyn leans forward, and his lungs compress; I'd say he's six feet, a hundred and seventy-five pounds, tending toward pudgy from the faint kettle-beginning-to-boil whistle of his breath. Likewise Schechter and Burg make themselves at home, Burg pacing as usual—the man can't sit—Schechter slouched into a chair by the window. I know these postures from a hundred similar chats, usually in Simon's private quarters, usually over Scotch, which Llewellyn will get to love. Simon serves strictly single-malt, and even I relax at the scent of the barrels and peat.

The atmosphere is congenial. What's not to be happy? All of these cameras expect to write books someday, and this scene will lend verisimilitude to their platitudes. For now, however, everything is off the record and Simon has a chance to play the plain-spoken man of the people.

"There's this politician . . ."

This politician sits by the edge of my bed, legs crossed comfortably, fancy Italian loafers idly and irritatingly tapping under the mattress, fingers still touching my left arm as if I'm a wounded soldier he's got to comfort. I've been through this routine before, with a different P.M. on my triumphant return from Lebanon, and Simon's been through this routine before with different soldiers; he knows the moves, but he doesn't realize—or doesn't care—that I will not be comforted by him or his policies. But even if I can't be counted upon to press the ben Levi lever during the next election, my presence in this photo-op will serve. Everything does.

"And he's retired. He's been out of the show for a few years."

In America, minor league baseball players refer to the major leagues as "the show." It's another piece of Yankee lingo Simon picked up during his matriculation across the ocean. Hey, maybe he and Chess crossed paths, dormed together.

"And he bumps into an old friend on Dizengoff Street. The friend says, 'What are you doing these days?' "

Simon's wording and pacing are impeccable and work even though everyone in the room besides Chess has heard the joke before. It's Simon's favorite. He tells it over and over again—when he's sure the recorders are off, because he knows that it does not reflect well.

" 'I've gone into the honey business, become a beekeeper.'

" 'A beekeeper?'

" 'Yeah, I'm doing fantastically. Making a fortune. I've got two hundred thousand bees working for me day and night.' "

The numbers change with Simon's mood. Sometimes its two hundred, sometimes four or eight hundred thousand or a few million. The night of the last election there were an even billion bees. You can take Simon's temperature by the number of bees his ex-politician owns. Two hundred thousand is low end, so, despite his usual boisterous performance for the media, I can tell that Simon is uncharacteristically sedate. Nonetheless, he loves the joke and continues.

"'Where do you keep them?' the friend asks. 'I mean,' he says, 'that must take a lot of hives and space and stuff.'

"'Not really,' the politician replies. 'I keep them in a cigar box.'

"'One box?'" Needing to gesture, Simon finally removes his hand from my shoulder and holds up a single finger and mimes the politician's friend's amazement for the portion of his audience that can see.

Noam chuckles appreciatively. Obsequious twerp.

"'One box. Two hundred thousand bees. But they must get crushed, their wings mangled. That's terrible.'

"Then the politician says, 'Eh, screw them.'"

Simon throws his head back and laughs, already in a better mood. "'Screw them!'" he howls.

Maybe you've got to be there.

As if embodying the excavation of layers in one of his son's digs, Simon descends from the devoted leader of the nation in our joint act for the larger number of cameras, to the hale fellow with a few buddies, and down yet further to the most primitive neolithic foundations when Schechter, Burg, and Chess leave and the only ones left in the room are him and me and Serena and a couple of faithful adjuncts who owe him their food, shelter, and underwear. Now that it's just family, he can finally reveal himself—all business. "They buried Rubinstein yesterday."

"Serena told me."

"Sorry about that."

Whether he's sorry that Rubinstein shot me or that Rubinstein was buried or that Serena told me is open to interpretation, but I consider this a concession to humanity and nod.

"A penny for your thoughts, Nathan?"

"I'm sorry about it, too."

"This sort of thing can happen anywhere. But the Shin Bet nailed him pretty quickly given the circumstances." He keeps talking, taking up every ounce of air in the room, and the less he makes of the event, the stranger it seems. Mr. ben Levi may have the morals of a guided missile, but he also has a missile's intelligence. Yes, his brilliance in public gets him the votes, however it's his brilliance in private that gets him in public. If I've perceived more than a lone loon at work here in the fields of the Lord, he has had the same perception—and probably before me, probably on the chopper back to Jerusalem—but seems determined to convince me otherwise and keeps blabbing. "They did everything they could to save him, though frankly I don't give a rat's ass."

Surely this dissembling is not merely to grant me peace of mind, ease the convalescence. I ask bluntly, "Who was the rabbi?"

"His name was Rubinstein."

"Not that rabbi."

"Which rabbi?"

I mean which rabbi officiated at the burial, because that makes a difference that ought to be clear. If it's Shlomo Bozer, who supported Simon during the last election, that's one thing. If it's David Ezrachi, who supported Weiner, it's another. Either way, I want to know what company Rubinstein kept, and Simon clearly wants to keep that data from me. No matter, I have my sources.

"This country." He slaps me on the back. "You can't spit without hitting two or three rabbis."

"Or two hundred thousand."

My reference to his joke stops Simon cold.

The second a number is mentioned, I can feel Serena's gears clicking. She's staring at me, figuring.

I'm figuring, too. Why am I on the outside all of a sudden? What the fuck is going on?

Then Simon picks up the slack and continues. "Rubinstein's brood is back in Brooklyn with their grandparents. Poor kids. Imagine having a father like that."

Simon is always concerned about the children and maunders on sentimentally, forgetting that the cameras are gone.

I think about Simon's own children, a messed-up bunch if there ever was one. His eldest, Natalie, has been through every kind of therapy and rehab known to man as well as plenty of men known to rehab via two—no, three—marriages and divorces to her shrinks; his "baby," Jonathan, sports a Mohawk that he recuts into the shape of a scimitar or a swastika as regularly as it can grow back after Simon shaves his head; and then there's Gabriel. The middle child, without the drama of the firstborn or the sullen resentment of the youngest, Gabriel ought to be the pride of his father's "brood." Handsome, well spoken, Hebrew U. summa, military honors, archaeologist. Israel is the only country in the world where archaeologists are, figuratively as well as literally, rock stars.

Gabriel was the kind of child any parent would die for. And utterly perfect for his particular parent when he swore it was his experience in the paratroopers that first turned him to archaeology. Flying above and then drifting down upon sites like, well, Tel Arnon led to a visceral understanding of how the past and present connect. Unfortunately, it also led to a visceral understanding of how the current Israeli war machinery and the ancient Judean courts and centers of learning are diametrically opposed. Gabriel became the worst sinner of all; he became a dove.

From Gabriel's first speech at a Peace Now rally until a week ago, father and son hardly spoke. They didn't even appear in the same room if either one could help it. Simon didn't exactly say Kaddish, but he might as well have. No one dared mention Gabriel's name in his presence. Hence the thrill of the scene in Tel Aviv. Had a reconciliation between the most famously estranged family in the country occurred on the P.M.'s turf, it would have been a coup. Local magazines would have gone wild. Other doves might have questioned their commitment to public peace once their most revered advocate signed a treaty with their most dangerous opponent.

As for Gabriel's private life, that was another disappointment to Simon. Unlike his sister, who did it too often, Gabriel never married, never bred, never gave Simon grandchildren good for photogenic knee-dandling. Though he's constantly listed as one of the most eligible bachelors in the country, Gabriel never appears in the papers' society pages escorting this lady or that tramp who would be delighted with his company. This has led to entirely unfounded speculation in gay circles that Gabriel is one of us. Ridiculous. Coming out as a dove must have been a lot harder for him than coming out as a *faygele* would be. But who knows? Maybe the personal is more difficult for Gabriel to wrestle with than the political. Maybe he secretly listens to Judy Garland records and subscribes to the Hebrew edition of *Christopher Street*. Nonsense. We should be so lucky. Homosexuals in Israel are like Jews in the Diaspora who parse genealogical tables to determine that Steve Case or Harrison Ford is a quarter Jewish and *kvell* over Barbra Streisand, whom we on the nether side also adore. But let's just say that half the happily married hunks hereabouts really do prefer boys. Let's say that all Gabriel needs is one good man. What good is that to me? We had our moment on the floor in Tel Aviv and I'll treasure the memory.

"Think of the memory they must have," Simon sighs for Rubinstein's orphans.

We're talking in circles. After the performance, after the jokes, Simon is in high evasion mode. First, he quibbles with my grammar, pretends that he doesn't understand me in order to determine what I understand, which appears to be as little as any B.P. does a bikini on the beach. Then he veers off on a tangent, forgetting the sad, fatherless babes to say something about the stalled peace negotiations with "the entity" that he claims I ought to be kept up to par on, because I'll be "back in the saddle" before the week is out. Satisfied, he stands and I hear the air sigh from the cushion he's been sitting on. "Noam, I want you to make sure Nathan gets anything he needs."

"Of course."

And they're gone, except for Noam, who picks at his teeth with a nasty clicking sound, and then says, "So what do you need?"

This is an opening if I've ever heard one, and I'm tempted to scream, "Eyes!" but won't give him the satisfaction. Instead, I smile and just say, "Flush it."

Before things get contentious, Doc Ivan, who slipped out of my room as soon as our earlier charade had been concluded, has wafted back and interrupts. "I'm afraid you'll have to go," he tells Noam. "The patient needs his rest. Doctor's orders."

Bullshit, of course, but I'm grateful. I have a lot to think about.

"I mean that," Ivan says after Noam sulks away.

"But I thought visitors were good for the spirits. Friends are important."

"Some friends you've got," Ivan snorts.

"It's bettah than Beirut."

"But not as good as Moscow, eh, boychick?" Ivan laughs and leaves, too.

Already I miss him. This hearty, messy surgeon who was probably working with a rusty scalpel in Brodzki Hospital a few years ago suddenly feels like my best friend here in the land of the Jews. I almost regret thinking of him in bed.

And then I think of the rest of them, Simon and his gang, in bed in a different way, because their bed is called the Knesset, that architectural travesty that we're stuck with, because it's on too many postcards to demolish. It's as representative of Israel as the White House is of America. Then I realize that the Knesset is not a bed; that's too cozy and copacetic an image for a building designed for a different era, now bursting at the joints with politicians and lobbyists and journalists and generals and their affiliated minions. It's a box; it's our little cigar box, every cubic centimeter of which is crammed with maneuverers of one sort or another, angling for space within the box and territory without. Eh, screw them.

# CHAPTER 4

"But I *want* to come and pick you up," my mother chuffs into the phone.

"But I don't want you to," I reply.

"But, Nathan, you're—"

"Blind, mother. I know. And I have been for years. I don't need anyone to hold my hand."

"The number twelve bus is so convenient. Just at the bottom of the hill."

"A mountain."

"And it's so quick."

"And it's only been blown up twice in the last year. Come to think of it, maybe it's not such a bad idea."

"Nathan, Nathan, Nathan."

*Toro. Toro. Toro.* Every conversation we have moves in the same direction, and makes me feel as though I'm five years old again, and begging to cross the street to wait on line for bread by myself for the first time.

Sometimes I think that my blindness is the best thing that

ever happened to her. It's given her a reason to live. "Besides, I have Goldie."

"I don't think she likes me."

"Goldie is a dog. Dogs don't like anyone."

"Of course they do."

"No, that's a myth. They really hate and resent people, but know they need us for their food and comfort. So they pretend to lick our hands when they'd prefer to bite them off." Pretend/prefer: an elegant contrast; the wordsmith strikes again.

"Well, Goldie doesn't even pretend to like me."

"That's because I've trained her, Mom. Every day, when she was a pup, I showed her the famous picture of you in the bonnet on the river, and then I whipped her. Now whenever she hears your voice she growls. Rrrr. Rrrr. Down, girl, down. Oops, I'd better go before she gnaws through the cord."

"I thought you were a speechwriter, Nathan."

"I am."

"What a shame."

I know it's a mistake, but I can't resist asking, "What do you mean?"

"It's a shame, because you missed your calling. You should have been a comedian."

Got me. I'll give credit where it's due. The woman knows how to lacerate, but she never had an opportunity to do so on a larger stage than her kitchen. If she hadn't grown up in Russia, she might have been like this country's other Goldie.

"You're just jealous."

"Jealous of a dog? Me?"

"You." It's true; the small codependence I and the German shepherd have is a needle in her heart.

"Anyway, the government's taking care of me. Noam will pick me up at five."

"I've never liked that young man."

At moments like this blood shows and I'm almost willing to give her the small pleasure of agreement. Nonetheless, I say, "I should be home by ten."

"Well, your bed's waiting for you."

Thirty years old, mixing with the most powerful people in the country, and I still sleep on a portable cot in the glassed-in porch of the small apartment they gave us when we first arrived here. Except on the nights when I don't, when no one except the man I find in Dregs or the Dread Bar hosts. Then my mother doesn't dare ask any questions, because she fears the answers.

I pack the leather overnight bag I splurged on when Simon and I really started traveling: New York, Washington, London, Geneva. It's a wonderful bag with compartments for clothes, toiletries, and papers. Everything in its place.

"Daddy," Room 404 moans. Thank God this is the last time I will hear his senile maundering. I am tempted to enter his room, which reeks of age, and shake his ancient shoulders and say, "He's dead. Get over it." Then I realize that that's the same thing I'd like to say to my own mother, and slink down the hall.

"Goodbye, Mr. Kazakov," the young nurse who has changed my linens and bedclothes for the last week calls out. She knows what my body looks like better than I do. I ignore her, but I'd sort of like to say goodbye to Doc Ivan, but he's somewhere else in the vastness of the institution. This would be a real test of my olfactory capabilities, see if I could trace that invisible wend of cheddar like a bloodhound sniffing a missing child's T-shirt and crashing through the woods in hot pursuit.

But Israel has no woods, and the country's founding fathers are dead, their generation's place taken by the likes of Simon ben Levi, the son who became a father of his country.

I stride past the nurses' station and travel down in the elevator, listening to the insipid beeps that irritate everyone else for my convenience, stop at the gift shop, and ask for cigarettes.

"I'm sorry. We don't sell cigarettes here."

"What do you mean, you don't sell cigarettes? What sort of place is this?"

"A hospital."

I had nearly forgotten, and will be glad to forget entirely. I push through the front doors into the blast furnace of midday Jerusalem.

Between doctors and nurses returning from expeditions into the world for lunch, and patients and visitors arriving or departing, and tourists flooding out of tour buses to see the chapel's Chagall windows, the entry is a madhouse, but Noam is waiting for me, his Mercedes parked illegally over the curb.

I can hear his screechy voice telling off a policeman who wants him to move, and start toward him. I wouldn't allow him to touch anything in my room, but I will allow him to chauffeur me. The only question is where I want to go. I've already told my mother that I won't be home, and I have no desire to go to the office. It's noon, so the Dread Bar will not be busy, but sometimes one companion is better than a crowd.

"Here." I hand Noam my bag as if he's a redcap at the airport and am about to open the back door when a tall man bumps into me. I feel the bristle of his beard on my forehead and the texture of his rough wool overcoat on my arm.

"We want Moshiach," he says and thrusts a pamphlet into my palm.

When did Jews start to proselytize? Isn't that against the nature of the faith? I always thought that it was a rabbi's duty to dissuade anyone who wanted to convert. Now the haredim aren't content with breeding like bunnies; suddenly they must lasso secular Jews to augur in the messianic age. They are omnipresent at airports and bus stations, and I guess hospitals are good hunting grounds, too. Where there's pain, they offer a scroll of prophecy for patent relief.

How does this system work? Do they receive marching orders in some central depot each morning? You, with the glasses, go and get a few soldiers to put on tefillin. You, the twins, go nab a couple of tourists at the Western Wall. You, big boy, find a blind man who doesn't know better.

"We want Moshiach," he repeats.

"*We* don't want anything you're selling," I growl.

"Read it," he says and pushes the pamphlet farther into my hand.

Read it, indeed! What an imperative. This one is a real loser.

"Read it," he says again, and just as I detect something familiar in his voice, his strong hand presses my finger into the corner of the glossy paper, which undoubtedly has a photograph of the late Rabbi Schneerson from America on its cover, and I feel something else, bumps, probably jabbed into the pamphlet with a pencil, forming shapes. Three bumps in an upside down L pattern form the letter *m* in Braille.

He swiftly rubs my fingers over a sequence of bumps and more softly pleas, "Read it."

Then, just as Noam shoves him away and opens the door, I catch a whiff of two more smells. The first is mothballs. Either the coat has been in a closet for a long time or it's rented. The latest fad. Sarcastic, secular Jews rent Hasidic garb for costume parties and to stroll the narrow alleys of Mea She'arim. They travel in mufti among the believers to observe the other half.

Simultaneously it occurs to me that the bristle from the beard did not feel authentic; it's a fake, from the same costume shop. Then the second smell hits me, the one buried underneath camphor and gabardine, a more literally earthy scent, the smell of the desert.

I can hardly wait to get into the car and read the letter from Gabriel. "A tobacconist," I order the driver.

"I think we should get to the office," he says and turns the radio to a local jazz station.

"Fine. Whatever."

Noam is droning; he's like a five-foot mosquito driving the car, ignoring lights to the samba beat of the alto sax as if he's crusing the hills above Rio. I can tell this, because I know that no normal vehicle can possibly cross Jerusalem without stopping once, and because we swerve wildly several times, leaving beeping horns and squealing brakes in our wake. But none of this registers beyond the scrim of consciousness, because my fingers are caressing the glossy brochure with the punched-out lettering.

The punches are awkward and unevenly spaced; it's like a child's handwriting, painstakingly executed, letter by letter. I can picture Gabriel sitting with a Braille handbook, transcribing the three triangulated dots of an *m* and the four zigzag dots in a *t* with two angled dots twice in succession for two *e*'s between them.

"Meet."

The *m* and the *e* repeat.

"Me."

Anywhere, anytime. When? Where? And why were you dressed in that ridiculous getup unless it was to make sure that nobody saw us together? One thing I know is that Gabriel is not a frivolous person. He may dress as if he's going to a costume party, but there's no party. The man is not playing games, and lest I forget recent history in the light—more light!—of today's strangely conveyed message, a bullet was fired.

"Four o'clock. Independence Park."

With my dancing shoes, dear Gabriel. My hand caresses the letter as we finally come to a halt beside the security booth in front of the state office building garage. Noam doesn't bother to open his window, but pauses to reach inside of his jacket—I hear the ruffle of material, probably silk—to find his pass to wave in front of the guard's face, and then hits the gas. The car takes one last accelerating burst past the concrete barriers into the garage, and the light from outside is obliterated by the shade of the overhang.

Home, in a way.

It's not necessarily quality time, but I probably spend more sheer hours in this building than I do anywhere on earth.

Minutes later we've walked from Noam's designated but distant parking spot, beyond the ministers', in the oil and metal sensaround of the garage to the elevator, and now we're going up. Goldie crouches at my feet while Noam stands in the front of the lacquered box, which responds immediately to his jab at the controls, both physically and audibly, with a series of beeps built in for my benefit. Israel is ahead of the curve in handicap access, because there are so many wheelchaired, hearing-impaired, and blind vets.

I reach past his shoulder and run my fingers over the Braille markings that number the floors beside the numbers themselves. I haven't forgotten what numbers and letters look like and love it when I find an embossed sign in one of the antique shops along Bialik Street, but they have a blunt architectural feel that seems less elegant than the sequence of dots B.P.s use.

I think of the dotted message that I tucked into my inside breast pocket before leaving Noam's car.

"Fourth floor, ladies' lingerie," Noam makes a joke as we exit and turn immediately leftward, past several soldiers, whose straightening I can hear as we stride past, and enter the executive suite.

There's a perennial clicking of computer keys and ringing of phones and a perpetual murmur of conversation from the various stations. Ellen Markowitz, the private secretary Simon brought with him from his early days as a Knesset representative from Ramat Aviv, says, "Hello, Nathan. Welcome back."

"Can't say I'm glad to be here," I reply.

"Don't worry. I can't say I'm overjoyed that you're back."

I like Ellen. All brisk efficiency, she treats everyone the same, like shit. I run my fingers over her face, and she nips playfully as my thumb touches her rouged lips.

"No tongue today?"

"Ham sandwiches for all. In the office." She presses a button underneath the desk and sliding bulletproof doors open with the same hydraulic exhalation as the hospital elevator doors.

Already. No decompression time. Back in the saddle.

Noam has veered off to his own office, so Goldie and I enter alone. The room is about ten meters square, with a stainless steel desk ordered from a Jaffa foundry, a conference table, and a separate seating area with a couch and cushioned chairs set about a coffee table. Simon is on the couch, Serena behind his desk murmuring into the phone, while a few others occupy the soft chairs. I can tell that there are at least two strangers present from the slightly raised temperature of the room and the rustle of napkins, a swallow of office coffee.

No matter what's available outside, office coffee always stinks. It's the same in the White House. I've drunk there. In fact, I've been drunk there. If you're ever there and given a choice between Scotch and coffee, don't be an idiot.

I stand in the center of the large Iranian carpet that was a gift of the Shah during an earlier dispensation. I could use a smoke, but Simon's a militant health advocate. No red meat in his diet, just lentils and groats and tofu grown in a scummy basement in the Arab Quarter.

"Gentlemen, this is Nathan Kazakov," Serena puts down the phone and introduces me from the desk.

"Hello, gentlemen," I say. "Who are you?"

It's Cyril Klein and Eli Khadoury. This explains Noam's rush from the hospital. I've never had reason to meet these men, but I know quite well who they are.

I extend a hand into the empty space in front of me and one of them grasps it, probably Khadoury. As the nominal chief of Shin Bet, otherwise known as Israel's FBI, he is accustomed to the manners of the outside. Not that he is merely a figurehead; the man runs the day-to-day business of the bureau and he's nobody's fool. Nonetheless, his very presence in the world acts as a glove to hide the dirtiness of his hands—enter Klein.

The latter's is the name that's never in the papers precisely because his are the bare knuckles that set in motion the events that create the ink: car bombs, kidnappings. Remember the Palestinian ambassador to Italy and his dive off the balcony of his seventeenth-story hotel room in Milan? Remember how the investigators said he was depressed? Maybe he was depressed for a few seconds because Klein held him over the edge by the ankle and . . . oops!

Cyril Klein was a hot-shot army colonel during my time in Lebanon and then disappeared from the ranks just as he ought to have been promoted to general. Rumor had it that he had become a renegade arms dealer based in Cyprus, but by then I knew better. He's in charge of all covert operations and must therefore be covert himself. He doesn't shake hands, but sits upright, attentive in his chair, and I feel his eyes upon me. I sit in the chair that wise Ellen has rolled in from the outside.

Khadoury takes the floor. "We asked you here, Nathan, because we have a problem."

"Yes, I know."

"You know?" Serena asks.

"Isn't it obvious?" I reach up to the bandage that still covers much of the left side of my face.

"Not that," Khadoury brushes me off.

Well, pardon me, I think, and say, "What, then?"

Simon speaks now for the first time. "Gabriel's disappeared."

---

Eyes give away emotions more obviously than the tooth grindings and sudden, shocking effusions of sweat that I have to rely on. That's why these experts in evasion cannot read the instantaneous apprehension that must flit across the scarred surface of my cornea and pupils like a lightning bolt. They can't hear the click of my teeth or smell the prickles of sweat that pop out on my chest as if I've been exposed to a rare spring shower. Unfortunately, my hand jerks reflexively upward toward the breast pocket in which Gabriel's letter rests. I remove a pen and hold it like the cigarette that I suddenly crave. "Disappeared?"

"He hasn't been seen since last night."

Last night? I haven't been seen in a week and nobody's called out the Mounties. "The man is an adult. In fact, how old is he?"

"Twenty-nine," Serena says. She has all the numbers.

"Surely a twenty-nine-year-old has a life. Maybe he got a call to the desert for a discovery."

"The people at the dig he's been working south of Ein Gedi haven't seen him, either."

"Maybe he went to Eilat for the weekend with his girlfriend." My glibness is clearly inappropriate here, and also a violation of my own utmost desires.

"Gabriel doesn't have a girlfriend."

Well, that's good news. I continue talking stupidly. "Maybe he had a hot date, got lucky. Maybe he's shacked up in a Herzliah condo with an El Al stewardess."

Khadoury breaks my logic into pieces, "The Prime Minister's son is under twenty-four-hour surveillance. If we say he's missing, he's missing."

"Yes, but if you say he's under twenty-four surveillance, you're wrong."

A mephitic odor comes from Klein. His voice, more of a rumble than an enunciation, travels slowly across the room with a trace of his parents' British accent. Klein's father was the highest-ranking Jewish officer in the English foreign service, loyal as a lapdog yet considered untrustworthy by his masters. Whether he spied on the Irgun or was a spy for the Irgun is still subject to debate. Like father, like son. Klein is the last remnant of the Mandate in the flesh. "Have you seen him?" Then he realizes the stupidity of the question and the rumble continues, "Have you heard from him?"

I twirl the pen that came from my breast pocket. "Why should I?"

"You were one of the last people who spoke to him back in Tel Aviv."

"I've been occupied since then," I say testily. Why am I being interrogated?

Serena moves to smooth over the awkwardness. "We played a tape from the briefing before Rubinstein came in, and you were speaking with Gabriel."

"It was a question from the audience. Besides, all this is on the record."

"Yes, but it sounded as if you knew him."

"Of course I know him. This whole country's no bigger than a Moscow subway station. Besides, he's an archaeologist."

"Did anything strange strike you about the assassination attempt?"

"Yes, a bullet."

What I don't say is that what's also strange is that there seems to be no attempt whatsoever to parse said assassination attempt from my perspective. Why is it not considered even theoretically possible that Reb Rubinstein actually hit the target he aimed at, even if he was two inches away from a bull's-eye, even if it was a blind bull?

"Nathan, we're looking for help here." It's Simon addressing me again. As I expected, he is lying on the couch and his shoes are off. Would he be embarrassed if he knew that they emit a faint, fetid odor that only I can smell? Probably not. It's one of the perks of the job. You can smell like a sewer, but everyone will perceive a rose.

"No, I don't think so," I say carefully. How I know to keep secret Gabriel's communication I'm not sure, but if he's hiding from his father and these people, he has a reason. "The last time I met him before Sunday was at a reception at the Israel Museum last May." Strictly speaking, this is true; that was the last time I met him *before* Sunday.

"We're worried because his guard was overpowered last night, and he hasn't been seen since then."

"Did he know his guard was overpowered?"

"He didn't know that he had a guard. He never believed he was in danger. We had to operate in disguise."

"What sort of disguise?"

"Why do you ask?"

"Just curious," I lie, and then decide to go on the offensive. "I deal in information. Maybe it's relevant. Maybe not. If you don't want to tell me because it's compromising some great state secret, don't!"

Of course, Khadoury responds. "Depending on the situation, our men can wear anything, be anything to be inconspicuous, just a guy in a suit reading a newspaper, a construction worker, even a Hasid."

So the outfit didn't come from a costume shop, at least not a commercial one, but some wardrobe these guys keep for their dress-up games. I can picture the humiliated agent, knocked out and stripped naked, but dare not ask for confirmation. If the agent called collect from a corner phone booth before he was arrested for indecent exposure, somebody may be on the lookout for an archaeologist dressed in beard and gabardines. Suddenly a tremor goes through me; Noam must have witnessed the Hasidic proselytizer at the hospital. But Noam isn't in this particular loop. He's sitting in his office, stewing for just that reason. "I'm sure he'll show up."

"Why?" Klein asks cautiously.

"Everyone does, eventually. Look at me."

"That's exactly our worry," Simon says.

"I'll keep a lookout," I say, and nobody even catches the irony. The meeting concludes.

Independence Park at dusk is an oasis in the midst of Jerusalem. Cars whiz along the perimeter as government workers from a hundred agencies speed toward home, but all is quiet inside the park's green boundaries. To the east, the Old City is coming alive with cafés and the suite lights at the King David Hotel. Soon, the Son et Lumière will commence along the crenellated wall near the Jaffa Gate. To the west, the big tourist hotels are gearing up for the evening.

It's not a large park, even for a B.P., but it does have open spaces and wooded areas, and I don't have any idea where to meet Gabriel. I don't think I was followed as I left the Knesset, but just to be certain I took a taxi to a café along Ben Yehuda Street and slipped out the back door to the Jaffa Road. I caught another cab and took it to a one way street off Keren Ha Kiyemet, where Goldie and I made a dash in the wrong direction before we caught a third cab to the King David Hotel several blocks from the park. I know I was worried, because I didn't even collect the receipts for reimbursement. I sit on a bench and wait until I feel isolated and decide to let Goldie take me where she will along the gravel path between greenery.

A few teenagers are already drinking beer on the pedestal of a statue dedicated to the martyrs of '48. One of them burps.

An old lady is scattering food for the pigeons that infest this place. I don't think it's bread, because the pellets hit the path with a faint clatter—probably seed or corn. It crunches under my feet and then again as footsteps approach me from the rear, so I slow down, but an Arab boy smelling of the falafel stand he probably works at during the day slides past and disappears ahead. There have been muggings in the park lately, much decried by the papers as a sign of the end of civilization as we know it, but I never feel danger. Muggers are afraid of Goldie, who looks fierce but is really a pussycat. She doesn't really growl at my mother, although I'd like her to. Maybe I will attempt to train her with that horrible sentimental photo that looks like something out of the Tsarina's family album.

A creaking sound, regular as a heartbeat, from the left. Strangely, the sound wavers, as if its source is moving in the wind, but there isn't any wind.

If I squint and strain to peer out of a crescent of unscarred tissue at the edge of my left eye I can sometimes make out a form—it was that that gave me the fleeting sense of Reb Rubinstein—and I suddenly catch a black shape, first closer, then farther, then closer, now farther.

I start walking toward it and Goldie halts at a low gate, and I understand. It's a children's playground, containing a sandbox and jungle gym and a swing set on which Gabriel is gently rocking. Back and forth. Back and forth. I'm hypnotized. I smell desert.

He watched me all along, knew that I would find him.

"Hello," I say, and start across the spongy material they lay down to protect children from skinned knees, although, it occurs to me, they should have special playgrounds with nothing to bump into for blind kids. A new civic advance.

A second later, I hear an alarmed cry and a comet strikes me. At least it feels like a comet, a vicious object crashing into my torso, knocking me to the ground, vengeance—or justice—for my cynical thoughts. One second I'm bouncing across the play surface, and the next I'm enmeshed in a tangle of limbs, my own and someone else's, someone whose hot skin I can feel, who's wearing a T-shirt and short pants and the sneakers that smashed into me a moment ago.

Goldie is barking, and the man on the adjacent swing is skidding to a halt, shoes braking him against the rubber turf.

A boy is on the ground, screaming at me, "Why don't you watch where you're going?"

What a comedy!

He was on the swing next to Gabriel, but I was so entranced I didn't notice.

"Can't you see?" he's berating me.

Calm, basically in one piece—at least he missed my wounded ear—and still happy, I say, "Actually, no," and turn my gaze upon him.

The boy sees the hard crust of burnt tissue that covers my eyes, breathes deeply—the intake is like a vacuum—and flees.

Now, at last, as he did in the pressroom, a ministering angel hovers above me. Nonchalantly, I jest, "We've got to stop meeting like this."

"Vat?"

His voice is thick, and in my daze I think that he's still in character, but then I realize the scent of desert is gone. And this gabardine does not smell of mothballs. Instead, it's soaked in genuine rabbinic sweat. I smell the mold of ancient texts and salami. A fringe from the *tzitzis* these people wear brushes against my forehead, where his hand rests, gentle in its own way. Who is this man? I wonder, and then realize in a blaze of obviousness: he's just a rabbi who's been interrupted in his strange, secular, childlike communion with his

God. For him, the motion of the swing must echo the cosmos that he believes was created by divine fiat rather than out of the rage of nature.

He is entirely at ease with himself and his world, and I know nothing. The chains by which he was suspended from the swing set's crossbeam might as well extend up into the Jerusalem sky and beyond, through the levels of the atmosphere, into the infinite ether where they're held by the same hands of God that once parted the Red Sea and established His dominion on earth at this very point in infinite space. I turn my face to the sky that I cannot see. It has already darkened in my short stroll through the park.

Who holds my strings, I have no idea. If not the deity who gave me to Mother in a flyspecked hospital room near the Ismailovsky metro stop in a land at the end of decades of failed social experimentation, who called me "Jew" and kicked me tumbling to my presumptive homeland like a boy with all the momentum his bare, pumping knees could create, and then, via the subagency of a cadre of Lebanese rebels, thrust me from the unremunerative—make that anti-remunerative—world of poetry into the position I now occupy but cannot comprehend . . . who, then? Simon would like to think he holds the strings, Mr. Master Marionetter, but that's not true. Maybe I hold my own strings, but any puppet who attempts that trick is bound to collapse in a heap.

In the presence of the rabbi's placid faith, I suddenly hate everything.

Like the boy who fled at the sight of my face, I stumble to my feet and run toward the exit, because I cannot see the face of God.

# CHAPTER 5

Out of the park, reeling down Agron Street.

I stagger over an upraised chunk of sidewalk, carom off a street sign. I'm a spectacle.

In comparison, I felt positively composed as I lay bleeding in Tel Aviv. And not only because of my deodorant. Usually, when I speak to the people who run this country, and with them to the people who run other countries, and, take my word, I've met them all, I remain unimpressed and unfazed by the glamour and the power of our mutual enterprise. Folks I meet say, "How can you deal with the pressure? The stakes are so high!" but what they don't know is that there's always a problem and it always occupies one thousand percent of everyone's time. If it's not nuclear war it's diplomatic parking tickets and I cope with each with equal aplomb. Government is by definition catastrophe management. So why, then, if high drama is my daily fare, has a minor playground accident thrown me off balance? If I can't handle this, it's a wonder that I can tie my shoes in the morning (though finding them is often a problem).

Is it that I've been stood up? It's not the first time, and, since I believe that the past predicates the future, it won't be the last time.

Is it the swirl of mystery that surrounds me like the vapor of cotton candy that adheres to a cardboard cone in a carnival midway? No, this, too, is terra cognita. I know the hidden agendas of political life too intimately to find the enigmatic incomprehensible or the incomprehensible enigmatic. Remember the series of secret meetings before the Canary Islands summit that led to the international anti-biological weapons concord? Talk about confusing. You couldn't tell the terrorists from the statesmen from the businessmen without a scorecard. And the debate: a gas that gives you a bellyache is a biological weapon, but a machine gun that rips your belly to pieces is not. Semantics! All weapons are biological; that's their point.

Ridiculous though it may be, it must be the memory of the trace of the sound and scent and more so the sense of that one man swinging in synch with the universe that makes my every step land uneasily, because I can't believe that there isn't a hole that will plunge me to Hades. I need grounding, and suddenly know no better place to find it than a barstool.

Conveniently located on an unnamed alley that spears through between Agron Street and Khativat Yerushalayim, Dregs is one of my favorite watering holes. It's next to a store that sells the usual Judaica crap to sentimental tourists: postcards, key chains, olivewood camels in small, medium, or large, velvet, knit, and suede yarmulkes, silver-plated kiddush cups and menorahs kept in a locked glass case to connote a value the things themselves do not deserve, and, of course, endless reproductions of the Wailing Wall on photographs, lithographs, woodcuts, jigsaws, macramé. But off to the side of the fluorescent-lit, *tchatchke*-filled window there's a wrought-iron gate and four crumbling concrete steps. Descend those steps to a dank hallway that leads to a steel door that opens into the room that is Dregs.

That's it, just the gate that creaks like a playground swing. No sign. You've got to know it's there, it's that cool.

Unlike the tasteful hangouts that serve strawberry daiquiris and yolkless omelettes to fashionable fags in the Billi District, Dregs has no pretensions. Not that Ezekiel, who owns Dregs, would have the chance of a snowball in the Negev of pretending anything given the nature of his premises.

Clear and simple, Dregs is a bar. On one side, scratched mahogany stretches toward the rear, where a jukebox plays everything from hard rock to show tunes, mostly American. About a dozen stools line the bar and a nipple-high shelf parallels them on the opposite wall. Though it measures a scant five meters wide, the establishment feels spacious because there are no tables. This keeps the patrons from nursing a single drink and facilitates what Ezekiel likes to refer to as "mingling." In the good old days, mingling often led to assignations in a back room, where many a good time was had and many a disease was spread. Sadly, the back room was closed down by management before the health authorities could insist and its semen-sodden pillows were replaced with a pool table. I hear the clack of balls like punctuation over Pet Clark as I enter.

"When you're alone and life is making you lonely." Indeed.

"Long time, no see," Ezekiel booms, happy for the company this early evening, well before the rush.

"Likewise," I say.

"Read about you in the papers."

"Read about my boss, too?"

"At your side in your hour of need."

"He's a prince."

"You know what he should do with these borders?"

Ezekiel used to be as pure a bar owner as Dregs is a bar, but over the years he's grown more and more involved with politics, even ran for district council once, lost, amazed that his black leather vest and chaps didn't go over better with the voters. Politics is the national pastime here, and Ezekiel indulges with his own particular, well, bent. For example, I'm sure that somewhere on the wall besides Mr. February and a chalkboard with the results of the latest football pool is a petition to legalize same sex marriage. In fact, I stopped dropping in so frequently when he started lobbying me seriously. "Don't forget the gay vote, Nathan," he'd hail me with that rise in his voice at the end of the sentence. This I can hear in the state office building. I come to Dregs for something beside politics. But here I am, and if I must listen today, I will, but first I say, "First, pour."

Ezekiel knows what I drink, vodka before five, whiskey after. He looks under the counter for a clock—bad business to have one in sight; it lets the customers realize how many hours they've wasted, the minute hand a constant recrimination—and pulls a bottle from the rack behind him. It clinks faintly against its neighbor to the left of the cash register. White liquors, vodka and rum and tequila, are to the right. Must be five-oh-five. I can smell the peat on the tip of the spout.

Ezekiel pours heavy and sets the glass on the counter. "On the house for a hero of the nation."

"How about a chaser for Goldie?"

"I hate it when Germans get drunk," he says. "Especially the old ones. That's when you find out how many people they killed. Where were you during the war, doggie?"

Goldie looks up with her warm, wet eyes.

"She says she wasn't even born then."

"Guilty. Guilty," Ezekiel pronounces judgment.

"But she's severed all connections with her parents. Hasn't seen them since she was a pup. Refuses to answer their letters. She even made Aliyah."

"Okay, okay, you're breaking my heart. I'll make an exception," he says, and cheerfully fills a shallow bowl with beer from the tap.

Ezekiel's dad spent some quality time in Mauthausen, and Zeke himself was a tank commander until he realized that he wanted to do more than take showers with the rest of his regiment. That was when his world changed. Still dichotomized, the split was no longer between German and Jew, between Arab and Israeli, but between gay and straight. Occasionally a gay German tourist will, however, confound him. Even a German dog. He pushes the bowl across the bar and says, "But I won't serve Beck's."

I say, "Goldie will just have to make do with Budweiser," and set the bowl on the floor beside my barstool, then straighten up and prepare to listen to yet one more person's ideas for solving the problems of the world.

Ezekiel's hand cups the side of my head where my ear used to reside. "May I?"

"Sure."

His little finger probes gently at the small hole in the bandage, and he chuckles with appreciation. "You do get weirder by the day, my man."

"Let's check out how you're doing," I reply, and extend my hand. He lets it flutter over his features. They've sagged a bit in the months since I've been here. Ezekiel's in his mid-forties, when age starts to tell. From the angle his head extends for my examination, I can tell where he stands, a good inch farther back from the counter than I remember; this may be an adjustment for a belly that has finally begun to display the beer he's drunk over the decades.

I remember Ezekiel's face from years ago, and I remember his body from the back room, where the same gentleness of his fingers worked in such contrast to the gruffness of his manner.

"Enough," he says, and takes a sip of the beer—Beck's—that's always in front of him. He allows the distributor to ply him with samples and never sells them. But today's lecture is not titled "What Murderous Beasts the Germans Once Were and Will Always Be." No, he's playing another one of his greatest hits: "The Stupidity of the Jews and Why Anyone in Their Right Mind Really Should Hate Us." This number begins as the jukebox changes to Edith Piaf.

"What ben Levi has to do is erase all the lines on the map. The hell with borders. But be sure to open bars everywhere there used to be borders. Gay bars, straight bars, as long as they're not those disgusting juice bars. People who drink can't think about anything but fucking, and people who fuck are too tired to kill."

Wisdom.

"Think of your famous serial killers," he continues. "Charles Manson or back to Gilles de Rey, or your plain political assassins, Lee Harvey Oswald, Yigal Amir. None of them got laid. You put those guys in bed and they shoot their wads, not their guns."

"But what about Reb Rubinstein with his six kids?"

"Oh, him."

"Yea, him. I have a personal interest."

"Well, how do we really know they're really his kids? Anyone do any genetic testing? They may be his rabbi's kids, for all we know. Besides, he missed."

I tune out, and Ezekiel goes on, something about a demonstration at the Wall and what a great thing it would be if I showed up.

Every day there's a demonstration at the goddamn Wall, women who just have to pray in taleysim, reform Jews who insist on their right to pray while nibbling shrimp, prayers for peace, prayers for war, all those thousands of folded slips of paper people stick in the cracks so that their most heartfelt desires will go direct to the deity who is as deaf as I am blind.

And yet . . . one lonely rabbi acting like a child in a municipal playground can turn around an entire world of thought. Whatever else surrounds me—the concrete floor, damp with a decade's-worth of spilled beer and poisonous human emissions, the Little Swallow of Paris warbling her heart out against a background of pool balls clunking into pockets, and Ezekiel's cracked gender politics—I'm still thinking about the swings. They're so vivid to my mind that I can still smell the desert. Specialists in B.P.s' disorders would call it an olfactory hallucination.

"Shalom," a soft voice whispers.

There's a body on the stool next to me. He must have slipped in like a fish.

Ezekiel will not impede business. He breaks off his lecture and shifts into bartender mode, "Can I help you?"

The presence, a confection of rubber sneakers, cotton T-shirt, and warm bread, addresses me directly. "Will you buy me something?" The voice sounds distinctly underage, but it bothers neither me nor Ezekiel. I like the voice; it's as soft when it speaks as when it whispers, and has an adolescent pitch and a Palestinian accent that would not be welcome in most bars in this town. Maybe Ezekiel's theories are right after all.

"What'll it be: homes or schools or hospitals?"

Silence. I guess he doesn't see the evening news.

I try again. "Anything you want."

"Anything?" he echoes with a sly, Arabic leer.

I nod to Ezekiel.

Ezekiel nods to the boy.

The boy nods. "Sabra. On ice."

Sabra: affectionate nickname for native-born Israelites and the nation's contribution to the world of liqueurs. What Sambuca is to Italy, Kahlúa to Mexico, and Bailey's to Ireland, Sabra is to Israel, grain alcohol mixed with pungent orange flavor, a digestive, an aperitif, usually sipped from a wide-mouthed glass on a short stem, like cognac, straight. With ice it's a contradiction in terms, hot and cold at once, the ultimate luxury for an Arab ragamuffin who, I suddenly realize, I've met before.

When? Half an hour ago.

Where? At the base of a playground swing.

First he kicked me in the head, then he tracked me, and he knows that I know it. While Ezekiel walks down to the far end of the bar where the liqueurs are stored, he takes my hand and, again whispering, says, "Can you follow me?"

I could follow a snowflake in a blizzard.

"That'll be five shekels," Ezekiel says.

I push ten across the bar. "Keep the change."

"Looks like you found a sugar daddy, kid."

The boy gulps rather than sips the drink he's probably only heard of, and coughs as the raw orange gasoline burns his throat.

"Let's go," I say.

The boy starts for the door, and in the background, Ezekiel has wittily changed the jukebox to start playing the jazzy brass of "Hey, Big Spender."

Anywhere for an assignation, the tawdrier the better. I wonder how much money I have on me, or if the sweet nurse at Hadassah H. relieved my pants of superfluous bills before Ahmed—call me racist, but they're all Ahmed to me—can do so. Unlikely, but my thoughts are a jumble as we march across town at a discreet distance from each other. At first he seems to fear losing me and turns frequently, but then he gains confidence in my shadow. Not to worry, my lad. I am as bound to you as Goldie is to my limp wrist. So what if my leash is invisible; it's attached to the invisible slap of your sneakers on the pavement and the invisible waft of the desert from your skin.

As if he can tell that I'd rather not enter Independence Park again, the boy walks two perpendicular sides of Jerusalem's meager greensward instead of cutting a corner, and then turns up Ha Kayemet. Branching off to the left and right is one of the original residential districts outside of the Old City, where urban descendants of the first rural kibbutzniks live. A car slows down beside me and then drives up ahead to accompany the boy for a minute, probably a police car.

His steps are more deliberate now, aiming for nonchalance, revealing tension.

What's wrong with this picture? the patrolmen may be asking themselves. If the Palestinian youth was pursuing the blind man, they'd see a crime about to happen, but the situation is the reverse, and they pull off after letting him know that they know he's where he shouldn't be.

We traverse the entire district of ivy-covered villas and cross one of the wide boulevards built in the seventies to connect the outskirts to the center. Jerusalem rolls over a sequence of hills, some chockablock with beige Lego housing, others reserved for government purposes. To the left is the Knesset, straight on Har Herzl and Yad Vashem, but we make a right and walk, alone on the wide sidewalk as commuters pick up speed on the broad macadam, in the direction of the big hotels and the Central Bus Station.

Please, not a bus ride. I don't think I can bear waiting for hours and then standing crushed in a smelly crowd—Israel may have handicap legislation, but Israelis still haven't learned politeness—while all the white people get off and stare at me for staying behind as the bus crosses an entirely visible line, complete with police barricades, that separates us from *them*.

Can't we just take a cab? Or maybe I'll call Noam and force him to drive me and this evening's boy around the city while we dally in the back seat like Emma and Rudolf.

Alas, my trick seems set on a particular destination and the bus depot looms beyond the Sheraton. Maybe he has a bomb and a bag of bent nails strapped to his belly, and we're on a suicide mission.

Nonsense. Besides, I can smell a bomb as well as Goldie's trained siblings.

But the liveried doorman at the Sheraton doesn't know this, and his attention is fixed on us from the moment we step onto hotel property. Then, more daring, more amazing, and despite his vigilance, we trespass farther. Instead of walking straight across the public right of way, we start up the sloping semicircular drive to the doorman's private domain. There is a sidewalk, but virtually nobody ever uses it. I can sense the bulk and smell the idling exhaust of half a dozen tour buses clogging the drive together with an endless chain of ubiquitous Mercedes taxis. What would Ezekiel think?

If the boy expects me to spring for a room in the Sheraton, he has another think coming. Well, actually, I will. After all, I haven't had any of my usual out-of-pocket expenses for the last week, so I can exceed my budget for pleasure. You want top shelf, sweet cheeks, you got it. Anything for a lad with a sense of theater.

The ground levels at the top of the ramp, but that's where the boy surprises me. Rather than enter through the revolving doors I've always hated, we veer away from the hotel's grand facade to a path that leads to a service entrance. Instead of setting our luggage down on the marble floor, instead of being soothed by the waterfall in the lobby, instead of receiving the snappy attention of an army of bellhops and concierges, we're immediately inside a vast kitchen, amid the steamy air of industrial dishwashers and the clatter of a thousand plates and the scents of a score of foods.

I hear Arabic chatter among the staff and think how easy it would be for Hamas to infiltrate this joint. It's a miracle that an exploding cake doesn't appear one day. If I were advising the other side, that's what I would suggest. Hit the Jews where they live. Two dead tourists might equal two hundred million dollars, not shekels, in lost revenue. That's what Islamic Brotherhood does in Egypt. Instead, these idiots focus on the buses ridden only by cleaning ladies.

The boy stops in an alcove that smells of grease and detergent, and I hear chains again. This time, however, they're not part of an innocent playground swing, but the workings of an enormous freight elevator clattering down its shaftway. Unlike the cabs tarted up with mirrors and jade inlay for the guests, this elevator has a heavy steel floor and unornamented walls. Even better, the freight elevator has no Braille buttons or signifying beeps for the blind. Visionless tourists must be treated delicately; as for blind janitors and chambermaids and waiters, screw them.

The boy presses a button, and we rise, and keep rising. I don't expect him to hit the stop button and blow me between floors, but I could live with that, too. No, he's going somewhere particular. Without beeps it's hard to figure out how high, but I count under my breath. At six seconds per floor, I arrive at ninety-five when the elevator starts to slow, and one hundred and four when it halts, no less than seventeen stories up. Nothing by New York standards, but high for the Holy Land. The hotel only has eighteen floors. The kid either lives in style or moves in interesting company.

As I follow him down the hall, my fingers trace the doorways. A standard hotel room is three to four meters wide, five to six steps apart. By the end of the hall, say seventy-five steps, I've counted four doors. We're definitely in the penthouse.

He knocks once, pauses, knocks twice, pauses, knocks once. Code.

The door opens and the smell of desert is as overwhelming as if a tidal wave of sand has poured out. There are two men in the doorway, one a hulking presence that anyone who's ever spent any time in government can immediately recognize as a bodyguard, and another, the source of the scent. If that wasn't enough, I also detect the odor of heavy wool gabardine that's clung to him even though I don't think he's wearing the garment anymore. I also recognize the breathing. This time there's no mistake. Before he can welcome me, I say, "Hello, Gabriel."

We walk across a room the size of his father's office. He reaches for my arm as if to guide me, and I allow this though I have no need. Goldie trots beside us; she will nudge my knee if there's a coffee table or ottoman in the way, as she will if there's an obstruction in a sidewalk or a hydrant by a curbside. But I don't mind appearing helpless for two reasons. First, this has all been too cloak-and-dagger for my taste, so it's better to keep my resourcefulness under wraps. Second, Gabriel's arm is comforting.

Someone else is sitting, and Gabriel introduces me. Unlike his father, Gabriel is polite. "Nathan, I'd like you to meet my friend, Gita Mamoun."

A husky female voice bounces against large plate-glass windows that surely overlook a panoramic view of the walls and domes of the Old City. "Mr. Kazakov, I've heard so much about you."

"Likewise."

The plot gets thicker.

Ms. Mamoun is a legend, and indeed, some people believe that she is literally legendary, since she is seldom seen and never photographed. A Palestinian in Israel, a woman in a strongly patriarchal society, she is rumored to be the most successful businessperson in her part of the world.

Born, like Simon, circa 1948, Gita was the youngest daughter of a Bedouin clan that roamed the barren hills north of Jerusalem in a mobile slum of ragged camel-skin tents while recalling their ancestral grazing lands on the green side of the green line. Amid these impoverished primitives, she was bred on goat's milk and resentment. As a child, she helped smuggle weapons to her older brother, Ali, who was one of the first fedayeen. She carried the parts of a bomb to him in the hem of her skirt or the panties beneath, because the Shin Bet hadn't yet learned to search the private parts of pubescent girls in those innocent days. Sadly, Ali was not as smart as his little sister and his bomb exploded as he fit the pieces together. Even worse, he wasn't killed immediately, but carried, in pieces, to the miserable tent, where Gita saw the torn body desperately in need of modern antibiotics or morphine. She had one gun left, which she sold to a competing terrorist faction for enough to purchase the drugs that eased her brother's way out of this world, but as he entered the heaven of martyrs she realized the extraordinary profit she had made.

As the legend goes, it was in that single luminous moment that Gita understood the twin goals for the rest of her life: she wanted to help her people and make money. Unfortunately, the latter was directly at odds with the former, since the only avenue open to revenue involved arms. She became a dealer, starting with small weapons and working her way up to grenades and then grenade launchers, and ultimately tanks and aircraft. By then money had become its own reward, and she ventured farther afield, anywhere a commodity was unavailable and desirable. Gita traded abstractions, dealt in contracts and options, never taking possession of actual objects. She played the international markets with the facility of a Jew.

Here's one, possibly apocryphal, Gita story: she heard that there were such exorbitant import duties in Chile that practically no one could afford to bring in goods that people with money were eager to buy. Anything that arrived in Santiago was impounded and parceled out to corrupt officials, and the leftovers were auctioned—but even the auctions were rigged. Only a few unwanted cargoes filtered out to the market for honest profit. According to the story, shoes were in great demand one season. So what did Ms. Mamoun do? She sent an emissary to the extreme north of Chile, where, according to shipping manifests, an enormous unclaimed container full of shoes was to be auctioned. Call it lot eighteen. Her instructions were clear: attend the auction and purchase the lot at any cost.

The day of the auction, the assistant frantically called her. Yes, lot eighteen consisted of fifty thousand shoes, all sizes, all shapes, but they were all left shoes. "Useless," he sobbed. "Buy it," she ordered, and hung up the phone. Buy it he did, for bupkes; even the greedy port officials didn't want fifty thousand left shoes. He paid his bill to the snickering of the customs crowd and hired a convoy of trucks to haul away the stupid purchase.

Later that day, however, twenty-five hundred miles away, another one of Gita's emissaries was buying another impounded lot at a different port in the extreme south of Chile. What was in the other container? Guess.

Gita asks me, "Would you like to feel my face?"

"Yes, very much so."

"I have read that this is the way you can determine what people look like."

"Sometimes I can detect looks from language, and sometimes I can make out faint portions of images themselves."

"Do you think this enables you see the truth beneath the surface, Mr. Kazakov?"

I tread carefully. "Do you think that you can see the truth beneath the surface despite the false impressions created by your ability to see, Ms. Mamoun?"

She laughs a deep, throaty chuckle. "We're going to get along very well, Mr. Kazakov."

"Any friend of Gabriel's is a friend of mine."

Gabriel is sitting on the couch now, like Simon across town. I can feel rather than see that he is wearing his usual pale shirt and pants, though his Hasidic overcoat is beside him, like the ghostly husk of a rabbi. He says, "When things started getting dangerous, I could think of no one else to ask for help besides Gita. We met through Rafi."

"Hey, big spender," the boy from the bar and the playground before whispers.

"What danger?"

"We'll get to that."

"How do you know Rafi?" I'm probably hoping that they met at Dregs, but don't really expect to hear so.

"He worked for me in the Negev. At night we would talk. Somehow, he led me to understand that he knew Gita."

I turn quizzically toward the boy.

He answers my unspoken question. "Everyone knows Gita. Except, of course, those who don't. But they benefit from her."

Homes and schools and hospitals. With the profits of her business empire, Ms. Mamoun subsidizes soup kitchens and blood banks. Her foundation trains carpenters and plumbers. Yet many people believe that the benefactress who lives to serve is a figment of the communal imagination. It's difficult for both Palestinians and Israelis to conceive of a heroine of the larger world who cares about a cesspool where the usual role models are killers and thugs.

"Rafi is a member of my extended clan," she says. "When he showed promise it was better that he work for an Israeli than one of his own people. It was easy to find him a job on the archaeological crew. In the West Bank, he would only learn to hate."

Gabriel interprets. "Gita is on the side of sanity."

And yet she has incorporated the grammar of separation. Note that she has Rafi work for "an Israeli" as if he himself is not one, because a Palestinian who resides in Israel is still a Palestinian, the kind who needs the homes and schools and the hospitals she secretly finances, and armies and covert operatives, too.

I contemplate the events that brought us together as reluctantly, partially described several hours ago in another meeting in another Jerusalem suite. If these people were able to overwhelm even the most incompetent Shin Bet agent—and I assume that it wasn't a rookie who was assigned to watch the son of the Prime Minister—I can understand why Klein was unhappy. Did he know that it was the Arabs? We're used to thinking of them as so buffoonish that they're more likely to blow up themselves than their targets, to the point that some wags have suggested distributing bombs to Hamas in order to eradicate it. Were they able to pull this off?

And did he know that it was done with the approval—no, not with mere approval, but upon the explicit request—of the subject of their protection?

Do Klein and Khadoury know about Ms. Mamoun?

Gita—it's so easy to fall into the personal with this woman—must know that she is not loved by everyone. She must maintain an elusive status because many people on both sides of the line clearly want her dead.

"Yes," she says, calmly answering my unvoiced question. "That's why I live here."

"You *live* here? I mean you live *here*?" I ask in amazement.

"You think I like Chile?" she replies. "I'd rather sell shoes to my own people, but they don't have money. Peace is the only way to prosperity."

"And yet your own profits were made from enmity."

She shrugs. "That's just one of the contradictions that makes life interesting."

Gabriel continues, "When I learned about the danger, Rafi got in touch with Gita for me. She invited me to join her. Where else is safer?"

Gita shrugged. "Room service leaves something to be desired, but at least you know who's next door, the head of UJA this week, AJC next week. Me, I'm just a reclusive South American heiress."

"And a traitor to your people."

This stings, and Gita stings back. "You are the one who works for the beast, Mr. Kazakov."

"Do you agree with your friend, Gabriel?"

"It's true, you do work for—"

"I meant, do you agree that your father is a beast?"

"He's in trouble."

"Who?"

"My father is circled by snakes. I must rescue him."

"Who are we referring to?"

"Klein, Khadoury, Noam Abravanel." He knows the inner circle as well as I do, and we share that opinion.

"What about Serena Jacobi?"

Gabriel has to mull over the answer to this one. Slowly, he says, "I think she genuinely loves him."

"As well as your mother?"

I am hitting below the belt, but Gabriel does not take up my challenge. The whole country knows about Simon's waywardness. He continues, "But I don't know if she loves him or his power, and whether she will sacrifice him for greater power."

"What greater power?" Now I'm uncertain. Simon is the undisputed lord of his party, and Labor under Weiner is in disarray. The last election was a rout. I don't need Serena to call up the numbers, sixty-two percent for Simon if you include the religious parties which are usually required to eke out a two-point majority. So what if the next election seems in doubt? There is still no greater power than Simon.

"That is the question." Gita Mamoun takes the floor. "We believe that a group, call it melodramatic but call it a cadre, of people deep inside the government wants to destroy him. Believe me, Mr. Kazakov, unlike every creature without a prick in this country of pricks, I harbor no attraction to and no affection for the current Prime Minister."

Fleetingly professional, I wonder who writes this stuff. I appreciate the parallel construction and more so the tactical vulgarity.

She concludes, "But we all require the rule of law before we can begin to approach the rule of justice. We believe that this group will stop at nothing to attain its goals. I'm talking about assassination."

"Are you saying that Rubinstein really was trying to shoot Simon?"

"No." Gabriel shakes his head, voice wobbling with trepidation. "He was trying to shoot me."

# CHAPTER 6

Just one more kick in the head. I'm standing in the lobby of the hotel and the echoes off the acres of marble—floors, walls, I wonder if the ceilings are marble—are smacking into me like marbles clattering in a tin can.

It's a lot to absorb, and I've got to think. Then I feel a warm, wet tongue which brings me back to earth. Goldie has licked my hand, and now she's nuzzling my thigh with her soft, triangular head. I reach down and massage her neck. Baby wants to go home. She hated the hospital nearly as much as I did, made her peace with the Knesset office she knows as well as the secretaries, enjoyed a brewsky at Dregs, and took the visit to the penthouse of the Jerusalem Sheraton in stride, but it's been a long day. Usually Goldie's head twitches with alertness, but now, whether its the aftereffects of the beer or whether she is as baffled as I am by the sequence of events, she's had it. She's ready to curl up in the corner of the small kitchen on Rehov Rambam. Transference, anyone?

"Come, girl," I say, and we leave the hotel. Immediately a taxi pulls up.

I give the driver my address and settle into the back seat with Goldie's head on my lap.

The driver has a Russian accent and can tell that I do, too, so he tries to open a conversation. "Is that a good neighborhood?" By which he really means: aren't there too many Arabs there?

Frankly, I think there are too many Jews on Rehov Rambam, but I've had it with parlor politics and don't answer him. Shunned, he turns on the radio and Yemenite music, all tinny tambourines and whiny Middle Eastern tunes, blasts out of the dashboard. It's his way of assimilation. I can't blame him; during my army days, I listened to the awful stuff, too, and I, too, spouted superpatriotic rot. First you try on the attitudes of your neighbors, then you adopt their music. And, of course, there's no doubt who my driver votes for. Simon scores big with the Russians and the "Yemenites," the latter meaning any Jews from Iran, Iraq, Morocco, and elsewhere in the Arab world; it's a strange coalition. All the formerly oppressed band together to oppress another people to the consternation of the liberals who liberated them in the first place. That's the way it is; immigrants swiftly learn any prejudices the natives have to offer. Oddly, the only taste that never changes is for food. No matter where we go, the scent of a foreign cuisine goes with us. Viz: Proust. I only read him in Russian, but a madeleine is as good as a blintz.

Yet certain traits are international, and bad driving is one. This guy doesn't drive like Noam, whose heedlessness of traffic regulations comes from a kind of politesse oblige. Instead I'm the back seat captive of a naturally pessimistic Slav who is taking out his world-historical rage on the pedestrians and other motorists of Jerusalem. There must have been charioteers like this in Rome, and even peasants behind oxcarts in Merrie Olde England who cut off or crashed into other peasants in oxcarts.

I can feel the tension in the wheels, the tightness of the turns, the frantic acceleration as we must be hitting yellow lights just as they turn red. We ride the hills like a roller coaster and once or twice hit a bump and leave the ground behind for a second. Leaves my stomach behind, too. But he knows his way, this guy, and I can feel the turn off the boulevard, the two rights, and the left into the street named after a medieval philosopher where Mother and I live. Numbers must be whizzing past; he can surely sense that 442 is leading to 444 is next to 446 and that 448 will be soon, but he refuses to slow, and jolts to a stop.

My head snaps forward and then comes to a rest.

A car is idling at the curb in front of us; I can hear the low purr of the engine.

I'm about to pay when I get another idea. Maybe it's the driver's recklessness, and maybe I just don't want to see Mother yet, so I say, "You know what, I changed my mind. Let's go somewhere else. The Jaffa Gate."

I'm waiting for him to say, "Is that a good neighborhood?" but this time he doesn't bite, and this time, on the return journey, his driving is careful. Maybe it's a personal or company policy: driving out of town may be fast and driving into town must be slow, or maybe it's because the Jaffa Gate is a destination for tourists that puts him in another mode, but that's fine. I need the time to think.

As soon as the cab pulls up the ramp reserved for buses during the day, I'm in another world. The smells of falafel and beer from the take-out stands that cater to the students and backpackers of the world assault me. Crowds are jostling past us, exiting the Son et Lumière, and someone, probably a New Yorker, calls, "Taxi." The travel agencies say that it's not safe at night here, though the byways are so narrow and covered with awnings and corrugated overhangs that it's hard to tell midnight from noon. Let's just say that it's not safe at any hour, although what is?

The Old City, old when Athens or Alexandria was new. I recall my first vision of this place an hour after I stepped off the plane from Vienna. That was the route out in those days. The former USSR wouldn't admit it was sending Jews to the renegade Zionist entity, so we all went to Vienna and then changed planes. From the land where Hitler was born to the land that would never have come to be if not for Hitler. Vienna's always been a good disembarkation point for Jews.

When we arrived in Israel the exteriors were pretty much the same as they had been for several thousand years, a jumble of cubes, once rough and grainy, smoothed by time to a pastel gloss, heaped atop each other like the blocks in a gigantic child's toy chest, but the insides of these small boxes that had fermented the imaginations of generations of god-besotted pilgrims—at least those in the Jewish Quarter—were all wired and plumbed as efficiently as the latest high-rise in Tel Aviv, and satellite dishes peeked off the wrought-iron balconies that once served for laundry, and the souk that used to sell cumin and rice to the locals was now filled with sandals and ceramics and Kodachrome cartridges. I'd never been here before, but I could tell that it was all the same as it ever was and all different than it had ever been, except for Abdullah's Café, which Abdullah swears his ancestors have owned and worked since the Crusades.

I imagine Richard the Lion-Hearted at the head of a column of tired Crusaders. "We'll take two thousand espressos to go." It requires a lot of juice to rescue the Holy City and slaughter the infidels.

It's Abdullah's that I'm on the way to, off to the left, immediately out of the main path that wends back toward the Wall. I cross the Via Dolorosa at Station Ten, where the Romans stripped the garments off the guy who would become the official God of the empire three hundred years after his death. Here, where the Christian Quarter abuts the Moslem Quarter, you begin to get a feeling for what the whole city must have been like until '67. Here the smell is human rather than commercial; here the rents haven't octupled with each passing decade, because the very name of the district still intimidates the Americans who think they're so daring. Two urchins start hassling me, "Dollar, mister. You have dollar?"

That's the disadvantage of my Russian countenance; the beggars don't bother the residents and can't tell that I'm not a Yankee tourist. I should have borrowed Gabriel's Hasidic costume.

I stride forward while comparing my unwanted companions to Rafi. If not for Ms. Mamoun, he might be here right now. Instead, he sleeps in one of the guest bedrooms in the same suite as the most mysterious woman in Israel and the most wanted man in Israel.

"You want Church of Dormition? You want Midnight Mass? We take you for dollar."

They'd take me for a lot more than a dollar if I let them. All I'd have to do is whisper, "Hashish," before they'd start salivating, thinking they'd have me in a basement.

They'd probably let me have them in a basement, too, if I wanted that, but my taste doesn't run toward adolescents. I twist Goldie's leash and she growls.

"Bad dog," I say. My Hebrew is excellent, but I do speak with an accent, so as far as the kids are concerned they've still got a dupe. Maybe not an American. A Finn, say, or a Laplander who left his reindeer at the hotel, a visitor from the Land of the Midnight Sun. "Bad dog," I repeat as Goldie, who may remember those words from her puphood training, rubs my leg to prove how kind and loyal she is.

But the boys are too obtuse to get the message, or maybe they just believe that a B.P. from any country is too easy a mark to let loose. "No. Good dog. Good dog." One of them reaches down to pet Goldie, but I turn the leash harder and she snaps.

The kid is quick, I'll give him credit. He yanks his hand back and laughs. "You right. Very bad dog, mister."

I decide to play a little. "Bad dog is German shepherd. She doesn't like Jews."

Now the boy is mortified. "But we not Jews. We Palestinian. We see Jews, we go *grr.* Good dog."

I'm getting tired of this game, and Abdullah's is nearby. I finger inside my pocket and pull out a handful of shekels. If I hand them to the kids they'll pester me forever, so I've got to abase the beneficiaries of my charity. I fling the money over my shoulder and the kids are gone before the coins clatter to the pavement. I turn a corner beside a shop that sells chipped seconds from the ceramics factory and can already smell the best coffee in Israel.

No matter that it's midnight, the café is full. There's a murmur of conversation punctuated by the clack of dice rolling across backgammon fields underneath clouds of smoke. Most, but not all, of the talk is in Arabic, but IDF soldiers on guard duty in the Moslem quarter fuel up on caffeine here, and set their guns down against the thick, stuccoed wall to the disdain of hip peaceniks who have also discovered the place. A cluster of young people in the rear beside a display case full of raisin-and-nut-filled pastries breaks into laughter. Everyone's money is good as far as Abdullah is concerned.

"Adoni Kazakov," Abdullah hails me from behind the counter.

I wonder if Ezekiel's ever been here, maybe even studied at the Arab's size-twelve feet. One sells coffee and other coffee liqueur, but they both have the natural host's manner.

Abdullah continues, "It is so good to have you back. The blessings of God must be shining upon my humble establishment." Of course this is an act, but he performs it with the gusto of a born impresario who knows his audience knows his routine, but enjoys it anyway. "We have never allowed anyone to sit at your special table," he says while gesturing to his daughter to clear my table of the old man whose old smell is almost as morbid as that of Room 404. "Many people want that table, but no, I say, this belongs to Adoni Kazakov, and it will wait for him as long as it takes."

Was Abdullah once like the two street urchins who followed me here? Is this flyspecked "establishment" the best they can hope for once they stop dreaming of a penthouse in Tel Aviv?

"Don't lay it on so thick."

"Not for you. Allow me to bring you a special. On the house."

"But—"

"I insist. Hannah!" he bellows to his daughter, the waitress and scullery maid.

Everyone's buying me drinks tonight. Nothing like a return from the dead to bring out the welcome. Besides, Abdullah knows that I tip well. He's even stopped overcharging me for the coffee.

This is my Jerusalem, not the panorama visible from the safety and distance of Gita Mamoun's suite, not the sacred sites that drive half the residents to murder the other half every other generation, but an idiosyncratic collection of small havens. Dregs and Abdullah's and a half dozen other favorite spots are the stations of my own transit through the holy city.

I sit in the chair that's still warm from its hastily vacated occupant, who has shifted two seats down against the wall and is probably casting an evil eye my way at this very moment, but too bad. I feel the warmth and comfort that almost make me forget why I'm here: to think.

Moments later, Abdullah's daughter has brought the coffee to a boil, let it simmer, then brought it to a boil again. Whether it's the grounds or the brewing technique, the sludge served in a fragile cup is different from any other coffee I've ever had, and better. The sheer kick may keep me awake until dawn, but it's worth it.

Abdullah stands for a moment, not exactly subservient, just waiting for a clue as to what's desired.

I'm tempted toward solitude, but as I did when the driver pulled up in front of my house, I change directions again. "Join me?"

"With pleasure. It is an honor," he says, and lowers his bulk next to me. "Hannah!" he calls again, and snaps his fingers, requesting a coffee for himself. He must drink so much he doesn't feel it anymore.

Together we sit silently until he, too, is served by the girl with a scent like cloves and honey. Now, since the first part of the ritual is completed, he can speak. "It is good to see you again."

He may even mean this. Yes, he robs me blind; yes, he is surely involved with anti-Zionist activity, but the proprietor's primary allegiance is to these few square meters filled with a dozen unmatched café tables and a few dozen unmatched chairs, this space with a sagging roof and cracked tiles and the copper pots he makes—or has his daughter make—his coffee in. He loves those pots as much as an alchemist does his alembic, and he knows that I love them, too. We have our bond. "Thank you," I say. "It is good to be here. How is Hannah doing?"

Somehow Abdullah squeezes out a sound that can only be characterized as a verbal shrug. Ever since she hit fourteen, Hannah has been a magnet for the boys. I don't need eyes to notice that not all of the other patrons of the café are here for the coffee. The direction of their attention is obvious. By now, at seventeen, she must be such a beauty that Abdullah would be wise to chain her to the dusty display case if he could. "Youth," he sighs. "She is dating a man twice her age."

"You, too, were young," I say.

"I don't think youth was so dangerous then." Abdullah distrusts modernity—usually in the shape of a Mr. Coffee machine—as much as the kibbutzniks who kvetch about their sons and daughters who have left the soil for the discos of Tel Aviv. Common cause if only they'd allow. War between generations can be just as fierce as war between nationalities. The big difference is that youth is bound to age, whereas a Jew will never become an Arab. On the other hand, maybe the Jews have already become like Arabs, blindered, blinkered like the workhorses on the West Bank, and maybe the Arabs have become like Jews, cleverly working the international media for their own benefit. Pity the poor victim. Look at how brilliantly the Shoah has served the surviving Jews. So if the first Holocaust gained us Israel, the so-called Palestinian Holocaust may yet gain them a nation of their own.

Though he's simply got to hang a green and white flag from his awning if he doesn't want his café to accidentally burn down, Abdullah is probably the only Arab who hates the idea of the West Bank. And Gaza, that nasty little cesspool, is beneath contempt. Abdullah claims that he's never left the confines of the Old City in his entire life, not for a moment to visit family or picnic in the hills. He's a consummate urbanite and might feel comfortable in London or Paris or Moscow. Once I ate lunch at a garment district cafeteria when Simon and I were in New York, and what struck me was that the steamy, dingy atmosphere felt precisely like Abdullah's.

Unlike the politicians who presumably represent him by using Jerusalem for its symbolic significance and genuinely want the lebensraum of the territories, Abdullah only advocates Palestinian territorial imperative to get rid of competition in the city. Let them have a casino in Jericho, a Hilton in Hebron, as long as they leave him to serve the remaining clientele that loves Jerusalem half as much as he does, which is as much as he loves anything on earth with the possible exception of Hannah his daughter, whose growth and maturity drive him to distraction.

"And the city?" I ask, knowing that I won't have to read the last week's newspapers after our conversation.

"Someone robbed Jacob Twersky."

"Really?" This is news.

As much of a local fixture as Abdullah, Twersky has a shop in the Cardo, the Roman arcade in the Jewish Quarter that has become a mini–Madison Avenue filled with boutiques and chic restaurants.

Mostly his clerks sell coins and worthless chipped amphoras to tourists, but in the back room the man deals in rarer artifacts that, rumor has it, are not entirely legal. All archaeological findings must be reported to the government, and yet where there's a market. . . .

Robbed, though? Twersky's shop may look like the others, but he's lived in the Old City since he arrived as a nearsighted lieutenant with the army in '67 and knows its dangers better than the police do. He even knows the dangers of the police better than the Arabs do. Besides, his premises have an alarm system to rival the Israel Museum's. That Twersky is vulnerable is as shocking as hearing that Abdullah has switched to decaf.

"Yes, he was here the other day and told me. I didn't understand entirely, but it was a sophisticated scam, a switched manuscript, a check on a Caribbean bank."

Though he's as observant as any rabbi, Twersky's a regular in the café, and Abdullah's kosher credentials are good enough for him. Sometimes, for a special customer, the antiquities maven will send a runner across the Old City to fetch a carafe of Abdullah's brew. Coffee is coffee.

I suggest, "Maybe he's losing it."

"We all do." Abdullah sighs, and I catch a hint of a tone that I can't yet identify before he continues, "Even you. To be shot by a man who never shot anyone before, an amateur, I was ashamed for you, Nathan."

Now we've reached first names, and Abdullah knows what I want to talk about.

"Is that what you hear?"

Reuters doesn't exactly maintain a terminal in the kitchen, but if Chester Llewelyn ever develops a fraction of the sources that Abdullah was born with, he'll win a Pulitzer.

"I hear many things."

Now it's my turn to sip. I cannot ask Abdullah what he hears; I can only listen when he chooses to speak. Those are the rules of this intricate game. Besides, he will only tell me if he perceives some benefit to himself. Fortunately or unfortunately, news of Jews eating themselves is always of benefit here.

"The papers deny it, but I've heard that Rubinstein was connected to Israel Ha G'dolah."

Israel Ha G'dolah means Greater Israel, and the group that goes by that name is a fringe of a fringe off Kahane Chai off Gush Emunim, a secret society that is allegedly planning for the return of the Temple and expects to usher in a new Messianic age.

"Your source?" I say, and immediately regret it. Suddenly Abdullah's a clam, just an honest coffee merchant, wouldn't know politics if they bit him on the ass.

But he's already let slip this one tidbit that must be chewed over. Perhaps Israel Ha G'dolah is what has Simon and Shin Bet so worried. The messianists consider the P.M. a traitor, but would they attempt to assault his son? Did Rubinstein have anything to do with this bizarre cult that wants to reinstate Temple sacrifices? Would Simon have brought in Gita Mamoun to help rescue Gabriel? And is the search for Gabriel by Shin Bet a pretense, even from me? I wonder why Serena Jacobi did not bother to inform me of this item. Even if it's false, the fact that someone believes it is interesting. Was I the only one in either the Knesset or the Sheraton who didn't know?

A chair scrapes across the floor. I was so immersed in private speculation that I didn't detect the approach of another person. "Speak of the Devil," Abdullah chortles.

"My dear, Nathan," a low, Yiddishly inflected voice announces itself. It's Jacob Twersky, undoubtedly dressed in a perfectly pressed white shirt and checkered vest with *tzitzis* fringes hanging out.

"Hannah," Abdullah bellows. "Another special for another sad case. It's victim's night tonight!"

"What is this I hear about a robbery, Jacob?"

"Nothing, nothing." He shrugs it off. "A mere inconvenience. The cost of doing business."

But I can tell that he is shaken, and I, too, wish to change the subject. "Everyone has to do business. Even Israel Ha G'dolah."

I can't see the round spectacles Twersky wears, but a glint of light reflects off their thin gold rims as he examines me with the frankness that people who can see apply to people who can't. Then the glint is gone as he turns toward Abdullah, the obvious source of this information. Finally, he turns back to me and, measuring his words like change from a large bill, admits, "There have been meetings. On both sides. The Yemenite is in town."

For a second I think of my taxi driver, but I'm being slow. A week in the hospital has changed my usual frame of reference. A second later, however, I get it. The Yemenite is not some dark-skinned émigré who owns a music bar on Ben Yehuda Street and maybe deals a little hash on the side, but the senior advisor to Palestinian authorities, and the only one who refused to attend the congress that voted to remove the plank calling for the elimination of Israel from the platform. Depending on your point of view, he's the last honest man or the last hard-liner. Either way, he's as crazed as any believer in Israel Ha G'dolah.

That's why Twersky mentioned this. As much as he and Abdullah have in common, they still stand on opposite sides of a psychic green line, and each wants to let me—and through me, Simon—know what the other side is up to. I feel like a fish contemplating bait.

The two men continue to contend for the status of the most informed man in Jerusalem, and now we're in the realm of vanity as each one ups the other, but what this has to do with my current predicament, I don't have the faintest idea.

Names and figures are swirling around me. Circles within circles. Simon and his advisors and military command, the reporters, Gita and Gabriel, Israel Ha G'dolah, and the Yemenite.

And then I sense a rumbling deep underneath the basement of the café as if we're housed inside a cello whose strings are starting to vibrate but aren't yet audible. If I didn't know better, I would think it was an earthquake tremor.

It's not only me. All conversation has stopped, not just that of the two men at my table, but that of the soldiers and the teenage boys hovering as close as they dare to the divine Hannah.

"Abdullah?" I ask with a jut of my chin.

"Demons," he answers, and Twersky laughs mildly.

It's the laugh that compels Abdullah to elaborate, but he addresses me directly, after scraping a match on the tabletop and lighting a cigarette. He exhales a fog of smoke and says, "Your government is being very tricky. I am surprised you have not written any pretty speeches about this, but oh, no, I forgot, it does not exist."

It? What? "Do abstract nouns exist?" I reply.

Now it is Abdullah's turn to perk a head like Goldie. I can tell because of the rumbling of his breath, like the rumbling of the earth. He hasn't yet told me what he means by demons, and I wonder if a doctor has yet told him about the demon in his lungs, the result of half a century's worth of hand-rolled tobacco. I don't need a medical degree to make a diagnosis.

"It's the fucking tunnel again."

Since the on-again, off-again "peace process" has not yet led to the construction of any tunnels under the Jordan and the only other river we have in Israel is the Ha Yarkon, which dribbles around Tel Aviv at a maximum width that a twelve-year-old could spit across, there's only one tunnel worth speaking about.

"Obviously," Twersky says. "Everyone knows it runs north beside the Western Wall. Somebody's probably changing a light bulb. You should call the U.N."

"If they're changing a light bulb, why do we hear it only at night, and why when we complain to the authorities do they claim that all excavations have been closed down? Why do they forbid Arab representation on these vitally important light-bulb-changing missions? They think we're idiots."

The rest of the café is listening to the argument, and the soldiers are quietly reaching for their guns.

"Nobody thinks you're an idiot, Abdullah."

"Sweet salve. This is interesting, it's a new technique. Usually the Israeli government broadcasts its triumphs to the world. *You* turn the desert into orange groves that *we* destroy. *You* have this wonderful air force and *we* have a camel corps. *You* have light bulbs, and *we* are so primitive that we must make do with candles."

While I can't help but think that this man could write speeches, Abdullah turns on me personally. "Usually *you* write the releases, Nathan. Now, instead of saying what you are doing, you are denying it."

"I am denying nothing."

"Which does not mean that there is nothing to deny. And, of course, you have been out of the loop."

I don't like being put on the defensive, and I don't like the feeling that even a coffee-based amity can boil over on a second's inadvertent provocation. Maybe more so, I hate the fact that Abdullah has intuited my own sudden, disconcerting ignorance. Nonetheless, I am not in a mood to argue and offer a halfhearted explanation/excuse. "I am sure that if anything worth noticing is going on, the public will be informed."

Abdullah snorts. "Does this mean that the Israeli government has finally learned shame?"

"No," I insist, as if correcting a pushy reporter, "there is nothing to be ashamed of. No shame; maybe discretion."

"But that is an Arabic virtue."

"Then maybe . . ." Twersky intervenes with the same perception I had earlier, "as you are becoming Jewish by using the media of the world to further your cause, we are becoming Arabic in our undermining of things."

Abdullah says, "In this case, literally."

My cup rattles across the table of its own accord, like the marker on a Ouija board.

I summon up the history of the tunnel from my early, enthusiastic immigrant studies course as refined by my ad hoc postgraduate degree in local politics. Discovered in the late nineteenth century by British archaeologists, it lay no more investigated for decades than any warren of rooms in a tavern basement. When Israel captured the Old City in '67, however, a new era began. Core samples determined that the half-mile-long "tunnel" was really a Roman street that had been built over in the Middle Ages—similar in fact to the Cardo in which Twersky maintains his shop. Unlike the Cardo, though, this tunnel remained underground, because it lay beneath the Moslem Quarter—until '88, when the government decided to make an additional opening to accommodate tourists. Since this was during the Intifada, the excavation was decried as a colonization of Arab territory. "Archaeological imperialism," they called it, and the new entry remained sealed.

That's how the situation remained until only a few years ago, when further research determined that a branch of the tunnel might extend beneath the Temple Mount. Then the tunnel—by then it was "the" tunnel—became the object of exponentially more furious dismay. Orthodox Jews were afraid that someone might trespass upon the forbidden site known as the Holy of Holies. They wanted all access to the site shut down.

That was the first time Gabriel ben Levi came to public attention. He had been the subject of a few profiles in the weekly magazines because of his father's rising stature and because of our country's fascination with the past, but this was different. Suddenly the shy scholar of ancient civilizations had relevance to the superheated world of present-day issues. Still, nobody could have expected that his statement would be any more notable than that of the usual suspects who maundered on about any given subject du jour.

Gabriel was interviewed by the national radio station at an improvised perch off the plaza beside the Wall where the tunnel began. I remember the speech well. The pain in his voice was evident. It was galvanizing. "The reason we look to the past," Gabriel explained, "is for the sake of the future. We believe that the knowledge we may gather will help people, but if people believe that such knowledge is too difficult at this moment, so be it. The tunnel has waited two thousand years; it can wait another two."

"It can wait" became a catchphrase that was revived years later when Gabriel's father came up for reelection. "We Can Wait!" signs followed Simon around, inflicting a torture he never publicly blamed on his son. Note the elision in my language: never publicly.

Bringing up those words now, Abdullah said, "I guess someone can't wait."

Ever since it was closed to the general populace, the tunnel has become the hottest attraction in town. Only VIPs—politicians and the big donors to UJA—are allowed access. No surprise; people get a frisson out of the special because it's special. After '67, visits to Golan Heights were the ultimate proof of status and now it's the tunnel. The place should have a red velvet rope at the gate.

The notion of a secret dig seemed ridiculous, and I assumed that the tremor below Abdullah's was a neighbor adding to a basement despite the zoning laws. Besides, until it hit the papers again, it wasn't my business.

What was my business?

Abdullah and Twersky were at it again, but this time in agreement, coplotting a demonstration to stop an American sportswear chain from opening a shop in the Old City. The rest of the room regained its hum as Hannah served the tables, but every once in a while her father and his friend returned to the elusive subject of "meetings."

Home again. Meetings over this, over that, meetings in public or private, Jerusalem is nothing but meetings, meetings of Israel Ha G'dolah or the Yemenite or Hadassah. A meeting to ponder the meaning of the assassination attempt. Their words seeped through my thoughts. "What's that? A meeting about me?"

"People are interested in you, Nathan."

I refrain from saying, "Yes, I've noticed."

# CHAPTER 7

Many of the Ottoman Empire's elite janissary troops were eunuchs.

"No surprise they were such good soldiers. I would kill, too, if you chopped my balls off."

Early twentieth century Zionist followers of Vladimir Jabotinsky wore brown shirts.

"Certain fashions are never out of style."

"You mean, certain fascists are never out of style."

Tolstoy found great satisfaction in going into the fields to help peasants with the harvest.

"Yeah, except his work clothes were made of silk, and when he was finished he went home to a mansion the size of the Hilton."

"Are you saying Tolstoy was a hypocrite?"

"I'm saying he was human."

Backgammon strategies.

The history of dice.

Fertilization of coffee plants occurs during a dry season.

Purple became the imperial color of Carthage precisely because it was so difficult to produce from crushed abalone shells that only the royal treasury could afford it.

Invention of modern currency was as great an accomplishment of philosophical abstraction as the discernment of God.

Conversation is the engine here, coffee the fuel. The café owner, coin dealer, and I veer from subject to subject until Hannah interrupts after most everyone else has left the café. "I'm tired."

"Go to bed," Abdullah says. "I'll close." We three have no need of sleep.

Edward Said's disingenuous plan for one joint Jewish/Palestinian nation, under one flag, a harmonious, democratic republic wherein each citizen has one vote.

"Yeah, and if there's one more of you than us, we'll have an ayatollah in the Knesset."

"You already have an ayatollah in the Knesset. The only difference is that this one has a wonderful writer." Abdullah playfully punches my shoulder.

"No need to spare my feelings."

"Hey, I mean it. Without your words ben Levi would be nothing."

"Please, spare my feelings."

We laugh.

Bored, the soldiers roust a hippie, find marijuana in his backpack, and shrug. They're soldiers, not police.

A new sushi restaurant is opening in the Armenian Quarter.

A beggar enters. I can smell his odor, hear the coins in his cup. Twersky donates a bright new shekel, Abdullah serves a leftover pastry, and I rummage beneath the folded message in my pocket for spare change. Could this be the father of one of the urchins I gave money to earlier?

I guess I mention this because somehow we're on to genetics. Are the children of beggars doomed to become beggars, the children of kings destined to become kings? Yes, the children of the leaders often become leaders themselves, but qualities of leadership are not always inherited with the position.

"The Sumerians had the right idea," Twersky says.

"What's that?"

"Kings must be worshiped and then they must be killed. They know this as they enter into the kingship. It is their function and their value. The people obey them and then eat their hearts."

It's this last word, meant literally, heard subjectively, complete with the sentimental apparatus of American Valentine's Day, that makes me think of Gabriel.

Many of the visual images of my past have receded so far into the distance that I can no longer recall them, and sometimes, more terrifyingly, I cannot recall having perceived visual images at all. The Kremlin's onion dome, for example, is more real because of the root vegetables I can hold in my hand, cut with a knife, smell, sob upon if they're pungent, than because of its looming perspective over the city of my youth. At other times, however, distinct pictures enter my mind. Unbidden and undistorted by reality, they approach a platonic ideal. Gabriel.

What did he mean by declaring that Rubinstein was aiming for him? And if the failed would-be assassin-turned-successful-martyr was connected to Greater Israel, does that mean that the group wanted Gabriel dead because of some archaeological discovery that threatens its dream of a Third Temple? Was Rubinstein's the opening shot in the ultimate battle between the secular and the religious? That would certainly freak out Simon, since he relies on a tenuous alliance to maintain his parliamentary majority.

Gabriel. What is he up to?

Indeed, any remarkable archaeological discovery has the potential to set the Yemenite and his caftanned cadre seething as violently as Israel Ha G'dolah, and that might be why Gabriel sought protection from Gita Mamoun.

Gabriel. I am struck by an image that must have appeared in one of the Tel Aviv weeklies when he found the so-called "new" cave at Qumran a few weeks before I joined the army. Wildly out of synch with the original Dead Sea Scrolls, the cave's nine crumbling parchments seemed to imply that the Essenes who lived there were gathering an archive of heretical texts of their era. The notion that these pre-Christians had the self-consciousness to establish a library of the forbidden totally subverted the concept of them as naive believers who cared only for their own idea of the holy. There Gabriel was, dressed in romantic archaeological chic, baggy trousers, short-sleeved khaki shirt showing off his muscles, and, slung low on his waist, a webbed belt with small picks and axes protruding like a Wild West marshal's six-guns. He stood with the dark opening of the cave beside him, the green-blue of the Dead Sea behind him. There he was in the midst of the literary necropolis, alive, blood coursing through his veins. And now I fear for Gabriel's heart, that mystical organ and physical pump that enables him to breathe and enter the world of my senses through memories of his visage and the more current scent of sand.

Gabriel.

I'm still mulling this over when dawn pierces rotted sections of Abdullah's corrugated tin overhang, and the time has come for us to call it a morning.

Twersky and I walk the narrow alleys that both of us know as well as we know our hands. With him to guide me away from any unexpected obstacles, a mound of dog shit or an upturned paving stone, I allow Goldie to trot ahead. Tracing the path of the invisible—it gives me satisfaction to know that it's invisible to everyone—tunnel, we pass under the Wilson and Robinson Arches that protrude from its underground vaults while hugging the shadowy buildings that abut the unexcavated portions of the Western Wall until we traverse the boundary between Moslem and Jewish Quarters. To the southeast lies the Cardo, where Twersky has his shop; to the northeast the vast plaza hacked out of the formerly Arab slum to accommodate pilgrims to the Wailing Wall. Twersky assumes that I wish to head south to exit at the Jaffa Gate and automatically turns right at the corner of a still-shuttered ceramics store and spice shop whose owner is opening for the day, but I have a sudden desire to make one more stop within the Old City.

Twersky takes an extra stride and realizes that I'm no longer beside him. "Nathan?"

"Goldie and I will take it from here."

He knows better than to ask if I need his help, puts a palm on my shoulder. "Shalom, my friend."

They're simple words, but they echo. One recalls the American President's farewell to Yitzhak Rabin. I nod and repeat, "Shalom."

Goldie and I walk through the awakening streets, yet before we can reach the Wall, both of us hear the cry of a muezzin. Atop the El Aksa minaret, he is calling the faithful to prayer. I wonder if Abdullah can hear, too, and if he pauses while mopping coffee spills and pastry crumbs from his floor to drop in the direction of Mecca.

I am jostled by several Arab children on their way to school, and reflexively check my pockets to find them intact.

A mule carrying a clatter of tin pots hee-haws from an adjacent alley.

Like a flutter of birds rising out of a nest, three or four Hasidic girls emerge from a courtyard, chattering in Yiddish. Their conversation halts for a moment as they see me.

A guard on lazy duty at the entrance to the plaza coughs as Goldie and I pass through the metal detector, and does not search me. Note to potential terrorists: get a dog.

Immediately I can sense the enormity of the space as my footsteps cease to echo. Down a flight of worn stone stairs and the distance ahead of several football fields is the Wall. According to legend, its huge base stones were set in place by Adam, Noah, Abraham, Isaac, Jacob, Joseph, and Moses. Never mind that Moses died in Sinai and never entered the Promised Land, and that the legend is in direct contradiction to the Bible. Imagine the very first man, recently ascended from apedom, newly exiled from Eden, shlepping a ten-ton stone to a site in the middle of nowhere, secure in the knowledge that twelve biblical generations later another man recently descended from Ararat would find his way to this same hill and do the same, etc., etc., until the structure that was actually, and no less grandly, erected by Solomon arose. It's a sight, the ultimate physical representation of the Holy Land.

Even I pressed my lips to the Wall's smooth contours once upon a time. Several days off the plane from Vienna, set down as mystifyingly as stones in the middle of the desert, Mother and I, along with the rest of that week's shipment, were bused by the Immigration Department from our temporary residence in a converted hotel to this spot to duly behold and appreciate our new lives. We had already started Ulpan lessons, but still didn't understand a word around us. That didn't make a difference. The Wall—by its antiquity, its solidity, its sheer mighty profundity—was enough. Standing underneath it tells you all you ever need to know about human weakness and the power of faith.

For that one moment, even I believed. All of us believed. Like zombies, we stumbled forward and automatically separated into men and women at the gate like two forks of a river. The women continued somewhat faster toward their destination while the men awkwardly donned black cardboard yarmulkes we fished out a receptacle before resuming our journey.

Oddly, the massive strength of the Wall was set off by hundreds, thousands, of slips and scraps of paper, mostly white though occasionally colored, wedged into the cracks. Some were carefully folded and stuck out like origami, while others were crumpled balls set on tiny ledges where the mortar between stones had worn away. Some appeared welded to the surface with bubblegum. Our guide explained that these were letters to God, but that we were not in need of divine intercession since our prayers had already been answered. Then he led us in recitation of Judaism's most basic prayer, the Sh'ma, syllable by incomprehensible syllable. Then we kissed the Wall.

It was my first kiss.

Years before, I had felt the initial stirring desire for masculinity when I saw a famous poet read in a café on Moscow's Arbat, but it would be years till I came out, and this unrequited adolescent peck on the Wall brought an unseemly blush to my cheeks. I looked around to make sure that no one noticed. One nearby yeshiva student caught my attention. Dressed in black with a wide-brimmed hat, he had long earlocks and a wisp of beard that floated outward from his chest as he swayed back and forth, like a rabbi on a playground swing. The fervency of his worship shook his body so violently that his head nearly smacked the wall with each beat of prayer.

Indeed, the same young man, or his sons, may be here now as I make my way through the ranks of early morning worshipers. They are davening Shakhris, the first of three daily services. This time, however, my vision is different. I can make out no more than an impressionistic flock of crows cawing on all sides of me.

This time, I tilt my head backward and cannot see the top of the Wall. I can, however, reach out to touch several of the slips of paper inserted into the cracks. What would I wish for? Sight? Foresight? Insight? Sounds like the basic premise for a speech. Peace on earth, good will toward men. No, though my desires are just as impossible to achieve, they are more limited in scope. Gabriel.

Palms pressed against the cool stone—it will heat up as the sun crosses the sky—I think, Help me if you can, but I do not write a note because I do not know if God reads Braille. This time there is doubt and, perhaps, disdain.

A tour group, aiming to get a jump on the day, arrives. They're Christian; I can tell because the guide is recounting the story of Jesus and the moneylenders. They're also American; I can tell because the guide makes a lame joke about having a friend at Chase Manhattan. Besides, Jewish groups tend to linger, whereas these folks obviously have places to go. This is a station for them rather than a destination. Nonetheless these American gentiles put on the same—maybe literally—black cardboard yarmulkes I once did and attempt to summon a properly respectful approach to the Wall, where they scribble their own notes for special delivery to an ecumenical God. Today will be a long day for them, and their guide is already getting ready to steer them to the Pool of Siloam and the Garden of Gethsemane and from there to some particular gift shop. "The best in Jerusalem," he'll claim, and the owner will kick back to him a small percentage of the receipts from their purchases.

I hear the click of a few dozen cameras, but one click is aimed in my direction. At first I think nothing of it. The tourists are taking pictures of the rabbis, too, and a blind man with a dog at the Wall is clearly a photo-op worth bringing back to the family in Des Moines. But Goldie growls. She senses something that I don't, so I step toward the source. What will I do? Demand the negative?

The photographer backs away and disappears while the group of

Americans is still gawking at the Jews. Soldiers are on duty, but they can't help me if God can't. It's time to leave.

After catching another taxi at the Dung Gate, this one driven by an actual Yemenite who has the cultural confidence to refrain from playing Yemenite music—or Russian balalaikas, for that matter—I arrive back on Rehov Rambam for the second time in ten hours.

The building is a four-story stucco construction with four apartments per floor, all accessed off a central stairwell with terrazzo treads without risers. There are bicycles and garbage cans on each landing, and a light switch on a timer that I don't bother to use. But the light is on; its electrical hum means that somebody has used the stairs in the last five minutes.

Aaron Litwak may have gone to work early.

I start climbing, and hear the television from Avram Tucker in 2A and the Paltiels arguing behind the door to 2C. Mother and I live in 3A. The key fits easily into the lock and the door swings wide through half the space the Absorption Ministry has seen fit to allocate us. By now I could pull a few strings and get a better apartment, larger and closer to the center of town, but Mother is comfortable and I don't mind being reminded of where I've come from and what I've come to. A little suffering is good for the soul.

We have a living room, and off it juts a single bedroom, a bathroom, a kitchen, and a glass-enclosed porch that serves as my quarters. Blinds between the living room and the porch provide privacy.

The living room contains two chairs, a low coffee table, a television, and a Danish modern couch which has a clean, geometrical wooden frame and three once-orange cushions that were grimy with sweat when I last saw them. They haven't been cleaned since.

My porch has an unmade bed, a freestanding closet for my clothes, a desk, and a bookshelf encased in glass like the porch itself. Otherwise, there are about two centimeters of floor space. I kick off my shoes and check the answering machine. I listen to multiple well-wishers and three hang-ups before padding into the kitchen to make myself a snack. For all the meetings after meetings of the last day, I haven't had a bite to eat since breakfast at the hospital and my stomach is rumbling.

Someone is sitting in the kitchen. The air has traces of human vapor; sounds are diminished by otherly presence.

Someone is sitting at the farthermost of the two chairs at the checkerboard-size table. Someone who knows that I'm blind, because he freezes when I enter.

How do you define fear?

Half of my speeches are designed to feed the mortal terror that you, Mr. and Mrs., or, if you're modern, Ms., Israeli Citizen are about to be exploded in a bus or slaughtered in your bed by rabid Palestinian terrorists. The other half are written to reassure you that if Simon is elected you will be safe from same. Since most voters are in fact not killed by Palestinian terrorists between one election and the next, Simon's presence is declared effective. He's a human condom, but if he breaks—you're screwed. Vote for Weiner from the grave.

Luckily, the someone in my kitchen doesn't notice that I pause for a second before continuing to the refrigerator. Whatever else is going to happen, I might as well eat.

I open the refrigerator to hear its welcoming little clicks and hisses, and remove a carton of eggs from its regular place under the drawer that contains cheese. I open the top and contemplate flinging the half dozen remaining eggs at the figure in the corner and fleeing, but I'm too hungry, and curious, too. I set the eggs down on the small counter between the refrigerator and the stove and fumble around on the rear of the counter for the mesh basket that contain potatoes and onions. I start humming, just in case my visitor coughs. I know that he knows that I'm here, but I'd prefer it if he didn't know that I know that he's here. I'll take any advantage that I can. I reach for a cast-iron skillet hanging from a peg over the stove.

I weigh the skillet for a moment and sense the tensing of muscles across the room. It's someone who believes he—or is it a she; there's a scent that is not necessarily male in the air—can cope with a flying frying pan.

I put the skillet down and reach for a knife, just to torture my unseen observer. It's a well-honed implement with a thick handle and a thin blade, but I couldn't aim it if I tried. I start slicing onions on a wooden carving board and push them into the skillet with the flat of the blade, pour a healthy dollop of oil into the pan. On an impulse, I stand between my observer and the stove and pour in more oil until the pan is nearly full. I run a safety match along the side of the box sitting beside the stove and take a moment of pleasure as my companion is made uncomfortably aware of the light. Then I place the match to the burner until fire flares out from under the pan and the onions start sizzling.

I drag the second seat away from the small table and sit down, careful to extend my legs into the center of the floor to avoid bumping into my guest. I try to stare at him, to imagine what he looks like and whether he is holding a weapon.

Luckily, I don't smell the metallic tang of a gun. Unluckily, I wouldn't be able to smell a knife or a bludgeon or any number of other, more exotic weapons, a garrote, say, or a blowgun with a dab of curare on the tip of a dart. For the first time since Tel Aviv, I am genuinely terrified. I've spent so much time contemplating what may be going on that I haven't really considered the effect.

I hear a car idling at the curb and recall that a car was idling when my Russian driver first pulled up to 448 Rehov Rambam hours ago. Someone has been waiting for me, and he has a friend downstairs. Perhaps it's a friend who took a picture of me in the plaza in front of the Wailing Wall, so that he can make copies and give it to other friends so that they can more easily recognize me. We're talking a minimum of two against one, and the one isn't used to wielding any weapon but a well-placed period. Some great writer said something like that. Who? Turgenev? Babel? Leskov?

I'm associating wildly, imagining myself with a blanket thrown over my head. Superfluous as it may be, that's the way these people do things, isn't it? Next, I'd be tossed into the trunk of that vehicle downstairs and driven across a border, back to Lebanon. Torture I've endured, but I can't bear the thought of imprisonment. Why do I assume that our destination is Lebanon? Something about the smell of my visitor is closer to home. It's organic but not vegetative; it's . . . muddy. I wonder if there are tracks on the floor.

I stand up, stretch ostentatiously, and turn on the radio on the counter in case my companion is wired. The radio is set to the classical station and the DJ announces, "Now for Lyons' Symphony No. 4 in D Minor." I wouldn't have recognized it. Despite the heightening of my senses, I've never been that attuned to music. I know the music of language as well as I know anything on earth—line breaks and beats, repetitions and variations on a theme, the subliminal emotional effects of sibilants and gutturals—but not the literal instrumentation played in concert halls. I enjoy music, but as background. Now I listen carefully.

The string section starts slowly, but gradually woodwinds enter, and then brass takes over.

Together we sit like a pair of devotees who dare not break the spell of the orchestra. But the first violinist in the Israel Philharmonic doesn't mind being watched. It's his job and his pleasure; he's an exhibitionist and the audience is full of voyeurs. They're both ecstatic, but me, I'm no performance artist. I live behind the scenes, and now I'm on the big stage, waiting for the curtain to rise, staring rigidly ahead; I'm about to scream. Then, just as the kettle drums start pounding, the phone rings.

I nearly jump out of my chair.

The phone is on the wall, beside the person opposite me. As I lift the receiver, the cord dangles and may tickle his ear. "Hello." My mouth is dry, my voice hoarse.

"I told you to rest!" The voice is angry, but not as angry as I feel at this interruption.

"Who is this?" I'm not even sure whether I'm addressing the phone or the body inches away from me. What if I swing the hard plastic receiver at his head?

"I thought that your supernatural powers could identify anyone. Or do you need the scent of an omelette?"

This reminds me of something, but I can't put a finger on it. Then I recognize the voice and gasp with relief. "Dr. Ivan!"

"It's Dmitri, but never mind."

"Yes," I sigh, and contemplate blurting out, "Help!" just as I feel the slightest tension on the cord. My visitor is ready to yank it from the wall. I ease back into the chair as if this is just a normal conversation and start chatting. "I intended to come home directly, but had some errands to do."

"What's that?"

"Errands."

"I can't hear you."

Is this a comedy? I turn down the radio and repeat, "Errands."

"And what is more important than your health?" He might as well be my mother, who must be sleeping on the other side of the wall. Or is she tied up, or knocked out, or dead with a pillow resting on her puckered lips? My God, I haven't even thought of her, but I can't now because the moment is too wrought. What is more important than my health?

"Oh . . . shopping." Immediately I regret this lie, because I haven't brought any bags with me, and the last thing I want to do is telegraph my awareness. I improvise swiftly, idiotically. "I'm wearing a new pair of shoes. That should be good for my health." Then I realize that Ivan does not usually make follow-up calls to patients at six in the morning. "How about you? Did you try to call earlier?"

"Yes, but I didn't leave a message."

That explains the hang-ups on the answering machine. "Oh."

"You sound tense."

He's perceptive, too.

"It's been a long day."

"Yes?"

"Don't be a shrink."

I don't mean to cut him off, but I feel my guest rising. He's pacing slowly, carefully, stretching with the arrogance of the sighted in the home of the blind. Only the sizzle of onions makes any sound.

"There was something I wanted to tell you."

"Oh?" I want to ask Ivan what could be so important, but I don't want my guest to become aware that there might be something as important as his visit.

My guest sits back in his chair.

"Yes, something happened at the hospital that I thought you should know about."

"Tell me, by all means." I try to sound chipper, as if this idle talk is part of my normal dawn routine.

"A few hours after you left, the nurse was supposed to prep the room for a new patient. Mandate from the administration. Occupy all beds, et cetera. But . . ."

"Yes?"

"It was already cleaned."

What are we talking about? The house is a mess; it's always a mess. Mother used to work as a cleaning woman until pleurisy got the better of her joints. Now she stays at home, plays mah-jongg with the local merry widows, and delights in the mess; it's a sign of freedom. I say, "Good help is hard to find."

"Her prepping was strictly professional; make sure the proper medication and machinery is available. Housing cleans at night. The room had been searched."

What is he telling me? "So maybe I came back because I left a picture of my grandmother next to the bed. An icon. A religious object. A subject of spiritual devotion." I'm ready to explode.

Ivan ignores me. "Granted, our security is not as good as the Knesset's, but no one is supposed to get past the desk without approval. Somebody did, and whoever it was had a particular interest in your case. They stole your medical chart from the foot of the bed."

"Is this especially private?"

"It does include your home address."

My ears are ringing.

"Are you all right?" Bless him, he can pick up on something in my tone as well as a B.P. Too bad he can't see through the wires.

"No."

"Are you alone?"

"No."

"Can you speak freely?"

"Not really."

The line goes dead.

"Who in God's name are you talking to?"

As if a light has gone on, the room is ablaze with talcum and cold cream. It's the smell of a woman fighting the onslaught of age, the smell of a woman who puts on makeup to go to the grocery store and flirt with the elderly widowers. There's no other smell like it. It's the smell of Mother.

Am I so jaded to the scent that infests this place that I can no longer perceive it? If I lived in a skunk's nest for ten years would I be unable to perceive that, either? Has she been sitting here all this time, using the occult powers of muliebrity to mask her aroma and torture me?

The onions are crisping, the oil sputtering.

"And what are you cooking?" Mother's voice is coming from the doorway.

The phone is ringing, Ivan calling back.

"Hello? Hello?" I cry into the receiver.

"Hello," another voice echoes.

For the first time in ages, I feel blind. Voices and scents are colliding around me, talcum and onions and mud. "Who are you talking to?" Mother asks.

"Who are you talking to?" Ivan echoes.

The blinds must be down, the kitchen dark, and besides, without her glasses, Mother's vision is also impaired.

"What's going on there? We were disconnec . . ." Dr. Ivan is shouting.

Bedtime odors, sweat, my own and someone else's sudden effusion. A workingman's sweat. A farmer's sweat. Onions, cooked and raw, straight from the earth. He's been cool until now, but scent is a telegraph. He's getting ready to react, and his body is telling me so. He's just waiting for a signal.

The click of a switch.

Why Mother bothered, I don't know. We're used to sitting in the dark, but now there's light, and the table comes flying at me, and I'm on the floor in a tangle of limbs and telephone wire.

Mother shrieks.

A heavy, booted foot kicks out.

I'm used to head injuries. From Tel Aviv to Independence Park, the site of my limited senses and spring of my unlimited imagination takes abuse, but this time neither Gabriel nor Rafi, his emissary, is there to comfort me. I reach up, my hand seared by the heat of the handle of the cast-iron frying pan.

The voice—it's as American as the tour guide at the Wall—gasps two words that I can't quite hear in the pandemonium. I almost hear them, but they don't make sense. All that registers is that he must be screaming about the frying pan or the lit stove or the hot oil. No, it's not quite a comment of the moment, on the moment; it's more of a question.

"Leave me alone, you brute!"

I don't know if he's grabbing her. I don't know if he has a knife or garrote or blowgun. I just know he's an invader. Without another second's thought, I grab the frying pan and wing it in the general direction of the ruckus.

More screams, at least one coming from me. He repeats the same two words and doesn't wait for a reply. The front door slams open. It's either someone else coming or someone leaving. A second later, I know: it's the latter. We're safe for now, but now I notice the pain that made me scream. I'll take pain over terror any day, but still . . . something is horribly wrong. First my ear—no, first my eyes, then my ear, then my fingers like a medieval penitent who's thrust his hand into a bonfire to mortify the flesh. Now my foot.

"I still don't understand what you were doing," Mother says as she wraps a bandage around my toes and ankle per Dr. Ivan's instructions.

He's still on the line, which she picked up after the intruder fled, presumably with a sizable lump on the back of his head.

Note that she didn't turn immediately to me. Mother can sense a medical degree as acutely as I can a predilection for the same sex.

Simon ben Levi, Prime Minister of Israel, could have been calling and she wouldn't have been impressed. The nameless son-of-a-bitch whom she hasn't seen since he impregnated her thirty years ago might be calling to see how things were going, and she'd be cool as a cucumber facial, but a doctor was different.

Stunned, probably in shock, I overheard half of their cheerful introduction—"Of course I remember you . . . from the hospital . . . Hadassah, such a fine institution. . . . And where did you train? . . . and when did you leave Moscow?"—while sitting with my foot bathing in a pool of boiling oil until the conversation finally came around to me, and she ran to the bathroom to retrieve a roll of gauze. Now she's alternately cooing at him and castigating me.

"Here," she says. "The doctor wants to speak to you."

Reluctantly, I take the phone. "As you were saying?"

"Good God, what's happening there? Do you live in an asylum?"

I think about Mother and nod, before reaching down to touch the skin that has puffed up like a pastry shell. Instead of collapsing, I compose myself sufficiently to ask, "What do you recommend for a burn?"

"I've already told your mother."

Once again, I'm out of the loop, but this time I have a certain self-interest and am determined to find out what's going on. I speak slowly, enunciating carefully, holding to each syllable like a drowning man to a scrap of floating wood. "Say, hypothetically, that someone has just spilled a pan of boiling oil on his bare foot. . . ." Why did I ever take off my shoes?

"What?"

"Hypothetically, what would you recommend?"

"Hypothetically," Ivan repeats my words, "I'd recommend that such a person come directly to the hospital."

"Say"—I'm biting my tongue—"that he won't do that."

"Then I'd say that he should immediately bathe the burned area in cold water. It will bring down the swelling and soothe the pain."

"Say that the pain is . . ."—I search for the correct word—"excruciating."

"Then take some aspirin, or something stronger, say codeine or several shots of vodka. Personally, I prefer Absolut."

"It figures."

"Use aloe if you have it, or a medicinal ointment if you don't. Give me the name of a local pharmacy and I'll call in a prescription. Wrap the area loosely and keep off it."

This is the advice that he's already given to Mother, who is following his instructions to the letter, straightening her silver hair with one hand while mummifying my foot with the other.

He says, "I'll be right there."

"Don't bother."

"I'll be right there."

"I won't be."

"Fifteen minutes."

"Too much."

"As your physician, I demand that you remain where you are."

What arrogance! Moreover, what insanity. The man still doesn't understand that we're talking about more than health. At least more than a foot's health. Somehow we're talking about more than the physical well-being of one beaten, pathetic speechwriter. "See you for my yearly checkup."

More than the pain, it's my denial of the entire medical system that convinces him that I must be serious. But Doc Ivan is good. His bedside manner extends to telephone advisory services, and he will match any patient's cynicism if that's what's called for. "At the rate you're going, you won't last out the month."

Hoisting myself onto the counter, easing my blistered and gauze-encased limb into a stoppered sink full of cold water scented by a few leftover shreds of onionskin, I remember what the intruder said before all hell broke loose. Two words: "Strange Fire."

# CHAPTER 8

The nice thing about sex is that during those minutes—how many is up to the individual man depending on how much of a man he is—one is no longer a disparity of parts. Oh, there may be the quite nice rubbing of toes, the warmth of thighs, the pounding of hearts, the soft wet infiltration of a tongue into a mouth, but basically one is reduced to a single organ. No matter how romantic rubbish would have it, you're all cock.

Now, like a jigsaw jumbled into its constituent elements, or a poem snipped with a scissors into individual lines, I'm the dead opposite of a sexual being; I'm an unlinked, disharmonious assemblage, each piece of which cries out for attention. I'm a ruined ear, a bruised forehead, and, mostly at this moment, a foot. In the past, I've experienced everything from tooth pain to shaving cuts to Lebanese torture to tiny, unpleasant clenchings of the heart muscle when I've smoked straight through a few packs of unfiltered Camels, but the sheer, searing anguish of my right foot is something new. Every step, my flesh or sinew shrieks from beneath the gauze wrapped around it according to Dr. Ivan's instructions. The sandal loosely strapped over the instep feels like sandpaper, the ground under the arch like hot coals.

Still I stride, easy left foot, brutal right foot, easy left foot, agonizing right foot, easy left foot . . . into the Jerusalem morning. Mother whined and threw herself at me and Dr. Ivan threatened to have the police chain me to my bed, but I had to go and had no other way to travel. If I could see, I could drive, but the notion of pressing this foot to a pedal is too much to bear. Besides . . .

I might have called a taxi, but worried about the line being tapped. I pictured a special car pulling up to the curb while the real taxi was en route. Mother could have checked the driver's credentials, but I wouldn't trust her to walk the dog, let alone determine whether a polite young driver happened to be carrying a gun. I could wait at the corner bus stop, but there, too, I would be easy to follow. Whether it was pain that blurred logic or my naturally suspicious nature or plain stupidity, I figured that the only way to escape was by using these miserable, blistered instruments that God presumably gave my forefathers when they flopped out of the primordial seas onto land on the sixth day of creation.

I trip over the roots of the date trees that break through the sidewalk in their crazed fecundity as I make my way down Rehov Rambam.

Goldie whines; she needs her sleep and wants to tug me home. But she's good and when she realizes that I am determined to forge on, she trots wearily forward.

I try to determine if a car is rolling slowly behind me, but I can't tell. I walk toward the corner and then veer suddenly, between 430 and 432 Rambam, slip between the buildings, into the yard separated from the yard behind it by a fence of preformed concrete blocks. I touch the fence. It's about as tall as I am. No glass on top. This is not an embassy neighborhood. Weight full on my good foot, I lift my bad foot as high as I can, boost up, and collapse back against a garbage can I hadn't noticed.

Usually I can smell garbage a block away, determine the quality of the neighbors' and strangers' previous night's dinners, tell who uses a condom by the earth/milk aroma of clotted semen, distinguish between those who read newspapers and those who read magazines by the way the different papers mulch. But now I'm so disoriented by the miniature sunspots that explode off my arch with every step that I haven't even realized that I have a tool here.

A garbage can. I adjust the metal lid and climb atop. This I can do. Now I stand on my good foot and hurdle the bad one across the fence.

What about Goldie? Without her, I'm chopped liver.

"Here, girl. Jump. . . . Jump, Goldie, jump." I extend arms into a semblance of a cradle and wait until a bounding fifty-pound bag of dog nearly knocks me off my perch. She licks my face and I drop her as gently as I can to the far side of the fence, then drop myself, less gently than I'd prefer.

We're in the yard of a family with young children. I trip over a toy truck and land in a sandbox. At least it's soft. I grope for Goldie's leash, find it, and allow her to lead me through the alley between buildings on this side of the fence to Rehov Rashi.

The streets in the Ma'alot Dafna District are named for rabbis, philosophers, and Talmudic commentators. Rehov Rashi intersects Akiva Street, which wends downhill to connect with Judah Loew Boulevard. Local Arabs have been petitioning the municipal council to acknowledge their heritage, too. They want Avicenna and Averroes Avenues, but names are destiny and the council would rather consider Himmlerstrabe.

Down another street until it dead-ends onto the highway somewhat farther than I'm used to. The glare of sun and the continuous rush of cars means that it must be nearly nine o'clock. People are streaming into the center to go to work in the ministries and museums and counting houses of the capital. And I'm hunted. Are any of these cars watching me?

Actually, all of these cars are watching me. Who wouldn't? I'm a spectacle, half barefoot, my head still half bandaged, staggering beside a panting shepherd.

Still uncertain, though I didn't hear anyone clambering over the fence behind me or the sudden acceleration of a car squealing around the corner of Rambam to intercept me, I feel relatively safe. Nonetheless, Goldie and I take the paths of most resistance. We get tangled in shrubbery and cut across a construction site where the crew shouts at us as saws whine, hammers bang, and a gigantic mixer chugs and emits the scent of liquid concrete.

We skirt the base of Annunciation Hill, heading toward the six lanes of Derekh Ha Shkhem. Dead ahead, eastward, across the highway, lies more Jerusalem sprawl. To the left is the great, wild northland, Jericho, the West Bank; to the south lies the city. I've been driven here hundreds of times, accompanying Simon to ceremonially mortar the foundation stone of the latest settlement, to pay respects at the site of the latest terrorist attack. Laptop on my lap, I've ridden these roads while writing the words that would be spoken within the hour. I know the highway's turns by heart, but not by foot, and my foot bursts with pain.

Yet Goldie and I continue, parallel to the buzz of the traffic, until we reach the point where two additional roads merge with Derekh Ha Shkhem. It occurs to me that I don't know if there is a traffic light here, because Simon's car blasts through intersections like a comet. I flick Goldie's leash upward, the gesture that means, "Go."

Afraid, she hesitates.

I flick the leash again, more imperiously.

Goldie is torn between her training and her master. What happens when twin imperatives conflict? She knows to avoid traffic, yet she also knows to obey. On the surface, Goldie is a shepherd, but beneath the fur, she is a German. She follows orders.

Goldie steps into the road, and I follow. A car honks. We continue. I feel the wind of more cars, but we zigzag like kids and step onto the far side with shared exhilaration.

Suddenly the air grows close. Two steps off the curb, we might as well be centuries away from the world of superhighways. Mea She'arim. I shunned this place when we arrived from Russia and sought it after I returned from Lebanon, because it felt more like the Old Country than anyplace else in this silicon-circuited, chrome-plated nation of ours. Of course, my image of the Old Country was false, because I never knew a homeland filled with Orthodox Jews. I met them for the first time when we moved into the flat on Rehov Rambam and a welcoming committee from the shul hosted an evening for newcomers. In those days, Israel wasn't overrun with Russians. We were a novelty that didn't yet threaten anyone's jobs. The neighbors were happy that Jews of any sort were occupying the flats that were popping up in every vacant lot between Arab shanties.

Even then, however, I was drawn to the Arab boys, who didn't attend school, and seemed to spend all day drinking orange soda and kicking a soccer ball back and forth, and took off their T-shirts when the game grew intense. Even then, I kept away from our "modern" Orthodox neighbors and more so from the anachronistic believers in Mea She'arim.

And yet I was drawn there when I first became blind. I don't know why; I didn't think about it, but I enjoyed walking the cramped byways of this tiny district after I ceased to see. Maybe it was because the Hasidim didn't really see this world, either, because they were so focused on the world to come.

No, that's not right. Yes, they're oblivious to everything except the presence of God, but in their service to their deity they're the most worldly people I know. To start with, they fuck like mad. Witness the dozen little ones behind every skirt. Or no less than half a dozen. All of these pasty-faced women bundled up to their double chins, all of their poor, bookish child-husbands. To look at them, you wouldn't think they could figure out how to insert tab A into slot B. Yet come Shabbes, every bed in Mea She'arim rocks according to rigidly prescribed rules that compel sex for the sake of something larger than themselves. Come Shabbes, they come.

They do this because that's how God tells them to behave here. And the here that they inhabit smells like restaurant row on Tverskaya, meatballs on the wind. It sounds like Pravda Square, too, their Yiddish inflected with Europe. Maybe that was why I was drawn to Mea She'arim after Lebanon, because the language and syntax were familiar in a world that had become utterly foreign. The only problem was God. Finally, I couldn't sever the texture of their language from its subject, and left.

I haven't been here in so long that I feel like a lost tourist as I wait for footsteps. "Pardon me," I ask someone coming out of a shop that sells smoked fish and dried fruits.

"Here," he says, and presses a few coins into my hand.

Suddenly I'm a Palestinian boy in the Old City, all of a kilometer away, somewhere to the left, in the direction of the sun.

"No, I don't need money." I earn more in a week than my benefactor does in a season.

"Keep it anyway." He thinks I'm proud.

So as he gives me his hard-earned money, I give him his mitzvah. I put the coins in my pocket and ask, "Do you know the way to the Jaffa Road?"

He replies, "Have you put on tefillin today?"

Goddamn Jews. Charity he'll give freely, but he's going to make me pay for the directions. Already his arm has clutched my elbow and started to steer me into the nearest *shtiebl*, where he plans to make me don the esoteric cardboard boxes and leather straps that represent the presence of God in the head and the heart and say a prayer for the good of my soul. "Hey," I want to tell him, "the leather I prefer is different."

My form of sex is abhorrent to him. Its very nonprocreativeness is more of an abomination than adultery. But doesn't the fact that homosexuality is biblically proscribed mean that it was extant in the days when the Holy Writ was written?

I have two choices. I can grant him this further satisfaction by muttering a few hallelujahs, or I can shun him and flee. Neither is appealing, because I'm in a hurry. Then a third alternative comes to me. I say, "How dare you insult me?"

"What?" He's taken aback.

"You ask a Jew if he put on tefillin?" So what if I'm clean-shaven—well, relatively, since I didn't bother to spruce up before leaving Rehov Rambam; so what if I'm not wearing a yarmulke? We're beyond rationality. If I'm a Jew, I must have put on tefillin. Anything else is inconceivable.

Ashamed, he murmurs, "I'm sorry."

"Never mind." I stumble forward, but hear him answer belatedly. "Two blocks forward, one block to the left."

"Thanks."

Good. From here it's only a short, excruciating stroll to the Jaffa

Road, and from there I know my way. I'm not about to wander for forty years in this urban wilderness. I have a specific destination in mind, the only place that may provide a guide for this perplexed man. Still, rather than taking the most direct route, Goldie and I detour through the Ben Yehuda pedestrian mall, scoot into an L-shaped café that allows us exit elsewhere from the entrance.

I assume that my limb has gone numb, because I don't feel quite the same level of pain as before. Although this allows me to place one foot in front of the other, something tells me that this is not good. Pain is what lets us know who we are. Without pain, there's no life. Fortunately, this is one boon I've never lacked. From youthful, poetic angst to mature agony, I've known it all. I pause to rewrap the gauze, and fluid oozes onto my hand. I hope that it's pus instead of blood. Less visible.

Whatever the hell I look like, I continue limping past a series of old garages converted into shops selling cheap clothing and kitchenwares. I devour the aroma of roast goose that floats out of Felderman's Restaurant when the door is opened—nearly lunchtime, it's taken me two hours to traverse the distance a government car usually does in ten minutes—beside the noxious, fumy parking lot of the central bus station, onto the long looping boulevard I've cruised along so many times before. There I stop, and instead of continuing toward the ministry, I hobble up the curved driveway that I last approached from the other direction early yesterday evening.

I can hardly remember the last time I slept, I'm so exhausted, but I've got to continue.

I'm tempted to circumvent the doorman and go through the kitchen again, but the thought of any kitchen makes my foot throb, and I don't think I can go any farther. Before the doorman can question me, I whip a laminated High Clearance ID from my pocket, wave it in his direction, and push through the revolving doors into the Sheraton lobby. Forget about separation of church and state; there's no separation of church and business here.

I press the highest button in the elevator and ascend. I walk the hall with fewer doors than any other floor in the hotel, and arrive at the last door on the right. It's open.

The room is empty. Goldie's sigh as she sinks to the rug and immediately starts snoring is the only sound besides that of my feet dragging across the nap of the carpet. A maid must have emptied ashtrays, cleared the coffee table of cups and cans of soda, swept, vacuumed. It's no hospital, but the atmosphere of the suite is void.

I navigate the space, finger trailing the rim of the wainscoting that's one of the marks used to distinguish this high-floor, high-rent district from that of the mere $200-a-night cubicles that fill the sixteen floors below. Am I leaving my own trail of blood and dust around the perimeter of the room? So be it.

There's a large television cabinet, a carved wooden buffet table, an opening into a kitchen. There are smooth Corian counters, a stove, a full-size refrigerator, and sink. I circle that room swiftly, maybe not wanting to be reminded of my recent experience in another kitchen, and return to the living room. I pass a sliding glass door behind the curved sectional couch that Gabriel and Gita Mamoun reclined on just yesterday. A hallway on the far side leads to three bedrooms, each with a king-size bed, each with its own television, desk and mini-refrigerator in case the occupants can't be bothered to travel all the way to the kitchen. Each bedroom has its own fully marbled bathroom with a Jacuzzi and a stack of warm, freshly laundered towels. I fumble through the end tables by the beds, hoping to find something, but the housing staff has done its job well.

I'm walking back to the living room, wondering if I should ask the desk what happened to the people in Penthouse C, but that's nonsense. They left suddenly, and didn't leave a forwarding address.

Somewhere in this city, a large, muddy man with a bump on his head doesn't like me, and somewhere else in this city, another person gave the large, muddy man his orders. I'm thinking so hard that I don't realize for a second that the air in the room is different. From the sound of her breath, I can tell that Goldie is standing. I pet her and feel the angry bristles. "There, girl."

I need to speak to hear my voice echo. The front door is still closed, but the air is different, literally. I feel a breeze. Shit! During my search, I forgot one thing. The glass doors to the balcony are open.

Okay.

I accept the invitation and walk outside, where the light hits like a thousand arrows as I try to recall what the exterior of the Sheraton looked like when I first arrived in Israel, and if I've ever been at a meeting or party in some room here that spilled into the al fresco. Years ago, hotels in Jerusalem were built facing the Old City just as those in Tel Aviv were built facing the Mediterranean. Thus, even the best hotels like the King David and the Dan had good sides and bad sides until architects realized that hotels built perpendicular to the most compelling views were more rentable, because every room had a sidelong peek at the sea or the golden Dome of the Rock. For the same reason, most hotel rooms in Israel have balconies, but they are sized for the individual rooms, perhaps three meters long, one meter wide. But as Penthouse C, situated at the blunt end of the edifice, is unique for facing directly at the Old City, it also has a full-size terrace rather than a tiny, cantilevered platform. I stride three full steps until I come to the railing and turn around, sensing perhaps five meters on either side of me, enough for several chaise lounges and an umbrella-shaded table with matching lawn chairs. All it's missing is its own lap pool.

"Hello, Nathan," a voice welcomes me.

"Hello, Cyril," I reply.

It's Klein, the head of covert operations for internal security, last encountered in Simon's office. "Hmmm," he murmurs. Why people are impressed that I can recognize them from their voices mystifies me. Sound is simply a sensory clue, like sight. Just as a computer finds the object of its search by matching up patterns of 1's and 0's, we match visual or auditory or olfactory clues to previous such clues stored in our personal memory banks. It's not all that different from Cyril seeing my foot and recalling similar wounds he may have seen on battlefields or at the site of civilian bombings. That's how we know things and make appropriate judgments. Empirical evidence.

"Has anyone ever told you that you're really a mess, Nathan?"

"Frequently."

"They're right."

"I know."

"Have a seat."

I need a seat. Now that I'm not moving forward, the pain in my foot flares and I can barely remain upright. I lower myself onto one of the lounges. It has a wire frame and soft cushions that I gingerly prop my sore limb on.

"You should have a doctor look at that."

"Thanks."

We sit silently, each contemplating the other, until Klein asks, "Are you checking in or just visiting?"

"Actually, I was passing through."

"You might want to stay awhile. You never know what you might find."

"I did my best to find whatever was here."

"You didn't do good enough. Given your talent for observation, I'm surprised."

"There's nothing here."

"You looked?"

"In my own way."

"Where?"

"Everywhere. The bedroom, the bathroom, the closets."

"Not everywhere."

"Well, I'm at a disadvantage. What did I miss?"

"We'll get to that. In the meantime, what are you doing here?"

There's no point in hiding what he obviously knows. "I was looking for Gabriel."

"Yes, me, too."

"Did you find him?"

"Did you?"

"No."

"Neither did I. How did you know he was here?"

"He told me. How did you know?"

"Someone told me." No point in asking who.

"When did you know?"

"Am I being interrogated?"

"Yes."

"Yesterday."

"Before our meeting?"

"No."

"Even if that's true, you could have informed us as soon as you heard. You might have saved a great deal of trouble."

"Actually, I thought that might create a great deal of trouble."

"You thought wrong, Nathan. You were under so many obligations to help us that I can hardly enumerate them. As a citizen of the country, you were obligated to tell security. As a trusted member of the Prime Minister's staff, you were under a personal obligation to Simon. And if you ever vaguely hope to help Gabriel ben Levi out of the extreme danger in which he is in, you owed him as well."

"I think that Gabriel may have a right to define that for himself."

"Oh, yes, all well and good, but he doesn't know what he's involved in, and the least you could perceive is that you don't, either. Everyone seems to think that you're a very smart man, but I think you're an idiot. In fact, you make me sick."

"Maybe you should see a doctor."

"Wit is not intelligence."

At this point, Klein stands. I can hear his own chaise creak as he rises and looms over me, blocking the sun. He takes a few steps to the edge of the balcony, from where he must be looking at the Old City. That Klein has discovered Gabriel's refuge does not surprise me. That Gabriel must have known that Klein discovered his refuge in time to escape does not surprise me, either. Then Klein does surprise me by asking one more question: "Do the words 'Strange Fire' mean anything to you?"

"No."

"Then our conversation is over. If you ever have reason to continue it, you know where to reach me." He starts to the entry to the living room.

But I have a final question, too. "Cyril?"

"Yes."

"You said that I missed something. That we'd get to that."

"Oh, well, I lied. You'll have to get to that yourself. Just use your powers of perception."

A moment later, he's gone, striding past Goldie to the door to the suite, which opens and clicks shut behind him.

I'm tempted to remain on the lounge and nap. Nap, hell, I could use Rip van Winkle's sleep, but Klein was just too pleased with himself, too provocative. There's something to find here. Klein may be an asshole, but he's smart, and he uses words deliberately.

I can play guessing games. What did I miss on my tour of the suite? There might be a purloined letter tacked to the wall, for all I know, or a box under the bed filled with kindling for whatever the fuck Strange Fire is, but those are forever beyond me, and Klein implied something else. Use your powers of perception, he said. I did. I smelled, I heard, I felt. And now I'm thinking. I smelled, I heard, I felt, but I forgot to use one power of perception. I forgot to taste.

Hauling myself off the lounge, gritting my teeth as my foot makes contact with the cement of the terrace, I follow the intuition that scares as it entices me. Something in me does not like this game as I pad back to the kitchen, rummage around further, investigate the cabinets and drawers above and below the sink, and pull open the stove, until I notice a faint beelike buzz. For a second I think about Simon's favorite joke, and then I realize what's causing the buzz: the refrigerator. I open the thick, insulated door and feel a blast of cold air that contrasts brutally with the regulated hotel air. I'm shivering all over as I reach inside and immediately touch the awful treasure. It has thin lips, a gently tapering nose, and heavy-lidded eyes that are open and staring at me. My trembling fingers flutter across its features in search of identification. Only when I come to the chin, from which thin wisps of adolescent hair sprout between the cleft, do I, in my own way, see.

Rafi.

# CHAPTER 9

"Tender shepherd,
Tender shepherd,
Let me help you
Count your sheep"

A round of celestial music surrounds me as I exit the elevator to the lobby. To the left, a choir of female voices repeats, "Tender shepherd, tender shepherd," while softly crooning masculine voices on the right offer to, "Let me help you . . ."

My first thought comes from the voices rather than the words. Male and female are separated as they are in Mea She'arim, but the song is not quite Eastern European.

Before I can piece together the logic, I recognize the literal meaning, and reach down to Goldie. "Not you, dear," I say, and stroke her, feel the hair of a living creature.

"Tender shepherd."

Did Goldie see Rafi, too? Does she understand the extreme violation of everything that is occurring as we breathe?

"Let me help you count your sheep."

Finally I catch the real meaning. There are as many Christian tourists as Jews in Israel, especially at this time of year, Easter. This is a group of evangelicals, probably American, because the tune they're singing is not a hymn, though it sounds like one, but a song from the musical version of *Peter Pan*. Idiots. I wonder if this is the group I passed several hours ago at the Western Wall.

> "One in the meadow,
> Two in the garden,
> Three in the nursery,
> Fast asleep."

The last notes fade amid the ongoing activity of the hotel, busboys dragging luggage from the entrance, conversation from the lounge, a page for a "Samuel Kahn. Phone call for Samuel Kahn." and another voice from the center of the sexually segregated choir. "Room keys over here," the guide says in the half-commanding, half-coaxing manner of a Boy Scout troop leader. "Pick up your room keys, and we'll meet in the lobby at two o'clock. Two o'clock in the lobby."

Everything is repeated twice, the directions to the tour group, the page for Samuel Kahn, tender shepherd.

Everything is repeated twice.

My fingers twitch as Goldie's living hair responds to my touch. I need to go to the bathroom.

How I made my way out of the horrible penthouse, I don't remember. How I found and pressed the correct elevator button, even if the Braille for lobby was embossed on the metal plate, I don't know. I felt like I was waking up from a long night's sleep when I heard the tourists singing, so happy to be in the Holy Land. But Rafi's eyes haunt me, and the drama of the last two days seems faint compared to the harsh reality in the refrigerator.

As soon as the next maid makes a quick check of Penthouse C—or sooner, if Cyril Klein has decided to make a phone call—the place will be aswarm with police, and I've got to get out first. But first I have an irresistible need to wash my hands, and stagger to the reception desk, where I barely manage to gasp, "Bathroom."

"Are you a guest of the hotel, sir?"

I'm a blind man, a half-deaf man, a wounded man, and if that isn't enough, I'm a man so enraged he's ready to grab the prissy young woman who dares question me, smash her brains out on the counter, and sign for a room in her blood. Bill me later. Instead, I grit my teeth and say, "I'm Nathan Kazakov."

Luckily for both of us, she recognizes the name and immediately complies. "I'm sorry, sir. It's right over . . . I mean, allow me to show you . . . I mean, I'll take you there."

"Never mind. You didn't do it."

"Do what, sir?"

"Nothing." Damn. Once the head is found, this woman will undoubtedly mention my presence, and I'll be in more trouble than I am now. Let's see, how hard would it be to find a blind man with one ear and a trail of bloody bandages on his right foot who was seen escorting the deceased through the hotel kitchen the previous evening by a hundred witnesses, and has left his name at the desk and dozens of fingerprints at the scene of the crime, including on the handle to the refrigerator, on the glass shelves, and, if it retains impressions, on the head itself? Oh, yes, he's got a tender shepherd, too.

I don't care. If I don't clean myself, I'll faint.

The receptionist directs me through the crowd of tourists jostling for their room keys until I round a bend between the lounge area and a video arcade for children. My hand trails over several public telephones and finds two adjacent doors. Usually the men's room is the first, so I push it open, smell perfume, and exit.

Seconds later, I'm finally where I belong, washing Rafi off my hands in the enormous facility that feels like a kitchen with its span of tile and porcelain. Minutes later, I'm still washing. I can't stop washing. I squirt another dollop of liquid soap from a container mounted to the wall into my palms and start again while another man enters and unzips by the row of urinals.

The sound of the zipper undoes the flap in my mind that separates the nightmare of the last forty-eight hours from the lesser nightmare of the rest of my life. For a few seconds, I can forget Rafi and the man with the muddy boots, and return to thoughts of sex and, incidentally, poetry. For a second, I dream of handing in my resignation and devoting my remaining days to recapturing the artistic impulses of my youth. I dream of settling down in a small orchard with a young computer engineer who goes off to work in the morning and returns to homemade dumplings I've baked between stanzas. It's sad how unreal my dreams are. Where do they come from?

I'm still standing at the sink, the water flowing over my hands, when I realize that there ought to be another sound in the room.

There's no gentle splash to my left; the man at the urinal is not peeing. Neither do I hear the small sighs and grunts or the jingle of coins in the pocket of a man coaxing his bladder to relax and release. There's a familiar scent of hair spray.

I have a choice. I can pretend that I don't know that Noam Abravanel is following me, or I can confront him, or I can wait until he confronts me.

I step into one of the toilet stalls and sit. I decide to examine my foot, but it won't lift off the floor in response to the order from my brain. I have to hoist the numb object up and set it across my good leg like a log. I unstrap the sandals and unwrap the bandage, which is wet and sticky with whatever fluid has seeped from my foot as a ridge of blisters grew and popped, grew and popped—everything happens several times here—like volcanic eruptions along my arch and toward the ankle.

I rewrap my foot with toilet paper, which adheres nicely to the form and soaks up further emissions. Then I lift my foot and leg again and plant it back on the floor.

I don't really have any choice. My flight across Jerusalem from Rehov Rambam to the Sheraton sapped any reserve of energy I had. I'm tired and terrified and in so far over my head that I hardly know where to go next. Let the chips fall. I open the stall and say, "Get me out of here."

For a second there's a pause and I expect a Jerusalem police sergeant to materialize. That's just one of the advantages of being a

B.P.; we have an endless, childlike capacity for surprise. Think of some gory horror movie. A teenage girl—probably dressed in a sheer nightie, but that's beside the point—wanders the halls of an abandoned mansion, opens a closet door, and a body falls out. She shrieks and so does the audience. Every moment of every day is like that for me, though usually not so dramatic.

"In a moment," Noam replies.

No surprise.

I suggest, "In the meantime, why don't you zip up?"

"Why should I? Are you tempted?"

I don't need to bother with this, not with him. Cyril Klein is a force to be reckoned with, contended with; Noam is just a glorified gofer with a private office and a fancy license plate.

"No, I just thought you might dribble, and then you'd have to clean up."

Noam snorts, but doesn't respond except to follow my suggestion and zip as surreptitiously as he can. He leans against the wall and I remain on my throne. Royal prerogative—until the door opens again, and this time it's a familiar face, even if I can't see it.

"No jokes about the venue, Nathan," Simon says.

"No jokes about anything," I agree.

But before we can get to the point, the door opens one more time and the rest of Simon's entourage flows into the room. There's Klein and his other half, Khadoury, and Serena. This must be an opportunity for her; we're in one of the few rooms in Israel where she's not welcome. She takes charge and says, "Thank you, Noam."

"You're welcome."

"Thank you, Noam," she repeats until he gets the message and slinks toward the door.

I address Serena. "We've got to stop meeting like this. Noam might think you're easy."

Excused for the duration, Noam doesn't dare add his two shekels, but Serena purrs, "I am easy for the right man."

I say, "Whoever that may be."

"Enough!" Simon commands, and takes his own seat, up on the baby-changing platform installed recently for the convenience of liberated American dads who perform domestic chores their macho Israeli counterparts disdain. Simon crosses his legs to the sound of silk on silk and continues from amid the residual aroma of poop. "I want my son."

"Yes."

"This is none of your business, Nathan, but we can only assume that Rubinstein's shot has warped your priorities."

Actually, I believe that Rubinstein's shot has clarified my priorities, but I remain silent as I think of the craziness that must exist beyond the bathroom door, the lobby invaded by security, a convoy of vehicles blocking the driveway to the consternation of the doorman and the tour guides. Boy, will this give the evangelicals a story to tell when they get home, the P.M. himself stopping by their hotel for a short pee. Make that a long one.

Simon has begun harking back to Gabriel's childhood. He's actually remembering a bicycle. Does he think he's opening an orphanage? Who is this show for? And the imagery! He's made the bicycle red, a violent color, rather than placid, patriotic blue. Call rewrite!

Something has broken in me. I was cynical before, sure, but basically content with my job and my place in life. Now I can't stand the presence of this man who took me out of the military hospital and gave me a home. I hardly realize what a privilege it is to be sitting here on a toilet in the fanciest hotel in the country listening to the private recollections of the most powerful person in the country.

Why this defeat? It isn't the abuse I've taken by bullet, park swing, which reminds me of Rafi, and frying pan—Lebanon was worse—and it isn't even Rafi himself, although that poor boy's head will stick in my mind forever. No, it's the sense—"sense" is a key word for me—that something is happening all around me that everyone except me knows.

But what difference does that make? Am I so shallow that the mere elitist insiderness of my position sustained me? Was all that I loved the childish bragging rights of, "I know something that you don't know. Nyah. Nyah. Nyah"?

As a Jew, I was born on the outside of greater Russian culture. As an immigrant, I lived on the outside of native Israeli culture. As a blind person, I was removed from a common, human inheritance. The one thing that connected me to anything larger than myself was language, in particular the language of politics. A failure at meter, I found my metier in the stump speech and its various offshoots: the policy statement, the parliamentary debate, the diplomatic apologia, and the ever-popular, sly, and underhanded public announcement that never means what it seems. It may be shabby, but it's mine.

And yet, as Simon maunders on to Gabriel's brilliant career at the university, and how proud ben Levi *père* felt at his offspring's accomplishments, I feel more and more inclined to reach behind my back and flush the toilet.

Of course, I won't. Nor will I stand straight or hobbled and march out of the room and the life I detest. My fantasy retirement is clearly nonsense. Besides, until this thing resolves itself, my job is the best tool I have. The special embossed identification card in my wallet will grant me access to just about anyplace in the country, and I don't know where I will have to go, although as Simon continues speaking, I begin to feel an intuition.

"Strange Fire," he's saying.

A spark leaps from his mouth to my ears, and I'm attentive.

"Do the words mean anything to you?"

Give the man credit. I have to keep reminding myself to avoid underestimating Simon. He may not speak beautifully when I'm not feeding him beautiful words, and he may have the morality of a tiger in a drought, but he's got a sixth sense for human response. He knows immediately when a line goes over well or falls flat. He knew long ago that I turned on him, and didn't care, but now he knows that I've turned to him. He's waiting.

Again, there is no point in lying, because he probably knows. That's one of the first rules in politics: never ask a question unless you're sure of the answer. "Yes, an unexpected gentleman caller in my flat mentioned the term, but I was too busy scalding myself to ask him to explain."

"My God, what happened to you, Nathan?"

He noticed.

"A small accident. Not so bad as the one upstairs."

"Oh, yes, that."

"I think you mean 'him'."

"Grotesque," Simon comments. "But that's what happens when . . . well . . . whatever happened."

I could have written that one better.

Simon finishes, "So what happened?"

"Ask him." I point in the direction of Cyril Klein, whose back is pressed against the bathroom door.

Simon must have nodded toward Klein, because the silent official replies tersely, "He was there when I arrived."

I continue, "Was his neck attached to his head at the time?"

"I've had enough of this pansy insinuating—"

"Now, now, Cyril, Nathan was a decorated soldier in the IDF."

"Yeah, what did you do in Lebanon that you acquired such affection for dark meat?"

That's another thing I hate, gay-baiting—along with the word "gay." Israel may have more cell phones and cappuccinos per capita than Seattle, but we're not what you might call a progressive society. Simon walks a perpetual knife edge between venture capitalists in Armani suits smooth as a baby's ass and the haredim in gabardines coarse as steel wool. Now he does what he always does when caught in the middle; he goes forward, ignores the trouble, and says, "Do you think it might have been the same person who visited your home?"

That's a good question, and I consider it. I simultaneously ponder why we're having this discussion. Simon is not a detective, nor is anyone else in the room. In fact, I assume that no policeman is anywhere near the Sheraton at this moment. Instead, a team dispatched by Mr. Klein is probably scouring Penthouse C of any traces of the murder that must have occurred there within the last twenty-four hours. I could call the police right now and they'd say, "Crime? What crime?" I could take the elevator back upstairs, use a pass key to the suite, and find the chief evangelical from the group in the lobby boffing two of his flock while they sing "Tender Shepherd." I could run to the kitchen, rip open the refrigerator, and find . . .

champagne on ice. When national interests are at stake, people disappear. I could be chopped into pieces on the baby-changing table and flushed down the toilet and no one would ever know.

"No," I answer the question. "I don't think it was my visitor. Rafi was killed while the stranger was in my kitchen. I'm his alibi." Also, I didn't smell mud upstairs.

"Rafi?" Khadoury, an Iraqi Jew himself, sneers. "You were on a first-name basis. Who else was there?"

"Gabriel. You know that."

Why I didn't mention the third name, I'm not sure. Not as slickly as I'd prefer, I try to shift the discussion away from what I'd rather not talk about and toward what I want to hear about. "What about Strange Fire?"

Amazingly, this works, after a pause in which Serena clearly looks to Simon for approval. She says, "We believe that a group of Islamic fundamentalists is aiming to create a major action in Jerusalem during the next seventy-two hours. We are not talking about a hopped-up teenage suicide bomber on a bus. We are talking about a highly sophisticated bomb placed in an extraordinarily sensitive location that will involve enormous loss of life and possibly lead to war. We also believe that this group that we have code-named Strange Fire may have kidnapped Gabriel as a part of their plot. Frankly, few Arabs have such resources. One does. Her name is—"

"Gita Mamoun."

Serena stops.

"There's only one 'her' with such capacities in this part of the world," I explain my knowledge. "But she subsidizes schools and hospitals."

"And armies," Simon finishes, quoting one of my more eloquent phrases.

"Please, Nathan," Serena continues. For a second, I think that she has been brought along because a female perspective is needed when a woman is involved, but in feminist terms Israel is quite modern. You have a country with only a few million people, you can't afford to ignore the potential talents of half the population. "This is an old story," she says before telling it. "What better way to hide a hawk than in dove's feathers?" she adds a nice rhetorical flourish. "We believe that Ms. Mamoun is involved in planning this event," she cuts to the chase. "Obviously, we are talking the most extreme danger and the highest possible security. Nobody outside this room knows what you know, so from this moment on you will have twenty-four-hour protection."

"Protection" means I am effectively under arrest. My friends are worried either about who will find me or what I will find. "How do you know this?"

"The young man that you called Rafi was our informant."

"What would you like me to do?"

"Obviously, Ms. Mamoun has seen fit to contact you for some reason. We can therefore assume that she may attempt to contact you again. When this occurs, you are to report immediately."

It's notable that no one asks *why* the so-called Strange Fire group may have contacted me. "But isn't she likely to keep away from me if I'm covered? The point of bait is that it floats freely."

"The point of bait is that it is attached to a line."

"I need freedom."

"And I . . ." Simon interrupts, "need my son."

This is the trump that stops all dialogue. I don't know who wrote the sentence, but Simon delivers it as well as Olivier. Suddenly politics is beneath consideration. Even the possible war that Serena evoked like a specter from the perennial lunacy of the Mideast takes a back seat. We're talking about a father and his child.

Never mind that estrangement if not outright animosity has been the hallmark of Simon's relationship with Gabriel since the latter's days at the university recalled by the former with such maudlin sentiment. This is not a matter of a particular father and a particular son. This is basic. This is biblical.

# CHAPTER 10

"Daddy. Daddy, please come home," the familiar voice moans.

"Hey, it's Room 404!" I'm delighted to hear the insane old crank.

"You remember your neighbor," Doc Ivan notes as he wheels me down the hall toward my usual room. It's sort of like Penthouse C at the Sheraton for someone like Gita Mamoun. I wouldn't stay anyplace else.

Of course I remember. My memory does not reside in my foot, which has already been anesthetized, cleansed of a sedimentary layer of Jerusalem dust, scraped, sutured, and bandaged again so that its swelling has gone down to the size of a coconut appended to the end of my leg. Said foot rests on the ridged steel plate that folds out from between the chair's chrome support. "How could I forget? He kept me awake for a week. How's he doing?"

"Worse than ever. I'm afraid he's not long for this world."

"At least he'll meet his daddy. Sad old fuck."

Yes, I'm back in the hospital. Everything happens twice in this country. By the time my audience with Simon concluded, it was clear that I was in a state of shock and that I needed medical attention if I was to be of any benefit.

"From the way you talked, I was sure that I would see you again," Ivan said when the P.M.'s car brought me to the emergency entrance several hours ago. He's a good man, his cheesy breath as comforting as the first shot of painkiller, though now that I think of it there's something odd about that breath today. Even stranger, Hadassah H. seems good, too; after one very long and sleepless day in the outside world, these antiseptic corridors feel more like those of a spa than a prison.

The nurses all greet me as we pass the station.

"Absence makes the heart grow fonder. If you play your cards right you can probably convince one of the girls to help keep you warm, Mr. Kazakov." Ivan chuckles and turns the wheelchair into the doorway I thought I'd never pass through again.

I smell the emptiness and say, "Home, sweet home."

"Your mother wouldn't like you to think of anywhere besides Rehov Rambam as your home."

I raise my neck up and turn to the left, but have a hard time hearing. I'll have to get used to making this minor adjustment. I swivel to the right and say, "You've been talking to my mother?"

"Yeah, I tried back a few minutes after you left and she sounded so distraught that—"

"But that was a telephone number. How did you know I lived on Rehov Rambam?"

"If you must know, we have your address in the hospital records. And if you'd like to know how I found it, your mother gave me the directions. A lovely woman, and an excellent cook."

That was the odd thing about his odor. It wasn't cheddar, but the sweet farmer's cheese Mother loves. I ought to have picked that up immediately. "You went there?"

"We drove all around the neighborhood looking for you and got hungry."

"Blintzes?"

"Best ones I've had since the Potemkin Cafeteria closed."

"I know that place."

"And why shouldn't you?"

"Well . . . it was illegal."

"Yes," Ivan sighs nostalgically, and it's his sigh that resigns me to his presence in my life. First he called, then he drove over. The man has no sense of privacy. It comes from living in communal apartments with six other families for too many years. It also comes from places like the Potemkin in which, even pre-Glasnost, individual urges emerged from beneath the wax masks we all wore in public. You only really appreciate water when you're dying of thirst.

A former club for the actor's union, the renamed Potemkin was a false front behind which drugs and poetry were semi-freely exchanged, though I was too naive to notice the former. Of course, the place was known to and tolerated by the KGB as an escape valve which incidentally provided a convenient way to keep tabs on Moscow's most undesirable and would-be undesirable citizens, including the overlapping categories of writers, Jews, and a handful of high school boys who found their way to its old oak doorway the way other, more ambitious youths found their way across borders. Thinking back, I wouldn't be surprised if it was actually owned by the KGB; the men in green hats who ruled Russia wouldn't mind collecting the illegal Western currency slipped across the bar in return for illegal Western liquor by those who disdained rubles and local vodka. First the customers ate the blintzes; then they drank; then they talked, too much; then they were arrested. It was a fool's game, but the lure of the forbidden was irresistible.

Unable to afford Scotch or the rarer yet jigger of Jack Daniel's, I went whenever I could, but I was so ignorant that once—it must have been the summer before Mother and I emigrated—staggering out to vomit in the garden behind the terrace, I was shocked to discover boys kissing boys under the eaves. Although the weather was sultry, I felt a chill that I attributed to the churning of the liquor in my teenage belly, but I was wrong. The liquor was purchased by a raven-haired Mafioso who probably wanted to take me home, and I probably would have gone with him if I hadn't drunk too much of the surprisingly potent Yankee bourbon. At the time, I simply couldn't distinguish the exotic vices sustained by the Potemkin from the ultimate shape of my daily life.

Thinking back to those days, I remember the sense of giddy courageousness with which we peeked at adulthood from afar. The world was filled with potential, be it for uninhibited romance or unmitigated danger. We assumed that our photographs were taken as we slipped through the portals of the Potemkin, our sins against the state recorded in the ledgers of the Lubianka, our homes searched while we partied.

Now the world is filled with a similar potential, as I feel similarly watched by a similarly elusive power. In fact, I suddenly recall what Ivan told me when we last spoke, that somebody searched the room I have just reentered. I wheel around the space, fingers probing everywhere, from underneath the firm mattress to atop the bank of sophisticated machinery beside the bed.

"Looking for something?"

Ignoring Ivan, I lift the edge of one of the framed pictures on the wall and search for a wire. I reach into the box beside the radiator controls. I glide into the bathroom, legally capacious enough for my chair to 360, and tap at the rear wall of the cool and smooth-faced—it's probably a mirror—medicine cabinet. But just as I failed to find Rafi in my initial search of Penthouse C, I find nothing. If there's a button-size transmitter in a flower pot or a video camera mounted within the television hung from the ceiling or a decapitated head resting on the pillow, I don't know.

I sit down, exhausted.

"You need rest."

"Hmph."

"A penny for your thoughts." Ivan presses a coin into my palm. Its edges are smooth and so is its surface. I can barely read the outlines of a face, and I can't identify the face, although I can make out an arch of floral pattern surrounding the face like a halo. It's an old coin, a very old coin, an antique coin. The flowers are a laurel wreath, the profile Roman. "Where did you get this?"

"It was stuck to your foot. I assume you stepped on it somewhere in your travels and just picked it up."

I turn the coin in my hands and can't quite grasp the significance. It's like the the twenty-four-hour span we call a day, even though it includes a night; it has two sides, intrinsically connected and impossible to see at the same time. Then I remember the change I picked off the table in Abdullah's Café. Jacob Twersky must have mistakenly placed it on the coffee-stained tile circle. It must have fallen out of my pocket when I changed, and then adhered to the gooey mess on the bottom of my right foot. It's probably not particularly valuable, or Jacob would have been more careful, but it may have been a good luck charm, and I should return it. Then again, I need luck.

Ivan says, "It looks quite interesting."

"I need money."

"Don't we all?" he sighed again. "I'm too old for this, but I have to work here for another five years to pay off the educational loan they gave me to study for the test that I could have passed twenty years ago in Russia. Then I can go into private practice and really make some moolah." He's playing the bearish buffoon, trying to distract me.

"Ivan, I need money, now."

"I can lend you some, although there isn't much to buy at the gift shop." He removes several bills from his wallet.

"This isn't enough."

"Then go to the—"

"Hush!" I jerk upright and put a finger to his lips. He mustn't utter the word. I am sure the room is bugged and I am doing my best to speak in code. This code has to be just clever enough to be incomprehensible to my unseen eavesdroppers, yet obvious to my intended audience. I run my hand over Ivan's bristly face, feel the hair and the furrows in his forehead. He is thinking, watching me as I nod. Usually urgency and seriousness are conveyed through the eyes, but I must do the same with the set of my lips and chin. I don't want to repeat myself. I don't want to give anyone else a reason to think. Nonetheless, I believe that Ivan understands.

He says, "Really?"

I nod.

He leaves my fingers in place and nods in return, but I can't tell if his nod is one of agreement or appeasement. I insist, "Soon."

I attempt to force my thoughts into Ivan's head. Without help, I will never get anywhere, yet he has no reason to help me. I think of any cards I can play to convince him: the doctor/patient relationship, the fellow émigré connection, the pleasure he must take in undermining authority, my mother. Jokingly, I say, "I'll get you blintzes once a week for a year."

"You're crazy."

"Patience."

"Patients!" he scoffs, and then, giving up or giving in, adds, "I will take care of everything. In the meantime, you need rest."

Indeed, my guardians at the door and listening to me on tape and viewing me on film ought to be happy that I will be healthy enough to leave, to make my travels more exigent. The trick is to elude them on those travels.

"Rest," Doc Ivan repeats.

"No," I refuse, but the next thing I know, I'm waking up. How many hours later, two or twenty-two, I can't say. Did he drug me? No, he didn't need to. I'm groggy with half-fulfilled dreams—of what? they're lost. something!—that dance away from consciousness as I rub my eyes for all the good it does, but now is the time. Somehow it feels like dusk, which might be the best hour to make a getaway. The day watch is probably tired, the night watch not yet on duty.

"Drink this," Ivan says—has he been here the entire while?—and fits a carton into my hand. A straw extends from the carton and I take a sip of thick, frothy liquid that tastes like a chocolate milkshake. In one long siphon, I devour the contents, realizing that I've been starved as well as exhausted. I never had a chance to eat the omelette I was making last night.

Ivan explains, "It's a special, high-nutrient mix. There are several more in this package, along with several changes of dressing for your foot. You don't know how close you came to gangrene and amputation."

"Big deal," I scoff. "A foot, an ear, I've always got another."

The doctor ignores my bravado. "Smear the ointment on the foot and replace the dressing every twelve hours when you get home."

Home? If I can miraculously manage to slip out of an enormous public institution amid the daily hurly-burly, I will be trapped inside Rehov Rambam. He's betraying me.

"I've also put some money in . . . so you can't say I reneged on our bet."

"Bet?"

He puts a finger to my lips.

Bless him; he's telling me that he's speaking in code, too, that he also feels that our words are overheard, that he has a plan. I kiss his stubby, smoky forefinger.

"Enough," he says. "Go in the bathroom and change. Your clothes are filthy. Here are the other ones you brought." He thrusts a second package into my hands.

Strange. I did not bring a change of clothing. Besides, the clothes I wore here may be filthy, but we're not going to a ball. But I'm too woozy to argue and limp into the bathroom. This is the second time today I'm sitting on a toilet for a purpose for which it was not designed. Everything happens twice in Israel.

I open the heavy, crinkly paper of the bag that feels like it came from a supermarket. The first thing I remove from it is, of all things, a sneaker. Is Ivan crazy? On the one hand, I'm supposed to treat my foot as if it's a Fabergé egg; on the other, he thinks I should wedge the damaged limb into this piece of molded rubber. I dig underneath the second sneaker and come up with the second surprise, a pair of satiny shorts, which is followed by an armless T-shirt of the same material. I run my hands over the shirt and feel something stitched to the back; it's a number, eighteen. The stupid thing is a uniform for some athletic team. I'm about to leave the bathroom and escort Ivan down to the psychiatric ward when he calls through the door. "How's it going?"

I tempted to say that Michael Jordan will be right out when something tells me to shut up. Ivan is too serious. So if he wants to play with costumes, I'll indulge him. I peel off my regular clothing, which—he was right—is stiff with dried sweat after a long evening and the morning's ordeal, and don the uniform. It's quite easy to get into, because the shorts have an elastic waistband and the shirt is no more than a scrap. The sneakers are trickier, although Ivan has chosen a large size that flops clownishly on my left foot. It's the right foot that's the problem. Despite whatever drugs Ivan's shot into it to alleviate the infection and bring down the swelling, it still feels tender and bolts of pain shoot upward as I insert the foot as gently as possible. I tie the laces in large, loose bows.

"Do you have everything on?"

I thought I did, but there's one more item to complete my attire. Beneath the sneakers and uniform lies a hospital robe. Although it flaps open to encompass me like a tent, I nearly missed the thing, because it was folded as neatly as a stack of napkins under a picnic lunch. The gown isn't so much a stitched or woven garment as an extruded plastic wrap of preternatural texture and thinness, like the Mylar sheets marathon runners don after a race. I remember to place the solid side to the front, leaving the back draping my satiny butt, and limp toward the door.

"Excellent," Ivan says. "Well, almost." He tucks the halves of the rear closer together to cover the uniform. "Your vehicle, sir." He guides me to my wheelchair, ready to go, like a chauffeur holding the back door to his limousine open at the curb.

Reluctantly, I slump into the seat.

We wheel into the corridor and immediately I feel the space come alive. There's a rustle of hastily folded newspaper and the faint static of a walkie-talkie.

If Ivan thinks that a guy in a wheelchair in such a ludicrous getup can evaporate in front of the sharpest eyes in the country, he's crazy, but I can do nothing but trust.

Ivan whistles as we pass the nurses' station and enter the elevator, which descends five levels from the fourth floor. We are in the basement, where another Shin Bet operative picks up the watch.

"Where are we going?"

"Oh, that little performance you noticed in the hospital bulletin, the one you asked to attend. It just started."

What the hell is he talking about? Forget that I never asked to attend anything. How could I have noticed anything in whatever stupid bulletin they issue to cheer up the bedridden unless there's a Braille edition, which, somehow, I doubt?

He starts whistling again, deliberately precluding conversation. His statement was for the benefit of the ears that are listening to us. Perhaps the chair itself is bugged. He's also establishing an alibi, separating himself from whatever is about to happen.

The subterranean corridor we're cruising along is a little like the service area at the Sheraton. The hospital cafeteria must be nearby, because I smell a lethal mix of overcooked vegetables and Jell-O while a laundry capable of handling as much linen as the Sheraton emits its own dank miasma. Drafts tell me when we intersect perpendicular corridors that lead to different regions of the installation. Most are filled with footsteps and human bustle, but a thin clanking emerges from one. It's coming toward us, and I calculate the trajectory. Before I can warn Ivan, an orderly in a hurry has pushed his cart filled with test tubes directly into our path.

"Whoa!" Ivan veers, and so does the cart.

The pitch of its wheels changes. Two legs must leave the floor. Then they land with a rattle. The test tubes shake, but don't break.

"Watch where you're going, dammit," Ivan shouts. He is a doctor, after all, and there is a hierarchy.

"Sorry, sir," the orderly apologizes.

"Could have been bloody," Ivan mutters, but I'm cheerful now for the first time and laugh.

"Everyone's a driver," I say.

"Except you." Ivan puts me in my place and sets us on the path again.

I think of the word "bloody." It's the kind of word that Cyril Klein might have used, but Ivan was not speaking in the slang that still infects this country half a century after the British Mandate ended. He was speaking literally about the contents of the racks of hundreds of fastidiously labeled test tubes on their way to the lab to reveal the evil present in the veins of hundreds of patients. Syphilis, cirrhosis, sclerosis, AIDS. Blood tells.

Wide twin doors open upon an airy expanse. "This is the recreational facility," Ivan says. "The courts are straight ahead."

Now he's a social director and this place feels more like a four-star resort every minute. They've got tennis courts and a golf course for the ambulatory, movie theaters for the lazy, poetry readings for the aesthetically inclined.

He's insistent and won't quit until I appreciate the extent of the "facilities." He's a tour guide on automatic pilot. "We're behind the main building," he says, and continues, "near the parking lot, that's about a hundred meters to the left." What does he think I am, a potential donor? Maybe they need a new parking lot and they'll name it after me for a cool million in cash or stock.

"Down the hill beyond the lot is the Church of the Visitation. Not that you'd ever need to go there."

God, am I obtuse. He's giving me the lay of the land, because he thinks I'm going to need this. And he wouldn't have to tell me if he was planning to go with me. What about Goldie?

He's locked her up, because she would identify me.

But won't the wheelchair and the gown? And what's with the dumb uniform?

"Ah, look . . . sorry. I mean, can you hear? The game has already begun."

I was wrong, too, when I imagined a tennis court. It's a basketball court. I hear the thump of a nubby orange ball as viscerally as I feel the elastic at my waist, and the pieces start to fit. Either my trust has been well placed or I'm booked to play one-on-one with the Harlem Globetrotters.

Odds, please.

No, the players are hardly as tall as Globetrotters. I hear several men calling for the ball, and none of their voices comes from more than a meter off the surface of the court. I also hear the distinctive whine of wheels turning and the glancing clash of colliding vehicles and realize that the athletes must be cripples in wheelchairs, probably vets. Basketball, because of its small, flat, wooden court, is the only major sport that can be played by people without legs. I'm pushed to the sideline and set among a group of crippled children for whom this game is being performed as an inspirational exercise.

It's also being played to win. One team breaks away with the ball, and a moment later, I hear a soft whoosh through the net.

"Twelve-six, Haifa," Ivan tells me the score.

The children are excited. They're rooting and cheering, slurping sodas that have drawn bees to this lovely outdoor event.

I hear the rustle of polyester nurses' uniforms and think of my own uniform, probably exactly like those on the court. Perhaps the children are wearing uniforms, too, with their favorite players' numbers. There are more wheelchairs here than in the rest of Jerusalem combined.

A referee's whistle blows.

"Three-minute warning," Ivan says. "Why don't you sit in this other chair. It's more comfortable."

I get up slowly and reach for the first package he gave me, the one I'm supposed to take home. His hand clutches my elbow, his finger stroking it thoughtfully. "Are you pressing something?"

I feel a button in the side of the package. There are only two answers. I say, "No."

His fingers squeeze my nerve.

I nod and press the button.

"Here! Here!" A player calls for the ball.

"Here." Ivan guides me to a free chair no different from the one I vacated. "I'll be back in a minute." He rubs my neck, leans down, and whispers, "Good luck."

The next minute passes slowly. The ball bounces, the team from Beersheva scores, the referee calls a foul. There's an ever more aromatic cloud of spilled soft drinks and buttered popcorn and chocolate melting in the sun, and smoke.

Nobody smokes in hospitals, and this is not the smoke of cigarettes. It's more acrid, more chemical, and it's coming from the direction of the package on the chair I left behind.

For a second, nobody else notices.

Then some fuse catches to another material, and the smoke is no longer faint. I find it overpowering just as a few people say, "Something's burning" and "What's that?" until there's a popping sound and a whizzing sound, and even I catch a flare of light to my left. For a second, there's a horrified, expectant pause, and then a familiar voice, Dr. Ivan's, shouts, "It's a bomb!" and all hell breaks loose.

My hands have been clenched on the wheels beside me, and I shove off as if a blanked gun has sounded, a flag waved, a race started. People are screaming, kids are crying, and wheelchairs are bouncing against each other like pinballs.

Gliding across the court, I relinquish my hold on the controls briefly enough to rip off the hospital gown—watch out, Gypsy Rose!—which flutters over my shoulder like litter tossed from a car window, and am suddenly just one more person in a uniform in a wheelchair on a field full of men in uniforms in wheelchairs. Instead of standing out, I am impossible to make out and take advantage.

Something bumps against my shoulder, a stray basketball.

Someone grabs for my chair. Either it's a nurse or one of the men who have been watching me. I slap at the hand, swerve sharply, carom off another player.

Following directions, I aim left, toward the parking lot. I remember Ivan's description of the premises as if a mental map has been etched into my mind. Wheelchairs are flying in all directions.

I hit the end of the court, catch a gently sloping path downhill, and pick up speed. Bumping over a curb, I am nearly thrown, but, like the orderly with the cart carrying blood, catch myself before it's too late. My chair smacks off the mirror of some doctor's car and scratches a wobbly line across the car's doors until its momentum is slowed.

Pausing for a second, out of breath although gravity has done the work, I decide to abandon the mobile apparatus that served me so well. I hop upright and push the chair into some bushes and start loping down the graded macadam that ought to lead to the exit. Ivan must have shot my foot up with some high-powered anesthetic, because I hardly feel a thing, though I know I will suffer later.

A few other wheelchairs occupied by children or basketball players who have set off in this direction by random chance whiz behind me, while others, followed by agents, are surely whizzing in every direction from the court. Shin Bet's probably going wild searching for me. This is Israel in a nutshell, and I'm happy.

I bump into a sign that clangs against my forehead. Christ!

I hear sirens. We are a rapid-response nation.

And I'm responding rapidly. Within minutes, the squad will determine that the "bomb" is nothing but smoke, while those who were watching me will figure out that the object of their observation has done more than flee; he has escaped. Whether they put the two together will be Dr. Ivan's problem to deal with as long as I have taken advantage of the situation.

God, do I appreciate Ivan. First, he placed me in a wheelchair in the only place where they are the most common mode of transportation. That makes tracking one particular chair, especially since it's no longer the chair with the bug, difficult. But he knew that I would be able to ditch my new chair at an opportune moment, thus leaving my pursuers doubly confused. It's basic psychology. If Nathan can't see, then he must not be able to walk, either. Until they find the chair in the bushes, they'll be looking for a man on wheels.

Of course, they'll question Ivan, but I'm not worried for him. Throughout our dialogue he never said a word that could be directly connected with this plan. I pressed the button on the package. I set the false alarm in motion. And I'm tricky; they already knew that. They'll be suspicious of Dr. Bear, but they'll have to accept his innocence. Some bear, he's more of a fox.

The one thing Ivan hasn't considered is this uniform. It served me well on a field of men in uniforms, but will soon stick out as sorely as I thought the wheelchair would. Where to go? Within minutes, there will be cordons at a short leash-length from the hospital. The only specific location I am aware of is the only place Ivan mentioned, the Church of the Visitation. I decide to visit.

Somewhere, someone is already typing a statement for the press, attributing blame or taking credit for the action at the hospital. One week ago, I would have been at the center of that action, but I'm too busy running, too delighted at not having to do anything but run to bother with public relations. One foot after the other, even if the right one is already starting to feel like miniature explosives are detonating under it with every step, I trot down the hill toward the church, but what's at the church I don't know.

I leave the chaos above while the sounds of the "bomb"-induced craziness recede. I wish I could go faster and am keenly aware of how difficult walking, let alone running, is without Goldie. Nonetheless, I understand why Ivan had to separate me and the dear girl; my escape would have been impossible in her company because even the doctor could not have rounded up two dozen shepherds to accompany two dozen men in basketball uniforms in wheelchairs after the fake bomb started smoking.

I arrive at a fork in the road. I can tell, because I've kicked the curb every few meters, stumbled over it once or twice, torn the skin on my basketball knees, and suddenly there's an intersection. On one side, the flat macadam flows onward to merge with the highways that connect the hospital complex to the rest of the country; on the other side, the road turns to cobblestones. Decisions.

It may lead to a dead end, but I follow the cobblestones and almost immediately realize that I'm on church property. If the entry to the Hadassah complex is busy with doctors and patients and tourists come to view the Chagall windows, the grounds here are serene. I smell flower blossoms and well-tended grass as I feel the bulk of the structure looming. The wind carries a hint of wet stucco, from workmen repairing the facade. Their voices drift down to me from a scaffold.

I've heard of this place, but even in the days when I had eyes I never saw it. On this site, Mary, pregnant with Jesus, visited Elizabeth, pregnant with John the Baptist. According to the Christian Bible, the two fetuses that would change the world communicated womb to womb while their mothers-to-be sipped tea and gabbed about morning sickness.

Without Goldie, negotiating the steps is difficult. They are broad but numerous, and at the top I am confronted by a huge bronze door embossed with cast figures representing moments of the New Testament. I extend my fingers and find a human shepherd surrounded by a flock of nubby sheep. The door is locked. Churches often have several doors, however, and there is seldom any need for more than one to open. I inch to the left and bump into a railing that must define the porch. I reverse directions and move to the right, where I find the central portal.

Inside is cool and vast. I feel light through stained-glass windows sixty, seventy feet above. There is a scent of incense—familiar from somewhere—and a burble of water from a low trough to my left. The pews must begin nearby because I hear an old lady murmuring prayers.

Then she stops. She's noticed me. A blind man in a basketball suit huffing and puffing like he's just run a marathon—not an everyday apparition in the Church of the Visitation. Maybe she thinks I'm the Holy Ghost.

I pad up the aisle, passing a few more elderly parishioners, who must come here daily. The place is so calm it could float away. But half a kilometer away is a scene of hysteria, which will soon encroach on these sacred precincts in search of me. I feel the hysteria mounting within. Was Ivan so clever in getting me away from Hadassah only to trap me here?

No, he must have had something in mind. Maybe there's a contact waiting with a priest suit to cover the incriminating satin shorts. I consider looking for the confessional. Father, I have sinned.

"Psst."

At last. A rough-edged whisper summons me down a row of wooden pews. It's not Ivan, but I smell eggs and smoke, so maybe it's a friend of his. Maybe they had breakfast together.

I bang my foot on an unhinged extension from the pew in front of me and the pain leaps straight up my spine. I trip and callused hands reach out from a roughly textured workman's shirt to steady me.

I sit.

He whispers out of the side of his mouth. Accents fade when the volume goes down, so it's hard to identify his place of origin, but this is neither native Israeli nor immigrant Russian.

"We do not have much time. Count to twenty and then follow me."

"How?"

"Oh, right."

This man is an underling. He has instructions, but not much understanding. At this moment, I don't have much understanding, either. I assume that he will take me back to meet Ivan somewhere. A safe house. But I have to help him to help me. "I can follow you at ten steps. Where are we going?"

"A car."

"Good. Where is it?"

"Parking lot, around the back."

I remember the driveway. "Can you pick me up in front of the church?"

This is not strictly according to plan, and Ivan's emissary hesitates.

I echo my last words, but without the "Can you" that preceded them they become a command rather than a question. "Pick me up in front of the church."

He feels better now, because he doesn't have to make a decision. "Five minutes."

I hear sirens in the distance. "Try to make it three."

A moment later, he's gone, but I track his steps across the flagstones. Fortunately, if not deliberately, pebbles or some sort of construction debris flaked off his shoes, and crunch beneath mine. Hansel and Gretel couldn't have done better. Again, I hear the soothing flow of water and smell the ranks of sacramental candles.

Now I know why the smell is familiar. Churches in Russia that had been shuttered since 1917 suddenly attained this aroma back in the eighties, post-Glasnost. Churchgoers carried it with them when they left, a secret signal only recognizable by believers and, presumably, the blind, though I wasn't a member of that particular tribe in those days.

Jewish houses of worship smell differently. Without wax, without incense, without the endless repairs involving glazing fluids, tiling grout, mortar, and brass polish, they smell of paper. Dried and desiccated with only a hint of mold foxing some fancier leather volumes, that's the scent of Jewish faith. I discovered this during my early days in the Promised Land, but the scent has been the same since the founding of Mea She'arim. It's an abstract odor that only a really refined sensibility can detect and it conveys both frailty and certainty, trepidation and serenity; it gives you the feeling that, though fashions may change and governments rise and tumble, the foundation goes to bedrock. I've always envied that sensation, but just couldn't believe it was true. Dig underneath the synagogue's basement and you'll finally find . . . nothing.

On the other hand, my belief in Nothing is strong and I'll take the earthly security of my cosmic insecurity over the delusions of a guy on a cross or a spirit in the sky any day. One thing I know is precisely what I don't believe.

Suddenly I can hardly wait to get outside, though that, too, is unusual for me. Hardly a nature boy, I'm more at home at Dregs and among dregs than aswim in the wine-dark sea or atop Masada or amid our great national forests, planted one tree at a time with seeds purchased with pennies from America, yet today the warm breeze is refreshing because enclosure feels like a trap.

I go down the steps easily, remembering that there were fourteen risers, and wait until I hear a vehicle cornering the church. It pulls up directly beside me, and the front door is opened from within. I enter, shut the door, and immediately realize what the stuff my guide's shoes left behind for me to follow was, because the interior of the car is suffused with its aroma: mud.

I've smelled this particular liquid earth before, in the kitchen on Rehov Rambam.

I keep one hand on the door latch, although leaping from a moving car is the last thing I need, when a voice from the rear says, "I'm sorry."

I turn around, facing the man I last encountered over a pan full of boiling oil and crisped onions.

He continues, "I didn't mean to scare you. I didn't mean to fight."

His tone is sincere, but I'm not in a forgiving mood. If he wants absolution he can go back into the church and look for the confessional. Besides, our battle is ancient history, and I need to keep up to date. "How did you find me?"

"Well, the doctor found me first. I was wandering around your neighborhood in a daze. That pan you threw, a slight concussion. I was lucky the oil had already spilled, but I have a few spatter burns on my neck."

Ivan must have jumped into his car the second we got off the phone. After blintzes with my mother, he must have found the man I had fought and took him to the hospital in my place.

"He bandaged my head, and I see he took care of your foot. He's a good man." My companion pronounces "gut" with a Yiddish inflection that gives him away. I'm no Henry Higgins, but I can tell a Brooklyn accent when I hear one. This man was born and raised within a linear mile of wherever Reb Rubinstein lived before he made Aliyah. The mud he reeks of must be that of the fields. I've got two settlers for companions and I know where we're going.

Ivan understood me after all. Yes, he shoved some cash into my pocket when I asked for money, and that will help me wherever I've got to go, but in the meantime he fulfilled a more important mission. When I said I needed money, I meant that I needed to go to a place where money is available. I needed to go to the bank. Not Bank Hapoalim, not Bank Leumi. Not the American Express office on Ben Yehuda Street. The bank I need to go to in order to find the source of my trouble is the West Bank.

And the "gut" doctor had one other patient who could take me there, because that was where he came from. Ivan probably agonized over whether to deliver me into the muddy man's hands, because he must have realized that we had met before. Two patients from Rehov Rambam with oil burns cannot be a coincidence.

It was a dangerous call. Obviously the muddy man and myself did not meet under optimum circumstances. But something about this guy must have made Ivan trust him. Indeed, his voice is genuinely regretful. Besides, Ivan also knows my determination and should have given me the credit to assume that I would have found my way anyway. And this way, Ivan will know where to find me if he must. The worst thing he may have done is made somebody's job easier and shortened my life by a few days.

By now, we've looped away from the tourist center and are angling south, since the descending sun is on my right. West is secular Tel Aviv, and the literal bank of the Jordan River is north, but the "West Bank" refers to the occupied territories to the south as well. Hebron is south.

# CHAPTER 11

Gradually the balance of scents shift and then reverse. To understand this, just imagine a boy, say five years old, who toddles downstairs and sees a cake. It's his birthday; he'll be delighted. If such an imaginary child was blind, he might smell the heavenly mixture of eggs and butter and sugar and fresh-baked flour and, depending on his mom and the extent of her desire to accommodate his taste, chocolate or vanilla or coconut or even almond marzipan bunnies in a ring about the perimeter. But if he could see, the boy might wonder about the irregularly shaped brown object sitting discreetly beside the candles, and if he could smell as well as a B.P. he might catch a whiff of something untoward in the mix.

Then say that one spoonful of the cake was removed and replaced with an equivalently sized spoonful of the same stuff as the odd object. Now imagine the cake disappearing bit by bit, and the object increasing bit by bit until, instead of a birthday cake with a turd atop it, the confection becomes a gigantic, artfully molded cylinder of shit with just one almond marzipan bunny ornamenting its disgusting circumference.

"I think I'll get off here."

"My name is Chaim," my companion answers.

I have no doubt that he isn't leaving Jerusalem unless I'm in his car. My only choice is whether to ride in the back seat or the trunk. "Glad to meet you."

"Look," he says, "I'm sorry. I mean, about the kitchen. I didn't expect anyone else, so I must have overreacted."

He doesn't say what his original intentions were, and what he would have done if Mother hadn't intervened, but I reply, "Think nothing of it." No one else does.

And so we drive for about an hour, say seventy kilometers. I smell humanity leavened by mud in the air-conditioned car, but as we leave the paved road, I start to smell more mud and less humanity. The car rattles and comes to an abrupt stop.

Checkpoint.

The driver rolls down his window, allowing a blast of desert air to obliterate the cumulative effects of an hour's cooling. "Shalom," he says.

A green-uniformed blur pokes into the window, clearly examining the passenger, me. In a rough, Brooklyn-edged voice, he says, "Delivery?"

"Der Alter wants him."

The voice immediately accedes. "Then bring him."

And the window shuts, but the scent of mud that's entered the car overpowers any other scent, and I feel as if I'm in a swamp the rest of the way into what must be a compound. I hear children at play and machinery at work, trucks and generators that produce electricity for this remote settlement.

"Welcome to Beis Machpelah," the driver announces, but I already know where we are.

Several kilometers away, the town of Hebron sits aswelter in the middle of nowhere with no reason for any of its inhabitants to be there except to torment the rest of the inhabitants. Hebron's only claim to fame is the Cave of Machpelah, in which, according to legend, Abraham, Isaac, and Jacob are buried. It's a holy site, and the city that surrounds it is a slum in the desert occupied only by those

Arabs unfortunate enough to have been born there and those Jews nettlesome enough to move there. The latter occupy the desert by volition, but any Arabs who wanted out could have applied for relocation by the Israeli authorities, so nobody besides the dead patriarchs has any excuse for such miserable residence. The contending factions of the local population deserve each other.

And Beis Machpelah, on the outskirts, is even worse, since it doesn't have any biblical pedigree. Founded early in the century, but brought to recent prominence by a Brooklyn rabbi, the settlement is an insult to the land around it and a continual thorn in the side of the army which has to protect it. Beis Machpelah was also the home of Isaiah Rubinstein.

We park the car and walk along a rutted drive to a large building, probably corrugated tin because it reflects the rays of the sun. The second my guide opens the door, a rush of mud smell—an olfactory mud slide—pours forth from within, entirely drowning the scent of humanity.

Nonetheless there are plenty of people inside the dense fecundity of the place. Several woman talk loudly above the clacking of conveyor belts that bring in the raw material, process it, removing pebbles and grit, and mix it with a squirt of neutral chemical ointment to give the final solution the requisite density to compete in the commercial marketplace. At the end of the line, a stream of plastic bags slaps down onto the belt, each to be filled with precisely four ounces of the precious substance. I smell a faint scorch as another machine heat-seals those bags, and sets them in cardboard boxes, two dozen bags to each box, for shipment to pharmacies and beauty salons in Israel and abroad. We're in a mud factory.

"Down a few miles."

"What?"

Out of the clatter of motors and the reek of mud comes a smooth voice scented with cinnamon-flavored tea. "Down a few miles, they mine potash from the Dead Sea, but that requires major capital investment. This is the only resource we have."

The voice is familiar, but I've only heard it in snippets, interrupted by any of a number of other voices, at least one of which I also heard in the last few days. I run through the Rolodex I've encountered since I was shot in my head: politicians, police, Abdullah and Twersky in Jerusalem, doctors, athletes, priests, most recently settlers.

Of course! Now I know who I'm speaking to.

Born as Moshe Zuckerman, my host changed his name to Moshe X as a youthful member of the JDL back in America in the late 1960s. This act of willful social provocation occurred before he discovered God and Israel in the 1970s and swapped his signature beret for a yarmulke. Yet even when the ordained and Aliyahed Rabbi X's beard reached his *pupik* and he became the venerable Der Alter in the 1980s, the fire in his belly still burned. Standing before me is a man whose voice I have only heard on television.

That's why I didn't recognize him immediately. He is on the news regularly, but not as a tour guide in a mud factory. The gentle rabbi is always good for a quote about the latest fracas in the West Bank, and invariably he delivers his lines in a high-pitched screed that trails off into an Ayatollah-like wail.

The last I heard of Der Alter was several months earlier when Zev Schechter, one of the journalists who accompanied Simon into my hospital room, wrote a series of articles on Beis Machpelah. Besides a colorful portrait of Orthodox customs and mating rituals in the desert, Schechter recounted rumors of gun smuggling that caught the attention of the Shin Bet, including my new friends Eli Khadoury and Cyril Klein. Unfortunately, by the time the IDF raided Beis Machpelah, any evidence had long since been removed and the embarrassed security forces were filmed hauling several tons of mud away from the innocent factory while Moshe X castigated them as soldiers of a police state.

Now he speaks with a p.r. man's professional aplomb compared to the TV's raging, hatred-filled hysteric. Either the tape misrepresented him or the tapers did.

"In a way it's simple, just another gift of God."

This is Moshe X's standard line, his stump speech. Whatever happens is a gift of God. Moshe's God might as well be Santa Claus, his bag filled with presents. One is the Torah, another the Holocaust, each a learning experience. Der Alter is determined to find the deity in every earthly event. Actually, I'm inclined to agree with him, but where Moshe assumes that each gift is an unalloyed good, I'm willing to judge the quality of the merchandise. I hold the Creator accountable for His actions on the same grounds that I do a rabid Hasid in a Tel Aviv auditorium, though I'll grant that my encounter with the latter was also a learning experience. Learning is necessary, but Moshe and I draw different conclusions from the same basic lessons. He always sees good, while I "see" whatever is there. Like everyone in Israel, I know I am right.

He continues, "The sediment on the floor of the Dead Sea is so filled with nutrients that it acts as a natural salve to clarify and beautify the skin. This . . ."—he dips his fingers into an unsealed bag and smears mud onto my cheek—"is the greatest natural cosmetic on earth. We export Zion's bounty."

The scent of the mud grows heavier as the enormous centrifugal vats swirl the mud around to provide a lotion for the complexions that require its rejuvenating. Kibbutz Beis Machpelah may have received a gift of God that allows its residents to earn the income to live here, but they have to provide something of their own.

"Of course," Moshe X finishes, "God helps those who help themselves."

Was he willfully quoting Emerson or whichever Protestant thinker would have thought in such a manner, or was he merely repeating a platitude because he was platitudinous guy? Or was he making fun of me? I try to parse his attitude and want to run my fingers over his face to find out if his eyebrows are arched with humor.

But Moshe X is not the kind of person you touch without permission. If I reach out, his acolytes will tackle me before I can blink. My kitchen antagonist and kidnapper, Chaim, probably born Harry, seems to have a gentle soul, but that doesn't mean that he won't use violence if he believes it's necessary, and he, like the entire population of Beis Machpelah, believes that whatever Moshe X believes is necessary.

Off in the corner of the factory, where an opening in the tin wall leads to a loading dock from which the shipments of mud will be trucked to a distribution center, a small uproar breaks out. I hear alternating shouting and crying in two languages, Hebrew and Arabic. The Hebrew shouting is loud and male, the Arabic crying low and female. They're the voices of a foreman and a worker, the latter probably bused in from Hebron to work the more arduous, less technically demanding procedures of industry.

"*Sheket!*" Moshe X commands, and immediately everyone obeys. Only the rattle and hum of the machinery ignores his presence. He continues, as mild as a medieval scholar, "God gave us this country thousands of years ago, complete with milk and honey."

"And mud."

"Yes," he says, and I feel his eyes on me. "And mud. And also potash, if we are willing to mine it from the depths of the Dead Sea. And oranges, if we are willing to drain the swamps and plant the fields." I can practically hear the national anthem playing the background.

"And soybeans, too, and computer software, for that matter, if we are willing to develop it. I assume you know about Kibbutz Ha Negev." He refers to a neighboring institution, only twenty kilometers of arid terrain distant.

I know, I know, a success story, a couple of teenagers in earlocks who just went public to the tune of several hundred million shekels, all belonging to the suddenly richest kibbutz in the country. So much for the honest sweat of the brow of the First Aliyah. So much for duck eggs and olive wood replicas of the Wailing Wall. But Der Alter isn't jealous. Anything that leads to Israeli prosperity is a gift of God.

Moshe X continues, "Jews have inhabited the Holy Land ever since the start of time. You, sir, are the beneficiary of that legacy. You would still be squirming under the communist heel if not for the State of Israel."

It's time to assert myself. "I am a representative of that state, sir."

"Rabbi," he corrects me.

I let it pass, though animosity remains like a current in the room.

Moshe X ponders me. He is an intelligent man and can tell what I think although my résumé might imply otherwise. "You work for a noble leader."

I might say that I work for the nation, but that isn't true. Whether Simon is noble or not, I work for him.

"Ben Levi may be a flawed man, but he is the best safeguard of our freedom and our future." He has assumed that my blindness has made me bitter, and maybe he is right, but he has shifted in the wrong direction and immediately adjusts. "We are deeply upset that one of our own attempted, well . . ." The good rabbi knows audience reaction; he's half spiritual leader, half showman. If he wasn't a man of God, he would have made a good press secretary.

"You didn't invite me here to apologize for the late Reb Rubinstein."

"No, but we do apologize and wish you know that when a Jew assaults a Jew we consider it in an insult to God."

I refrain from pointing out that his statement makes no reference to God being insulted when a Jew assaults an Arab, or that, in actual fact, his Jews seem to spend most of their time fighting other Jews: in the Knesset, in the Supreme Court, on the neighborhood religious councils. There's a thuggishness beneath Beis Machpelah's sacred vocabulary that I don't care to test. Also, it occurs to me that nobody knows where I am and that I could easily disappear in the desert. I could be dumped into one of the mud-mixing vats and churned into cosmetic cleanser.

"But you're right." For the first time, Moshe X surprises me. "I didn't want to see you merely to apologize. At this point, that is between Isaiah and God. Come along, I'd like to show you something." He takes my arm, and I allow myself to be escorted as if I required the assistance.

We exit the rear door of the mud factory and gradually leave the smell of earth and its liquids behind as the sun bakes everything dry. It must be over 100 degrees, but feels hotter because the rays absorbed by the macadam burn through the soles of the athletic sneakers I still wear. "Over there, I mean to the left," he corrects himself, "is our new social hall, and beyond it are dormitories for the children and a nursery for infants. To the right are the original buildings, used for administration and as a shul. Our gardens, which you will soon sss . . ." He halts awkwardly, and plows on, more careful of my sensibility. "Our gardens are in development, but in the meantime the mud factory provides the income. Ahead is a water tower; that's our lifeline. Without it, the kibbutz could not exist. Beis Machpelah was founded in '28 by sixteen Jews from Russia. Just last year, we installed a plaque in their honor."

He is playing on what he assumes are my sympathies.

"Today, over two hundred families live here. We divide our time between working and praying and tending the Tomb of the Patriarchs. How many children do you have?"

"None." I wonder if he knows about my tendencies. I don't hide them, but neither am I am a popular cover boy. Not photogenic enough, I suppose.

"That's a shame; if the First Aliyah reclaimed the land, our job is to repopulate it."

Suddenly we hear a burst of machine gun fire, but none of the guides reacts. In addition to domestic and commercial installations, the kibbutz also maintains a firing range.

These aren't the illegal weapons of Schechter's notorious article, but their rattling is eloquent. I can almost feel the frown in Moshe X's countenance as his expansive, nothing-to-hide tone turns terse. "We do, as I said, have to protect ourselves. As Israel is an island in a sea of enemies, so Beis Machpelah is an island amid a sea of enemies within greater Israel."

Israel Ha G'dolah. Der Alter never used the term "West Bank," never mind "Palestine." He never acknowledged any diminution of borders tacitly and presumably soon-to-be legally acceded to by the Oslo, Wye, and Cancún agreements. He and I live by the same basic tenet: words are truth. If you name it, it is.

"But you know this, too, Mr. Kazakov," he strokes me. "You were in the army. You suffered and paid a great price on behalf of the nation, and we are grateful."

I nod.

"What you must know is that we pay a price, too, every day of our lives. Our children must play behind barbed wire as if they are in concentration camps. Our men must serve guard duty at night after their normal day's work. Our women must shop under military protection. Our holy places are defiled, while our soldiers are set to guard their holy places. This is not a normal life."

But nothing in Israel is normal. That's why I couldn't live anyplace else. As much hypocrisy as I see, however, I also see that Moshe X could be honest, that he'd really prefer to live in peace with his God. In methods, however, lies morality.

Shadows slide over my face, relieving the heat for half a second. Then they disappear, then reappear, then disappear again. We are standing underneath a structure that has a hundred perforations, a miniature Eiffel Tower. The water tower.

"We were told there was a chance of water at two hundred feet, but by the time we hit four hundred it was still dry. There *is* a water table everywhere."

"Seek and ye shall find."

"God provides." Moshe X repeats his bottom line, ignoring my sarcasm. "At four hundred and twenty-three feet, there was a rumbling, and by four thirty a flow. We were at a level beneath the Dead Sea, where the salt had leached out through the sedimentary layers, which clarified the water into as pure a state as it arrives into the Dead Sea from the Jordan River. We were drinking mountain water in the desert." I hear a knob turn, the faint grate of metal on metal, and then I hear liquid splash. Moshe takes my hand and places a tin mug in my grasp. "Drink."

Parched in the sun, I put the hot metal to my lips and sip at the coolest, freshest liquid I've ever tasted. A drop descends from my lips to my chin where it immediately evaporates. I haven't had anything to drink or eat since the chocolate-flavored nutrient shake at the hospital and I feel as if I could guzzle a barrelful, but I don't ask, because I understand too well the subtle lesson I'm being taught. Between the thick ooze of mud in the factory and the pure water and the hot air, I'm in a place where life is at its most and most dramatically elemental. These people live at the base level. Nothing else exists in Beis Machpelah besides earth, air, water, and fire, nothing except God.

"From here we must take another method of transportation," Moshe announces. While talking, we have left the paved roads of the original settlement and walked eastward, along a dirt path as hard as paving, toward the perimeter of the kibbutz, away from the sun, the rays of which prickle on the back of my neck. I hear and feel the spray of surrounding irrigation and smell something organic. Moshe explains, "Here are the gardens I mentioned. We are growing soybeans, cabbages, eggplants, tomatoes, and more. There are marvelous new agricultural techniques that we hope will eventually allow us to be entirely self-sufficient. Over on the other side of the kibbutz we have chickens and cows."

But as Beis Machpelah itself peters out into the desert that stretches, depending on which direction one takes, to the Dead Sea or the thin belt of civilization that trims the Mediterranean coast, so the promotional tour that must have been scripted for visiting American donors ends, too. I smell a burning cigarette and hear the impatient pawing at the ground of what I assume is a horse. I smell manure. Moshe asks, "Are the animals ready?"

A new voice, half Brooklyn, half Sabra, replies, "Yes."

"We will have to take donkeys from here on, because there aren't any roads."

I should have known. Horses would be just as useless as cars in the Negev. "I've ridden worse."

"Gut." Moshe slaps me on the back. We are joint participants in a grand adventure.

Five donkeys await us along with two new settlers, both introduced to me as Avi. That makes things a little simpler, but I wonder if all new settlers are named Avi. The Avis' voices, native but inflected with the accents of their parents, are more youthful than Chaim's; perhaps that's why they've been chosen for this mission. Old habits die hard, and a previous generation is less accustomed to present-day customs, which in this case involve primitive pack animals instead of taxis. Chaim still has one foot in Brooklyn and can be trusted behind a wheel, whereas the new blood adapts more easily to local means.

"We'll be back tomorrow," Moshe informs Chaim, who departs without another word, feet crunching on the path. Then one Avi with strong hands helps me onto my hairy mount, while the other Avi assists Der Alter.

The elderly rabbi grunts and laughs. "Back in the saddle."

Suddenly, unexpectedly, Avi grasps my burned right foot to thrust it into a metal stirrup. He is as professional as a shoe salesman, but I let out a gasp.

"What?"

"Never mind." I gingerly slip the injured limb to rest against the comforting warmth of the beast's belly and grip the pommel that protrudes from a thick leather saddle.

Then the two Avis leap effortlessly atop their mounts, and we start off with a bray from the last donkey, which carries our provisions: jugs of fresh water and food and camping requirements. It seems like we'll be gone overnight.

From Moscow to Jerusalem, I've always been an urbanite, so the ways of the natural world are foreign to me, but I trust our native guides and allow them to lead me and my docile companion off into the desert as the misty revolutions of the irrigation machinery fade behind us.

The gait of a donkey, though slow, is not smooth. Even before we hit rocky ground, each step of the beast jostles me from side to side, and soon I'm seasick with the swaying motion and my rump aches nearly as much as my foot. I try to push myself up off my safely stirruped left foot to allow an inch of air between one ass and the other.

Avi trots beside me and says, "The best way to ride is to maintain full bottom contact. You will get used to it." I picture a new breed of cowboy, wearing a dark suit that must be intolerable in this climate, and a narrow-brimmed felt hat that is hardly justified by the tiny penumbra of shadow it casts over his forehead. He probably sports a wisp of beard, which will grow in the fullness of time into a rabbinical bush. He undoubtedly carries a pocket prayer book in his jacket, but he is as much a creature of this wilderness as his donkey and he knows the ways of the desert as well as his forefathers. If Abraham could cross the wasteland, Avi can, too.

We ride for several hours, during which I become aware that life exists even here. Birds twitter and flap breathlessly across the sky, and the hot wind rustles some sort of vegetation that clings tenaciously to cracks in the rock, its roots searching down, perhaps as deep as Beis Machpelah's well, to draw sustenance from below. Lizards slide back and forth over the land with a whisper, and the desolate howl of some creature—all I can think of is a coyote—pierces the dusk.

Likewise the scent is complex, a mixture of salt from the Dead Sea and further mineral exudation from the landscape. I can tell the color ink someone is writing with from its odor and Brie from cheddar on a doctor's tie at ten paces—and the smell of sex lingers like an afterthought—but I wouldn't know shale from basalt from quartz to save my life. For a moment, I think I catch a whiff of more synthetic smoke, but neither of the Avis has lit another cigarette and the smell dissipates in the beginning of a breeze that blows down from the mountains. Perhaps one of the bushes my donkey brushes against has caught fire in the final piercing glare of the setting sun.

What am I doing here? Once again, in the calm of the desert, I trace my path from my companions' companion's misguided bullet—misguided to greater or lesser extent depending on whether or not it was aimed at me, but misguided any way you consider it, because it didn't kill anyone—though, to put it plainly, my kidnapping. Okay, so far it hasn't been as painful as Lebanon, but that's only so far.

What am I doing here? I could have remained in the hospital until my foot healed and then gone home and then to work. I could have written the speech Simon would have recited when I first returned to my office at the Knesset. If I was really as disillusioned as I pretended to be, I could have quit and gone into advertising. If I could sell Simon, I could sell anything.

Yet something has kept me going. Something made me convince Doc Ivan to thrust me into this situation on the West Bank. That something has a name: Gabriel. I remember the last time I met him before Tel Aviv. It was at the party I alluded to back in Simon's office, at the Israel Museum, for the opening for a new exhibit of recent discoveries at Megiddo. They weren't Gabriel's disoveries, but he was at the party as a peer of the archaeologists reveling in their discernment of the difference between ninth and tenth century B.C. artifacts, and I was there as Simon's representative.

I drank wine; I ate cheese. I couldn't look at the recently discovered jugs or jars or whatever they dug up, so I was looking forward to the end of a tedious evening. I was probably thinking about dropping into Dregs for a nightcap when someone next to me asked, "Can I get you something?"

I'm not even sure how I knew it was Gabriel. I had met him years before when I first started working for Simon, before the estrangement, but even then he had kept his distance from the campaign, tolerating a few happy family photographs and no more. Perhaps there was something in the timbre of his voice that reminded me of his father, or perhaps I remembered his voice from the famous "We can wait" broadcast. In any case, we didn't have to introduce ourselves. Of course, it was entirely logical that he would be here.

I replied, "A new job?"

"Work should provide more than a salary."

"That's very nice. But not everyone can do what they love." I knew. That afternoon I had written an especially unpleasant piece for Simon defending the B'nai B'rak religious council's decision to ban women from synagogue libraries. Oh, we claimed our defense was based on local determination, but it was really based on votes. Now that I had six feet plus of ben Levi genes that I wasn't beholden to, I took out my resentment toward the father on the son and continued sarcastically, "The world needs street sweepers as well as archaeologists."

But rather than take offense, all Gabriel did was laugh kindly and say, "More."

So I laughed and added, "More than speechwriters, too."

"Street sweepers of the world, unite."

"Um . . ." I was about to ask him if he wanted to go somewhere else and have a drink, but uncharacteristically chickened out. "Tell me about this stuff." I waved my hand in the direction of the exhibit.

"Really very fine. Megiddo's been a treasure trove for years, but they've found something new that explains a lot."

"What?"

"Here." He escorted me through the wine-swilling patrons of the museum until we stopped amid a particularly dense cluster admiring something set on a flat-topped pedestal. "Here," he said again, and placed a large, curved object in my hands, a bowl.

Immediately, a satiny curator was on us like a guard dog. "Please!" he demanded.

"Don't worry," Gabriel refused. "Mr. Kazakov won't drop it."

"And if I do, Mr. ben Levi will catch it."

We were having a great time.

The man stuttered, "T-t-touching is strictly f-f-forb-b-b—"

Gabriel interrupted midstutter. He had his father's imperious air of command. "Touching is strictly necessary to find it, to unearth it, and to display it. In this case, touching is strictly necessary to perceive it. What else is a museum for?"

Principles aside, Gabriel wasn't entirely right, and I was feeling eager enough to want to impress him and cheerful enough to ease the curator's quivering distress. I replaced the bowl carefully upon its platform and leaned forward to smell it. Of course, eleven hundred years of burial had expunged any trace of what it contained, grain or wine perhaps, but I thought I detected the faintest possible whiff of smokiness. "A good year."

"No, actually it was a very bad year. Reach out one more time and feel the external layers."

Usually I bridled at assistance, but there was nothing patronizing about Gabriel's manner. He was a natural teacher, correcting me when I was wrong—firmly, but kindly—and leading me in the direction of discovery.

"One is smoother than another."

"Yes, that's because there was a fire. We can tell from the carbon deposits. That's why this is so important. Most of Megiddo was burnt circa 970 B.C. That may explain why its name became the derivation for Armageddon."

"Not bad for a would-be street sweeper."

I remember that bowl and suddenly think of the Strange Fire that destroyed its world. Megiddo is north toward the Jezrael Valley, but it functioned as an ancient crossroads, like Hebron, and once again

I swear that I can smell smoke on the desert horizon—clearly a product of my poetic imagination.

Disconcertingly, the dying embers of poetry inside me are being fanned these days. It's the mystery of the contemporary Strange Fire that both Cyril Klein and Chaim referred to that's creating a draft, sucking me up a flue toward an unknown sky. Unlike the conflagration at Megiddo that probably had a quite mundane cause, a cooking brazier accidentally tipped askew or a flame-tipped arrow deliberately delivered airmail by a besieging enemy, this mystery is symbolic rather than chemical and therefore more dangerous.

No, I can't underestimate the danger. Whether chemical or symbolic, the separate fires may have similar results. Megiddo's destruction was mysterious, too, until the archaeologists solved it with the aid of a single bowl. Somewhere in the museum there must be human bones that reveal the same patterns of smoothness and charring as the bowl. Somewhere in the museum there must be dozens of other bowls broken into so many shards that all the king's curators will never be able to put them together again. Still, one bowl remained, miraculously intact.

That's why I'm here, but I've been rushing from site to site so swiftly that I haven't had time to understand until now. I know that I'm in danger, and I believe that Gabriel is in danger. I want to save him as an ironic providence saved the single bowl from out of the orange and black maelstrom that engulfed Megiddo. I didn't drop the bowl that night in the museum, and I don't want to drop it now. Maybe, later, I'll find the strength to invite Gabriel out for that drink. And then . . . maybe.

# CHAPTER 12

My thoughts are interrupted when Avi reaches across my waist to grasp the reins that lay limp in my hands. I guess that we've arrived at our destination. We dismount, probably at a signal Moshe X relayed the moment he received a divine signal from the firmament. The rabbi says, "Ma'ariv."

We have stopped to pray.

Three times daily, morning, afternoon and evening, in Shakhris, Minkhah and Ma'ariv services, the Orthodox bespeak their dedication to God. Moshe X hands me a prayerbook.

I know what it is from the velvety smoothness of its pages and the cracked leather of its binding. How many times is the best novel read, how frequently a favorite poem recited, how often a dictionary referenced? This book is read three times a day, every day. "No, thanks," I decline.

The rabbi snorts as if to say, "Your funeral."

But I am more concerned with the body than the soul and take advantage of our break to stretch and try to further discern where that persistent waft of smoke on the air comes from as Moshe and the Avis face northward to Jerusalem. Their prayer is quick and businesslike, a murmur that varies in pitch rather than intonation. They pray like a hive of bees.

I remove my right sneaker to apply a dab of medicinal unguent to the blistered flesh. The air feels cool in the dusk, though the temperature couldn't have yet dipped below eighty or ninety. A pink residue of illumination must be glimmering up from behind the hills to the west, but I pretend it's already dark and relish the thought, because darkness equalizes. At night, nobody can see. At least this is true for genuine night, without street lamps or automobile headlights or the spooky blue glare of a television through a neighbor's window, and the closest bulb to this desolate spot comes from the kibbutz kilometers behind us. I wish I could tell if there was a moon, rising, falling, or in full lunar glow; if I could pray, I would pray there wasn't.

For a moment, I feel close to absolute peace as my companions commune with their own absolute. I feel like dancing—or hobbling—into the desert, waving my arms and running wild like some ancient mystic. Then, as if they can read my thoughts, Avi One clicks on a flashlight to banish the dark and Avi Two shouts, "Don't move."

"Don't move," Avi One repeats with calm urgency. "Not an inch," he says, as I hear Avi Two unzip a bag. There is a click, like a pebble dropping; it is the distinctive sound of a revolver safety shifted into unsafe position. Have they escorted me into the desert to kill me secretly? Will they bury me in a shallow grave this close to the patriarchs? I lift my head skyward, awaiting a coup de grâce.

The gun explodes, and a spray of sand splashes against my foot.

I freeze as Moshe X, his smell of age and cinnamon tea and musty volumes obscured by the cloud of burnt powder that suffuses the gentle desert atmosphere, rushes forward and kneels before me. He rustles in the sand and then stands up and presses a small object into my hand. It is a hard, ridged shell with several rubbery wires dangling from one end. At first I think it is a ruined transistor radio, but then my hand feels wetness, and my forefinger probes under the shell to a soft, fleshy interior.

Avi Two says one word, "Scorpion."

"Good shot," Avi One compliments him.

"Put on your shoes," Moshe tells me.

Beis Machpelah is situated in a bowl-shaped depression circled by a ring of hills. Gradually we rise up into those hills, carried aloft by the donkeys' sure feet, and then, gradually, we start to descend along a wadi created by a neolithic stream that dried up thousands of years ago. Several times the path is so precipitous we have to switch back, and stones loosened by the donkeys' hooves clatter into the night.

Finally we round a particularly steep outcropping, its sedimentary layers jutting out like bookshelves, and I know we are near our destination, because of three small events. First, the wind that has been steady at our backs suddenly dissipates. Second, instead of enclosure, I feel a vast opening ahead. Last, a pebble dislodged by one of the donkeys skitters ahead of us and comes to rest with a tiny splash.

We are at the Dead Sea, and we haven't crossed any roads, which means that we have entirely circumvented not only the western shore with its spas and tourist hotels and retirement homes, but the southern shore that serves the potash works. We are in uncharted territory and might have crossed the green line into Jordan.

We follow the shore for another hour, though our progress on the flats is even slower than it was in the hills, because the salt water that laps at our animals' feet has dried into razor-sharp crystals. Several kilometers away, the tourists who bathe in these miraculous, recuperative waters do so wearing sneakers. Finally, we stop for the night where a cliff has eroded over millions of years to form a natural, protective cove. The Avis set fire to a heap of brittle twigs they gather from the surrounding underbrush and unroll several sleeping bags, which we all check for more scorpions. We eat chicken cutlets prepared by the Beis Machpelah kitchen and cooked on a frying pan Avi Two retrieves from the pack in which he also keeps his gun.

I wonder if the faint smell of smoke I detected during the first leg of our journey was a premonition of the genuine smoke from Avi's cooking or the barrel of his weapon.

I wonder many things, mostly what we are doing here, and what is going on in Jerusalem, and where Gabriel is, and if the scorpion really had been about to sting me or whether the episode was a charade designed to obligate me to Moshe X. It would have been an easy game to play with a B.P. Just find a scorpion, kill it, fire a bullet into the ground, and say, "Here's what we found."

But the blood was wet.

I fall asleep and dream of scorpions.

"Shakhris" is the first word I wake to. Whether the Avis have been up for hours I don't know, but by the time I open my eyes—a reflex without consequence—they are shuckling and muttering again, thanking God for the new day.

Dawn is just beginning its rise over several thousand miles of Arab and Islamic lands to the east: Jordan, Iraq, Iran, Afghanistan, Pakistan, much of India, the Malay Peninsula, and the Indonesian archipelago. The nearest Jew in that direction is probably in San Francisco and he is probably gay. This reminds me that, according to Leviticus, I am an "abomination" to these people, but then again, they have no use for me as a strong masculine poet, either. They recite the verses of their dead ancestors three times a day, but cannot tolerate the poetry of the living.

Avi One hands me two hard-boiled eggs and a mug of coffee he brewed over the smoldering fire. "If you want salt, just dip," he says, and I do.

I like salt. Whether it's a Russian or a Jewish taste, I don't know, but I put salt on everything before I taste it and then I usually put on more salt. At home, we dispense it by the pinch instead of the sprinkle. Mother keeps a cup of salt in the center of the kitchen table. Sometimes visitors mistake it for sugar and put a spoonful in their coffee before we can stop them.

Moshe X repeats exactly the same words he used at the edge of Beis Machpelah. "From here we must take another method of transportation." He should learn to vary his sentences.

But this time there is no further guide to meet us, at least not yet. The Avis disappear up the slope that guarded us and return a few minutes later grunting. Whatever they are carrying is heavy; I can hear their exertion and then their relief as they drop their load into the Sea. It is another method of transportation: a boat.

Avi Two explains, "If we dragged it across the ground, the salt would rip a hole in the bottom."

Despite the Dead Sea's famous natural buoyancy, enough weight would sink in the shallows, so Der Alter enters first, and I feel like saying, "Ride 'em, sailor," but refrain. The rest of us push the nautical "method of transportation" from the spiky shards on the Sea floor and then, soaked to our knees, climb aboard.

I sit in the prow, Der Alter in the stern, while the Avis occupy the middle, each with an oar. Avi Two explains, "A motor would be destroyed by this water in a week."

The sun still hasn't had an opportunity to cast its rays directly upon us before we arrive at a cove similar to the one we sojourned in the night before. We walk across a lumpy field of salt formations while Avi Two explains. His role, it seems, is press secretary to the press secretary. "As you know," he begins, "the Dead Sea originates in the snow atop Mount Hermon. After it melts in the spring, streams descend and collect to create Lake Kinneret."

A.k.a. the Sea of Galilee

"From the southern tip of Lake Kinneret, the outflow creates the Jordan River, which delineates the border of Samaria."

A.k.a. the West Bank

"The Jordan passes about thirty kilometers from Jerusalem and then, farther south, empties into this natural basin. As you may have noticed, however, it is hot here." Avi allows himself to appreciate this moment of understated levity and then goes on with the lecture. "The Dead Sea is the lowest spot on the face of the earth, one thousand three hundred feet below sea level, and has only two inches of rainfall per annum. What creates the Dead Sea is the unique combination of evaporation and replenishment. But . . ."

There's always a "but."

"But recently the ancient balance between evaporation and replenishment has been altered. This is a result of increasing agricultural usage in the north."

"And also," I add, "nearby."

"Our well does its own part in lowering the water table, but that is *de minimus*."

"A gallon is a gallon."

"Yes," he concedes, and continues. "The road Chaim drove you on to reach Beis Machpelah used to hug the Dead Sea. When that road was built in the 1950s it was less than ten meters from the water."

"I remember."

"You remember?" These are the first words Moshe X has uttered since his morning prayer.

"Well, not the 1950s, but thirteen or fourteen years ago."

Less than a month after I arrived in Israel, certified as a Jew, registered to vote, enrolled in language lessons, ensconced at the Villa Rambam with my mother, I was ushered into an Egged Company tour bus and driven, together with forty or fifty other new arrivals, from one end of the country to the other. It was part of our indoctrination package, overseen by a Russian-speaking guide from the Ministry of Immigration whose aim was to pack as much inspirational history as possible into five days. We started in Jerusalem and saw the Western Wall, various synagogues, tombs ancient and modern from King David's to Theodore Herzl's, as well as my two future alma maters, Hebrew University and Hadassah Hospital. We made a pilgrimage to the Holocaust Memorial at Yad Vashem and then zipped around the corner to the Knesset, thus drawing the explicit line from one to the other. Never forget.

Never imagine, either. Life will surprise you. Treading the soft carpet in the Knesset lobby, gawking at the assembly hall, I wouldn't have believed that within the decade I would know these premises as well as I already knew the thirty-five square meters the noble legislators of Zion had allotted me on Rehov Rambam.

We visited the former British military outpost at Latrun that had recently been converted into the world's only tank museum. We cruised past Ben-Gurion International Airport and entered Tel Aviv, where we snacked at a café on Dizengoff Street that had been bombed by a Palestinian teenager two years earlier. A bronze plaque commemorating the dead was attached to the wall beside the menu. Another version of the same lesson. Never forget.

Dizengoff was no busier than Gorky Street, but it was dramatically different from Moscow's main drag in two ways. The first was commercial, as most of my compatriot expatriots noticed. Agog with abundance, they took each other's photographs in front of fruit stands and the windows of clothing stores and electronics stores filled with merchandise that anyone—anyone!—could simply walk into and buy. Whether I was a good Communist or a bad capitalist I can't say, but I was immune to the lure of the purchasable. Instead, I feasted on the sheer human profusion of Tel Aviv. That was the second difference between municipalities. Dizengoff Street was an ongoing parade of young women and young men wearing short shorts and ribbed T-shirts; for me, they were the ultimate expression of openness and democracy . . . and sex.

From this heavenly fleshpot, our bus swung north to Roman ruins at Ceasarea, Ottoman towers at Acco, the placid Baha'i church of Haifa, and the village of Safad, home of mystical Kabbalist lore from Isaac Luria in the sixteenth century until today. Finally, we visited the region beside the Dead Sea. We swam—or, rather, floated like animate balloons—in its weird, viscous depths and then we drove to Masada. Instead of taking a cable car to the peak where a besieged community of ancient Hebrews killed themselves rather than surrender to Roman tyranny, we climbed the mountain—just like American teen travel groups and regiments of paratroopers in the spirit-bonding ritual that concludes their training. Several kilometers of steeply ascending trail later, we collapsed atop the plateau that jutted into the sky, the thing itself and suddenly, magically, transformatively, ourselves as well, symbols of Israel resurgent. And then we took the cable car down, reboarded our bus, and returned home, each to our respective thirty-five square meters. Yes, I remember that road, and especially the bus.

For all the historical and emotional weight of our whirlwind tour through our new homeland, what I remember best about that journey is the bus. In power and speed, it dwarfed anything on the roads of Moscow. And inside! The thing was as plush as the Hermitage. It was carpeted and air-conditioned, and, most amazingly, had its own bathroom. A bathroom on a moving vehicle! I think that we forty Russians peed as much as all of Odessa in those five days just to experience again and again the delirious thrill of exposing ourselves and urinating in the little closet while ocean, mountain, and desert scenery hurtled past the window.

Der Alter brings me back to the present. "That road is now fifty meters from the shore. The Dead Sea is shrinking."

Surely Moshe X has not brought me here to deliver an ecological sermon, and besides, we've already agreed that his few hundred holy souls are doing their part to turn the Dead Sea into the Dead Pond into the Dead Puddle approximately twenty years from now if the deliquidization of the basin continues at the current pace.

Besides, this is old news. Just two months ago I sat in on a hearing held by a Knesset committee appointed to deal with the problem. Simon cared about the fate of this most godforsaken body of water on the planet for several reasons. One was health, by which he really meant money, and the other was heritage, by which he really meant money. For decades, local cottage industry catered to curiosity-seekers and people who believed that the unique muds and salts and sulfur springs of the region had curative properties. Entrepreneurs humped coolers full of Pepsi-Cola across the salt-crusted beaches, Mom and Pop mudpacking operations sold the stuff to those too lazy to dredge it for themselves, and the spa owned by the kibbutz at Ein Gedi was booked years in advance. But that was small change, and the Dead Sea has recently gone big-time. In the last few years an entire new city of hotels and time-share condos for arthritic retirees has sprung up. Named Neve Zohar, it's Israel's Phoenix, Arizona, growing with an aging Judaism. Hobble as they might, these people pay taxes; they also vote.

Nonvoting but even more important are the tourists. The Dead Sea is a natural wonder that is an international attraction. Where camels once plied trade routes, an endless stream of Dan and Egged buses shuttle thousands of people a day to Masada and the beach. Without the green vista below, Masada is just another ruin.

Lastly, there are the environmentalists. Genuinely unconcerned with financial repercussions, this noisy, phony bunch rails on about the ruination of the "natural" world while sending out enough p.r. faxes to deforest the acres planted by pennies from the Jewish

National Fund. No less than Moshe X, they've made a pact with God. They'll chain themselves to the truckloads of potash mined from this site and all He has to do in return is to protect their cell phones and veggie burgers.

At the hearings, we talked about diminishing the gallonage taken from the Jordan or increasing the capacity of our desalinization plants sufficiently to satisfy the agriculture industry, but the most interesting proposal was that for a canal from the Mediterranean, thus artificially providing presalted water for the thirsty basin. Cutting across lower Israel like an abdominal incision, it would be the most massive engineering project in the country, reviving the Dead Sea, producing thousands of jobs and, not incidentally, creating miracle mile after mile of ribbon-width waterfront.

Nonetheless, Moshe X continues as he leads me along the shore, away from the Avis, who remain behind with the boat. "Five years ago, the ground we are walking on was underwater. Of course, it could have been explored, but that would have required expensive diving equipment. Once the water level dropped, however, it became more accessible. Perhaps this made exploration inevitable."

Things are beginning to come together. Fearfully, expectantly, I ask, "What sort of exploration?"

"Archaeological."

Of course. "Gabriel."

Moshe X's leather-shod feet fret at the salt crystals. "Yes."

We say nothing more as he leads me into a narrow crevice between twin overhangs of solid rock. From here, we walk single file and occasionally have to squeeze sideways between jagged stone pincers.

Ten paces later, the narrowing gap in the earth above us seals entirely and we hunch over until we are reduced to a crawl. I smell the fetid waste from the elderly rabbi's rear end. We take a leftward fork in the tunnel and continue crawling until we are compelled to adopt a snakelike slither. Every minute we slide farther down the evolutionary scale. I smell the rabbi's socks.

Diamond-hard spikes of petrified salt tear at the shirt and pants the Avis gave me to replace the green nylon uniform Dr. Ivan gave me. I feel as if I am entering a tomb and worry about how we are ever going to be able to turn around. Then a whisper of air caresses my cheek. There is an opening somewhere. Der Alter squeezes through a final hole in the rock and rises to his feet. I start to do the same when he blocks me with a gnarly palm. He says, "If you come in here, you will lose three months of life."

The man is serious, and I am curious. I stand.

We are inside a cave; the dimensions feel roomlike. The rabbi's flashlight clicks on, and I perceive a vague beam in the dark. I am not able to make out anything the beam lights upon, though, so I circle the room, fingers trailing the rough walls, half expecting to come upon . . . what? Something archaeological, for sure. A bowl? No, that's Megiddo. A headless statue? No, that's Roman. An urn filled with papyrus? No, the scrolls of nearby Qumran were preserved by the arid, moistureless atmosphere. If this cave has been submerged, any documents would have turned to mud. Besides, what discovery could be important enough to lead Rubinstein to try to kill Gabriel? The ark of the covenant? The skeleton of Jesus?

I finish my circumnavigation of the premises. Nothing. Not even a refrigerator with a severed head. If the treasure has been removed, why did we have to visit the site of its discovery unless the site itself is the discovery? I think of the Lebanese funeral chamber I was once trapped in. But the walls of this cave are unshaped by human hands. And what did Der Alter mean when he said that I would lose three months of life? Is this cave cursed? I think of the Holy of Holies atop the Western Wall, a spot so sacred that anyone who trespasses—even inadvertently—will die immediately. At least, that's what the rabbis believe. "Three months?" I repeat.

"More or less. It apparently depends on your body chemistry. We have already been exposed long enough. It would not be wise to linger."

"Exposed to what?" I keep groping along the walls and find one smooth mark, a few inches long, an inch wide. I rub it contemplatively with the ball of my thumb. A chisel has sheared away a chunk of rock.

The flashlight clicks off. Moshe X says, "Pardon me, but I don't know how completely blind you are. Can you see anything?"

"Occasionally I can make out a shape or a color. Now I can see nothing. What do you see?"

"The glow."

So the walls are phosphorescent.

Moshe continues. "Can you feel anything?" Whether he knows it or not, the rabbinical teacher is a Socratic, preferring to lead his students to their own conclusions rather than deliver wisdom from on high.

I concentrate. I feel dampness and enclosure, but could have felt both those qualities in the mikvah that surely exists back in Beis Machpelah to serve the ritual needs of the community. I rub my thumb and forefinger together, keep rubbing them together. My thumb is irritated, as if a splinter has lodged beneath the surface of the flesh. My thumb tingles.

I separate the two digits. My forefinger tingles. My entire body tingles, as if the cave itself is vibrating. There must be an expression of comprehension on my face, because Moshe X says, "We've been here long enough, but I had to bring you, because you wouldn't have understood otherwise."

I still don't know precisely what I understand. "Where are we?"

"A cave."

"What is the cave made of?"

"Uranium."

"There is no uranium in Israel."

"That's the problem. We're not in Israel."

Most journeys seem shorter on the return than they do on the outing. Uncertainty about distance or the validity of directions dispelled, one has a sense of pace and recalls landmarks—in this case a bend in the mineral-rich tunnel at the moment when the earth opens into a crack above our heads. Moshe X and I ascend the evolutionary path we previously descended, slithering on our bellies, then crawling on all fours, then hunching, then standing upright. When the crevice opens further, we move from single file to a comradely side by side, and Der Alter tells me the story.

"Gabriel ben Levi found this place several months ago. He was searching for the remains of Sodom, but that evil city probably lies under the portion of the Dead Sea that is still underwater. Instead, he may have found a scientific explanation for its destruction."

I am shocked that the spiritual leader of Beis Machpelah might tolerate a scientific explanation for what the Bible describes as deitific intervention. "But I thought—"

"God works as God wishes. If He wished to choose fire and brimstone from the sky on a sunny day, there would have been fire and brimstone from the sky, but if He wished to choose a spontaneous atomic blast from the elements of the earth, so it would be. The fact remains that according to the Bible Sodom was destroyed as a result of its people's iniquity at the precise moment when Avraham Aveinu was shunned and threatened by the Sodomites. This is not a coincidence; this is a miracle. It's also a miracle that such a deposit exists in a location for which there is no geological explanation whatsoever. That is why nobody found it before. People do not find what they do not look for."

The mixture of "facts" and "miracles" in his mind is dizzying, but I trust Gabriel's discovery. Still, threads need to be connected. I ask, "How did Rubinstein find out?"

"We are not primitive people at Beis Machpelah. Simple, perhaps," this very complex man insists, "but not primitive. When archaeological investigation disturbs an ancient graveyard, we consider that a terrible sin. When a shopping mall wishes to build upon an ancient synagogue, we consider that a terrible sin." His calculated repetitions have the pattern of any good speech. I appreciate the technique. "But when an honest researcher, whether religious or secular, a man who wishes to honor the past rather than destroy it, comes along, we are grateful. Gabriel ben Levi's past is our past. To the extent that he can bring it to life, his work is a blessing."

I can see the next step. "Isaiah Rubinstein helped the blessing."

"We are the closest settlement to this place. Ben Levi found it on his own, but he required a staging ground. He asked for my assistance. I gave thought as to whom I should recommend. Frankly, someone like Chaim has a good heart, but . . ."

"Not such a good head."

Refusing to denigrate one of his settlers, Der Alter says, "Isaiah was always an intellectual."

Instinctively, I reach for the left side of my head to the sore spot where my ear was blasted to pieces by the late intellectual.

"I am sorry," Der Alter sighs.

Back in the car that brought me to this neck of the desert, Der Alter's henchman, Chaim, also apologized. It makes me uneasy. Why is everyone sorry all of a sudden? "It's not your fault," I say, though I still have my doubts.

"It is no excuse, but Isaiah was aiming for ben Levi," he says, confirming Gabriel and Gita Mamoun's suspicion. "Intellectuals do not make good terrorists."

"They do when their weapon is the pen."

Der Alter's beard rustles across his chest as he nods.

I ask the next logical question. "Why?"

"Of that we cannot be sure. Isaiah did not confide his plans to anyone at Beis Machpelah. The Shin Bet conducted an investigation, and we conducted our own investigation, which I can assure you was far more intensive than the government's. Our people have come to distrust the authorities as they sell us, as they say, down the river. I personally spoke to everyone Isaiah had any contact with. Not his family and not his friends, nobody knew what he was going to do."

Whether Moshe X is protesting too much, I can't say, but I listen to him and inquire further, starting with practicalities. "Why did he choose that one day, that one place, Rabin Square? He could have aimed to conclude his . . . mission . . . in private. He could have done it here and nobody would be the wiser. Was he making a political statement?"

"I don't know. Perhaps things I said led him astray, but not intentionally. We do not enjoy violence. Perhaps the radiation damaged Isaiah's brain. Perhaps he already had a problem. You know that a few of our followers are a little . . ."

"Crazy?"

"I prefer 'overenthusiastic.' "

No matter that this man of God lights the fires that lead to such "overenthusiasm." No matter that he keeps the fires stoked, and that the same or similar fires led Baruch Goldstein into the mosque at Hebron with a Galil rifle and led other Jewish believers to stone other Jews who dare drive cars near Mea She'arim on Shabbes and to bomb Jewish butchers who sell unkosher meat. I take his statement for as much of an admission of responsibility as he is going to make. I can imagine the fevered Rubinstein stalking the beautiful archaeologist. Yes, he would have been wiser to shoot just about anyplace else, at Gabriel's home or at the university. But he struck when he had the chance. Maybe the pitch of Simon's speech as scripted by yours truly drove him over the edge. Homes and schools and hospitals and armies. Anyway, there are other questions I need to ask. "What about his motivation?"

"Of that, too, we cannot be certain. Ben Levi was still keeping this find to himself, but he would have written about it eventually. Perhaps Isaiah felt that this was a form of forbidden knowledge. Surely, it is dangerous. We believe that the uranium deposits here are a "nervous isotope" that is rare and theoretically adaptable for nuclear weaponry. Think of the destruction of Sodom. If that could happen spontaneously, the same elements could be harnessed for more awesome destruction. I assume that Isaiah thought that if Gabriel ben Levi was dead, we could keep his discovery secret."

"Secret from whom?"

"From everyone. From the Arabs to whom this land . . ." He pauses, not willing to use the word "belongs" since we are beyond the wildest zealot's definition of Israel Ha G'dolah. He scratches at his beard, which must have gotten itchy in the heat. I think of Gabriel removing his fake beard in Gita Mamoun's hotel suite, and I think of Rafi, who also knew the secret that effectively lopped off his head like a razor-sharp swing. Knowledge is like politics; there's no stopping it from having its effects. I don't say that if all that I'm hearing is true, then Rubinstein's bullet might have been too late even if it hit its intended target.

Der Alter keeps on. "Also from the Jews. You see, you do not believe me when I say that we want peace as much as any disco-liberal in Tel Aviv. We do want the land that God gave to us; we do not want any other land. We certainly believe in strength, but only for safety. If this secret becomes known it will upset the balance of power, and if the government feels a need to rectify that balance, then catastrophe will ensue. That is why we call it Strange Fire."

Der Alter is upsetting the balance in my own mind. For all his lunacy in the media, the so-called "rabid rabbi" works through a sophisticated projection that echoes the debate the United States and Russia struggled with for decades. He is talking disarmament—to be accurate, his notion is more like nonarmament—at the same time as his yeshiva boys are being trained in small arms use back at the kibbutz. He is a man of multiple, conflicting agendas. I'm beginning to like him. Not that I am ready to enroll in Talmud Torah or forget what the thigh of a soccer-playing friend from Haifa feels like in a secluded grove on Mount Carmel, I ask the next, and perhaps last, question. "What do you want me to do?"

Angry conversation filters up the crevice from the beach where we left the Avis half an hour earlier. An English voice I heard once before is protesting loudly, "You can't do this."

"Sorry to be blunt, but we can and we will and we are," Avi Two explains as patiently as he told me how to ride a donkey.

"Is this your property?" The first voice is prudish and self-righteous.

"No, but this is my gun."

"You wouldn't use it."

A single shot echoes.

"That's my boat."

"It's sinking."

We emerge from the defile, and Der Alter enlightens me. "An inflatable raft of some sort. Now it resembles a pancake."

Avi Two goes on. "You're right, I won't shoot you, but I might not offer you a ride home, either. It's a long and potentially unpleasant walk. Now, what were you doing following us?"

Immediately I recall the hint of smoke that I detected in the desert. It must have been the exhaust from some all-terrain vehicle which must have contained the inflatable. Who is this, James Bond? Does the vehicle sprout rotors and turn into a helicopter on demand?

"I thought this is a free country."

"Papa, this man is making me angry," Avi calls in our direction.

"Papa?" I repeat.

Moshe X laughs, the first humor I have heard from him. "Be fruitful and multiply."

"What should I do?" the good son asks.

"See if he has any identification."

"I refuse to be searched without proper authorization."

It's the Yankee arrogance that gives him away. I make the introductions. "You don't need to search him. Moshe X, meet Chester Llewellyn, the new *Times* bureau chief for the Holy Land."

"Chess," the reporter corrects me.

"I guess we're all friends here. Chess, meet Rabbi Moshe X. I am sure you will be writing about him quite a bit if you survive your first weeks in Israel."

"Mr. Kazakov, or may I say Nathan, a pleasure to see you outside of the hospital. I assume that your doctor recommended the desert air for your recuperation. Pleasant spot, what?" Llewellyn acts as if he's supping at the Boston Press Club.

Suddenly I am on the side of the settlers who brought me here. I, too, want to know, "Why were you following us?"

"Us?" Llewellyn replies with mock innocence, already adopting the Jewish manner of answering a question with a question. He might fit in after all.

"Me, then."

"You indeed. And quite a merry chase it was. They're still plucking wheelchairs from the gardens at Hadassah. I was following you, Mr. Kazakov, for the same reason I do anything here, because I heard there might be a story."

"And where did you hear this?"

"Tsk, tsk. You must know that a journalist never reveals his sources."

Well, this isn't entirely true, but for a man as self-consciously upright as Chester Llewellyn it might be. He could survive abandonment in the Negev, but not a wound to his professional ethics. "Fine. May I ask instead what you found out?"

"Read the morning edition."

"He came putting up in that little balloon as if he owned the place," Avi says scornfully.

"That 'little balloon' was an excellent bit of equipment. And so was the engine, now full fathoms five."

"And not a tempest in sight," I murmur.

Llewellyn clucks, "Always glad to meet a fellow Shakespearean, no matter the circumstances."

Stalemate.

So he followed me from the hospital and was deft enough to continue to the church, where he must have had a car waiting, because he knew what to expect. Perhaps Doc Ivan put him on my trail as a precautionary measure. The more I think of it, the more likely that seems. Ivan gave me to Chaim, the muddy man, because he knew that I was going to get to the Bank whether he liked it or not. This way, he arranged for an independent witness who could testify in case anything happened to me. If I disappeared, the *Times* would tell the world. Small comfort.

Why Llewellyn thought it was a story was another matter. Or maybe a lead was just a lead, and the events on the basketball court proved irresistible.

Another shot rings out. For the second time in as many days, I feel the spray of sand blown by a bullet. This one isn't as close as the other; it lands midway between myself and Der Alter.

"Idiot," Avi One hisses at Llewellyn. "You were so busy following us that you let yourself be followed."

"No more Jewish humor, please." A new voice comes from the ledge above us. I smell sweat and dry fabric and feces. I smell goats and camels. Call me racist; I smell Arabs. I don't care if they are Bedouin nomads or Jordanian soldiers. I relapse into atavism. My own people are not my friends, but they are not my enemies.

Llewellyn, too, knows his people. "I'm not J—" the blue blood insists, and the gun rings out again.

The journalist's body hits the sand.

Avi Two lets out a stream of bullets in return. They clatter off the rocks, and more bullets whistle around us.

"Run for the boat," Moshe X shouts, and I'm happy to oblige. I splash into the water, thrashing wildly for the vessel until I smack my wrist on the edge. I clamber over the side, hurt my knee. I hear more gunshots and more shouts and a wild yell from the ledge, where Avi's aim has apparently connected. But if one of them was hit, there is another to take his place. How many are there?

"Nathan," Der Alter calls across an infinite expanse of water.

"Here, here!" I shout back stupidly. Of course, he knows exactly where I am.

A bullet thumps into the side of the boat. Luckily, wood is not rubber, so all that happens is that a spring bleeds salt water.

"Papa," one of the Avis shouts.

"Shoot," another Arab orders, in English, the universal language of guns.

"*Gei*," Der Alter cries, relapsing into the Yiddish of his Brooklyn childhood. "Get the hell out of here, and find it."

I have already grabbed the oars and am paddling as swiftly as I can, in what direction I can't say and don't care, out, out, away, away, into the Sea. I know what I have to find: Strange Fire.

# CHAPTER 13

Suspicious of everyone, with no one around to suspect, I row till my arms ache and the sounds of battle fade. I'm in the middle of several hundred square kilometers of water. That's less than there was ten years ago, but the shrinkage doesn't help me an awful lot. Hey, I think, this place didn't help Lot's wife, either. I'm getting giddy as the sun beats down. I peel off my shirt and wrap it around my head like an Arab burnoose and let the boat drift and bob for a few minutes while I try to reconnoiter. If I can find my way around the maze of Jerusalem, I ought to be able to navigate this salty emptiness. I extend a hand, palm open, and try to discern the angle at which the rays hit.

Despite everything that happened since Moshe and the Avis woke me for breakfast and morning prayers, not much time has elapsed. It can't be any later than ten o'clock, but the sun already throbs with feverish intensity. It seems to be coming from the right, which means eastward and Jordan, so I angle left, toward Israel. The last thing I need now is to be picked up by the single cutter that serves as the Jordanian coast guard.

Ahead, due north, lies the vast potash and bromide mines of the

Dead Sea Chemical Works. Fearing grounding on one of the evaporation pits erected to hasten the natural processes that create the mineral wealth of this region, I row harder alee, aiming to travel parallel to the shore on which I can, if necessary, walk straight up to Neve Zohar, Ein Gedi, and, if necessary, Jerusalem.

The bullet hole in the hull still gurgles and water sloshes around the bottom of the boat, but I am not in danger of capsizing. I sing, "Nathan, row the boat ashore," and my words seem to float on the still air. I probably nod off, because I think I'm back in the uranium cave with Moshe X until I start awake to a tingling sensation. Is it really possible that a statue-seeking archaeologist could discover something that the Chemical Works engineers haven't? Even though I distrust certain Israeli politicians, I share the same naive faith in Israeli technology as the most romantic UJA "mission"-goer. These are the people who made the desert bloom.

When I get to Jerusalem, I'll have plenty of research to do, but all I really want is to visit my favorite old haunts and forget about the last week. I daydream about a shot of dark whiskey in the back room of Dregs or a cup of Abdullah's heavenly sludge. Abdullah! The fat café owner triggers thoughts of the murderous Arab on the beach. Why? Peaceful, cynical Abdullah is nothing like that. All he wants is to sell coffee and see his daughter grow to maturity, yet something he said during our conversation connects to the attack, and suddenly I know the identity of the attacker.

It's obvious. I haven't thought of it before because I'm logy from the heat and delerious from exhaustion and pain and the frenzied pace I've been keeping since I was shot. The Jordanians don't patrol the desert like sheriffs in the Wild West, and they certainly don't shoot American reporters if they can help it. Neither do nomadic Bedouin tribes; they live at subsistence, eat nothing but goat milk and groats and are glad if they can afford a battery-operated television. Only Hamas or Islamic Jihad or one of the other "revolutionary liberation" factions attacks without warning, but they traded their camels for Soviet-made jeeps a generation ago and specialize in assaults on urban transit. The only person who combines the murderousness of the better-known terrorists with quaint adherence to the lifestyle of the prophet is the Yemenite. Most people think he's as legendary as Robin Hood, but Abdullah heard he was in town.

It is odd and perhaps appropriate that Der Alter and the Yemenite should encounter each other by the Dead Sea. This is the only terrain as harsh and unforgiving as their respective philosophies. They're flip sides of the same coin, minted in the same forge, holy men with guns. I witnessed the shoot-out at the Oy Vey Corral.

American westerns are still popular in Israel, and the cable channels are filled with *Gunsmoke*, *Maverick*, *Bonanza*, and lesser-known TV oaters from the 1950s. Sure we've got access to the latest Beverly Hills Teen Cop Vampire in a Hospital Coffee Shop shows, too, but the archetypal lone just man in the desert has an enduring appeal here. Clint Eastwood could probably become mayor of Jerusalem if he wanted the job. I could write his campaign slogan in my sleep: Clean Streets and a Black Hat.

Now that I think of it, Simon isn't all that different from Clint. He's strong and he means what he says. At least the people, or at least fifty-one percent of the people, or at least two or three splinter parties he cobbles a coalition with in return for a ministry they can plunder at leisure, believe him, at least until they discover that he lies.

I probably believed Simon, too, for the first few months of our association. Naturally wary as a born Muscovian, viciously cynical since Lebanon, even I couldn't help but share the excitement of those early days when he and I and Ellen Markowitz rode in a used Toyota to a clubhouse meeting in Ramat Gan to wow the faithful with the possibility of "new leadership."

Simon's timing was excellent. The tottering, septuagenarian elders of the party still carried a semi-mythological air, but mythology didn't carry the weight it once had. They were still fighting the virtuous wars of '48 and '67, which had long been supplanted by the more ambiguous conflicts of the last few decades. They were pioneers not politicians, freedom fighters not modern managers, and the election results showed, as one after another incumbent fell to the likes of Weiner, who yearned for a less heroic place in history. The founders spoke the language of the Bible and orange groves,

Simon the text of the Internet and smart missiles. He advocated the same hard line, but in terms of the real rather than the ideal. Thanks partially to me, he spoke no less strongly yet more subtly, palatably, in a more fashionably modern voice, than those he did not have to denigrate as "old."

Word spreads swiftly in Israel, and Simon's insurgency became a threat to the established order. We junked the Toyota and invested some of the early donations in a bus. We hired a staff that grew along with our audiences. Suddenly I felt that I had an effect on the world. I just didn't bother to notice what the effect was.

Six months later, at the party convention, Simon stood up after the wheelchaired general he had whipped announced retirement and reluctantly passed the torch. The applause wouldn't let candidate ben Levi sit down. One of the most vigorous cheerers was a woman in the front row. I could tell it was a woman because I could smell her perfume and sense Simon's neck craning across the dais to peer down the slope of her décolletage.

Serena came backstage—how she got past the green room guards I don't know—and said, "That line about the problem with democracy didn't go over the way it should."

Simon didn't take criticism well. He turned to me. "Nathan?"

"Ms. . . .?"

"Jacobi."

"In your opinion, Ms. Jacobi," I sneered, "what was the problem?"

"It made them feel that they were the problem, and that's not an opinion."

Serena's assertion captured the room. Besides perfume, I smelled coffee and raisin Danish—builds strong politicos in twelve different ways—and heard nylon as she took a seat and crossed her legs. "If I had had a hand set, you'd have seen the vibration."

"A hand set?" Ellen Markowitz asked.

"Well, we wouldn't have used it here, but at a preliminary focus group you give people this gizmo. They turn a dial to the right for approval, to the left for disapproval, second by second. A computer averages the responses and prints out the data against the speech like a musical score underneath the lyrics."

Simon picked up on the most important word the stranger uttered. "We?"

"Studios use hand sets to gauge initial reactions to movies. This enables them to edit the scenes when they're slow or rewrite individual lines before a movie is released. I can order one immediately, if . . ."

Simon exuded a manner of smug approval. "Go on."

"If you agree that you need one . . . as well as someone to interpret the results. But of course if you don't agree, then I wouldn't want to work for you."

"But you do."

"Of course I do. The rest of the speech was excellent. With a little help, you're going to be Israel's next Prime Minister." She turned to me and said, "Congratulations." Just like that our relationship was set in mutual comradeship, mutual respect, and mutual animosity.

From then on the entourage included Serena, who analyzed voters by age, sex, economic status, country of origin, religious affiliation, etc., etc.—everything but politics, because that was superfluous. As far as we were concerned, everything was politics.

And although a room was always booked for Serena in whatever hotel we were staying in, from Haifa to Beersheva, Ellen Markowitz considered it a waste of resources. In private, Ellen called Serena's the "dressing" room—as opposed to the "undressing" room where Simon stayed.

As for me, no longer best boy, I stifled my resentment and did my job. I wrote whatever was needed: terse single-line statements, evasive paragraphs on the issues, jovial banquet blather, you name it, as long as it was approved by the hand set and the hand job.

Together, we marched into the Knesset the day after Simon's victory, as triumphant as IDF soldiers reclaiming the Wailing Wall after two thousand years of exile.

Politics, however, is a strange game. You spend so much time and energy on getting where you want to be that you forget what you may have to do once you get there. After Simon installed Ellen at the gates to the kingdom and ordered his stainless steel desk from Furnesthetics in Jaffa, he suddenly had to live up to his promises, which proved more difficult to enact on the ground than they had been to deliver in the air of the campaign.

Israel's local culture wars between religious and secular authority, between ancestral customs and modern conduct, were not exactly soothed by Simon, who spoke like the former, lived like the latter, and suddenly satisfied neither. Also, whatever the opposing sides thought of each other, they both worried about their pocketbooks when inflation remained high, leading to a popular joke that swept the country. "Why is it cheaper to take a taxi than a bus?" Answer: "A bus you pay for when you get on, a taxi when you get off."

"Get off the taxi!" Labor began a new campaign the minute it lost the last. I'll admit, a purely professional response, I appreciated the writing.

From the day we took office, Weiner was at Simon's feet like a mongrel dog, tearing the cuffs and pointing out how ragged the emperor's clothes were.

Worse, our major plank, national security, was as precariously balanced as a frayed rope bridge over a chasm. No matter how high the military budget, how excellent the army, how tight the cordons around "them," paradise-bound Palestinian suicides managed to slip through and remind us of the truth we pretended to ignore: they existed. This became brutally obvious when a bomb exploded in a shopping mall in Netanya.

Shit happens. Everyone knows that. But this time it was scooped out of the toilet and arranged on a platter for public display. Ten soldiers who parachuted into Lebanon in search of the bomber's operations center were captured. My bowels tightened and my eyes twitched behind their mask of scar tissue.

Not that anyone made the connection, and not that I wanted them to. Besides, one Russian boy from the regular army was insignificant compared to ten sabras on a special mission. I just gritted my teeth and wrote the P.M.'s speech to the nation, fully aware that Weiner had always said that Simon couldn't protect us, and that it suddenly appeared that he couldn't avenge us, either. Now, due to the first two failures, he had to fulfill the hardest task of all. At this point, he had to redeem us.

But how? There were three basic options, each with a hundred permutations. The first—ignore the situation—wasn't tolerable. The second—bomb the hell out of everything north of thirty-three degrees latitude—wouldn't do the hostages any good. The third—attempt to rescue the rescuers—was the wild card. We discussed the possibilities into the night. Ellen ferried in pot after pot of coffee while Simon and the top brass pored over satellite photos of the vicinity surrounding the "safe house" where the men were held.

Serena and I sat quietly on the couch as each branch of the military offered its own iffy, unsatisfying solution to the intractable problem until the door opened unexpectedly.

I assumed it was Ellen with more coffee and Danish, but Serena sucked in her breath and exhaled, "Christ."

The debate ceased and every eye in the room except for mine focused on the intruder. Finally, Simon broke the silence and said, "What do you want?"

"I want . . ." the voice of the man at the door started softly, but then gathered strength, "to help." I recognized that voice immediately as the others had recognized the speaker a few seconds earlier.

Simon snorted, "I don't think this is a situation for an archaeologist."

Noam Abravanel, present to sharpen pencils, echoed his master. "What are you doing to do, bring in your little teaspoons and dig the hostages out?"

Gabriel ignored him and spoke directly to his father. "The radio says that it's likely that our men are in the village of Al Khayom. Is that correct?"

Simon remained silent, but Colonel Schmuel Shahev, hero of '68, head of the air force, answered, "Yes."

"When I was in the army on maneuvers, I did some personal exploration in the area because I thought there might be an interesting site nearby. Here." He strode toward the enormous table on which the maps were unfurled. "The village is set on a hill that overlooks the valley you'd need to traverse to get there, but there's a long wadi adjacent to the town that you probably don't know about."

"If we don't know about it, it doesn't ex—" Noam started.

"Shut up," Shahev snapped.

"It's right over here." Gabriel traced a line along a smooth quadrant of the photograph. "By these tiny white squares. They're houses, maybe sheds."

"Why doesn't it show up, then?" Shahev asked directly.

"Because the satellite camera isn't an X ray and can't tell what's underneath the surface. The wadi has eaten into the side of the hill, probably in the midneolithic age. That's why I investigated. I thought it might hold remains." I heard a crinkle as Gabriel bent the map into an S curve. "Look from the top down. Can you see the indentation?"

"You're sure it's this village?"

"Look up my army records. See where I was stationed."

Ignoring the strategic opportunity, Simon wanted to know, "Why are you doing this?"

Gabriel didn't answer. Maybe he thought the answer should be obvious.

Colonel Shahev said, "Let's do it,"

But Simon still hesitated. "I don't throw good money after bad."

Shahev merely replied, "This isn't poker."

The P.M.'s head swiveled around the table, but nobody could help him. The shekel stopped there.

Even Serena was inadequate. Simon would have liked her to conduct an overnight poll, but the hostages were about to be moved to Syria, and the clamor for action was intense.

Gabriel's fingers tapped the table.

Simon paced the office, went over the possibilities, sought advice, paced again, paced again. I could feel Shahev's impatience mount as minutes passed. "It will get harder, sir," he said.

"Yes, but—"

"But what, sir? We didn't wait at Entebbe."

The room hushed; a magic word had been uttered. Entebbe. Occuring midway between Israel's founding and the present, the IDF's rescue of a hijacked airplane in Uganda had the power of a primal legend. Also, politically thinking, a dramatic rescue would make everyone except those mourning for the victims of the bomb and the original ten commandos forget about the flaws in security revealed by the original bomb.

"What should we call it?" Serena asked. Though the decision

hadn't yet been affirmed, we were in her realm, and she took the floor with confidence.

"I don't understand what you mean." Gabriel was baffled.

"Ever since Desert Storm, every operation has to have a name for the press. Nathan will need something evocative to play with."

"To play with," Gabriel sarcastically repeated her glib language when there were lives at stake. "How about Operation Vale of Siddim?"

"What's that?"

"Genesis," he said, waiting for someone else in the room full of Jews to recognize the reference. When no one did, he sighed and turned into a teacher. "Chapter fourteen. Several tribes in the so-called vale by the Dead Sea took Lot captive from Sodom before it was destroyed. Abraham set out to track the kidnappers and rescue his brother. And the Bible says," he quoted, " 'he and his servants smote them, and pursued them unto Hobah, which is on the left hand of Damascus.' "

"Perfect." Serena clapped. "Who said you were no good?"

"Who?" Gabriel repeated.

"Let's do it," Simon said, his decision made at last. This could be his finest moment.

Alas, every moment passes, and, due to Simon's delay, the mission set off after 0300 and arrived after dawn when the light gave it away. Operation Vale of Siddim was a massacre, with too many casualties on both sides. Several of the rescuers escaped via Gabriel's wadi, and all of the hostages were killed.

The bomb, the hostages, the bungled rescue. Strike one, two, three. Now the heat was really on. The papers demanded an investigation. Weiner's party collected ballots for a parliamentary vote of no confidence that would have entailed a new election. Simon Commander-in-Chief ben Levi had flinched in battle, but wasn't going to make the same mistake twice. He gave Colonel Shahev a cyanide pellet and commanded him to bite.

Or the equivalent. For a soldier to confess his failure under pressure was tantamount to suicide; and if it wasn't really his failure, then his confession was pure sacrifice. In either case, Shahev's thirty-year career of service to the cause he believed in was over. I swear, I could amost smell bitter almonds as I wrote the speech the colonel delivered on national television.

Shahev obviously wasn't the lieutenant who had rescued me from a different situation over the mountains and through the cedar woods half a dozen years earlier, but I thought of that officer and the way he allowed me to pause in the midst of the pandemonium to find and touch the scarred foot of the boy who had captured me. Nonetheless, I wrote, and Shahev recited, "We did the best we could. I accept full responsibility for Operation Vale of Siddim. No further comment."

The kind of man who saved me, who might have saved the hostages if he had been allowed to, took the fall stoically, a soldier to the end. He pushed through the crowd of press and disappeared from public life. He probably retired to a bee farm. Screw him.

It wasn't Simon's hesitation that I held against him; who could know the right thing to do? Nor was it the Prime Minister's cowardice; ask me and I'll say that bravery is a synonym for stupidity. It wasn't even the ruthless way in which Simon avoided the blame that was rightfully his that gnawed at me. It was his failure—uniquely combined with his success. Simon *had* to save those boys, but only saved himself. From the Vale of Siddim on, I needed to be saved from the well-paid, well-perked, well-respected governmental safe house I was locked inside.

You can look at me in either of two ways. From the outside, I was a fragile ancient bowl just waiting to shatter; from the inside, I was a shattered bowl that needed repair.

I still need to be saved, and my foot hurts. I think of the boy in Lebanon and then of Rafi in Jerusalem as I row into a shadow, and the perpetual dark that surrounds me grows darker. Unless the first storm in the region since Abraham left Sodom several chapters after the Vale of Siddim episode is scheduled for today, the sun must have slipped behind an object of bulk. Yet even Masada does not cast a shadow until dusk. I must be closer to shore than I thought and virtually underneath one of the twenty story hotels at Neve Zohar.

"Watch where you're going!" a crotchety, elderly voice calls out from a few meters ahead.

I backrow to halt myself.

"Hey, it's the ancient mariner," another voice comments.

Swimmers' voices are usually effected by liquid pressure on the lungs and somewhat breathless, but these voices are hearty. Of course; the salt-laden water makes it impossible to sink or remain submerged here. I am surrounded by a circle of tourists bobbing like corks. It's a matter of relative density.

I let the gently lapping waves carry me forward until the bottom of the boat scrapes on the bottom of the Sea.

I lower myself awkwardly over the gunwale and stagger onto land, where it takes me a few minutes to regain my balance after hours of rocking from side to side. I am tentatively upright now—physically, not morally—amid sounds that can be heard on any beach in the world: towels flapping, children chasing each other, parents calling out, "Mimi, wait until we put on the sunblock," and roving vendors hawking Eskimo Pies, as well as sounds unique to this beach: "Mommy, the water burns my eyes." I also hear the thick glop of silty mud that Beis Machpelah sells by the truckful. Here it's scooped by the free handful from deposits in channels along the shore, slathered by individuals over their own calves, thighs, stomachs, and shoulders, and applied to each other's unreachable backs by giggling adolescents.

Most enticing, I hear the stream of open-air showers of fresh water piped down from the hotel to wash the caked mud and salt residue from acres of mud and salt-reinvigorated skin.

From the stench of Beis Machpelah's factory to my endless trawl from beyond the Chemical Works, I've had enough of the Dead Sea's mineral bounty and crave only the shower. I step near enough to feel its spray and land on a pad of roughly poured concrete. Surely I look like some horrid apparition from the deep, no eyes, one ear, limping again from the renewed pain of my swollen and blistered foot, naked from the waist up, red as a ripe tomato.

Either the shower obliterates all nearby sounds or the shock of my appearance has frightened everyone else away from the area. I don't care. I grope for, find, and pull the chain that lets loose a cascade of heavenly wetness. My flesh is so hot that the water practically steams off me. I gulp some and let the rest run, sopping my pants and sneakers. I don't care. I clutch the chain as if it's a life rope, and let the water run and run as I remain there until I feel as if I've been immersed for nearly as long as I've been asea, but eventually I have to stop.

The second I let go of the chain and the flow dwindles to a drip, a guttural voice asks in English, "Do you need help?"

I turn toward the person who must have been watching my record-breaking shower, and perceive the instinctive cringe that usually meets me. A sign of my weakness, I cringe, too. Maybe this is another ambush, but God, yes, I need help. If the person speaking to me were Stalin himself I would say the same thing. "Can you take me to Jerusalem?"

What a request for a foreign vacationer! Fifteen minutes earlier, he had been basking and bathing. Maybe he thought that the poor B.P. needed directions to the hotel, or even a handout, but a ride, how ridiculous. Surely he knows the most basic of rules: never give lifts to strangers.

The stranger—a teenager, from the sound of him—confers with an invisible companion in his native language, German. Israel is acrawl with German tourists. They love the place; they love to spend money here. They tip well, dance at Jewish discos, and can't get enough synagogues. Every night, they pray that the miracle in the desert continue.

For my purposes, this young Hun is a good bet. It's unlikely—though not impossible—that he is an agent from Beis Machpelah or Shin Bet or whatever the Yemenite calls his organization or the *New York Times*. "I can pay," I say, nearly begging. "One hundred shekels to Jerusalem." This is several times the cost of a taxi, but I am desperate. I am so desperate that I start negotiating with myself before I receive an answer. "Make that two hundred."

"Okay, but one thing, please."

"Three hundred."

"Please." He sounds forlorn. "There will be no need to pay."

Then what's the one thing?

Shyly, the boy from the Rhineland asks the most important question of all. "You are Jewish?"

For a second I think this is anti-Semitism and, of course, I am right. It's anti-Semitism in the guise of philo-Semitism. If I were a blind and wounded and oil-and-sunburned Christian, I wouldn't stand a chance, but God bless Germans and their endless, undying need to make reparations. I turn my noble-nosed, kinky-haired, olive-complexioned profile to the Dead Sea, and would let down my pants if necessary. Jewish? *Moi?*

Ten minutes later we're in his car, a late-model Volkswagen that Egon, my good Samaritan, and Kathy, his girlfriend, have driven down from Regensburg, stopping in Vienna, skirting the Balkans, and checking out various nude beaches in Turkey on their way to the Holy Land. I don't mean to be rude, but just as Egon starts telling me what his grandfather did in the war I fall asleep and don't wake until the people's vehicle jolts to a halt and the noise of Jerusalem traffic drives through the window like water from a spigot. Home.

"Where for?" Egon asks.

He would be delighted to chauffeur me anywhere as long as I don't convert en route. He would take me dining as long as the restaurant is kosher. So, as they must say in Germany, where for?

I have to get to the Knesset eventually, and I also want to ask Abdullah what he really knows about the Yemenite—in confidence—but I'm in no shape. If I don't get some real rest, I won't be able to accomplish any more than a caterpillar in a cocoon, and no mere doze under the hottest sun on earth or nap in the coolest car is enough to sate my need for sleep. I need to go home. Rehov Rambam. "Left at the corner."

We retrace the route I last took barefoot; was it only two days ago? We take the curve at Derekh Ha Shkhem in such a cautious fashion that Goldie could be driving. When the light turns yellow we actually stop, causing the driver behind us to honk furiously. Nobody in Israel besides German tourists obeys the traffic laws.

I smell the last tiny copse of blossoming date trees that marks the entrance to our development. A grove once covered this entire hillside, and the three or four remaining trees now serve as a lonely vestige of a previous way of life. I can't justifiably say that I am nostalgic, because I never knew that way, but I imagine something simpler and yearn for it.

Home. "Make a right at the next corner, third house up the block, just after the street lamp."

Egon obediently follows my directions, slowing to a crawl, as if reluctant to relinquish his precious Jewish cargo. Finally, though, he has no choice.

"Thank you," he says.

"Thank you," I reply, and then, curious, and also because I know it will give him infinite pleasure, I reach out to touch his face. He is crying. I wonder if the tears that run down the side of his nose are as salty as the Dead Sea. I reach into the back seat to touch Kathy's face. Her hair is chest-length, straight, undoubtedly blond. Her nose is sharp with a blunt, probably cute flattening at the tip, her eyes recessed, undoubtedly blue. A delicate webbing of the skin beneath them could be a result of late nights or the sun or both, and her mouth . . .

Her lips are thin; she is panting lightly; her tongue flicks out to my finger. Her tongue is dry.

Her mouth. Extending from its left corner, a thin indentation etches a path across her cheek. It is probably invisible underneath her tan, but I can trace it as easily as Gabriel could an ancient riverbed in the desert. Kathy has a scar that neatly bisects the right side of her face from her mouth to her temple. Well, Egon, old habits die hard, or maybe I'm being unfair.

I leave the car.

The Balaban twins are playing goomi with a long, elastic oval strung between the newel post and a garbage can on the patio in front of 448. Goomi is a kind of cat's cradle for the feet. Kids, usually girls, hop in and out of the oval, creating increasingly complex patterns with the elastic. The game continues until the thread gets tangled. Sometimes one kid trips and skins her knees, but Natasha, neighborhood champion, hops back and forth with a tap dancer's skill, the heels of her sandals a tattoo on the sidewalk. Molly sits on the grass, waiting for her turn, and calls out, "Hi, Nathan."

"Hi, girls. What level are you up to?"

"Sixteen," Natasha answers breathlessly, concentrating on the goomi equivalent of a triple axel that turns the elastic into a distended star.

"May I?"

"Oh, Nathan, you'll ruin it."

"I hear that Yossi's store just received a new shipment of Gummi snakes."

Gummi candies are all the rage among Jerusalem's preadolescents. They adore the neon-colored gelatin molded into the shapes of grotesque animals. There are Gummi bats and Gummi beetles and Gummi frogs, but the snakes are the favorites. Gummi, it strikes me, goes with goomi. Also, the best Gummi beasts are imported from Germany. Black Forest brand. Maybe Egon is the Gummi heir, touring on the income from home.

Molly is on her feet in a second. "Really?"

"Well, maybe." I finger through my pockets for change. "Ten shekels ought to buy a healthy supply."

"C'mon, Natasha," Molly squeals.

Finally, Natasha misses a step on level seventeen. "Drat, I was going for the record. You distracted me," she whines. But her stubby little fingers grab the change from my outstretched palm. "Okay. Your turn."

Me, corrupter of little girls. I inch forward until my left ankle touches the elastic. I place my tender right foot inside the loop. I jump and shift my left foot forward, my right foot back, making a figure eight. It hurts like hell, but I jump again, crossing my feet in midair, forming a double helix. So much for level one. I try a tricky sidestep to enter level two—a feat I have only recently accomplished after months of coaching from my two seven-year-old rabbis—but my right foot is laggardly, and the elastic twangs free.

"Oh, Nathan," Molly sighs.

"I'll practice," I promise. "Now off with you. Yossi may run out of snakes."

The girls skip happily toward the ramshackle shopping arcade that serves our district while I trod wearily up the open-air staircase. Step by step, my feet grow heavier and my head lighter. Once again, I hear the television from behind the door of 2A, the occupant of which, Avram Tucker, a retired postal clerk, might as well serve as a life-support system for the remote. Perhaps it was my ill-advised attempt to reach the second level of goomi, or more likely the trauma of my trek through the desert and my time asea, but the pain from both extremities of my body, ear and foot, is immense.

Luckily, it's easier to carry two heavy shopping bags than one, and each opposing pain makes the other minimally more bearable. I feel like a speck of iron hovering between two electromagnets.

I find the strength to dig my key out from the depleted coinage in my pocket and insert it into the hole. It occurs to me that the last time I entered these premises an unexpected visitor had been expecting me, so I try to prepare myself for another Chaim. In fact, every time I arrived anyplace for the past week, from Independence Park to Dregs to the Sheraton to the Church of the Visitation to the cove beside the Dead Sea, someone has been waiting for me, so I half anticipate Serena Jacobi or Gita Mamoun or Cyril Klein or Der Alter or the Yemenite or Noam Abravanel or a young boy named Rafi, living or dead.

Instead, the only person I should have expected is the only one there: my mother. "Nathan!" she screams. A starched bundle of muliebrity flies into my arms. "Nathan, Nathan, where have you been? I've been so worried." Her hands flutter across my face as if she were a B.P. trying to read my character in my countenance.

But Mom is not the most perceptive person in the world. She hardly seems to notice that my skin is like dried clay and that it grips my cheekbones like shrink-wrap. She probably assumes that I've been out carousing. "Why didn't you call, Nathan? Oh, Nathan," she repeats my name, reinforcing my presence. "Everyone wanted to know where you were."

Everyone? "Who?"

"Your office must have called a hundred times. When they said that you didn't come in to work, I was really worried. And that nice doctor from the hospital. And . . . and . . . oh, people called, Nathan, I don't know who. Are you hungry?"

In Russia we were always hungry, but we wouldn't have thought to ask about it, because there was no way to rectify the problem and the question would have exacerbated the actuality. Here in Israel we are never hungry, but constantly ask. Mother has never gotten beyond a pidgin Hebrew, yet she's taken to the stereotype of the Jewish matriarch like a Marxist/Leninist to Talmud. Her life is spent between the beauty parlor and the butcher shop.

Usually I eat in sullen silence, begrudging her generosity, but today is different from all other days. Today, I am hungry. I am starved. "Yes," I reply.

Her hands fall away from my face. "Really?"

"Mother, I am as hungry as I've ever been in my life. What do we have?"

She is like a teenager giddy with delight, or perhaps younger, more like Natasha and Molly, their faces probably smeared by now with cherry-colored Gummi goo. She runs to the tiny kitchen and starts removing pots and pans from the cupboard under the sink. "Latkes?" she calls.

And I discover that even I can be a good son and give a mother a bit of pleasure. I say, "To start with."

So satisfying is the taste of grated potatoes mixed with onions and an egg and salt and matzoh meal and fried in boiling oil that it doesn't occur to me that the same pan full of the same oil has caused much of my recent agony. I just ladle spoon after spoon of sour cream onto the small pancakes as fast as Mother can spatula them out of the cast-iron pan and set them down on a brown paper bag which soaks up the excess grease and leaves them crisp on the outside, warm on the inside.

I am feeling so sentimental that I coin a word. The way native Israelis are known as sabras, the indigenous cactus, because they are supposedly prickly on the outside and sweet on the inside, we Russians ought to be called latkes because our history has left us hard-skinned yet warmhearted.

But that's just bad poetry. I'd rather write speeches than greeting cards.

Still, I eat the latkes until Mother's knuckles are raw from the grating, which leads to the joke as traditional as the recipe: no latkes are complete without a drop of blood.

When I am as full of potatoes as a ten-pound sack, Mother says, "Soup?"

For years I haven't eaten more than an occasional omelette at Rehov Rambam. I live on take-out from the government commissary or banquet food when I travel with Simon or, at night, alone or with sophisticated friends, the "continental" restaurants that have popped up around Jerusalem like mushrooms—and serve mushrooms of a hundred different varieties in a hundred different styles, basted, buttered, sautéed, and served in a scallop-shaped dish. I live well, but I don't live, well, honestly. "Soup would be good."

Ecstatic with gratitude, Mother stirs the pot that simmers perpetually on the stove. She's adopted some sprightly, sophisticated manners recently, but when it comes to the kitchen, she's strictly Old World. Every time she removes a bowlful of glistening chicken stock from the pot, or a boiled chicken leg for herself or her bridge-playing friends, she dumps in another cup of water and another piece of fowl. She could write a book: *Zero Sum Cookery*.

Depending on when she serves this delicacy again, some of the chicken practically dissolves in the bowl while some is effectively raw. Eating mother's food always entails a risk, but I have become a risk taker since my shooting. I put the spoon to my lips and let the warm soup slide down my throat to coat my blood vessels with barely liquefied fat. Either I have chosen a good day or I am in a good mood; the stuff is delicious.

"More?"

"More."

I swallow another bowl of soup and another until I can't take another spoonful, and then I have three helpings of apple crisp Mother has removed from the freezer and heated in the oven until it's charred. No mind. As long as I keep eating, I am absolved from thinking about where I have been and where I have to go.

Finally the sink is filled with dishes and bowls and utensils and there is nothing else to do but conclude this anomalous domestic feast and return to life.

Mother says, "You must be tired."

I nearly cry with relief, and she is just as grateful to have her child returned to her if only for a day. I lean heavily on her plump, chicken-filled frame and allow her to lead me to bed. She tucks me in.

# CHAPTER 14

Bali, Nebraska, Zimbabwe, Peredelkin where Pushkin is buried: I have no idea where I went while I dreamed. For all I know, it was as mundane as the Jaffa Street market. Actually, it was the market. There were sponges and linens and soap wrapped in thin paper. But where were the spices? The market, which ought to have been redolent from open barrels filled with paprika and caraway, smelled like a hotel bathroom or . . . something else in a hotel. What? I struggle to wake, to escape the confusion. I reach out, feel a face, and recoil.

I'm in my sleeping alcove. I smell my foam-rubber pillow and feel the lumps and springs of my rollaway bed. The sounds of Rehov Rambam are real, too. There is the twang of pre-school goomi play and the clatter of a garbage truck. Sun shoots through the blinds at a familiar angle. The face isn't a dream.

It's hovering like a cloud above my bed, thick-lipped, puckered with ancient acne—or is it smallpox?—scars, hairy-chinned. I waver between dream, memory, and actuality. There is a face in the dream and a face in actuality, but the first is smooth and the second is rough. There are sponges in the dream and the smell of something like a sponge flickers in my memory. Eggs are cooking in the kitchen, but the sulfurous aroma of eggs is closer than the kitchen.

My fingers explore the tangle of beard and find a soft clot of congealed yolk. Then the three forms of perception merge. Sponges are also found in hospitals. Doctors have faces and one doctor, despite dire warnings about cholesterol, eats eggs.

My fingers must telegraph my awareness. As soon as I identify Dr. Ivan, his beard pulls away from my fingers, leaving a single curly hair within my grasp. "Good morning," he says.

"How did you get here?"

"How do you think?"

"Mother!" I call.

She calls back from the kitchen, "Food will be ready in a minute."

Ivan sits heavily on the foot of my bed and calls back familiarly, "We'll be there in a minute."

"We?"

He ignores me and says, "For a disabled person you are able to get into an awful lot of trouble."

"That's because I've developed coping mechanisms."

Phrases like "coping mechanism" and "disabled person" ought to have been aborted before they entered the language. I prefer "blind guy" and I'm sure that the basketball players at Hadassah prefer "cripples."

"Hmmph." The doctor snorts at my mockery.

"So," I say, "what's up, Doc?"

"I rebandaged your ear, cleaned up your foot, and treated the nastiest case of sunburn I've ever seen. Luckily, your mother's soup had already stopped the dehydration. Wonderful stuff, that soup; if I could package it in a hypodermic I'd be rich. You ought to be out of bed in two weeks."

"Two weeks?"

"Preferably three."

"Where are my clothes?"

"Oh, Nathan."

The paternal sadness in Ivan's voice is intolerable, but at least, at last, we are on a first-name basis. "What?" I snap.

From the kitchen, Mother answers, "They're in the machine." Hesitantly adapted to Israel, but entirely unadapted to modernity, she calls every electricity-powered device in the house a machine, and leaves it to context for me to figure out whether she is referring to the washer or the dryer or the television or the telephone or the fax or the can opener.

Ivan sighs again and hands me a bathrobe.

Well fed, showered, and shaved, dressed in clean clothes still damp from the "machine," which in this case turned out to be the ineffective dryer in an unventilated closet off the kitchen, I need one more thing. I open the blinds of my room and lean out the window. "Goldie?"

Down below, the dog stands in her usual spot under the single dwarf tree that has managed to take root in the rocky soil, ruffles the dust from her coat, and barks. Whether she found her own way home or whether Ivan or someone else brought her back, I don't know and don't care. She's home, too. "I'll be out in a minute, baby."

Goldie paws at the dirt and whimpers with pleasure.

I cross the living room and open the front door.

Behind me, Ivan says, "Where are we going?"

"We?"

"How do you expect to get anyplace without me?"

"Goldie and I managed before."

"Not very well. Besides, it might, I mean just theoretically, be helpful if you had a pair of eyes."

"That's what Goldie is for."

"She can't drive."

That is true. But cabbies can. Relatively speaking.

More importantly, Goldie isn't able to read, except for traffic signs, which she probably knows better than most Israeli taxi drivers.

The problem is that I need to read more than "Stop!" The computer in my office can download most government archives through a remarkable Braille punching system, but somebody has to select one document instead of another. Using a voice-activated interface, I only know my way around the sites well enough to find the data I require to script speeches. Now, instead of finding what I need to read, I might not know what I need to read until I find it. And what if, God forbid and as I suspect, Strange Fire has received the most secret of designations: For Paper Only? Can I trust Ivan? Do I have any choice? "Don't you have any other patients?"

"None that are likely to present me with such interesting medical problems. Besides, I'm done with work for the day, and I hate the beach."

"You work short hours."

"Not really. What time do you think it is?"

This is a trick question, but I fall into the trap anyway. I think of Molly and Natasha, due at the local school at eight-thirty, and guess, "Seven-thirty?"

"Not bad, as long as you're telling American time. Only an hour and a half off."

Six o'clock? The girls never wake that early. Then I realize that I've slept through one night and the following day. The light, similar at dawn and dusk, fooled me. It is eighteen hundred.

Mother can see the writing on the wall and wails, "Take good care of him. Wait, I'll make you a sandwich."

"I'm not hungry," I say, opening the door.

"I am," Ivan says, shutting it.

I shrug. Maybe she was speaking to him anyway.

We wait for Mother to smear congealed chicken fat on a few slabs of rye bread and spear a breast out from her eternally boiling pot, and double-wrap the "snack" in two layers of aluminum foil as if we were packing for an Arctic expedition. I lie, "I really was thinking in American hours."

I settle into a leather seat controlled by a series of switches that move the seat forward and back, pivot the base, angle the rear; the thing has more positions than the Kama Sutra. Cool air blasts from half a dozen vents set into a polished mahogany dashboard. Probably a Mercedes. "Nice car," I comment.

"Should be; it cost a hundred thousand shekels."

Definitely a Mercedes. "That practically makes you a sabra."

"I'd rather be a Yankee," Ivan snorts as he hits the CD and "Light My Fire" throbs from the speakers.

"An old sabra?"

"Eternally youthful." Ivan squeals away from the curb and enters the traffic. He takes the curves on Derekh Ha Shkhem with a racer's aplomb and lights a cigarette. "Where to?"

I think of my German driver yesterday who said, "Where from?" To or from, everyone with a car in Israel seems eager to drive me places. "State Office Campus."

"West side. I know a shortcut." He yaws across several lanes of traffic and slides through the near north neighborhood that spreads beyond Mea She'arim. The streets are rigidly geometrical, so each turn involves a screeching right angle whenever the Doors' music hits heights of instrumental frenzy.

"So, um," he comments awkwardly, "your mother lives alone?"

"If you don't count me."

"From what I saw, you don't really live there."

"Depends on what you call living."

"How about your father?" Ivan's tone is casual, but his intent seems prying.

"He doesn't live there, either," I reply with factual brusqueness that ends the conversation.

We drive a few more blocks and then pick up speed along the Jaffa Road. Eventually, Ivan resumes his inquiries, "What are we looking for?"

I worry that Ivan's previous question about my father was an attempt to determine what resources I have available—none—and that he's now trying to find out what I know—nothing. Could he be working for . . . who? Moshe X, the Yemenite, both are unlikely. I think about dumping him until I realize that I don't have a choice.

Besides, I brought him into this, and he has a right to know. So his question wasn't the most subtle gambit into my mysterious mission. Ivan is used to medical forthrightness and might have been asking, "Where does it hurt?"

"What do you know about science?"

"Knee bone's connected to the hipbone."

"Is that all, sawbones?"

"Actually, I don't even know that. Surgery's not my specialty. I do ears."

"And house calls."

"And freelance psychiatry. But you also appear to freelance, Mr. Kazakov."

Apparently we've returned to a formal mode of address. "What do you mean?"

"Well, you seem to be in a pretty dangerous business for a poet."

"Poet?"

"Your mother showed me a small pamphlet titled *Persimmon Blossoms*."

"Pomegranate."

"Yes."

Printed in a hidden annex behind the Café Noir on Arbat, the five hundred copies of *Pomegranate Blossoms*, three hundred and fifty of which emigrated to their present home in a cardboard box currently stowed underneath Mother's bed on Rehov Rambam, were intended to be lyrical on the surface yet deeply political between the lines, their evocation of a Zionist dream implicitly contrasting with a Soviet reality. It was a precocious first book, much adored by a small crowd of like-minded would-be illuminati who met at the Noir to read and discuss poetry. That accounted for about a hundred copies, while the other fifty were sent, anonymously, to various magazines and critics who received it with universally resounding silence. Months passed and years, while the author perused the literary columns, waiting for one—just one—sage to say something like "inspired and incendiary."

I'd almost forgotten about that book, the passion of its composition, and the humiliation of its reception. Now, it has found its first reader on a new continent, the volume thrust into his hands by the poet's mom. What a ridiculous circumstance. If only a friend of the doctor's—a publisher, say—had passed it along, saying, "Of course, I can't take a risk on an unknown, and the translation would cost too much to justify the revenues, but take a look at this interesting book that crossed my desk." Even if the cover merely caught Ivan's eye while he was perusing the used book stalls by Weizmann Square on his lunch break it would have been fine. If just one copy of *Pomegranate Blossoms* beyond the box on Rehov Rambam made the journey from Moscow to Jerusalem in the luggage of some émigré who later sold it, surely only to buy food, the volume would have been alive, sitting beside Mandelstam and Akhmatova in the midday sun.

But that isn't the case.

Mother must have dug through the dusty genizah she carts about wherever she goes like a camel carries a saddlebag while her son's self-appointed personal physician was sipping her chicken soup in the late afternoon. Absurder yet, her forwardness immediately taps the lode of vanity buried deep inside the author's soul. I don't want to respond, but I can't resist; carefully nonchalant, I say, "So what did you think?"

Ivan blows out a plume of smoke that curls off the windshield and comes back at us on the wave of air-conditioning. "Pomegranates, persimmons. One fruit's just like another. The lack of natural knowledge was the only thing about it that was authentic. As for the rest of that kvetching, it's adolescent drivel. What do you think?"

Aside from thinking that my driver is a heartless bastard, I think that he is an excellent literary critic. "You're right."

"Right." He coughs. "You're better off where you are."

"Where am I?"

"State Office Campus on your left."

Instinct is powerful. Conscious that I won't see anything more than a blur of sandy beige, the building itself indistinguishable from the hills behind it, the hills indistinguishable from the sky, I nonetheless turn to the invisible bureaucratic castle where I belong.

We park in the visitor's lot rather than attempt to brazen our way past the guard. There will be enough of that inside. No need to squander energy for the reward of a six-meter space in the underground garage. I reach for the door, but then one thing occurs to me. "Ivan . . . I mean Dmitri?"

"Yes?"

"Were you ever a poet?"

"Everyone in Russia's a poet."

"And Israel?"

"Everyone in Israel's a politician."

Is he flirting with me? I tend toward slim boys—Rafi-like wraiths. Still, I can't help wondering: What would it be like to bed this bear? Would he spurt honey?

Suddenly, gruffly, the doctor interrupts my sweet meditation. "So who are we visiting?"

"Not who," I answer evasively as I open the car door and step out. I slam the door with a solid, Germanic thunk and give him a clue. "What?"

"What, then?"

"I already asked what you knew about science, but all you wanted to do was joke about hipbones. We're looking for anything to do with uranium deposits by the Dead Sea."

"There is no uranium in Israel."

"First off, I didn't say it was in Israel."

"If there's no uranium in Israel, there's no uranium in Jordan, either."

"That's what I keep hearing, but if there is it may be designated by the code name Strange Fire. If we find that, we'll also find a who, Gabriel ben Levi."

My own mention of Gabriel's name brings my quest into clearer focus. The assassination attempt in Tel Aviv—no matter who the intended victim—was a crime, pure and simple, which ended seconds after it began. Only later did I realize that Reb Rubinstein's action was the result of a conspiracy, impure and complex, because it's still aiming to fulfill itself and has, in the process, led to at least two successful killings. I try to think logically, mathematically, about what might be going on, but the various interested parties from Cyril Klein and the Shin Bet to Moshe X and the settlers at Beis Machpelah are like vectors angling in opposite directions that have only one point of intersection, Gabriel.

I think of the young, helpful archaeologist explaining the Vale of Siddim to his father, offering a precious bowl from antiquity to a helpless B.P., and suddenly, irrationally, I'd like to help, too. I'd like to be the kind of person who helps. The way Gabriel sifts sand in the desert to reclaim a common human inheritance, I sift clues now to find and reclaim Gabriel. And until someone offers me a better one, the best clue I have is the term "Strange Fire." I have to find out what the Knesset knows.

I am so used to slipping into the office by way of the P.M.'s private entrance that I don't realize quite how many other people use this building. Even after hours, the lobby is buzzing with clerks and secretaries and officials. Most are leaving, but many are commencing night-shift duty that might lead to an urgent page for me if an embassy in Buenos Aires or Melbourne is bombed. I am also surprised by the level of security that protects this enclave. Everyone, from ambassadors to generals and judges to pizza deliverymen, passes through metal detectors at the front door, and that is only the start.

Throughout the searches and ID checks and cross-checks and phone calls to see if so and so is expected in the Department of the Interior or wherever, all I can think is that we could have used a little bit of this back in Tel Aviv.

A soldier runs his fingers around the underside of Goldie's collar. "She's clean," he says to another soldier.

"No fleas," I banter, and sign in for myself and my visitor.

"Shalom, sir," the clerk at the desk says, unaccustomed to my level of clearance.

We are checked again at the elevator, but upstairs, where I know everyone, it will be easier and harder. I can only hope that most of the staff has already gone home by now. Maybe we should have waited until midnight, but that would have created its own problems. "What are you wearing?" I ask Ivan.

"What do you mean?"

Two soft chimes have already rung, signifying the floors we passed. "I mean . . . Oh, Christ." There is no time to explain. I reach out and let my hands flutter over his shirt and pants. Cheap polyester, probably white; it feels like white. Excellent. He is wearing his doctor's garb, probably came directly from the hospital to Rehov Rambam. The door opens. "Follow."

"Evening, Mr. Kazakov," Benjamin, the guard at the desk in front of the locked, bombproof glass that seals off the executive wing from the world, welcomes me. "It's good to see you back."

Instead of returning pleasantries, I stride straight past this genial relic of some prior war, muttering, "Medical emergency. This is Dr. Tatarsky."

"Wha? Huh?" Benjamin's hand reaches for the phone.

I reach out and place my finger on the little nub that cuts off the phone. "It's . . . private, Benjamin."

What I am implying by this—Simon and Serena on the couch, a heart attack?—I don't know, but secrecy is the one way to guarantee attention in this country. "Buzz us in."

"Oh, um . . ." Benjamin swiftly calculates his responsibilities. Nobody is supposed to enter without authorization, but an emergency is an emergency, and besides, nobody ever questions the harmlessness of B.P.'s.

"Now!" I command, and Benjamin's finger hits the buzzer.

"This way, Doctor. Hurry."

Most of the station desks are manned, but none of the senior people appear to be on the premises, so there is no one to impede our passage. I jerk at Goldie's leash to signal her to move faster within the maze of shoulder-height partitions. On either side of us, aides murmur to their coequals in other government offices across the globe or to the lovers they expect to meet later this evening—I don't care.

We pass the last of the cubicles and approach the rear of the floor, where the special elevator I didn't want to take opens onto Simon's domain. I smell lilacs and recall the guardian I had forgotten. Doesn't she ever leave? Is she chained to her post like Syrian soldiers in the Golan? Suddenly a "medical emergency" will not wash.

Ellen Markowitz sits ten meters distant, behind a desk that would have done a CEO proud. The phone rings. Ellen picks it up, a sign of her own stature. The operators downstairs wear technology like a tiara, because that is all they do, but Ellen has her own mysterious functions that require mobility and intelligence more so than mere transfer to the proper line or transcription of messages. She answers curtly, "Yes."

Nobody who has this number needs to waste three seconds listening to "Prime Minister ben Levi's office. How may I help you?"

"They haven't come in yet. . . . Any minute. . . . The director should be waiting at the restaurant. . . . Reservations have been made. . . . After the screening. . . . Yes, yes. . . ."

From Ellen's answers to a series of questions I can tell that she is talking to someone from the personal or political rather than the operational side of the office. State business occurs in the ministries, election business here.

"And we have a surprise visitor." Ellen's tone turns cheerful as she catches a glimpse of me. Then she says the one word I wish she hadn't. "Nathan."

Ivan—I mean Dmitri—and I are nearing her desk, and she is telling this to someone who must know me on a first-name basis.

"Do you want to talk to—" Cut off abruptly, Ellen pauses and the air around her turns serious. I can tell at a distance, but she can't tell that I can tell. "Yes," she says, and hangs up. Then she changes gears again. "Well, if it isn't the . . . Wandering Jew."

Somehow, I know that she was about to say "prodigal son," but the potential reference to Gabriel might have been awkward, so she quickly substituted another archetypal figure.

"Returning from my many travels."

"Home, sweet home."

"So who were you gabbing with?" I try to keep it light.

"Oh, those idiots in the basement. My parking sticker must have expired and they wanted to tow my car."

"Well, I guess that's a problem I'll never have," I say with a laugh. "By the way, this is a friend I've been meaning to invite to lunch—I mean dinner—for a long time. Ellen, this is Dmit . . . Ivan." Better to use his fake name.

"Pleased to meet you." Ellen extends a dainty hand.

"Likewise." Dmitri shakes the hand, quite properly. We might have been at a diplomatic reception.

"Can you buzz us in?"

Of course, she isn't supposed to, but Ellen is so relieved to stop dissembling that this is better than a medical emergency. "No problem," she says, and presses the button under her desk.

The heavy glass doors swing wide.

"This way," I say, and Goldie and I start down the hall.

Practically stepping on my heels, Dmitri whispers, "She wasn't talking to the garage."

"No kidding, Einstein. We don't have much time."

Seconds later we are in my office, fifteen square meters that define the position I hold and the position I don't, windowed for all the good it does me. "Can you use this?" I sweep a hand toward the computer on my desk.

"Sure, what disease do you want me to look up?"

"Strange Fire."

"Dot com?"

"Hit the search."

Dmitri is defter than I could have hoped. His fingers play across the keys without a moment's hesitation. He scrolls and reads me the results. "Besides a few mentions of arson in Haifa, there seems to be a biblical citation."

Moshe X would have named his discovery after some Torah or Talmud reference. This is no help at all. I guide Dmitri through the sequence that leads into government files while the clock ticks. I figure that we have fifteen minutes before whoever Ellen was speaking to, whoever told her to refuse to tell me who she was speaking to, arrives or sends a cool, firm emissary, fifteen minutes tops.

The system is empty.

I don't like the next step, but it's the only step to take. "Let's go into Simon's office."

Dmitri is quiet. For all the damage to my body and for all the cloak-and-dagger misprision that got him into the sanctum, I don't think he fully realized the seriousness of my position or my pursuit until this minute. Until now he was humoring me, doing a little extracurricular pro bono medical work for a particularly interesting case. Even now, even if he clearly shouldn't be here, this is my office. But trespassing into the P.M.'s suite is different.

Simon's office is only two doors away from my own, but it is another world entirely. Fortunately, it isn't a locked world, simply because it is inconceivable that anyone would dare enter unbidden. There are procedures; there is rigmarole. Armed guards downstairs,

Markowitz upstairs, plainclothesmen surrounding the chief himself. The eight-foot cherry-wood door swings without a creak.

I walk between the conference table and the couch Simon naps and ponders and fucks upon straight to the desk in front of the window that looks out to the Old City Simon is prepared to defend with the lives of every eighteen-year-old in Israel. The steel surface is clear except for a telephone, a crystal paperweight, and a picture frame. I pick up the frame and turn it to Dmitri, who, fearless in his hospital world, stands on the far side of the desk as if a fiery chasm lies between us. "Who is this?"

"I don't know."

"Describe, please."

"A young man, approximately thirty years old, sandy hair, tanned, wearing a white shirt. Sweat stains under the arms. I can't tell how tall he is. The shot was taken from the waist up. He's standing in front of a rock, looking straight at the camera, not smiling. It seems as though he's just turned, as though he didn't expect a photograph and doesn't like it."

"Close your eyes."

"Yes."

"Can you remember the face?"

"Yes."

"Open your eyes and look at it more carefully. Commit it to memory. If you ever see this person when we're together, in a room, on the edge of a crowd, anywhere, tell me immediately. He may be wearing other clothes, a hat, a disguise, even a beard. Anyone who even vaguely resembles him, no matter what else is going on, tell me."

Dmitri nods; I sense the motion. He understands that I understand. If we find nothing else, this is good. Instead of relying upon Gabriel to contact me or not as he chooses, I have a surrogate pair of eyes.

"Okay," I say. "Now get over here and help me." I sit in the cushiony leather throne, pausing for only a second to sense the world from Simon's perspective. It is the neck of an hourglass, all of Israeli and Jewish history funneling down to this single narrow channel from which it will descend into the future, grain by grain, as the occupant of the chair permits. At this moment it seems like the pivot point of eternity, yet the second the last grain of sand has dropped, a celestial timekeeper will turn the glass upside down and another person will sit here. I open the drawers.

"Should we be doing this?" Dmitri is still hesitant.

He has been witty before, but this is the first time I laugh. "Of course not."

And if my seriousness and my terror failed to convince him, my laughter does. "Oh, well, then, if it's okay with the Tsar." Not that he's *that* old, but something about this reference makes me realize that my companion is older than I thought, but I don't dwell on it. His professionally competent hands, used to nudging aside a liver to get at a spleen, rummage swiftly and effectively through Simon's private belongings.

I hear the thin tinking of small metallic objects, the same paper clips and scissors likely to occupy any desk. Enjoying himself now, Dmitri plucks a rubber band and riffles a deck of cards. "Man must play solitaire when he isn't protecting the faith."

"Next drawer."

The gliders are so smooth I hardly hear it open.

Disappointed, Dmitri says, "Empty."

Now I am disappointed. "Totally?"

"Like from the factory."

"How many more drawers?"

"One."

"Do it."

This time I hear the glider; the bottom drawer weighs more than the top.

Dmitri says, "Bingo."

"Maybe. What do we have?"

"Built-in file rack, multiple folders, neatly tabbed."

Simon has to keep some papers nearby for immediate reference. Of course, Ellen would whisk into his office with whatever he needed in twenty seconds, but sometimes twenty seconds is too much. "Read the tabs."

" 'Polls.' "

It figures that would be the first.

" 'Weiner.' "

Simon's Labor opponent. This folder will be filled with whatever nasty stuff Cyril Klein has been able to dig up. I wonder how thick it is, because I could be expected to transmute gossip into allegation, but we don't have time. The clock is ticking. "Keep going."

" 'Tel Aviv,' 'Jerusalem,' 'Haifa,' a couple more city folders." Dmitri picks up one at random and flips through the pages. "Seems to be about local issues, a proposal for a new concert hall in Beer-sheva."

"Keep going."

" 'Military,' 'Judicial,' 'Housing,' 'Transportation,' 'Immigration.' " As Dmitri lists the titles, the folders slide from rear to front. Sand through an hourglass.

" 'Finance,' hmm, there's a folder inside the folder. Outside one is stuff about currency, the stock market. Inside one seems to be a statement, a portfolio. Hmm, nicely diversified."

"Never mind." Any stocks Simon owns are supposed to be kept in a blind trust—interesting term—to avoid conflict of interest. I wonder if Weiner has a folder titled "ben Levi" that includes this tidbit, but I don't care. "Keep going."

We run through another five or six, stopping fruitlessly to examine anything that might make reference to uranium, until we come to a national sequence.

" 'USA,' big fat one, 'Germany,' 'Italy,' 'France,' 'South Africa,' 'Soviet Union,' little matter of nomenclature there, should be 'Russia.' "

"Simon's a Cold Warrior."

"Hmm, 'China'. . . what's this, 'Honduras'?"

"Cross-filed with 'Military,' probably. Just business."

" 'Palestine.' "

"On paper only. We never use the word in public."

" 'Saudi Arabia,' 'Syria,' 'Iraq,' et cetera."

"Generic," I curse.

"Two more. 'S F' and, get this, 'Holocaust.' "

"Big issue here. 'S F'!"

"Need any help, gentlemen?"

The doctor acts like a bomb went off during an operation. He drops the folder and pages fly over my lap.

Damn that lockless door. "Ellen," I say. "We were just—"

"Don't even try, Nathan. I'm sure that you desperately needed some insignificant item to insert into Thursday's Chamber of Commerce speech, and that Simon will be delighted to hear it, but in the meantime you can just hand that to me." Her heels click across the floor until she stands on the other side of the desk and her arm shoots forward with an audible snap.

Ellen and I have always had a friendly relationship that went beyond her necessary bond to most of the rest of the people in the office, but she came up through the ranks with Simon and her fidelity to him is absolute. So, unfortunately, is my violation. I can't claim that this isn't what it looks like; it is exactly what it looks like. My trespass is more than unprofessional; it is criminal.

Alerted to something unusual about my presence by her telephone connection, Ellen must have guessed that she ought to keep an eye on me. Perhaps she was ordered to do so. She probably didn't enjoy that; I could tell from her awkwardness in the reception area. Her tone had shifted from formal with her unknown conversant to friendly when I appeared on the scene to frosty when she was compelled to lie. If it wasn't Simon on the line—and her voice had not conveyed the special trill reserved for the bossman—it was someone who could speak for him. She really had no choice but to allow me to step into the trap that I myself created. She is disappointed and she is furious. "I want those papers now," she says.

Dmitri is gathering the spilled documents and slipping them back into the folder. I hope he is glancing at the contents, but can tell from the trembling rustle of the pages that he isn't. Resourceful in his hospital home court, he is ready to surrender here.

But I have another plan. It isn't a particularly good one, because, barring an act of God or Simon, it is all but guaranteed to lead to more trouble, but I have nothing to lose.

Ellen forgot one thing. She is not dealing with the viciously cynical yet basically obedient Nathan of yore. Freed from the velvet yoke of the job I have probably just lost, I am a loose cannon. I take the folder from the doctor and hold it forth with my left hand. Ellen reaches out and I grab her wrist with my right hand.

"Nathan!" she squeals. Relying on a combination of her unquestioned authority and our previous friendship, she hadn't felt any need to call in security. If she had, six burly men in nondescript jackets would have already stormed into the room, guns drawn. Instead, we're alone.

I yank her onto the smooth surface of Simon's desk, and the phone crashes to the floor.

"Hold her," I shout to the doctor.

Perhaps the executive desk reminds him of an operating table, and the thrashing secretary of a patient in a seizure, but Dmitri acts swiftly. He presses her belly flat with one thick forearm and clamps his free hand across her mouth like an anesthetic mask. "Now what?" he asks.

"I don't suppose I can rely on your word to keep quiet," I address the terrified Ellen, whose smells of sweat and lilacs mix in a fearful bouquet. Thinking out loud, I say, "We have only two choices. We can take her with us or leave her here."

"You're the doctor," Dmitri says.

"Let's tie her up."

"There's Scotch tape in the desk."

"Somehow I don't think that would work."

"What, then?"

I can't look around, but I can hear the scratch of Ellen's legs squirming beneath Dmitri's grip. "Stockings."

"How?"

I lift the crystal paperweight and say, "Ellen, we don't want to hurt you, but we *are* going to leave with this folder. I am going to tell my friend to let you go for a minute. You will take off your stockings and we will secure you, as comfortably as we can. Do you understand?"

I take her muffled response as affirmative.

"Bear in mind that if you scream I will hit you with this." I show her the lethal weight. "Do you understand?"

Again, she grunts.

"She's nodding," Dmitri says.

"Let her go."

"Nathan, you are stark-raving—"

Dmitri's hand clamps down again.

"No commentary, Ms. Markowitz. You will certainly have an opportunity to tell your story later."

This time Ellen acquiesces. I sympathize with her rage and humiliation as she hoists her bottom off the desk and tugs at the waist-high, five-shekel drugstore purchase that is all she can afford on a government salary. She deserves better and I make a mental note to send her a pair of silks in the mail. "Now lay down again."

Unfortunately, the stockings aren't nearly long enough to wrap around the enormous desk. "What now?" Dmitri asks.

"Here." I vacate my chair. "Get up and sit down, Ellen."

"Oh, Nathan." Her voice is pathetic. I know what the problem is. Despite the grosser violation of her person, the one thing she can't bear is to sit in Simon's own seat. Ellen is smart enough to see all the failings of Simon's character, and I always thought that she probably disagreed with his politics, and might even have voted against him, but she loves him nonetheless and is loyal above all. "Please, Nathan."

"I'm sorry, Ellen."

She stands quivering, knees locked, physically unable to usurp Simon's chair. How does he engender such loyalty? "Ivan."

Gently, he lifts and lowers her, and a last, sad gasp escapes from the lady's mouth as she faints into her lord's throne.

Goldie sniffs curiously at her waist.

"No." I shoo her away.

Now it's easy. We find the scissors in the desk, cut the stockings into strips, and tie Ellen Markowitz's hands and feet to the chair's arms and legs. Just in case she wakes before we're out of the building, we also tie one strip around her head and softly breathing mouth.

Approximately one hundred steps to freedom. We cross the office, enter the hallway, and press a button to open the enormous glass gates from the kingdom. Ellen's own desk sits between us and the elevator. Someone is sitting in her chair. Call me observant. I know because he is humming the national anthem.

"You go to the elevator," I instruct Dmitri while I step up to the desk. "Any messages for me, Noam?"

Why is it that people don't mind being identified by other people who can see, yet get the creeps when a B.P. does the same thing? Maybe it's prejudice; maybe the Anti-Defamation League should get involved.

Noam Abravanel in particular should know better. He has seen me perform the same parlor trick a thousand times. Still, he misses a beat and loses track of the last line of Hatikvah.

I supply the missing lyrics. "*B'eretz Tzion b'Yerushala-ah-yim.*"

"Glad to see you're still patriotic, Nathan. Ellen will be, too, whenever she returns. I wonder where she is. I always thought she was strapped into this chair, peed into a cup."

"Very funny."

"I hope you provided her with a cup. Oh, you wonder how I can tell about things that I can't see. Maybe I've got the same ESP you do. Or maybe it's the magic of the intercom button. You should have picked up that phone you dropped. Receiver's off the hook."

"And me?"

"You're on the hook. But don't worry, I can swear that you were never anything less than a gentleman to Ellen. Oh, you have the 'S F' file. That should provide interesting reading."

If little Noam wants to play, I am willing to. Besides, we both know that another button at his fingertips will summon security unless I jump him, which I won't unless I can fly better than I can see. "What do you know about this?"

"About what?"

"Strange Fire."

"Just remember that you said it, I didn't. Okay?"

Noam is having far too much fun, but we can't stop now. "Okay."

"Well, then, I know that you are messing with things way beyond your control."

"Things like . . ." I think I'll give the twerp a taste of his own medicine, show that I am ahead of the game. "Uranium."

But I'm the one taken unawares when he starts laughing, not the snide, something-to-hide smirk he specializes in, but an authentic belly laugh. When he finally settles down, he gasps, "Uranium. Oh, my, that's a good one. Moshe X has been ranting about that for years. Fulfillment of biblical prophecy in modern technology. Right?"

"But . . . I . . . felt it."

"Let me guess, in a cave near the Dead Sea." He doesn't wait for me to display surprise. "Buildup of sodium hydrophosphate. Does that to everyone. It's salt in the atmosphere crystallizing on your skin. Don't you tingle when you get out of the water? That's basic, Nathan."

Grasping for straws, I stammer, "What about the Yemenite?"

"You've met him, too? For a guy who needs a bitch to cross the street, you get around."

Noam has always hated me. Whether it's envy at my closeness to Simon or some deep-rooted detestation of B.P.s—you'd be surprised how often I come across that; it's like they think we're extraterrestrials—or maybe plain old-fashioned homophobia, maybe caused by plain old repressed homosexuality, I don't know and never examined. Motives never interest me anyway, actions do. Noam was on the phone with Ellen, possibly from down the hall, possibly from the other side of town, and got here as soon as he could.

The elevator door opens.

"What are you waiting for?" Noam sneers.

There is an edge to his voice. Either he isn't saying everything he knows or there is something he doesn't know and wants to.

As for me, I don't know what's in the precious folder I've gone to such lengths to steal. If it doesn't help me, I'm lost, and don't have the time to wait for someone else to pop up and lead me to the next step. I have a brainstorm. "I'm waiting for you, Noam."

I say this prepared to threaten him with an imaginary pistol, though such a threat isn't likely to succeed. Nor do I think that I could use the same force on Noam that worked so well on Ellen. But the bastard surprises me again. He says, "I never thought you'd ask," and we all descend.

# CHAPTER 15

I am tempted to force Noam to drive, but it's more important to get to the next place than to put the upstart in his place. Dmitri pops the locks of his fancy German car with a clever little clicking mechanism and sits behind the wheel. I take shotgun, stroking the incendiary folder on my lap while Goldie curls up like a mat at my feet and Noam stretches out in the back. Let him enjoy himself for a few minutes, pretend he's the chief.

"Where to?" the doctor/driver asks.

"In."

Unlike Tel Aviv, which spreads north and south along the shore like an oil slick, modern Jerusalem developed in concentric semicircles rippling from the Old City to the west. Thus, every direction starts with either "in" or "out," depending on which ring you're starting from and which ring you're going to. Like a tree, the innermost rings are the oldest.

"Good," I say. I prefer in to out. Also, I feel that the answers to the secrets swirling around me are to be found at the center.

We pass the rest of the government campus and the big tourist hotels and the residential district Goldie and I walked through a few days earlier. We take the transverse through Independence Park, which makes me think of Dregs, and thirsty.

"Take a left."

Most traffic flows in the opposite direction as the people who work at the stores and financial offices of the center head for their flats in the outer rings, but evening Jerusalem is commencing to come alive. Young people gather at the cafés that have been empty since lunch and theater marquees buzz and glimmer with neon displays.

"Go past the King David and take a right."

Slowed by double-parked taxis, we cruise the block-long remnant of British imperialism. Built in the 1920s, blown up by Menachem Begin and the Stern Gang during the underground war against occupation in the 1930s, rebuilt but somewhat down-at-the-heels by the 1950s when it was literally a stone's thrown from the border, the King David has been entirely renovated and updated into the only five-star hotel in the country besides those on the western ridge owned by Western corporations. The Hilton and the Sheraton are arriviste colossi that serve well-heeled suburbanites from America, while the more authentic King David attracts a crowd of international sophisticates who stay at the Gritti Palace in Venice or Claridges in London.

"Another left."

Boulevards have long since given way to avenues, which became streets, which will diminish from here until they disintegrate at the gates of the Old City, after which even the wealthiest traveler must disembark and walk.

But, contrary to my expectations, we don't make a right toward the crenellated and golden-domed epicenter.

"Stop at the next alley," Noam orders.

I know our destination. Raucous Klezmer music and the smell of paprika spills out of a small courtyard surrounded by a late Victorian apartment building, all filigree and balconies. Unless we are meeting one of the elderly residents upstairs, we are going out for dinner at the Ghetto Café.

Actually, not all of us are going. The second Dmitri opens his door, Noam tersely tells him, "You wait here."

I can't imagine why Dmitri doesn't like Noam, but he replies, "If Nathan says so."

Reluctantly, I nod. This is Noam's date, and I have to let him set the rules. "Don't worry. I'll bring you a doggie bag."

"Good. I can share it with Goldie."

As a sign of disdain for Noam, I let Goldie guide me between a dozen limousines jamming the courtyard. The Ghetto Café isn't exactly hidden, but neither does it advertise. Founded thirty years earlier by Jack and Sarah Fisher, a refugee couple who owned a restaurant in Warsaw before the war and never quite adjusted to kibbutz life, it was originally the only place in town where Israeli Holocaust survivors could feel at home among their own kind. Fortunately for the Fishers' bank accounts and unfortunately for the café, it became popular despite itself with the bizarre upsurge in "Holocaust-consciousness" during the 1990s, and is now regularly featured in "insiders" guides to the city. Still, the elderly, daily-shrinking remnants of Eastern Europe are always welcome and automatically receive a different, cheaper menu than the tourists. Again, I think of Ezekiel at Dregs, a few blocks away; his parents probably hang out here.

Noam trips on a paving stone.

Inside, the Ghetto Café is wall-to-wall noise. There's no ersatz continental savoir faire here. A waiter bumps into me and yells, "Can't you see where you're going?"

"No," I reply mildly.

He must have looked me and Goldie over for a second, but instead of choking with the embarrassed chagrin that usually meets us, he laughs, "I guess not. Hey, who ordered the pickled herring?"

I like the place and recall descriptions of it. The brick walls are plastered haphazardly with theatrical memorabilia from some ancient actor's trunk. There are costumes and props and posters from biblical melodramas, from *The First Man and the First Woman* to *David and Absalom*, as well those advertising classic performances like Itzhak Yaroslavksy in *Merchant of Venice* and Bessie Boibrovitch in *Uncle Tom's Cabin* ("A flood of tears," says the *Tribuna-Ludo*).

Above the posters, below the low ceiling, a strand of barbed wire is gaily strung with hundreds of tiny white Christmas lights. If you ask, the Fishers will tell you that this is a "Jewish chandelier." They know history and irony, and so does their clientele. Yiddish is the dominant language as snippets of conversation burst from the clamor like bubbles. A millennium after liberation, an *alte cocker* regales a table of comrades with a story he has to have repeated a million times. "So I told the *kommandant* I'd rather be hung tomorrow than shot today."

Entirely unkosher, the Ghetto Café specializes in chicken paprikash and beef stroganoff heaped with buttery egg noodles followed by lush Linzer and chocolate tortes covered with whipped cream. For drinks, it serves vodka mixed with any flavoring, from lemon or currants to pepper or horseradish. You order a bottle and the waiter throws away the cap.

"That's it," a gravelly voice announces from a makeshift stage in the corner as the music stops. "We're going to take a break. Just remember, tips are optional . . . if you like pee in your soup." He shoots one final blast of notes from a clarinet and the room breaks into applause.

"This way," Noam says.

The tables in the Ghetto Café are about as close together as the walls Der Alter and I squeezed between to find the cave at the Dead Sea that Noam so glibly discounted. I still don't know whom to believe. Either man could have lied to me, but the rabbi paid more dearly for his statement. I don't even know if he escaped the ambush, unless, of course, it was a performance staged for my benefit. Noam, on the other hand, voices the logical, conventional wisdom that is hard to deny.

A solitary female singer takes the place of the band and starts her set with a Yiddish folk ballad in a minor key.

"Make way," the same waiter who bumped into me a moment ago cries. "Who ordered the borscht and blini?"

Voices yammer away about the War. "What we went through!"

Appreciative tourists not yet drunk on their overpriced vodkas gaze at the regulars with fascination. "What they went through."

Noam, then Goldie, then I walk up two steps into a raised alcove separated from the main room by a bead curtain and two large-shouldered men who pat me down before I can stop them.

Here's Simon on the town. Surrounded by his retinue and a few special foreign visitors, he's at the center of a U-shaped table, telling another familiar story. I've heard this in Hebrew, but he's speaking in English for the visitors' sake, his voice tinged with a Massachusetts accent so that no one forgets where he learned the language. "So Arafat says I'd better watch out, because if I don't give him what he wants and he takes it anyway, he'll hang me from the nearest lamp post."

"He didn't!" a credulous American gasps.

"Sure he did. The man doesn't know how to lie."

I enter into the cup of the U. "Is that a virtue or a flaw?"

Of course Simon notices me, but I'm not going to let him ignore me. I am Noam-the-retriever's partridge dropped at his master's feet, alive and squawking.

"Nathan. It's about time. We're nearly finished with dinner. Why don't you order something?" He lifts a finger and the waitress assigned to the alcove is beside me in a second.

"No, thanks."

"Have a drink, Nathan. Richard, let me introduce you to Nathan Kazakov. Nathan is the best writer who doesn't work for you."

I hear liquid gurgling into a tumbler and the glass is thrust into my hands by one of Simon's assistants, ecstatic to be invited out with the big boys. He smells of drink. The crew has been here for hours. Like any office cabal, they often go out after work to parse the events of the day, but I am never invited and the P.M. himself virtually never attends. There must be a dozen of them, most gravitating toward Simon. Only two figures sit on the periphery, opposite each other, the first exuding ill will and impatience, surely Cyril Klein, and the second slouched with a born bar hound's ease in his native environment. The latter is also someone I'm sure I've met, but can't yet identify.

"*L'chaim,*" I toast, and down the shot of straight vodka with a licorice aftertaste.

"Good. So Arafat says he'd hang me tomorrow and I say—"

I steal the punch line, "I'd rather be hung tomorrow than shot today."

Simon slaps his glass down on the table.

The American says, "That's why I never allow my writers onto the set. They always ruin their own best lines."

While the claque laughs, the familiar figure in the corner opposite Cyril Klein summons me. It's Zev Schechter, reporter. He says, "Don't let him bother you, Nathan. American moviemakers, they call them films, are all idiots. The man is in heaven here. He thinks the Holocaust was a redemptive experience. He wouldn't know Strange Fire if he sat on it."

I join him while the lights flicker and focus on the stage, where the ancient chanteuse, husky bass trembling with nearly a century's worth of tobacco inhalation, sings "My Yiddische Momma."

"What's going on, Zev?"

I can imagine his eyes squinting before he speaks. "Just out with the P.M. and the honcho from Hollywood. Great human interest piece, the two showmen. Great place, too. Have you tried the chulent? They leave a pot on forever, take out a piece of meat, put in a piece of meat, take out a piece of meat, put in a piece of meat. Sometimes you get it cooked, sometimes you get it raw."

The Ghetto Café is as hot and crowded as a New York subway in August, but a chill runs up my spine. Schechter is describing my mother's pot. I try to think if I described her culinary technique to Dmitri in the car, which might have been bugged or might not have had to have been bugged if the doctor spoke to the press. Did I describe her food to Moshe X and the two Avis over our campfire? I am losing track of what occurred when. Schechter has probably interviewed my mother, trying to find out where I was, and all he got was a recipe. I repeat my question. "What's going on, Zev?"

"You really want to know?"

"I've been shot at twice, hit once, burned twice, kidnapped, and followed everywhere I've gone. Yes, I want to know."

"The truth?"

"Try me."

"I don't know."

"Who does?"

"Gabriel ben Levi."

"And where is he?"

"That's the million-dollar headline. Best guess is that he's somewhere in Jerusalem. Maybe in disguise. Noam blew it when he didn't catch on to Gabriel's first approach to you. That's why he's in the doghouse. That's why he was so eager to fetch you here, get a scratch on the head. Stupid turd."

"How do you know all this?"

He shrugs. "Sources. But I promised I wouldn't write about it until it was over . . . in return for an exclusive."

"Well, if you really want me to help deliver your scoop, you've got to fill me in."

Schechter pours himself a shot of plum-scented slivovitz from a bottle on the table and leans back. We are alone at the corner of the U while Simon monopolizes attention at the center, blustering, "That's nothing. Let me tell you what happened when Saddam Hussein asked for a meeting. . . ."

"As far as anyone can figure it out, the operation started with some of ben Levi's explorations in the desert. He found something, not that stupid cave Der Alter took you to, a genuine archaeological find, a large one, a lost city. We don't know what for sure and we don't know where. Rubinstein was helping him, but so was some Palestinian boy. The boy told his aunt."

"Gita Mamoun."

"Her sources are as good as mine. She met Gabriel, probably offered to help him. If he went through channels, applied for grants, he'd be digging with a spoon until funding came through. It was the opportunity of a lifetime, he thought."

"It wasn't?"

"He's a fly in a web the size of Siberia. Mamoun has to stop that excavation at any cost."

"Why?"

"Money. The lady is overextended. She owns empty office towers in Riyadh, empty hotels in Kuwait City, and a ruined petrochemicals plant in Basra. While the smarter sheiks were getting their cash out, investing in Citibank and EuroDisney and the American stock market, she thought she was building the infrastructure for a democratic pan-Arabia that didn't pan out."

"What does that have to do with Israel?"

"It has to do with Israel because the propaganda is true. Call me a sentimental patriot, but the interests of the press and the nation coincide. Saudi Arabia and Kuwait and the emirates are a handful of billionaires and a revolutionary proletariat waiting to explode. Jordan and Syria are national slums. Lebanon had the same chance as Israel, but blew it. Forget a Palestinian state. You think it's bad now, if Arafat gets his country, Gaza will make the South Bronx look like the Riviera. Israel is the only political and financial success in the region, and Ms. Mamoun has one investment in Israel that can save her mysterious hide."

I tap my glass.

He continues "The Dead Sea Canal. You've been thinking about that one, haven't you? It's real, and Ms. Mamoun has options on half the desert between bodies of water."

"So she can hold up the project?"

"What are you, Kazakov, a fucking poet? No, she doesn't want to hold us up; she needs us to go forward. We won't have to seek eminent domain through the courts; she'll cede right of way in a second, because it will mean ownership of the new Tel Aviv. You know the intracoastal waterway that runs up the Florida coast? It's like that. She'll subdivide, sell off parcels, keep choice lots. Thousands of condominiums, dozens of hotels, millions of square feet of leasable commercial space, high-tech research parks. We're talking the real estate bonanza of the century, Kazakov. Woman might as well be a Jew."

"And we don't want that?"

"You still don't get it. Of course we want it. Let her make her money. We want housing; we want jobs; we want taxes. Prosperity is good for everyone. I told you, the propaganda is true."

"So what's the problem?"

"Moshe X and his sacred cemeteries. The whole project will stop on a dime the second they excavate the first synagogue. Think about an army of student interns cleaning shards of pottery with tiny little brushes. Oh, that won't derail the project, but they will delay it. Archaeologists think long-term. A decade, two, three. And you know what, as far as we're concerned it doesn't make too much of a difference. Yes, we'd prefer the canal. For all the above reasons and also because it would take care of the Dead Sea shrinkage problem, but we can wait because we also have a long view, but Ms. Mamoun doesn't. She can't. Her banks will dice her first."

Something about the journalist's use of the plural first person bothers me. "*We* can wait," he said. "As far as *we're* concerned," he said. He might as well be a speechwriter, crafting the candidate's syntax to compel the voter to adopt the candidate's view. Schechter has hammered Simon plenty in his column, but no one really knows where he stands. I ask him, "So why didn't she just kill Gabriel?"

"She had to find out who else knew about this."

"How do you know?"

"I told you. The Palestinian boy works for us."

Us. Across the prongs of the U-shaped table, Cyril Klein takes a call on a cell phone.

I think of "the Palestinian boy." What an awful, anonymous term. I say, "His name was Rafi."

"Was?" Obviously, Schechter doesn't know everything. He's been given certain information to give me and no more.

"I have my sources."

"If he's dead, she killed him, and that's why she killed him." Schechter traces a fingernail across my neck.

It makes a tawdry sense, but not all the details fall into place. I have more questions. "What about the name, Strange Fire?"

"It was Gabriel's term. The lad is his father's son. Everything in government is operation something or other. Why he picked this, I don't know. Maybe because it fed into Moshe X's mania."

That made sense. After all, it was Gabriel who came up with the Vale of Siddim. He thinks biblically. "And Rubinstein? Where did he come in? If Gabriel's assassination would ensure Gita Mamoun's development, why would he help?"

"Three possibilities. Either he really believed the uranium story and thought that it would be best to keep it hidden or Mamoun got him to believe that the archaeological excavation itself would violate the premises. In either case, he thought he was saving the land."

"You said three possibilities."

"Yes. Maybe he was paid."

"Ridiculous."

"I agree. So you're left with the first two."

Schooled in rhetoric, Schechter set up the straw man so that when it was knocked down the first two possibilities would seem stronger. He lets me absorb the situation and then suggests, "Let's say hello to Simon."

By now the famous moviemaker has left and Simon has dropped his genial hostly manner. Whatever liquor he downed in search of a campaign donation is flushed from his system and he's all business, conferring with Noam and a handful of aides. A late arrival, Serena Jacobi, sits in the moviemaker's vacated seat next to Simon. The question Noam called the office about before he found out about me had to do with the latest polls. Serena asks him, "What's it look like in the north?"

Noam hangs his head as if he is personally responsible. The polls are negative. After a flurry of support after the assassination attempt in Tel Aviv, Weiner has recouped ground by claiming that Simon's militaristic stance damages the economy.

"Numbers," Serena demands.

"Down two points in Haifa."

If the home of the nation's largest naval base isn't happy, the rest of the country is a disaster. The party is over unless the political magician pulls one last rabbit from his hat.

The clarinetist returns to the stage and joins the singer in "Bei Mir Bist Du Schein."

I have another question for Schechter. "What about the Yemenite?"

"Alas, poor Chess, I hardly knew him well, and he didn't know this country at all. He was a lamb in a lion's cage. I advised him to stick close to home, use the telephone for the first few months, but he thought I was just protecting the front page. Of course, I was, but I was also protecting him. Community of peers, competitive yet supportive. Instead, he got his headline, all right, but I got the byline."

Smug bastard. "Congratulations."

"You probably missed the story while you were sleeping it off. I would have waked you for a quote, but I didn't need to. The rabbi and his two sons exchanged shots with an unidentified band of Arab terrorists. One casualty, fatal. The culprits will only be identified when the big story hits the news. But off the record, what went down was precisely as appearances would lead you to believe. The bad guys followed a naive reporter. What I also didn't mention was that they were working for Gita Mamoun, aiming to stop you, sir, from finding Gabriel. Moral of story: don't ever trust an Arab, Mr. Kazakov."

"Nathan!" Simon calls out, his voice shooting from the center of the table like a toad with wings.

"Thanks," I say to Schechter, and step forward, ever the loyal retainer until otherwise released from my vows. Obviously, Ellen Markowitz's predicament is not a matter of overriding concern. If all turns out well, it will make a famous anecdote. There will be fences to mend, but if Simon says so, they're mendable. I'll send her flowers tomorrow, a lot of flowers. "Mr. Oscar gone?"

"Eh," Simon replied, "guy's a liberal. Screw him," and turns earnest. "We need your silver words, Nathan, and I need you. Help me find my son."

Simon's voice trembles, and I have to remind myself that he can play any song he wishes on this versatile instrument.

"Help me help Gabriel, Nathan," he repeats the theme with a slight variation.

I can't see his eyes, but they must be focused on me, because I can feel their power—and their vulnerability, which gives them yet more power. Whatever this man's manifold flaws, he has a father's passion to protect his young. I wish I had someone who looked after me with such vigilance, but all I've got is the weirdly unmotivated assistance of a Russian doctor who smells of cheese.

Reading my insecurity as uncertainty, Simon hammers home his point. "Look, I won't pretend that my son and I haven't had our—differences, but I—I love him. He's my son, and no one knows how close we really are. Now, he doesn't even know what he's running from or where he's running to. You seem to be the only one Gabriel trusts, and he may be able to contact you one more time. This time, help both of us. Bring him in, so we can talk. I don't care about anything else; I don't even care what happens in the election."

Suddenly a nasty little twinge shoots up my spine. Simon has gone one step too far with his line about the election. Okay, so he's overstating; it's his manner. He's still a father, and that word has a particular, painful meaning for me.

The chanteuse finishes her set with "The Partisan's Hymn," and every octogenarian in the room hobbles onto his or her variously prosthetized and varicose limbs to join in.

Informed by their tour guides, the lucky tourists also stand, repeating the ardent lyrics a beat after the survivors, and so does Simon. I can almost see him, clenched fist to his heart, eyes ablaze, as if there is a camera in the room.

# CHAPTER 16

"Let's leave the car here," I suggest.

"Is it safe?" Dmitri hesitates.

"No, one of those hundred-year-old freedom fighters is going to steal your hubcaps."

I've just heard about a conspiracy to kidnap and kill the Prime Minister's son and all my companion is worried about is his spanking new German set of wheels. But he can't follow the intrigue, so I can't blame him. We set off on an amble through the narrow streets of the oldest part of Jerusalem outside the Old City itself. We pass under sagging balconies that practically touch each other across byways built for donkeys and new construction of million-dollar town houses for wealthy Americans who want a piece of the Promised Land. On nearly every block we hear an incongruous mixture of prayer and Europop music. The latter blares from discotheques with names like Zoot or the California Club while the former seeps out of fluourescent-lit, single-room yeshivas and churches of every denomination and minor mosques emitting the wailing singsong of Islam.

Living in secular, political society, I certainly know about and pander to the multiple voting blocs of the faithful, but I have never really understood what God means to them. The presence of a deity—however they define Him, or Her, or It—is palpable, and a thought strikes me: neither they nor I can see what we believe in.

My right foot starts to ache and my thin cotton shirt rubs against my burnt shoulders like emery cloth. Organ music from an evening requiem in the Church of Four Saints bleeds into a nearby dance club's retro-Farfisa version of "96 Tears." Both are a long way from "Bei Mir Bist Du Schein," nor are they close to the ancient liturgical melodies of Der Alter and the Avis. I have to sit down, but these streets aren't yet the right spot for contemplation.

We leave the warren of alleys and pause in front of Jerusalem's City Hall, a building I know well.

A newspaper truck rounds the corner and dumps a wired bundle of tomorrow's *Ma'ariv* by the side of a kiosk.

A woman argues with a clerk in an all-night pharmacy. "Go home to bed," he says.

"But I can't sleep," she moans. "That's why I'm here. I'll bring you the prescription in the morning, I promise . . ."

"If I had a shekel for every promise . . ."

A beggar stops us and Dmitri gives him some coins.

A man at a bus stop asks us if we have been saved by Jesus Christ.

We walk onward until we've circled back to the King David Hotel, its carefully tended shrubs fragrant with night-blooming jasmine. A woman emerges from a taxi fragrant with perfume. "I need a cappuccino, Myron," she says to her companion.

"Oh, come on, Stella," he replies, "you'll never get to sleep."

I think of the woman in the pharmacy.

I need a coffee, too, and a place to rest. I have questions to ask and a thick binder of material someone has to read to me. Labeled "S F," the thing is tucked under my arm like a newspaper from the kiosk. Before Myron finishes paying the taxi driver and dealing with Stella, I slip into the back seat with Goldie and beckon Dmitri to join me.

"Where are we going?"

"Old City, Moslem Quarter, Herod's Gate."

"You sure?" the driver asks skeptically. He speaks with a youthful American accent, so I assume he's a college student, moonlighting to pay the tuition at Hebrew University, and proud of his skin-deep knowledge of the city. Most Americans never set foot in the Moslem Quarter, and certainly not after dark.

"Drive," I say, and ten minutes later we pull up to the least impressive of the Old City's seven gates. There is always activity at the Jaffa Gate and a few late worshipers are likely to be entering or exiting the Dung Gate beside the Western Wall, but the rest of the entry points are silent. Dmtiri pays and we enter the sleeping metropolis.

Stray dogs, hidden during the day, patter on the road beside the shuttered stalls that encroach on the gate and Goldie gets excited. She pants and strains to follow some dark and scrawny guy to the right. This happens occasionally. Goldie is as heterosexual as a bitch can be. Despite veterinary advice, I've never had the heart to spay her and therefore have to tolerate her cravings. It seems fair; she has to tolerate mine. I grip her leash and tug her to the left and say, "Another time, girl. Let's go."

Reluctantly, she obeys.

"Nice dog," Dmitri makes uneasy conversation. He obviously agrees with our taxi driver, who makes an illegal U turn to return to the King David as soon as possible.

Prohibited from a nocturnal liaison, Goldie grudgingly leads us toward our destination. We enter a lane that makes those in the vicinity of the Ghetto Café feel like boulevards. Instead of culminating in a grand City Hall, the lane merely intersects with another narrow passage at a needle-thin triangle with the stone cap to an ancient cistern at the center. Beneath the rough street, the cistern is probably more spacious than the triangle at which a few veiled women draw water into heavy buckets they lug home like their distant ancestors. Even at this hour, I hear the clanking of a chain and the pouring of liquid.

I think of the wells of the Bible, gathering places where people met to share sheer animal sustenance and human companionship, the Ghetto Cafés and California Clubs and Dregses of their era. Moses and Tzipporah, swinging singles, Rachel and Jacob, who would eventually be buried together with his father, Isaac, and his father, Abraham, at the Cave of Machpelah.

The smells are spicier here than in the Jewish Quarter, the air greasy with residue of lamb roasted with cumin or tarragon. Water is rare, fire common. What about Strange Fire? I catch a whiff of hashish before we come upon two geezers sitting at a folding table playing cards—I can hear the riffle. Silent as we arrive, they remain silent as we pass. So quiet are the streets that, a block later, I hear one of the card players claim, "Gin!" and slap his hand onto the table.

Dmitri walks closer to me. His body is hot and anxious; I could take his temperature. No matter his hundred-thousand-shekel vehicle and, I guessed, a flat in one of the new high-rises in Mevaserrat decorated like the inside of a Mercedes and a summer cottage overlooking Lake Kinneret—or maybe because of them—the ostensibly sophisticated doctor is basically bourgeois and terrified of the Arab underclass. I, on the other hand, don't mind a bit. Although Dmitri left Russia a generation before me, I have ranged farther from Moscow than he ever will. I could have sat down and played gin with the Elders of Fatah—if the cards were Braillle. There's nothing like a "disability" to level social distinctions.

Dmitri was totally unaware that his kindness to a semi-famous patient would lead him down these dark streets. Fear wafts off him like jasmine. He doesn't dare ask if this is "safe" because he doesn't want to hear the answer.

But it is safe. Incidents happen everywhere and no more frequently here than in New York, London, or Buenos Aires. We pass a throng of Christians en route from Midnight Mass at the Church of the Dormition. They found the Way to heaven and lost the way to their hostel, but I give them directions, "Praise the Lord."

"Did they say 'Braise the Lord'?" I whisper.

Dmitri nudges a hard elbow into my rib, but whispers back, "They only do that in the South Seas," and I can tell that he feels more at ease, and more so as we turn into a livelier lane where we hear exactly the same sounds we did in the Jewish part of town: disco music, prayer, and the omnipresent hum of televisions playing CNN, videos of *Titanic*, and reruns of American situation comedies dubbed into

Hebrew. No matter their political and spiritual differences, Christians, Moslems, and Jews share the modern communion wafers made in Hollywood. "We're almost there," I say.

"Wait!" Dmitri stops short.

"What?"

"Let me try."

I am eager to arrive at our destination and also, if truth be told, not quite as one hundred percent comfortable in the Arab streets as I pretend, but if the good doctor has obliged me so far, it is only polite to oblige him in return. I have no idea what he wants to "try" and a thought flits through my mind. Maybe he wants to kiss me. In the movies, stress often elicits ardor. "Fine."

We pause under a tin overhang. An exaggerated inhalation rattles through clogged nasal passages. Is he snorting cocaine? Stress often elicits drug abuse. I haven't heard any preparations, but he may have tipped a packet of white wonder powder onto his wrist as we made fun of the Christian seekers. I didn't hear him roll a ten-shekel bill into a tube, but perhaps he is adept enough to sniff it directly from his skin. His supply probably comes directly from the hospital, 99.4 percent pure. The least he could do is offer me a hit. I like dangerous hobbies.

He sniffs again, greedy man, and says, "Eggs."

Alas, no cocaine today, and the eggs are from yesterday. "You'll have to smell farther than your own beard."

He sniffs again and says, "Shit."

Goldie has taken advantage of our delay to deposit a small dump in the gutter. "Better," I say, "but not good enough."

The doctor's attempt to call forth the same olfactory skills that I use every minute grows more concerted. He takes several deep breaths, his chest rising and expanding, stretching his hospital whites. "Dust, stone, laundry, sky."

I laugh. "You think you're smelling, but your nose is telling you what your eyes are seeing. Close your eyes and try."

"My eyes are closed."

"Then your nose is telling you what your brain remembers seeing. It remembers these two- and three-story dwellings and the channel of night visible between their roofs and the clothesline that stretches between their windows that contains, if I'm not mistaken . . ." Using a simple knowledge of what people wear while focusing on the nature of the flapping of the laundry to discern its shape, I am like a mind-reader on a stage, telling a stranger what's in his pockets, using every trick at my disposal to wow the audience. "A shirt, two long robes, several socks, and . . ."—the pièce de résistance—"a brassiere."

"Amazing." The doctor exhales. His gentle fingers touch my eyes. "Are you sure you're blind?"

"As the day is dark. Here. . . ." I reach out to turn his body away from me, though once I hold him I am tempted to exercise another too-long-unused sense.

"Is something wrong?"

"No." I overcome my inclination. "Face this direction. Now try one more time. This should be easy. It's just around the corner."

"I don't think I can—no, wait . . . wait . . ." His audible sniffs come more swiftly, like Goldie investigating another dog's private parts. "Unless it's in the beard with the eggs and cheese and toast . . . I may have crumbled, but I didn't spill. It's strong. It's almost physical. . . ."

"Actually," I correct him, "it is physical. The objects we smell emit atoms of themselves. The world is constantly exploding. Billions upon billions of molecules of dust and stone and laundry are flying off their imperceptibly ever-diminishing sources, like the Dead Sea evaporating. Think of particles like motes in air, but infinitely smaller. The nose is merely a receiver that recognizes what literally hits it." I explain how the body works to the doctor.

"The shit?"

"Obviously. Goldie's poop is inside your nostrils. And worse, if it hits your nose, it's also in your beard along with the eggs and toast, and in your mouth and covering your face and clothes; that's why people wash their laundry."

"Some more frequently than others."

"Right. When you smell someone else sweating, their sweat is all over your entire body."

"That's disgusting."

"It's life, Dmitri. Get out of the hospital."

"I am out of the hospital. I couldn't get any farther away from the hospital. I'm standing on a fucking corner in the middle of the night, surrounded by a million Arabs who want me dead, standing with a failed faggot poet who's looking for some mystical nonsense called Strange Fire, and I'm covered with laundry and dog shit. We're both covered with laundry and dog shit and . . ." He halts, then nearly yelps, "Coffee!"

"You thirsty?"

"I smell coffee."

I smile. "Congratulations. We'll make you an honorary B.P. yet."

As expected, Abdullah's is open and busy. Most of the elaborately inlaid tables are filled with the usual crowd of backgammon players and lounging observers. I can't detect any Israeli soldiers—there is always a slight tension in the room whenever they're present—but there are several clusters of young tourists who chatter enthusiastically in English and Norwegian about their Israeli adventures.

"Effendi Kazakov!" Abdullah booms from behind the coffee machine.

Home away from home.

I let Goldie slouch onto the cool tiles beside the open doorway and lead Dmitri between the tightly packed tables to the rear. "Hello, Abdullah. Business is good."

"Ach, business is never good unless you are here. *Now* business is good," he effuses in his best hostly manner, and nearly crushes me in a bear hug.

"You say that to all the blind people."

"I say that to all the people with money in their pockets, but I mean it for you."

"Abdullah, let me introduce you to my friend Dmitri Tatarsky. He is a doctor and has money in his pocket."

"Any friend of Mr. Kazakov's with money in his pocket is a friend of mine."

The two large men shake hands and seem to get along. "A doctor," Abdullah exclaims with the same impressed respect as a Jewish mother. "I have a pain."

To which, finally at ease and glad to get off the streets, Dmitri replies, "A café owner. I have a thirst."

"Of course, of course. It is my honor to serve. We have . . ." He rattles off a list of hot and cold caffeinated beverages and finishes with a description of half a dozen Middle Eastern pastries. "Baklava, sesame cake, apricot layer, whatever you wish. If we do not have it, I will obtain it, should I have to go to the King David Hotel itself. And for you, Nathan, the usual?"

I nod.

Dmitri says, "Make it two."

After the convivialities, I am eager to get at the folder I am still carrying, but that can wait. I have questions to ask Abdullah. "And," I add before he can hasten to the counter to boil up my usual, "if you'll further honor us, make it three."

Sitting between the two huge men, I feel like a penis dangling between giant thighs. No, that's unfair to them. We're three penises together, one thin and two thick. No, that's unfair to me. I sit like a thin man between two fat men, somewhat fearful of being crushed if either of their frayed rattan chairs collapses.

"Okay," Dmitri says to Abdullah as he sips the potent coffee. "So where's your pain?"

Abdullah throws a heavy arm around my burnt shoulder—I wince—and asks me in mock intimacy, "Does this man know that if I show him my bruise, I will not be able to charge him for the coffee?"

Refraining from removing the arm lest I offend him, I reply, "As well as you know that if you do not charge him for the coffee, he will have to look at your bruise."

Abdullah claps his hands together delightedly. "Then we have a deal." He leans toward me, chair creaking ominously with the weight shift, and peels up his damp rayon shirt to display his side. Layers of love handles slide over each other like greased tires, creating a scent that is half sweat and half sour. "This mark won't go away. I must have bumped into something six weeks ago, though I don't remember what, but it's been tender ever since."

I smirk at Abdullah's hypochondria. Weighing no less than two hundred and fifty pounds and worrying about a black and blue mark, he is a twenty-eight-cubic-foot refrigerator complaining about a quart of spoiled milk on the bottom shelf.

But Dmitri doesn't make any jokes. His beard scratches his shirt as he looks down. "Does this hurt?" He palpates the area.

"Not more than usual. I told you, it's tender."

Dmitri's hands press into Abdullah's belly, then reach for his neck. "Any other marks?"

"Plenty. Over here." He swivels on the tiny chair to show the other side of his huge belly.

"This is an old wound. Probably an exit."

"June seventh, 1967. Courtesy of the Israeli army. I was shot in the back. I can show you the entry, too."

"No, thanks." Dmitri ignores the politics. "I meant any organic marks, any moles that may have grown recently."

"Actually, there is one." He slides up his pants leg.

Dmitri looks and touches. Then he leans back and sips the delicious coffee. "How about other symptoms? Fever?"

"I've had a cold."

"Joint aches?"

"This whole joint aches." Abdullah spreads arms wide to encompass his domain, then answers the question. "A little, maybe with the fever."

"Sores in the mouth?"

"Perhaps."

"Bleeding with the stool?"

"You live on an all-coffee diet, you don't look too carefully into the bowl."

"Weight loss?"

"Does it look like it?"

"Relatively speaking."

"I haven't used a scale in thirty years, but I don't think so."

"Good."

"And what's bad?"

"I can't be sure of anything."

"Don't shit a shitter, Doctor. You used the word 'symptoms.' Symptoms of what?"

"I'd like you to come into the hospital tomorrow. You can see me first, but call Dr. Levine at this number and make an appointment with him. Use my name." He scribbles a note on a napkin and holds it forth, his arm hovering over the table.

Abdullah downs his own coffee in a single gulp and places the fragile eggshell cup back on the table. He has served millions of cups of coffee over the years, but this time he sets it down too hard. I hear the cup crack. He asks one last question. "What sort of doctor is this Levine?"

Still extending the piece of paper, Dmitri replies softly, "He's an oncologist. That's—"

"I know what that is," Abdullah says. "And I guess I knew all along what this is." He slaps his side and pulls down his shirt. "Now, what can I do for you gentlemen?"

"Levine," Dmitri repeats, and leaves the paper on the table.

Suddenly Abdullah slams his fist down as if one of the million flies that occupy his café alit. Although I have sensed curious glances from the other tables, the noise draws all the attention in the room. "Hannah!" he bellows to his daughter. "Another coffee for my guests. And a selection of pastries. And . . ." he stares around at the rest of the customers, many of whom probably grew up with him. "And a round for everyone. Empty that fucking pot."

Instead of hopping to obey as she usually does, the girl approaches the table cautiously. She smells like the city, dry and laundered and emitting her own molecules of youth and vigor like a holiday fireworks display. She stands behind me, between the doctor and the patient, her hair brushing her shoulders with a whisk as she looks at each of them in turn. "Is everything all right?"

"What's not to be all right?" Abdullah hushes her. "Talking politics makes a man hungry. And I can't afford to lose any weight. Hah! Now, what was it you wanted to ask me, Nathan?"

Still, Hannah lags, and then finally departs to satisfy her father's rare generosity.

I listen to her steps echo on the tile and realize that I haven't said that I wanted to ask Abdullah any questions. The man is smart. There is no point to dissembling. I plunge in. "The Yemenite?"

"A great man in a world of little men, a freedom fighter in a world of politicians."

"And you are still a bullshitter in a world of bullshitters." I say this humorously, but also seriously, and Abdullah knows it.

"I don't know much, and I may not wish to tell you what I know until I have a good reason. That reason will have to do with who will be helped and who will be hurt. Though I love you like a brother, Nathan, you are not a brother, Mr. Kazakov."

"Have you heard anything about Gabriel ben Levi?"

"The whole world has heard about Gabriel ben Levi."

"How about Gita Mamoun?"

"She was occupying this very table minutes before you arrived."

"What!"

"Yes, she and Princess Di were having tea."

Unless I give him a reason, Abdullah is not going to reveal anything. "What if I told you that Gita Mamoun was trying to kill Gabriel ben Levi and that if this occurred, it would not be good for the Arab people?"

"It would not be especially good for Simon ben Levi, either, and for him I have no love. Shall I ask if anyone else in this room has love for your revered leader? Perhaps such a person exists and would be willing to help you."

"I'm not here on Simon's behalf. You and I have sat up late enough for enough years at this very table that Gita Mamoun and Princess Di just left minutes ago so that I think you know that. Besides, I believe that my own days working for ben Levi are numbered. In the meantime, an innocent person is in extraordinary danger. I won't pretend that Simon isn't interested, but this has nothing to do with politics. Simon is also . . ."

I deliberately wait until Hannah returns with a tray of coffee and pastries. She sets them down and picks up the cup Abdullah cracked while he reaches up to stroke her hair.

I finish, "He is also a father."

"You bastard."

I fill him in on the rest of the story, starting with what he knows from the newspapers and moving on to my first encounter with Gita Mamoun and my subsequent adventures with the Yemenite in the desert and ending with a veiled allusion to the assertions that Zev Schechter made about the mystery of Strange Fire.

"Okay, okay, I've heard enough. May ben Levi—ben Levi the elder—rot in hell, but in the meantime I have heard rumors that a significant action is about to be undertaken. Killing ben Levi Junior would qualify, but this stuff about money and real estate is nonsense. Everyone in the Bank knows that Mamoun practically owns the Bank. She is short on funds like Rothschild."

"But why would Schechter—"

"Oh-ho, the famous journalist."

Until now, I've been careful not to mention my sources. I bite my tongue.

Abdullah continues, "Under what circumstances, may I ask, were you made privy to this information? Were they tainted? No need to answer. Schechter is the worst kind of liar because he thinks he's telling the truth. He believes he's independent when he's really in the pockets of the powers-that-be. You were told this to mislead you, to besmirch the reputation of one of our most established citizens, one who, incidentally, I do not always agree with. Mamoun is a liberal. She channels money to Peace Now."

"If she works with Jews, could she have been working with Moshe X and Rubinstein?"

"Don't be silly. She works with the kind of Jews who wouldn't touch the settlers. Besides, she'd be the last person to engage in such a plot. A demonstration is one thing; even a bomb or an attack, though I do not fully support those, either, is essentially more of the same, and that might be something the Yemenite would be interested in, but the assasination of the Prime Minister's son is something else entirely. You could be talking about war, Reb Nathan."

I repeat some of Abdullah's words. "Do not *fully* support bombs." I wonder if Abdullah and Lebanon's Doc Ahmed could have been brothers. "How partially do you support them, Abdullah?"

"I am a patriot, Mr. Kazakov. But don't worry about me, I'm a harmless patriot. I may tithe to Fatah, but all I really care about is my daughter and selling a few cups of coffee and stopping the noise from underground from driving me crazy."

Indeed, I notice the same distant rumbling as I heard the last time I was here. It isn't loud enough to shake the café or strong enough to rattle cups, but Abdullah's senses are sharpening as his life force is weakening.

"And Ms. Mamoun is a patriot on the same terms," he goes on. "That's why this stuff with the young boy, the one named Rafi, it's impossible. For a Palestinian, the family is everything. You find whoever killed him and you'll find whoever is threatening your precious Gabriel. And if you really want to find who killed him, I suggest you look closer to home, Nathan. This is too complicated for simple Arabs. We're too stupid for such machinations. I tell you, this smells Israeli. Look under your own educated nose."

His statement makes sense even if it takes me back to square one. I tap the folder I carried from Simon's desk. "What about Strange Fire?"

Abdullah shrugs. "I have no idea. I can make inquiries and leave a message at your office."

"Make it my home instead."

"If that is all, I have other customers to attend to. The *alte cockers* are getting jealous of the time I spend with an enemy. They don't understand; it's nothing but business. Right?"

"Right." I shake his hand.

"Shalom," he says, and stands.

"Oh, Abdullah?"

He turns.

"Don't forget your paper." I pick up the napkin Dmitri wrote Dr. Levine's name and number on and hand it to the businessman.

He wipes his mouth with it and drops it in the garbage.

There is one more item to take care of before we leave the café. I push the folder across the table to Dmitri and say, "Read."

He sits still. The doctor, accustomed to receiving all manner of confidential information, hadn't heard the unabridged version of my last week until I told it to Abdullah. Is he jealous? He and I may be dual landsmen, but I've known Abdullah for years. His café was the first place I felt alive in post-Lebanon. I discovered it one summer afternoon after a frustrating Braille lesson at the Jerusalem Lighthouse. Goldie was a pup. We entered the warren of the Old City, confusing for a native, and swiftly got lost in its twisting alleys. We obviously passed the invisible border between quarters, but in those days the smells of different cuisines were not so distinct to me. I did, however, know the sounds of languages and could tell that the voices around me were no longer speaking Hebrew. We entered a courtyard through a narrow, shaded archway. Half a dozen boys had been talking in the courtyard, but hushed immediately. I guessed that they were adolescent. In the army, we learned that teenagers were the most dangerous adversaries.

A ball bounced rhythmically, like a clock ticking. I urged Goldie to find an exit. One hand holding her leash, the other touching the wall, I traced a stone facade interrupted by windows and a door. The ball slammed into the wall behind me. A boy laughed.

We reached a corner and walked along a second wall, and again the ball hit the surface, harder this time. I felt the tremble in my trembling fingers. We walked a third and fourth wall, each broken by a single flowered window box and a single door, propelled forward by the insistent ball that came closer with every kick. The boys had been playing soccer, but stopped for this newer, better game.

After four walls, we still hadn't returned to our entry point. Perhaps the walls weren't at right angles and the courtyard was pentagon-shaped. We walked a fifth wall and felt a fifth door. Perhaps it was a door to the courtyard, which the boys had shut.

One boy kicked the ball to another, the second to a third, the third back to the first, the first to a fourth. It skittered across the pebbled stone ground.

The fourth kicked it at me, by mistake or on purpose. It hit my legs. I tripped and let go of the leash.

"You," one of them called.

I pressed up against a window box, the flowers tickling my neck.

Was I about to be ritually disemboweled in this isolated corner of this ancient city?

The window flew open behind me.

I jumped into the center of the courtyard among the boys, and a harsh female voice screamed at us.

I didn't know what she said, though I detected names, furious imprecations, and dire threats. Immediately the boys ran. I followed their footsteps, bumped into a wall, found the exit, and fled.

The Moslem Quarter was even less integrated into the city in those days than it is now, and I found myself in a market filled with the bustle of Arab women shopping for dinner. I heard the clucking of live chickens and the sound of their decapitation. One headless foul must have hopped off the chopping board and started dancing at my feet. I felt its blood and its feathers about my ankles. "Goldie!" I cried.

"She's dead," someone laughed.

"Goldie! Goldie!" I wandered aimless and frantic through the lanes, searching for the lost dog who was supposed to guide me. Just when I was about to give up, a girl's thin voice spoke to me in Hebrew. "Is this your dog, sir?"

"Hello?"

"Here, let me help you." The girl's sandals stepped toward me and a tiny hand took my sweating palm. She led me into the cool interior of a café, seated me at a table and lowered my hand almost to the floor, where it came in contact with the soft ruff of a dog's neck. "She's so pretty. What's her name?"

"Goldie."

"My name is Hannah."

She introduced me to her father, who explained that his daughter had learned to speak several languages through the patrons of their café. He hoped she would grow up to be an interpreter. Then we argued about politics.

I try to explain this to Dmitri as a reason for my willingness to be forthcoming with Abdullah, but he waves off my explanation. "Never mind."

"Then please read."

"I already did. When you were in the Ghetto Café. I also ate those sandwiches your mother packed. They were delicious."

Of course. He was alone in the car with the folder for a good hour earlier that night. But he had withheld his knowledge for the rest of the time we spent together. "Yes?"

"It's nothing."

"What do you mean, it's nothing? The folder has a hundred pages in it. More." I grab it out of his hands. "Are they blank? Maybe there's invisible ink."

"They're not blank. They're printed, double-sided, I read all of it."

"And?"

" 'S F' doesn't stand for Strange Fire. Your boss has a secret that he must consider shamefully lowbrow. That's why it was hidden in his personal drawer between Palestine and the Holocaust. You're holding lists of the Hugo and Nebula Award winners for the last fifty years. Capsule biographies of Isaac Asimov, Ray Bradbury, Arthur Clarke, addresses of web sites where fans of the genre can "chat." It's got cast lists from *Star Wars* and *Star Trek* and every other one of those movies. By the way, didn't I see a director who made some of this Star Dreck come out of the Ghetto Café?"

I nod miserably.

"There are also a couple of xeroxes of what I guess are favorite stories, stuff about robots and intergalactic civilizations. I'm sorry, Nathan, 'S F' stands for science fiction."

# CHAPTER 17

"How long does he have?" I ask as we amble toward the Jewish Quarter and the Jaffa Gate. The city is quiet and appears utterly safe. I'm not afraid of teenagers or terrorists. The greatest danger comes from within.

"I'm not an oncologist, but the mark on the shin looked most like leukemia, a fixed, hard nodule that probably means the cancer has already spread. It could be in the lungs, the lymph, the brain. Six months is the usual diagnosis, could be more, could be less."

"Hmm."

"Hannah, the daughter, seems like a nice girl. What will she do?"

"The café isn't a gold mine, but Abdullah's been robbing tourists for decades and socking it away. She'll close up shop, sell the lease, go to the university. She'll be all right."

"I hope so."

"I do, too."

We continue without speaking, taking one twisty turn after another as automatically as rats in a laboratory maze who have learned where the cheese is. Goldie trots easily beside us, but I might as well be leading her. Finally Dmitri breaks the silence. "How do you do it, Nathan?"

I know what he means. Like all sighted people, even the doctor can't quite believe that B.P.s inhabit the same world he does. I answer, "There's a famous story about Mandelstam. Late in his career, before Stalin killed him, an admirer asked the poet how he did it. From the story, it's unclear whether this was an aesthetic question: 'How do you write so beautifully?' or a moral one: 'How do you find the courage to insult the strong man of our time?' but it doesn't make any difference. Mandelstam answered both questions in the same words. He said, 'I don't know how to do anything else.' "

We pass through the Jaffa Gate and immediately feel air. The Old City was built on a hill that descends gradually to several valleys along its perimeter and rises again to a sequence of ridges that swell and fall with diminishing ardor until the coastal plain. The first ridge west of the first valley supports the King David Hotel. To its right is the district where the Ghetto Café snuggles amid the back streets. Farther away, the skyscraper hotels poke up beyond the intervening metropolis. All of this is visible if you have eyes to see it. Likewise, we are visible from any number of transient and permanent dwellings. A wide, sweeping drive leads in either direction.

"Ready to go home?"

Is this Dmitri's way of saying, "Your place or mine?" I am ready to answer when I hear another sound and realize I have one more stop to make. I say, "Close your eyes."

"Okay."

"What do you smell?"

"Nothing."

"What do you hear?"

"Nothing."

"What do you remember seeing?"

"Nothing."

"So much for your honorary membership in the society of B.P.s. Don't be obvious, but open your eyes and tell me if there's a car idling to the left with its lights off. Tell me if you can smell the exhaust and if—now listen carefully—you can hear the faint sound of jazz guitar.

It will be difficult to make out his features, but tell me if the driver appears to resemble our old friend Noam Abravanel."

"You are absolutely incredible, Nathan."

"That's what I get paid the big bucks for. Besides, Noam's driven me before and he's the only one I know who listens to bossa nova. The only question is how he knew we'd be outside this gate since we entered another."

"Um," Dmitri sighs. "At one point I thought we were being followed, but I didn't say anything."

"For Christ's sake, why not?"

"It seemed ludicrous, that's why."

I put a hand on his shoulder. "From now on, trust yourself. Intuition is the best sense any of us has. But don't blame yourself, we couldn't have done anything about it. There were probably several others that you didn't notice backing up whoever you spotted. Besides, I have a few questions to ask Noam and this saves me the trouble of having to find him. Good night."

I start walking down the drive in the direction of Noam's car.

"Wait!"

I turn and repeat, "Good night," but that isn't enough. Dmitri wants to help. He *has* helped. He is involved. As they say in the movies, he knows too much. But I am the only one who knows how much he knows, and the least I can do is to protect him as much as possible. He is already in a stew of trouble, but he ought to be able to talk himself out of most of it—doctor/patient relationship, et cetera. From here on in, that will become increasingly difficult. I'm beginning to formulate a plan that will take me far over the edge, beyond the pale. "Thank you," I say, "but I've got to do this by myself. Noam doesn't trust you and won't speak freely if you're around."

"You expect him to speak freely otherwise?"

"I have reasons to believe so, yes, but I can't tell you what they are. This is business."

"But—"

"I appreciate your concern, but there's nothing you can do about it. Go home, take two aspirin, and call me in the morning."

---

Reluctantly, the physician follows doctor's orders as I continue toward the parked car, from the window of which Astrud Gilberto's smooth voice is singing, "And when she passes, each one she passes goes 'Ahhhhh.' "

But this is not the place for a private discussion, so I pass the car and no one goes, "Ah." On the other hand, perhaps I go, "Ah," as I hear the car make a gear-grinding U turn to pursue my shadow. I hope that Dmitri has set off in the other direction, toward his own car, and isn't attempting to follow Noam and me, and I hope that I've made the right decision. Actually, there's no other decision I can make.

It's a lovely, warm night with a calm, reassuring breeze that sweeps off the Arabian desert and washes the rooftops of the Old City. Goldie and I stride at a regular pace, though I can tell she is tired. "There, girl." I stroke her. "We're not going far."

We walk downhill into the valley and then uphill toward the King David. I consider avoiding a steep flight of steps that climbs the terraces to make it easier for Noam to track me, but going out of my way might seem suspicious. Anyway, I have to assume that by now the rest of his team assigned to the other gates of Jerusalem has been summoned and stationed at pivotal locations along my likely route.

A man standing under a streetlight ruffles a newspaper conspicuously.

A woman walks a dog on the other side of the railing that bisects the steps.

Traffic has slowed in front of the King David, but the doorman might be communicating with the garbage collector at the curb with a walkie-talkie.

"Suspect headed eastward along Rehov Zion, approaching Independence Park."

I enter a side street and pause to allow Goldie to pee and Noam to catch up. The street is dark, but I sense a glow from a neon beer sign in a window. Unless I have a key to an apartment elsewhere on the short block, this has to be my destination. I push open the wrought iron as creakily as possible and enter. Luckily, the place feels empty. "Hello?"

"Twice in one week," a voice answers from the rear. The owner of Dregs is fiddling with a television suspended over the bar, and static competes with the last notes of "La Vie en Rose" from the jukebox. "To what do I owe this privilege?"

Cutting to the chase—no time for chat—I hasten to the last stool and blurt, "I need a favor, Ezekiel." If he hadn't been here, I don't know what I would have done, but thank God queers keep late hours.

"I never loan money to customers."

"I need a lot more than money."

Like Abdullah, Ezekiel is good at reading his patrons' moods. It's a professional skill. "How about you tell me about it over a drink?"

"Pour two, one for me and one for the guy who's going to join me in approximately three minutes."

"An assignation?"

"Is anyone in the back room?"

"Two boys, but they won't mind company."

"Can you ask them to leave?"

"Nathan, they just paid."

"Refund their money. You're closing early, and before you hesitate, let me warn you, it gets worse. This favor, this series of favors, is major. But first, do you remember that guy who used to come in here three or four summers ago, drank too much?"

"That describes most of my customers."

"Shy guy until he drank, then acted stupid. Always wore a vest and bow tie, worked for some European bank. Behind his back, we called him the Mouse."

"Hah." Ezekiel remembers. "The Mouse because he always claimed someone had given him a Mickey."

"Right, that way he could have rough sex and pretend that it wasn't his doing."

"What about him?"

"Any truth to his claims?"

"Maybe once someone gave him a tuie or some Exstasy and he woke up in the back of a truck. It's even theoretically possible for lightning to strike the same place twice. But this doofus used to pull the same act every week."

"He couldn't have ever been given something across the counter?"

"What are you getting at, Nathan?"

"Here's what I need."

I have no particular claims on Ezekiel's loyalty and nothing special to offer him in return. Money isn't irrelevant to the owner of Dregs, but he refused to cash out when an American theme restaurant offered to buy the premises. Besides, I don't have a lot of money. I consider playing the Holocaust card with him as I successfully played the father card with Abdullah, but something tells me to hold my breath.

When Ezekiel finally replies with the lamest possible objection I know I made the right choice. He says, "But Nathan, I put that equipment away ages ago."

"You can find it."

"Besides, the equipment is second-rate. It's for pretending."

"Then let's pretend, Ezekiel. Just follow my lead."

The clock ticks, and Noam will enter any second. Finally, Ezekiel makes up his mind, places two glasses on the bar, and says, "It's after five, dark liquor, right?"

"Make it Scotch."

He pours the drinks, places one in my hand, and stirs the other. "Now I will ask the lovers in the back to cease and desist, but it will take me some time to make the rest of the arrangements."

I nod and sip. I need the drink.

Several sips later, two slightly winded young men emerge from the back room zipping their flies. "Exit's that way, gentlemen," I say. They leave, muttering, and before the door closes fully it opens for the last time this evening.

"We meet again," Noam says.

"Actually, I've been expecting you." I pat the barstool next to me and gesture to the drink.

"Sure," he says, and sits down. "Come here often?"

"Do you know anything but clichés?"

"I guess I need a personal writer."

"You can't afford me. In fact, I'm not sure that Simon can afford me any longer, either." I mean the word "afford" to have two meanings.

"Well, after your behavior earlier this evening, you may not have to worry about that. Once she was untied, Ellen was fit to be tied."

"You spoke to her?"

"Everyone speaks to everyone else."

"Do they tell the truth?"

"Sometimes."

"That's probably why I needed to be alone. I've spoken to too many people lately."

"Shall I leave?"

Both of us know this is not an option. I swivel around on the barstool and walk over to the jukebox. "Preferences?"

"Jazz."

" 'Girl from Ipanema' okay?"

"What are you telling me?"

"That I know you've been following me," I say as I flip through the selections, which I know by heart. B-2 is the original version that was playing in Noam's car, but I am tempted to play C-3, a campy knockoff titled "Guy from Ipanema." No, there will be plenty of time for games later. I drop in a coin and punch B-2 and say, "I want to know why."

"Didn't Zev Schechter tell you? Didn't Simon practically beg you? Don't you want to save Gabriel ben Levi?"

All of the above is true, and I am certainly willing to work with people I detest for the sake of a goal I desire—as apparently are they—but I have to be sure that we're on the same side. When I left the Ghetto Café, I believed this was true, but Abdullah placed enough doubts in my head to make it debatable. More importantly, so did Gabriel, back in the Sheraton. On the other hand, the simple archaeologist doesn't necessarily know what is good for him. "Yes," I agree, "but how?"

"He found you once; he'll find you again. When that happens, don't be stupid."

"And that's your message for tonight? You're just a carrier pigeon. Now you can fly away home."

"No, I have another message. It's not to believe anything that the fat Arab told you."

Was the conversation in the café taped? Was one of the Norwegian tourists really Shin Bet? Noam is willing to tell me what he already knows I know, but nothing more. I say, "The fat Arab's name is Abdullah and he's very convincing."

"His café has served as a dropoff point for weapons and information for years."

"Right, I bit into a bullet in the baklava."

"Do you deny that he's a known Hamas sympathizer?"

"I wouldn't trust an Arab who wasn't a sympathizer. Would you trust a Jew who wasn't a Zionist?"

"Nonetheless he's dangerous, and so is the Mamoun woman. Don't be naive, Kazakov. She's obviously in this up to her black and kinky cunt." Noam proceeds to cite chapter and verse that he couldn't have made up on the spot. In addition to repeating Zev Schechter's allegations of Gita Mamoun's financial woes, he tracks her initial financial success to Saudi investors. He names her best friends in college, at least one of whom is currently serving a life sentence in an Israeli prison, and goes on to delineate an amorphous relationship she maintains with a certain "charitable" organization suspected of illegal political activities. He proves that she has, as they say in American courts, means, motive, and opportunity for engaging in terrorist action, but he doesn't prove that she has engaged in such action. What Noam doesn't mention, however, is who else might have different means, motive, and opportunity. I have to find out, and this is probably the last occasion on which I have my own means, motive, and opportunity.

Astrud Gilberto sings from the jukebox, "Tall and tan and young and lovely . . ."

I reach out to clink glasses with him. His sounds empty, but I have to make sure. "Ready for another?"

"Sure, but where's the bartender?"

I am wondering the same thing myself and am about to circle around and serve the both of us when I hear Ezekiel's heavy steps rising from the basement.

"Last call," he announces.

"The same?" I ask.

"Sure . . ." Noam is starting to slur.

"The exact same," I say emphatically, and Ezekiel pours another round. Below the bar, he stirs one of the drinks before he serves them. Then he walks to the front door, locks it, and returns to his station, by which time Noam seems hypnotized by Stan Getz's wonderfully smooth saxophone.

The glass slips from Noam's hand and he slides from the stool. "I . . . I have to . . ." He kicks the glass across the floor. "You've . . ." His hands flail, pat himself. I hear the rustle of fabric. He stumbles into me, holding something hard.

He reaches across me, yet before I can respond to the situation something else slams down on the bar and, I suppose, Noam's wrist.

Noam yowls and staggers backward into the jukebox, which starts skipping. "She looks straight ahead, not at . . . straight ahead, not at . . . straight ahead, not at . . ."

Ezekiel is out from behind the bar in a flash, standing over Noam, who has slumped to the floor in a heap. "You didn't tell me he had a gun."

"I didn't know."

"What else didn't you know?"

"That you had a baseball bat."

"Hmph," he snorts. "It's the business."

"Let's get him downstairs."

"First let me take care of this." He kicks the jukebox.

"She looks straight ahead, not at meeee."

Ten minutes later, the dead weight we hauled past the bar and pool table is installed and secured in the basement storage area that had, years ago, been called the dungeon. It is a low-ceilinged brick room with sweating pipes and exposed wires and several dozen cardboard boxes filled with whiskey and beer. A bare bulb dangles from the socket that once shed weird black light on several dozen young men engaged in the performances that would eventually kill many of them. I wonder where Ezekiel kept his stock in the glory days.

"How long till he revives?"

"Hm." Something is on Ezekiel's mind. "Oh, not long. These things work quickly and wear off quickly. And by the way," he says, "I never served the Mouse a Mickey."

I shrug. "You're innocent until proven guilty."

"No, you're innocent until you are guilty. Proof is something else entirely."

Ezekiel has never told me any stories about his parents during the war, and he doesn't now. We sit quietly, each in our own worlds, and then Noam starts to wake.

Quite inelegantly he snorts and shakes. "I . . . I . . . what the hell is this?" He starts at me, but the equipment, though second-rate, holds fast. "My wrist, Christ, what have you done? Look at it."

"Unfortunately, I can't do that."

Again, the prisoner rattles his restraints and relapses into moans of pain. Noam is handcuffed to several iron rings that hang off a steel rod bolted into the brick basement wall.

"Go for it," Ezekiel says.

I will, but first I reach out and touch my partner's face. It is thick with decades worth of drink, eyelids puffy, nose wide, lips full and set. His expression is serious.

"Okay, Noam, I've heard what you had to say. That is, I heard what you *had* to say. Now we'll hear the rest." It's time for the truth.

"Let me go immediately."

"No, that's not going to happen, not unless you oblige."

"You're insane."

"Maybe."

"You, bartender, if you don't unlock me this second you are going to be in trouble like you've never known. I am Noam Abravanel, special assis—"

"Special assistant to Simon ben Levi, Prime Minister of Israel," I recite his title. "My friend is entirely aware of who you are and why you're here. We're not leaving until I'm satisfied. Incidentally, these walls are quite substantial. If you'd like, you can scream for help just to make sure none of your friends in the street can hear you, and then we can get to business." I hope this isn't a bluff.

"What do you want to know?"

"What is Strange Fire?"

"I don't know."

"What is Strange Fire?"

"I don't know."

"What is Strange Fire?"

"I don't know."

"Ezekiel, the equipment."

Without saying a word, the master of the former dungeon unsnaps a trunk that must have been sitting among the cartons of beer and hands me a heavy cast-iron implement. I run my hands to nipple-pinchers at the tip.

"Nathan, I . . ."

I heft the tool in one hand and let it swing low like a golf club until it smacks into Noam's shin.

"Yeow!"

"I'm sorry, it's not supposed to be used that way. Shall I use it appropriately?" I reach out and rip his shirt open; mother-of-pearl buttons bounce to the cement floor.

"You wouldn't dare."

I affix the pinchers with a tiny tightening screw. "Believe it or not, some people like this, but if you don't, then you'd better tell me: what is Strange Fire?"

"I don't know."

I squeeze the handle.

"Uranium!" Noam shrieks.

"There's no uranium in Israel. What is Strange Fire?" I squeeze again, harder.

"Arabs. It's an Arabic code for . . ."

I squeeze as hard as I can, and his nipple comes flying off like a pencil's pink eraser.

"Please stop," Noam begs.

"Not until I get the information I want. Ezekiel, what else do we have?"

Rummaging through the trunk, he names the rest of its contents as coolly as a nurse informing a doctor of the contents of a medical satchel. "Whips, clamps, ball gags, nut weights, waist cinchers, a spiked necklace, various genital castigators. Any need for a bondage mask?" He hands me what feels like a leather sack with a zipper across the front.

I slap Noam's face with the mask. "What is Strange Fire?"

"I don't know."

"Put this on him."

"No!" Noam shrieks again. The mask frightens him more than the more brutal toys.

"Why not?"

"It's a term Gabriel invented. It . . . it . . . " He tries to satisfy me. "It doesn't mean anything. No, wait. He told Moshe X there was uranium in the cave. There isn't. Ben Levi knows that. But he was afraid."

"Of what?"

"Of being killed," Noam sobs, afraid of being killed. "It was the code name he made up for his own assassination."

"Assassination by whom?"

"The Yemenite."

I wave the mask in front of him.

"No, that's not true." Noam is eager to help now. I just have to wait. "But it is true. They would kill him. They'd kill anyone. We sent them to kill you." He slumps down, but jerks upright at the pressure on his wrist.

I am calm. "Tell me about it."

"It was a mistake, before we thought you could help us."

"Never mind the minor offense. Tell me."

"There are channels. For communication. We fed information to the Yemenite. We hoped he'd get rid of you. Stupid, incompetent Arab. Never trust an amateur."

This is the arrogant Noam I know and despise. I think I have one more question. "Who are 'we'?"

He shrinks back toward the wall.

"Who are 'we'?"

He hides his head, fucking ostrich.

"Who are 'we'? . . . Ezekiel, the fire."

There isn't any fire in the trunk so far as I know, but Noam responds. "I can't. We, I mean he . . . he'll kill me."

"Better to be killed tomorrow than today. Who is 'he'? Now!" I demand.

In a whisper, almost more terrified of his imagination than the actuality in front of him, Noam whispers, "Klein."

I pause to contemplate his answer, and murmur, "I thought so."

But if our session is over, Noam has one question of his own to ask. "Then why did you hurt me, Nathan?"

Suddenly we are having a conversation. I reply, "Because thinking and knowing are different," but even as I speak I wonder if I am telling the truth. I wonder if I tortured Noam because I hate him, and the fact that I hate him because he hates me is meaningless. I wonder if I tortured him because I enjoyed it. Does my aim to save Gabriel justify this? I'm just as bad as they are. Worse. I drop the mask.

"Are we done?" Ezekiel asks.

I can tell that he is looking at me with disgust. Not the disgust that regularly meets my blank eyes and deformed forehead which looks more like bark than skin, but disgust at the far uglier character that lies beneath my rough countenance. He wants to lock away the toys of his trade and unlock our pained and degraded prisoner and never see either Noam or me again.

I haven't smashed any babies' heads against his cellar wall and I'm not Dr. Mengele, but after I leave, the son of Mauthausen might call his beer distributor and order several cases of the German beer he has perennially refused to sell. What's the point of holding a half-century-old grudge against an entire nation when the new, enlightened nation that took its place includes the likes of me?

I don't blame him. I am repulsed at my own actions and the avidity with which I pursued them. I took a malicious pleasure in breaking one pathetic human being down into something less than a human being. Thinking I was taking the moral high ground, I have actually dug a trench and buried myself six feet under. Yet thinking and knowing *are* different, and I am determined to pursue this to the end. Maybe I can't think of any kinder, gentler way to get the information because I have no imagination. Or maybe this is just the direction my imagination naturally runs. Anyway, in for a shekel . . .

"No," I declare. "We're not done."

"What?" both Ezekiel and Noam gasp at the exact same moment, united in their mutual fear and detestation of what I have become and where that might lead.

"I have more questions for you, Noam." This is not the time to question myself. When the Strange Fire has burnt out and cooled to cinders I might indulge in self-analysis, self-recrimination, and penance, but in the meantime I am steel. Ezekiel can call me a *kommandant,* but I have a mission and I will fulfill it.

"What?" Noam asks softly.

"Why?"

"Why, what?"

The special assistant is being cagey and this lends me strength. However flawed my methods and my motives, I still have to get the information that he has still withheld. "Why did Klein want to kill me? No, that's obvious." I work through the logic out loud. "He wanted to kill me because I was interfering with some original plan. The original plan was to kill Gabriel ben Levi. Why did Klein want to do this? And how did he convince Rubinstein to do his dirty work?"

The last question is a bit of a stretch, but I know it is on target. In fact, I already know the answer to that one, too. The chief of Shin Bet convinced the settler the same way he had the Yemenite, with some dubious rationale tailored to his discontent: uranium or ancient cemeteries or whatever. Directly or through "channels," he fed the true believer the poison on a semi-self-regulated drip that drove him crazy and impelled him to act unwittingly on Klein's behalf. It's his modus operandi. He turns other people into puppets and sits in the audience applauding.

Things are beginning to come together, but I still lack the most important piece of the puzzle. I repeat, "Why did Klein want to kill Gabriel?"

"I don't know."

"Shall I repeat the question?"

"No! I don't know. I swear on the Bible that I don't know. He doesn't tell me."

I put my hand to Noam's face and feel his wet cheeks twitching. I believe him. He can tell that I believe him and that his ordeal is almost over. He sighs.

I move my hand an inch away from his mouth and let another sigh flow through my fingers. It is one sigh too many. The first was relief that he would soon be free. The second was relief that he had managed to keep something hidden.

Steel yourself, I think, steel yourself and do what you must. Lie and hurt. "One more question, Noam. But if you're a good boy, I promise that this is the last question."

Ezekiel exhales in exasperation.

"Yes?" Noam answers weakly.

"What question have I failed to ask? What else do you know? What haven't you told me?"

This was probably the worst question I could have asked. All others had their answers even if they were truly "I don't know." But now I'm not asking Noam to inform on the merely lethal Cyril Klein; I'm asking him to inform on himself. I can feel the wimp's face tense with resolve. He has a little steel, too. He says, "Fuck you."

I turn to the silent observer in the room. An hour ago, in the bar, I told him what I needed and he reluctantly agreed because I convinced him of its importance. Perhaps I am no better than Klein, insinuating my way into other people's hearts, imposing my will on their minds, but so be it. I only hope that I haven't lost all credibility, because if Ezekiel refuses to play his part, I'll have to concede defeat and let Noam go free—that, or kill him.

Whether Ezekiel is simply fulfilling his earlier promise, or whether he still believes that I was right when I insisted that this was the only way to save the innocent Gabriel, or whether he is protecting Noam from me or protecting me from my evil inclinations, I can't tell. In any case, he stands.

"No, Noam," I state coldly. "Fuck you." I unzip his pants and pull them down to his ankles. I slide my fingers into the elastic waistband of his Italian silk briefs and slide them down, too. His legs and lower cheeks tremble like his upper cheeks. He presses himself back against the wall, but I use an elaborate pulley system attached to his chains to twist his torso around. I strap a wide leather sling under his belly to raise his rear to the most effective angle. Bent over, feet splayed, he doesn't say, "What are you doing?" because he knows.

Ezekiel unzips his own pants.

Noam tries to squirm away, but he is locked in place. Still he says nothing as Ezekiel steps forward, preparing. It isn't easy; the bartender doesn't believe in forced sex. I can hear the stroking sounds as he tries to arouse himself.

I am tempted to suggest something or even assist, but think better. Ezekiel and I never had a thing, and by now I am probably the least erotic creature in the world to him.

Finally semi-rigid, Ezekiel rubs himself against Noam. Skin on skin makes a sound like no other.

I don't need to say, "Last chance," because Noam must know this, or think he does.

Gripping Noam's waist like a bareback rider, Ezekiel enters the captive.

Noam's teeth grind, but he doesn't utter a word. A horrible thought comes to mind: What if he enjoys this? What if, as I've occasionally suspected, Noam has tendencies himself? In the best of all possible worlds, rape might free him to come out as his natural, gay, and lighthearted self. Next thing you know, we'll be sharing breakfast in bed.

Sadly, none of the three of us in the cellar inhabits the best of all possible worlds.

Ezekiel pumps and heaves so hard that Noam's head occasionally thumps into the wall with a nasty crack. I assume that by now Noam is bleeding from the head and butt as well as his torn chest. Yet both of the actors remain mute and I sit there like a blind teenager in a porno theater, listening to the sound track.

On it goes, the liquid slapping of flesh against flesh, until Ezekiel's panting grows rapid. I don't know if he signals me, but I can tell: the time has come. If deviant Eros couldn't force Noam to relinquish his last secret, Thanatos will. I have one final trick up my sleeve.

I speak with the measured cadence of a royal executioner reading the condemned man's sentence. "Okay, Abravanel. Enough is enough. We're nearly done, and I give you credit for your silence. You're tougher than I thought. Might as well be a true sabra. You will, however, when I explain the situation, wish to break the silence.

Here's why. There are probably a number of small tears in your rectum already. Those tiny cuts may act as a conduit to your bloodstream for bodily fluids including semen. Note that Ezekiel is not wearing a condom. Now, he may have dripped a bit already, and we can't do anything about that. But he hasn't come. And the thing is, Ezekiel hasn't been well lately. His T-cell count dropped last week and the virus has spread to . . . well, you don't want to hear the details, or do you . . . from your own doctor."

Between thrusts, Ezekiel gasps, "I'm ready."

"Stop!" Noam shrieks.

"Stop," I say.

Ezekiel pulls out.

"If you don't start talking before I finish this sentence, Ezekiel will go back in and may not be able to restrain hims—"

"The tunnel," Noam cries.

"What?"

"The tunnel. The tunnel."

For a second, I think he is speaking in metaphors and referring to his own rectal passageway. "What the—"

"The tunnel under the Western Wall, for God's sake. Please, please don't start again. I'll tell you everything." At last, he is crushed.

I unstrap the leather sling under his stomach and hoist the chains so he's upright. I wonder if he has an erection, but I don't check. I go to a slop sink in the corner of the basement and pour a glass of water from the tap. I return and hold it to his lips and say, "Go on."

"All I know is that Klein's first plan with Rubinstein failed in Tel Aviv and that the second plan is to occur in the tunnel. Ben Levi's been doing some minor excavation there. That's where he'll be killed."

"How?"

"I don't know."

"When?"

"I don't know, I swear it. I wasn't supposed to know this much, but one of the men I had trailing you met with one of the men Klein had watching the tunnel and he said too much. I don't know, I don't know, please, I don't know, I don't know, I don't know," he repeats long after I stop asking him anything, until his body jerks spasmodically and he faints.

"Happy?" Ezekiel asks, zipping his pants.

"Satisfied," I answer.

"Can I let him go?"

"Yes, and don't worry. You won't get into any trouble. He wouldn't dare mention this to anyone."

"I'm not worried, though maybe I should be. After all, how can I be sure that he was safe?"

# CHAPTER 18

Home again, home again, jiggety-jig.

Home again, home again, to eat a fat pig.

I can't resist. On the road to Rehov Rambam, I instruct the taxi I hailed outside of Dregs to stop at Lerner's Boucherie, provedore to fancy restaurants, foreign embassies, and native apostates. Located in an industrial district in the near northeast, Lerner's refrigerated warehouse opens at 4:00 A.M. for the chefs who need to start cooking before breakfast in order to serve lunch.

Aside from the pretentious Gallicism of the name, the single remnant of a misguided upscaling effort by the heir to the original butcher shop, there is no pretense about the place, or maybe it's a more sophisticated pretense to lure seekers of authenticity. Bourgeois gourmands love parking their Subaru coupes among the battered trucks that hearse in the dead cows and chickens from local farms and more exotic meats from the airport. They love climbing the perilous loading dock and pushing through the swinging doors into the frigid interior. Mostly, they love the company.

Everyone, from suburban housewives clutching shekel-stuffed kidskin wallets—Lerner's is not cheap—to teamsters guiding gigantic cadavers shackled to a hanging conveyor belt system, enters through those same heavy doors. Inside, the beefy men hoist the glistening produce to their shoulders and deliver it to Lerner's own *bouchers*, who wield cleavers and hacksaws to cut and chop the great carcasses into their constituent parts and send them forth to their final rest on blood-soaked racks beneath the whir of machines emitting the endless flow of arctic air that keeps the dead fresh.

And what glorious variety of species' inner fluids greases the floors until a day laborer spreads sawdust to absorb the excess! Lerner's stocks buffalo from the United States, reindeer from Finland, caribou from Canada, and pig from a ranch in the Loire Valley that supplied the tables of the Louvre before it was a museum. Beyond the mundane meats fit for greater and lesser kosher and nonkosher mortals, Lerner's also carries giraffe, gazelle, antelope, and bear, as well as wild boar and turtles for soup and quenelles and a score more animals better known for their pelts. It carries lions who lay down with lambs in the peaceably dead kingdom as well as those eternally bitter enemies, mongoose and snake, and a dozen other kinds of birds, including the rare Brazilian diving fowl that Noam Abravanel would have loved.

Rumor has it that there is a secret back room containing the edible corpses of endangered species.

Strolling the wide, reddened, sawdust-strewn aisles, I wish I could read, because the signs, reluctantly deciphered to me once by a friend, are the exact opposite of the institution's own idiotic name. Instead of some dumb euphemism like "Sweetbreads," Lerner's has "Brains" along with everything from generic "Guts" to "Lamb Tails" to "Pig Knuckles," "Pig Butts," "Pig Loins," "Pig Snouts," and, in a galvanized tin in the far corner, a heap of triangular "Pig Ears."

Unable to read, I let my fingers drift over the merchandise, touching the smooth hunks of a hundred creatures from farms, forests, mountaintops, and veldts. I lift slimy slabs of liver and a mesh of lungs like thickened cotton candy and the pebbly tongues of kine lined up in mute complaint. Rafi could be in the next aisle, Noam brought in on a hook on the conveyor belt that resembles the "equipment" in Dregs' basement. We're just meat.

Lerner's is wonderful, because no matter how dear the deer, pork, and steer, philosophy is always on the house. Yet besides the dawn rush from the restaurateurs of Tel Aviv, I have the necropolis pretty much to myself. A few stoned teenagers with noplace else to go giggle unseriously and the usual array of psychotic late-night loners shuffle their feet and click their teeth. For them, it's Lerner's or the bus station news depot. But I only want to buy a few rashers of bacon for my table, and I know where to go.

Third aisle down and to the rear. I twitch Goldie's leash.

"We'll be out in a few minutes," I tell the driver, who waits at the door.

I lift up a few packages of recently packaged strips of pig flank and sniff, waiting for the one that wants me to purchase it and devour its contents. This is a minor personal ritual I perform whenever I've had an especially hard day at the office. Some go home and watch pornographic videos, some drink to excess, Simon and Serena screw on the office couch, and I go to Lerner's. Here, I know peace.

My mother must be able to identify the scent that rises from the griddle as the slices sear and sputter until they attain maximum juiciness, but she pretends ignorance. Whenever I cook pig, she doesn't even suggest soup from her endlessly boiling cauldron. Russians aren't known to be the most traditionally observant of Jews anyway, a problem for the religious parties who seek their votes while avoiding confrontation with their habits.

Once, this created a stir when Simon was presented with Chicken Kiev at a banquet celebrating new immigrants. He cut into the dish and a mini-geyser of telltale butter spouted forth. Of course, Simon was practically weaned on cheeseburgers at Jimmy's Corner in Harvard Square, but cameras didn't follow the undergraduate. "Nathan?" he hissed at me as I ate my own delicious dinner three seats away.

Tempted to let the glorious leader stew, I passed him the napkin I had already hastily scribbled upon the second I perceived the crisis. To eat or not to eat, that was the question.

No sane—or successful—politician ever refused to break bread with potential voters, but in Israel the dietary police are always ready to pounce on the slightest infraction of ancient customs. The Knesset cafeteria keeps a *moshciach* on staff and all state functions are rigorously monitored. Simon, reading my barely legible scrawl, announced, "Israeli margarine is the best in the world," and happily ate dinner.

When, later, it was determined that each serving of chicken contained no less than half a stick of melted butter, the meal had long since been digested and deposited into the bowl of the P.M.'s private toilet. Everyone makes mistakes.

In public, I eat as my boss; in private, I do as I wish. I lift the pig.

"Who's your rabbi?" A husky female voice speaks from the far side of the pork-stuffed steel rack.

Above me, luminescent blue bug zappers fry any stray flies that have managed to enter the premises through the swinging doors.

Lerner's lends itself to idiosyncrasy. People are always wandering the aisles muttering to themselves or their dinner, so I don't think much of the voice in the next aisle. I tuck the package of rashers under my arm like a briefcase and turn around. The taxi's meter is ticking.

"Is he righteous?" the woman asks a second question, although there hasn't been a reply to her first. She is alone and speaking directly through the rack, her voice just loud enough to roll over the gently rounded portions of meat and arrive in aisle three. She is talking to me.

I stop, ears—make that ear—on alert. Lerner's is the site of frequent demonstrations by the black hats against secular Israeli society, but the courts have ruled that the *boucherie* has a right to sell what it wishes as long as it's not illegal.

In the same ruling, however, the courts also declared that, because Lerner's is a public facility, anyone has a right to enter the store even if there is no intention of buying its legal fodder. Thus, for months Hasidim have patrolled the aisles, attempting to intimidate lapsed Jews into obeying religious laws by their presence.

"Is he powerful?"

But only Hasidic men have made the sacrifice necessary to step foot into the repugnant precinct. Am I the beneficiary of a new offensive by the women of valor? Do the same trucks that cart in dead cows set forth from Mea She'arim each dawn with teams of matriarchs as big as cows to keep the chosen people kosher? They probably wouldn't do that if they knew what I know about smells. Once they smell reindeer or walrus or pig, the molecules of forbidden meats also enter their mouths. Fortunately for their mission, unfortunately for their targets, the soldiers of God are as ignorant of science as most of Lerner's patrons are of deity.

"Is he good?"

I focus through the rack and smell goat, not the goat that lies humbly athwart aisle four together with mutton and other déclassé inhabitants of the barnyard, but the more glandular scent of skin. Either an animal has escaped the slaughterhouse unscathed or someone is wearing a vast, shape-blurring cape consisting of half a dozen hides sewn together. Hasidim don't wear such outfits and neither do secular Jews. I smell Arab.

And not just any Arab. The voice is too subtle and self-assured to belong to the hoi polloi that habituates Abdullah's Café, just as the garb is too outrageous to clad the sophisticated ambassadorial class that shops regularly at the *boucherie*. The tone is chic, the getup sheik.

And the questions themselves: Who is your rabbi? Is he righteous, powerful, good? Simply put, they are too complex to come from a fundamentalist of any faith. I might as well imagine Moshe X participating in a literary symposium on Oscar Wilde.

The voice stops asking questions. It starts humming a familiar melody in a warm contralto.

Freed from language, basking in music, I don't even notice that it is the Israeli national anthem wafting across the aisle like smoke until a moment later. Instead, I recognize the hummer, though she didn't sing in the Sheraton. "Hello," I greet Gita Mamoun.

"Fancy meeting you here, Mr. Kazakov."

"Likewise."

"Lerner's has the best kebabs in the Middle East."

"The world."

"The Middle East is the world."

It must be, if the only disguise a modern Arab woman can don is the costume of an older Arab man, just as Gabriel's version of Moshe X's mufti would be outrageous anyplace else. I ask, "Are you alone?"

"Several friends are watching me."

"That's not what I meant."

"Well, about a dozen closed-circuit cameras are making sure that you don't try to steal that package of pig."

"That's not what I meant, either."

"Did you make sure it has a rabbinical seal?"

She can't get over my culinary apostasy. Arabs, too, eschew pork. Here is another example of intra-Semitic cultural unity, if only the separate Semitic cultures would see it that way. I say, "The right rabbi can make anything kosher."

"So who's your rabbi?" She returns to her original question.

"Where's Gabriel?"

"He's safe, for now."

"Thanks to you."

"Is that a statement or a question?"

"Is that a statement in the form of a question?"

"Nicely phrased," she says, and I nod my head. I always appreciate anyone who appreciates my syntax.

She steps around the end of the aisle, where pure pork gives way to sausages. "Let's keep moving."

Whether Ms. Mamoun is suspicious or afraid that Lerner's eye in the sky will get suspicious I don't know, but I agree. It is always better to keep moving.

What a pair—or trio, if you count Goldie—we must make, but the *boucherie* is so idiosyncratic that it is just about the only place in Jerusalem where a deformed blind man and a woman dressed in Ayatollah drag won't draw attention. If Moshe X in gabardines and Ezekiel in leather chaps joined us, we could set up a folding table and play bridge—if the cards were Braille.

"So," she says, as if we are neighbors who just happened to bump into each other on normal shopperly rounds, "what do you know, Mr. Kazakov? Or should I say rather, what do you think you know?"

I pause to grope around on the racks, where several birds larger than chickens but smaller than geese or turkeys lie. Avoiding her question, I ask, "What's this?"

"Penguin."

"How much is it?"

"Eighteen-ninety-nine a pound."

"Probably tastes like chicken."

"Half the meat in here tastes like chicken. It's the universal flavor."

"Bacon doesn't taste like chicken."

"I wouldn't know."

We leave the birds, avoid the feline aisle out of consideration to Goldie, who would go crazy, and enter into the domain of beef. For all Lerner's exotica, the humble steer still pays most of the rent, and a ranch's worth of steaks from all over the world spread forth. Besides more common Israeli and American steaks, there are steaks from the pampas and milk-fed Japanese Kobi steaks as pricey as perfume. Gita picks up the latter and discusses its qualities, though it occurs to me that this might be a performance to illustrate her financial well-being. "What do you know?" I ask her the question she asked me.

Although we aren't going to get into an infantile, "You first. No, you first," argument, we continue our delicate dance like mating bowerbirds, displaying then hiding our colors. Finally, Gita Mamoun speaks, slowly, carefully. "I know, or think I know, that you have received information about me. I assume it is wrong. I also assume that you cannot be sure if it is wrong. That is why you can no longer trust me."

"Correct."

"And because you can no longer trust me, I can no longer trust you."

"Fair."

"And yet we both care about the same things." She speaks sympathetically.

"The problem is that we may care for different reasons and therefore desire different results."

"Stalemate."

"What's this?" I touch a package of meat set inside an oddly ridged container.

"Alligator."

"You sure it's not crocodile?"

"Yes, the crocodile's over here." She hands me a similar package. "From Egypt. International trade knows no enmity."

"And internecine rivalries know nothing else?"

"You draw quick and accurate conclusions, Mr. Kazakov. I see why the ben Levis trust you."

"Ben Levi . . . *s*?" I emphasize the plural.

"You are working for both of them, aren't you . . . in a way?"

"I suppose so."

"Perhaps you'd better make up your mind which you prefer."

"What do you mean?"

"There are multiple agendas at work. They are in conflict, between and among multiple constituencies. No two people involved in Strange Fire want the same thing."

"I don't even think any two people mean the same thing by Strange Fire."

"This is possible. I . . ." She stops talking as a large cart with a squeaky left wheel rolls down the aisle toward us. It is pushed by a muscular Palestinian worker who smells of overly sweetened morning coffee and baklava. "I just wanted to make contact. I have to leave." She sets off opposite to the approaching cart.

"Wait, you haven't told me anything specific." I hasten to catch up with her and bump into a display of tinned Pekingese.

"I can't tell you anything specific, because you wouldn't trust me."

"Are you saying that, because we've established that I can't trust you, I should now trust you?"

She stops for a moment and chuckles, a soft, enchanting gurgling from beneath her kaffiyeh, as if she finds great humor in the nearby array of veal chops and cutlets and chunks and scallopines. "That's too perverse."

"This whole thing is perverse. I don't get it. What has Gabriel done that he is in danger?"

"He was born."

Again she sets off, leaving me to mull over her simultaneously absolute and enigmatic reply. "Wait," I call again. "How did you know I was here?"

She turns in front of the entrance, a blur of gray costume against the blur of the swinging doors, says, "Enjoy breakfast," and disappears.

At home, I set the individual strips of bacon in mother's cast-iron frying pan, turn on the gas, and head toward my bedroom to change.

"Is that you, Nathan?" Mother asks as I tiptoe past the door to her room. She's got hearing like a B.P.

"Yes, Mama."

"Is everything okay, Nathan?"

"Yes, Mama."

"You're working so late. You should relax, get out and play a little."

I tilt in the direction of her bed. I smell talcum and a mineral ointment she smears across her face at night for her complexion. I wonder if the ointment comes from Beis Machpelah, but I don't ask. "Yes," I say. "I intend to relax once the election is over."

"How is Simon doing?"

"Well, the polls don't look so good, but he's a magician, and I think he'll pull it out in the end. He always does."

"I hope so."

"Why?" I am curious. Perhaps this one-woman survey might refute the polls.

"Well"—she turns on her side and exhales into a pillow which smells of the barnyard, its feathers probably plucked from the same birds that fill the aisle at Lerner's—"he's a strong man and this country needs a strong man." This is the ex-Russian speaking. Though Stalin shadowed her childhood like an evil cloud, she believes in the catechism of "leadership," an interesting synonym for dictatorship. Like most Russians, she fears that democracy will lead to anarchy, which seems worse to her than fascism. "And besides," she says, "what about your job?"

"You know, Mom, I'm not worried."

"I worry."

I hear the usual fretfulness in her voice, but take greater notice of it than I have for years. I've been so involved in the spurious glamour of my position, the splendid seediness of my encounters, the ironic and maudlin self-pity of my own little world, that I haven't realized that my mother has had her own life. I step into her room and sit on the edge of her lumpy mattress to stroke the hair she wears under a net to preserve its vitality. Who is she kidding? Her hair feels brittle; she's dyed it again, probably the color of precious metal, gold or silver. She's dyed it to keep from feeling like she's dying. If she wants to fool herself into believing she's still young, I won't be the one to disillusion her.

Thirty-some years ago, when young people were dancing in New York and London, when Israel was fighting its most ferocious battles against the assembled Arab world, when there were no such things as personal computers or videotapes, when the world was a different place, she lay alone in a dingy, disease-ridden Moscow hospital—think of Chekhov's Ward Six—to give birth to a boy-child whose father she would never see again. What an indignity: one season's romance in return for ten hours of labor and a lifetime of obligation.

On her night table a gilded picture frame sits propped against an alarm clock. If Rehov Rambam 448 was burning, this is what Mother would grab first. Perhaps I would, too. I feel the glass protecting the photograph that I used to stare at for hours.

Who was that young woman lolling against the rim of a rowboat afloat on the Moscow River, wearing a broad-brimmed straw bonnet? Where did she get the bonnet? Who was the young man who snapped the photograph and then took her to his apartment and removed the bonnet, unlaced its satin tie and the rest of her clothing? Was the fraction of a second when the camera shutter clicked the pivotal point in her life? Before that, she had a name; nine months later, she was just "mother."

Has the trade been worth it?

"Nathan," she sighs as I stroke her head.

"Yes?"

"Don't you think you should get married?"

I feel her eyes on me and reach down to feel what I remember as gray-green orbs set high in a Slavic plane of cheek. They're still wide and, to the shopkeepers of the world, vivacious, but her flesh is papery around the socket. I suppose that I received my narrow features from the invisible photographer. Oddly, she says, "What if I'm not here to protect you?"

Can anyone protect anyone else?

I think of Gabriel, whose father is the most powerful man in the country—actually the region, arguably between Rome and Hong Kong—yet spends every waking or sleeping moment at risk these days. If Simon can't protect him, how can I?

"Nathan?" Mother murmurs, allowing her eyes to close, allowing herself to dream.

What can I say? I try to think of women, from Serena Jacobi and Ellen Markowitz to Hannah, the soon-to-be café owner, to Gita Mamoun to a nice lesbian couple I occasionally drink to excess with. None are quite suitable, none, with the possible exception of Serena, quite what Mother dreams of for a daughter-in-law. Dreaming myself, I can't help but think of men, the innumerable men of my romantic history. I think of those I saw back in Russia and early in Israel when I was still worth being seen; I probably pass some of the latter and possibly the former on the street every once in a while and don't recognize them, although they probably recognize me. When I was rescued from Lebanon it was front-page news; years later, in the Lighthouse Library, I read the *Ma'ariv* edition for the blind. But I wasn't dating in those days, because I couldn't reconcile myself to my ugliness. The saving grace of my condition was that I couldn't see myself in the mirror.

Poetry was the problem. If truth was beauty and beauty truth, the ghastliness of my countenance meant that I could no longer connect with literature, either. Until then, I had regularly disported with friends on the "private" beaches south of Tel Aviv, after which we'd hit the discos of the city, where, after a few drinks, I'd recite my latest epic or my greatest hits—*Pomegranate Blossoms*—until it was late and I'd toddle home with some muscular paratrooper. But the world of buffed poetry lovers in camouflage was suddenly, absolutely, and forever closed to me, and I hadn't yet discovered the subculture of wart queens.

Then Simon saved me. I started writing again, if not art. Life turned around. I found Dregs, where I learned to appreciate the fat and hirsute, the scrawny and twitchy, the malformed and misbegotten, and love them for their flaws as they loved me for mine, as long as they were male. I think of those I caressed and was caressed by in Ezekiel's dark basement, which leads me inevitably to those I have met or merely come to know better than I wanted to in the last week.

Besides Noam, the thought of whom makes me cringe and rage, regret my actions and crave more, and Klein and Abdullah and Ezekiel, there are the journalists, arrogant Israeli Zev Schechter and dead American Chester Llewellyn, the settlers, Moshe X, Chaim, and the Avis. I imagine Avi Two in bed, pausing before penetrating to pray. Hasidim are known for kinkiness.

I think of the Yemenite atop a salty promontory, but he probably has a harem of veiled women waiting for him in a tent on the dunes, though Arabs, too, are known for their affection for boys. I think of Rafi, and then try to stop thinking of Rafi.

None of these are really my type. I think of Gabriel. Gabriel, like Keats, true and beautiful. Prince of the desert. I wonder if he's been sleeping with Gita Mamoun as they've slipped from one safe house to another. Safe from whom?

Strange Fire flashes through my mind like summer lightning, but I shun it. For one last, kind moment, I want to bask in thoughts of the flesh rather than its dangers. Yet none of these many males I've encountered, not even Gabriel, adhere. They, too, are as evanescent as lightning. With none can I construct a fantasy that might, for a second, satisfy myself, let alone Mother.

"Really," she says. "Think about it."

I've lost track of the conversation. "Think about what?"

"Marriage."

We all have our dreams, and they are equally ridiculous, but some are so absurd that . . . One more man jumps into my head. I think of Dmitri, big and big-hearted, smelling of tobacco and cheese.

I smile to myself as I consider telling Mother that I have "Good news and bad news. The good news is that I'm in love; the bad news is that it's a man." Or conversely: "The bad is news is that I'm in love with a man; the good news is that he's a doctor."

Instead, I say, "Go back to sleep," stroke her head one more time, and go into my room.

My clothes are stiff with sweat and tinged with the mildewy odor of Dregs and the meat of the boucherie. I peel them off and step into a shower. I turn the handle as far as it will go just as the phone rings. I step under the spout. Cold water pours off the top of my head and cascades past my broken ear and blistered shoulders and soaks into the bandage still wrapped about my burnt left foot. Still, I can hear the phone ringing. The hell with it. That's what answering machines are for.

Finally, reluctantly, I shut the spigot and feel for a towel. To suit me, Mother has learned to set everything in its place, so, though filthy, the apartment is impeccably organized. I wrap the towel around my waist and pad out to the telephone. I press the button to repeat the last message.

A gruff voice says, "Nathan, did you go to Jacob's yet? He called again. If . . ."

I don't recognize the voice at first and I don't know who Jacob is. Rather, I do recognize the voice, but have never heard it on a telephone or an answering machine.

Before the message concludes, I press the button again. This time, it is clearly Abdullah saying, "Nathan, did you go to Jacob's yet? He called again. If you haven't left, don't."

I press another button to listen to a previous message. "Nathan, this is Abdullah. Why the hell is your phone unlisted?"

"To avoid unnecessary calls," I answer the answering machine.

"Never mind," Abdullah continues.

"How did you get the number?" I wonder out loud.

"I had to call a friend with . . . connections," he says.

"Get to the point."

"Anyway, Jacob Twersky came in a little while after you left. We got to talking and I mentioned your mysterious 'Strange Fire.' He laughed at first, because he said it was so easy, but when I told him more about the reason you were concerned, he turned serious. He said you must contact him immediately. He wouldn't tell me anything else, but he said he would wait for you at his shop. Nathan, I've known

Twersky longer than I've known you. The man is capable of buying a two-thousand-year-old coin and waiting another two thousand years to sell it. I have never heard him use the word 'immediately' before. I do not know why I am helping, but I . . . suggest . . . you follow his advice. You know the address."

I listen to the entire thing again, without interrupting, and then listen to the follow-up. "Nathan, did you go to Jacob's yet? He called again. If you haven't left, don't."

Bacon. I smell burning bacon and run to the kitchen, bumping my shin on the coffee table in the intervening living room. Goldie yaps at my feet.

The kitchen is already filled with greasy pig smoke and I reach down, but yank my hand back at the last second, the first smart thing I've done in days. I turn off the gas and grope around for a pot holder to lift the cast-iron skillet. Even through the dense weave of cloth, the pan practically burns my hand. Quickly, I set it in the sink and turn on the water, and a geyser of steam mixes with the smoke.

When I am sure that none of the cabinets have caught fire and that the pan is safe to touch, I poke around in the simultaneously ashen and sodden residue. So much for breakfast. I tilt most of the oily, lukewarm water down the drain and set the skillet on the floor. "Here, girl." I offer Goldie the remains. "Someone might as well enjoy this, but hurry. As soon as I get dressed, we're going back into town."

# CHAPTER 19

By the time we leave—me starved, Goldie sated, both of us exhausted—the best way to travel is together with the morning's commuters. Since parking space is precious downtown, everyone, butchers, bankers, artsy-fartsy candlestick makers, takes some form of vehicle for hire, a descending scale from limousine to taxi to the modified vans called sheruts to the fumy public transport that departs at five-minute intervals from the palm-shaded corner of Rehov Grossman. Jerusalem is a vortex; it sucks people from the periphery to the center. Only as workers funnel into downtown do they exit in greater numbers than they enter, to disperse to their separate destinations.

Goldie and I don't bother to consider the alternatives. We climb aboard the first number four bus that arrives and wedge through the SRO crowd. I smell three-score riders who have eaten three-score different breakfasts. Some chat with friends from the neighborhood or the daily ride, some read newspapers folded as intricately as origami, and some retreat into a Zen trance. Briefcases and shopping bags jab into my side. Ten minutes after I hung up the towel beside my shower in Rehov Rambam, I am sweating.

Goldie yips at a fat woman who stepped on her tail.

"Here." A man who must have gotten on the bus in a distant suburb touches my arm to offer me his seat.

"No, thanks."

"Please." The only benefit to my benefactor's long commute is a guaranteed seat, so his politeness is begrudging but insistent. He stands up and slaps the covers of a book together.

"No, really."

"For the dog, then."

Goldie rubs against my knees.

The man, smaller than me, smells of rough detergent and clean clothes and shoeshine and metal. He shifts an object from one shoulder to another and it hits the plastic back of the seat in front of us. It is a gun, and he is a soldier. Giving me his seat is his duty. I wonder what he was reading: *Leaves of Grass* or an infantry manual.

"Thanks." In fact, my foot has started to throb again and I appreciate the seat. Hemmed in to left and right while the bus rattles around corners before stopping to squeeze yet more passengers into the jammed aisle, I realize that my destiny is to become the object of public charity—if I'm lucky. So much for the most famous blind person in Israel.

I have always taken comfort in the thought that although I am not a notably happy person, at least I'm not mundane, yet poetry is long gone from my life and so, too, soon enough, will politics. After Strange Fire is over, I might be able to wangle some civil service job, flacking for the sewage authority, but my days in the suites are numbered. I never left Rehov Rambam because I didn't want to, but now I won't be able to. I've been a captive my whole life, in Russia, in Lebanon, in my mother's house, in the P.M.'s office, and I always got used to it. Now I'll have to get used to the number four bus. It doesn't bother me. Actually, it seems honest.

The bus pulls up at the central depot and about half the passengers transfer to other lines. I stay put, because the Old City is the last stop on the number four. Goldie stretches out under my seat and I carefully stretch a leg into the aisle. Suddenly there is room in the vehicle, but people transferring from other buses promptly take up the slack. I tuck my foot back under the seat and rub my toe against Goldie's heaving midsection.

I don't know where I will go after I speak to Jacob Twersky, but I have been acting like a child working on a connect-the-dots drawing since I left the hospital. Ignoring Abdullah's warning, I now assume that the next dot will be visible from the last one.

The bus pulls into the Jaffa Road, which once served as the main connection between Tel Aviv and Jerusalem, but has been superseded by more modern highways. The next stop is the commercial district near Ben Yehuda Square, the next Town Hall, and then the end of the line. Traffic grows denser and a bicyclist angrily bangs the side of the bus under my window when the driver changes lanes.

We stop at a red light and a woman several seats in front of me says, "What's that?"

I don't know who she is talking to, but the atmosphere in the bus immediately turns electric. Conversations cease, and the standees in the front press toward the rear, preferably the rear door. Goldie stands, too, ready to charge, bolt, or die.

"What?" the driver, a Moroccan, calls nervously.

"Stop!" the woman cries. "There's a package."

That is all she has to say. The Pope and Barbra Streisand could have gotten on the bus at the depot and nobody would have blinked. We could have driven past the oldest temple or the newest concert hall in the world, and the passengers wouldn't have glanced up from their newspapers lest they be taken for tourists. After three thousand years of history, Jerusalem is the most jaded metropolis in the world. The ghosts of Babylonian, Roman, Crusader, Ottoman, British, and Arab invaders contend with Microsoft, McDonald's, and Sony on every corner. But all dangers and invaders, past and future, evaporate in the presence of the ultimate threat, a single untended package on a bus.

"Whose is that?"

Another woman frantically rephrases the question. "Does anyone know who brought that on?"

Nobody dares mention the *B* word, but a businessman with a cell phone puts in a call to the emergency operator and a girl across the aisle from me starts sobbing and a religious man in the front starts praying: "*Shma Yisroel,* Hear, O Israel."

We hear. We hear. The driver immediately pulls over to the side of the road, blocking a line of buses and cabs behind us. In seconds, police responding to the call divert traffic and clear the sidewalk. The rear door hisses open and people hastily descend the oversize risers. Nor do they stick around to rubberneck. Rubberneckers in Israel sometimes lose their heads.

"Everybody exit slowly, one by one. Don't push." The calm voice giving directions belongs to the soldier who gave me his seat. Soon he and I are the only ones left on the bus.

"Now you, sir. Here, I'll help you."

"No, I'll help you."

Before he can stop me, I walk to the front of the bus, reach down into the void that has been the center of attention, and find the package.

"Don't move!"

"Why, is there a scorpion here?" The soldier doesn't understand the reference as I hold out a plain paper shopping bag, standard supermarket issue, wrapped around with rough twine.

Goldie sniffs curiously.

"Sir, put that down, please." The soldier is paralyzed between conflicting imperatives. He doesn't know whether to jump me or jump for the door.

I'll admit, I worry. I've read the headlines; I've written the speeches that followed the headlines. But I, too, am feeling a tug in opposite directions, neither of which permits interruption. First, I am too comfortable to leave the bus, especially now that it's so quiet. Second, I have someplace to go. I unravel the twine and rip open the paper, the soldier ducks, and something large and round drops to the floor. The bus is parked on a curb, so the object rolls down a slight incline to the open door.

It hits the first step and doesn't explode, a good sign, hits the second step, ditto, and lands on the sidewalk with a liquid splat. There is a pause and then a dozen police in riot gear start laughing.

I reach into the bag and pull out a second melon that one of the early riders must have tucked under her seat and forgotten at the central depot. "Here." I toss it in the direction of the abashed soldier, who has risen from his hiding place.

He catches the melon.

I say, "Take it home to your mother."

He taps the end and I hear a solid thunk, a sure sign of ripeness.

After the police find him nervously sucking down an iced tea around the corner, the driver remounts the bus and takes his last three passengers—including Goldie—to Town Hall, where none of us depart, and thence to the Old City, Lion's Gate. The soldier is reporting for duty at the Western Wall, but he has already done a full day's work.

I can feel his hesitation as he allows the crazy B.P. to exit first, but as I touch the first step, he can't resist. He has to comment. "Excuse me?"

"Yes?"

"You shouldn't have done that."

I shrug. "What were the odds?" Indeed, what are the odds of any of this shit? How could Rubinstein's bullet shave off my ear without piercing my skull? What sort of fluke was that? Or that it would lead me, ipso facto, presto chango, gallakazam, from Hadassah Hospital to the Sheraton Hotel and off to the desert, the domain of Der Alter, where I'd be shot at by the Yemenite, in and out of Jerusalem like a yo-yo. What are the odds that a mild-mannered, blind speechwriter will end up in the middle of a conspiracy that he doesn't begin to understand?

On the other hand, what are the odds that a lonely adolescent homo from Moscow would end up halfway across the world, able to vote and sway votes, a participant, no matter how minorly, in the life of his times. I don't delude myself. The world would be different if Simon ben Levi hadn't been born, but Simon could have as many writers as Rice Krispies if he wanted. I have talent; Simon has genius. I am fungible; he is unique.

I tell myself that each individual is unique, but that's the kind of nonsense the early morning worshipers at the Western Wall believe. Jews or Christians or Moslems in the Mosque of El Aksa pray as one in the faint, ludicrous hope that God loves them for themselves. Priests from ancient Canaan to the current papacy, imamship, or chief rabbinate play the same old standards for the ears of their adherents. Even with one ear, I hear their siren plaint offering comfort and immortality in return for the smallest denial of reality. Believe and ye shall be saved.

No, thanks.

Only the priests are great, and their greatness is a direct result of the spell they cast upon the masses. As for those masses, screw them. If the bag of melons on the number four bus had been a bomb, and if the bomb had exploded, the riders of the number four bus would have been obliterated in the gross aggregate rather than as the sum of our particular, personal selves. The headline would read "THIRTY-TWO SLAIN!" and if you think the subhead might acknowledge "Author of *Pomegranate Blossoms* Among the Dead" you'd be wrong. No, that line would be reserved for "Prime Minister Ben Levi Vows Revenge," and my successor in the office two doors down from Simon's would write the text before Mother said Kaddish.

I am inside the warren of the Jewish Quarter by the time I finish composing my own obituary. To the left is a café that sells rancid salad dressing, to the right one of a hundred Jew-mongering souvenir stands, complete with everything from five-for-a-shekel postcards to three-dimensional portraits of the Old City made of different colored beans, lentils and limas and red and green beans, to taleysim woven with strands of genuine silver and gold threads. Judaism triumphant.

People who have lived in the Old City for decades supposedly get lost in its maze, but B.P.s don't have the luxury. We learn. I hup Goldie two turns to the left, another turn to the right, past the remains of the first Sephardic synagogue, until I arrive in a district where jumper-clad girls in pigtails play the same game of goomi that Natasha and Molly play on my doorstep and their brothers play soccer just like the Arab boys across town. Aside from childish recreation, however, these Jews' lives are devoted to God. The kids attend yeshivas, the mothers stay home, and the fathers spend their days in prayer and study. Of course, they're utterly impoverished, but these families live in flats expensively renovated by funds donated by Jews from America, so that they can fulfill a biblical mandate the donors themselves have long since abdicated.

The low buildings are all constructed of beige slabs of native stone and laid out along the impossible pathways determined by the random motions of donkeys dead for millennia. I turn right again and left on my way to the Cardo, a Roman avenue several layers beneath the present elevation of the city, excavated and renovated into a high-toned subterranean shopping mall. When the Cardo opened, the Jewish Quarter was still pretty grubby and tenants had to be enticed into its vaulted recesses, but over the years it's become one of the most desirable locations in the Old City, and the original risk-taking lease-holders have been proven wise. Beside a few clothing boutiques, a camera store, a branch of Steimatsky's Bookseller, and an Italian restaurant that lays out its antipasti in enticing display, is J. Twersky, Numismatics.

I think of Jacob as Goldie and I descend the smooth stone steps from street level to the underground arcade that surrounds a mosaicked reflecting pool and several truncated pillars. Born in south Jerusalem shortly after the War of Independence, the son of a rabbi who was the son and grandson of rabbis, he spent most of his youth gazing across the dusty no-man's-land of the Hinnom Valley to Mount Zion and the Jordanian-ruled Old City. But Jacob wasn't aware of the spell those ancient, untouchable turrets and ramparts cast upon him as he memorized entire tractates of Talmud. Then, in the spring of 1967, when the nation seemed threatened by Nasser and the assembled Arab world, Jacob shocked himself and his father by enlisting in the army. As a yeshiva student preordained for the rabbinate, he was eligible for release from military service, but, as he later put it, "I wanted to conquer."

"And so you did," Abdullah comments whenever Twersky tells his story. "Bastard."

"Look at the bright side." Twersky laughs. "If I didn't, we never would have met."

Lieutenant Twersky was in the first battalion to breach the walls that bounded his youth. Yet in fighting for the spiritual home of the Jews, a terrible thing happened to him; he lost his faith. He still wore tzitzis beneath his military uniform and a yarmulke beneath his helmet, but by the time the troops under his command clawed their way, block by block, building by building, casualty by casualty, across the uncharted labyrinth to the Western Wall, he discovered that he was suddenly unable to pray. Confronted with the holiest site in Judaism, he stood in the narrow alley later to be expanded into the vast plaza of today, and stared at the huge foundation stones, and discovered that he had conquered . . . what?

No longer at home in the Beis Midrash, neither was the massively decorated Captain Twersky at home in the army. He resigned his commission and took up a bachelor's life in a small house abandoned by its Arab owners. There, amid the rats and debris, prior to indoor plumbing and electricity, he found the real meaning of his life; it wasn't God that he loved, but Jerusalem.

He couldn't get enough of the place. He wandered obsessively until he knew every inch of it. He found archives that had moldered away in basements for centuries and he found objects. Way before sites like the Cardo were set upon by teams of archaeologists, he laid claim to eroded architectural ornaments and glassware that contained cooking oil when Jesus lived and still served Arab kitchens in the latter half of the twentieth century. One night, under a full moon, he wandered into an octagonal courtyard where a two-meter-tall statue of Venus reigned over a lesser cohort of Roman gods, intact. He hired a few Arab day laborers who had remained in the city because they had no place to flee to, and set them to carting the pantheon to his residence. Later, with pain, he sold the Venus to the Stuttgart Museum, and opened for business. J. Twersky, Antiquities.

By then, however, he had competition. Other dealers set up shop and laws were passed laying claim to the "heritage" on behalf of the state. Bulk became a problem, so Twersky looked for the most easily transportable objects of value. He was mulling over this question one day before the Yom Kippur War when he purchased a tube of toothpaste at an Arab store and was given a strange coin in change.

It was neither an Israeli shekel nor a Jordanian dinar nor any of the stray pennies or pence or lire or marks that filtered into the country through tourists' pockets. Slightly eroded, it still bore the likeness of a man wearing a laurel wreath and a barely legible inscription that read, "CASAR."

Instead of demanding proper currency in return for his banknote, Twersky asked the store's proprietor if he had any more curious coins. On the spot, he offered to exchange "new money for old."

Rare coins were to be had in those days by sifting through jars and brass carafes in the *souk*, which had not yet started selling mass-produced sandals and crockery and postcards. The inspired entrepreneur and amateur historian went to a print shop and ordered new business cards that said "J. Twersky, Numismatics" before he fully knew what the word meant.

Given up for an apostate by his religious father who declared him dead and sat shiva, Twersky never abandoned the learning he had imbibed along with the faith he could no longer abide. Indeed, Talmud served the new secular Jew well, because it taught him how to teach himself. Rather than matriculate at the growing Hebrew University, he immersed himself in autodidactic lore. He subscribed to coin dealers' magazines and attended coin dealers' conventions. Occasionally he purchased a forgery, and occasionally he sold a forgery—with or without knowledge has always been subject to debate—but over the decades he became the city's main authority on the currency of the ancient world.

Jacob operated privately until the space in the Cardo opened and he decided that a public presence was not a bad idea. The rent was cheap, and he loved the location. Most of his more serious business still took place abroad or haggling in his back room, but he enjoyed selling the more common denominations and less-than-mint editions over the counter. Customers off the street weren't experts, but he gave them credit for seeking out his shop rather than the tacky souvenir stands. He even appreciated the window shoppers and set up his premises as a mini-museum of Middle Eastern coinage, with framed and matted displays of all but his most valuable specimens, which remained in a safe built into the wall of the house he has lived in alone since '67.

The inside of Twersky's house is a mystery that I have never been honored enough to share. Rumors about it spread through the insular Jerusalem community, but I pay no attention. I assume that I am also the subject of rumors, most of which are true. I sometimes wonder if Twersky is gay, yet never bump into him in the various scenes I inhabit, high or low. We have a relationship based on banter, gossip, and argument about matters of mutual concern, as does he and Abdullah or me and Abdullah or any two locals. I like Jacob Twersky, but I don't flatter myself that I know him. He is private.

My fingers run over the entrances to Effervescent Fashions and the Jewish Quarter Florist and Cardo Camera until they arrive at J. Twersky, Numismatics' plate-glass facade. I open the door by means of a pull custom-welded out of a score of silver dollars, and a buzzer rings. I suppose that the pull is a joke that means, "American money welcome here."

The front room is an unoccupied six-by-four-meter rectangle, but Jacob never leaves the store unlocked, so I assume he is in the back room, going over accounts or doing business with a foreign buyer. I pace beside the window onto the Roman arcade and imagine centurions marching outside, boots clanging against the stone, buckles jangling, greaves whispering of imperial glory.

I lift a handful of coins Jacob keeps in a dish beside the door as gifts for children, twenty-year-old tinny agorot worth nothing after successive devaluations. Tomorrow's antiques? Maybe, but in giving them away, Jacob is doing his bit to inspire tomorrow's collectors.

I run my hand over the wood-trimmed glass display cases inside of which lay somewhat more valuable coins, mostly Roman and Phoenician, but also British and continental. Once, when Jacob invited me back to the store to continue an especially vigorous discussion about tax policy over tea and cookies, he handed me a heavy Spanish silver doubloon worth a hundred times its mineral weight. Twersky's is an international trade, though he specializes in the native produce.

A nasty shock jumps through my skin.

There is a crack in the glass.

My finger throbs with the splinter that would have been invisible even if I could see.

I rub the ball of my thumb carefully over the crack, which extends the width of the case. At first I worry that someone has entered the store before me, punched a hole in the glass, and fled with a handful of coins, but the plate remains firmly in place despite the crack. This is odd. Twersky is a neat man and keeps his premises immaculate.

"Hello?" I call.

No response.

I step around the counter and feel a crunching underfoot. I bend down to feel the shattered remains of a clay pot. Besides coins, Jacob has a few old jugs and amphoras for atmosphere.

The door to the back room is open. The flow of air tells me the bad news before I enter. I smell shit. I remember that particular shit from Lebanon. It isn't incontinence or diarrhea, but the voiding of the bowels that occurs at moments of extreme trauma.

Goldie whines; she doesn't want to enter.

"Stay," I say.

Someone was alive in the room not long ago. Beneath the rank fecal aroma, a soft tobacco odor infuses the enclosed space. Perhaps that is another form of death, but I seek its comfort and desperately yearn to light up.

I slide my feet forward across an Oriental rug, expecting the obstacle I almost immediately encounter. I bend down and feel the back of a head. Wiry short hair, Jacob Twersky's.

No surprise whatsoever, but to make absolutely positive, I reach under the face crushed into the expensive carpet. I feel Jacob's familiar mustache and wire-framed glasses, but something is wrong with his features. The musculature is taut, bloated. His mouth is stretched open so wide that his upper and lower lips have cracked where they meet, like a pane of plate glass.

"I'm sorry, Jacob," I murmur. It is obvious. Whoever killed the coin dealer has done so to keep him from speaking to me.

Touching lower, searching for a bullet hole or a knife wound, for more information though every piece of information I find seems to lead to another death, I feel a curious scarf wound twice around Twersky's neck before it disappears beneath his collar like an ascot. Unlike an ascot, it is made of a thin and shabby fabric at odds with this dapper man's usual style, and knotted once at the nape of his neck tight enough to cut the flesh and cut off air. I pull the end loose and feel the fringes. Twersky has been strangled with the sign of a faith he doesn't share, tzitzis.

Suddenly I feel a violent craving to leave: this room, this city, this country. It isn't fear, but repulsion. The dead do that, more so than the deformed. From Adam's son, Abel, to Yitzhak Rabin to Jacob Twersky, the first story of the first tribe is murder. Maybe there's something in the Mideastern air that creates a culture where killing is the automatic response to conflict.

And yet all of those murders involve sacrifice, too. Abel's literally, Rabin's politically, and Twersky's personally. The coin dealer knew he was in danger; that's why he asked Abdullah to make a second phone call, to warn me away, to protect me.

But I came anyway, and I have to find whatever it is that Twersky had to tell me. I go through the dead man's pockets and find several slips of paper, none of which have holes punched in them to spell out a message for the blind. I grope further and discover a coin on the floor next to his head and another coin and yet more scattered across the carpet, as if he were a child playing with a collection when he was interrupted and strangled.

Coins are reliquaries of renown. So Jacob once told me. Before lithographs, before oil paint, coins were the method by which kings and emperors sent their image into mass distribution. That's how we know what Alexander the Great looked like. Statues were for temples in population centers, but every inhabitant of a realm kept the ruler's image in a leather bag attached to the waist. Later, of course, coins became avatars of nations, a daily reminder of the state's ability to define value clanking in the citizenry's pockets.

One of Twersky's hands is bent upward toward his neck, trying ineffectively to loosen the deadly knot, the other stretched outward, under his elegant credenza. I follow the direction his stiffened limbs lead. Centimeters beyond his fingertips, the leg of the credenza ends in a carved lion's paw. My mind races. Jacob in the lion's den. Was his reach a last futile attempt to escape or was he reaching for something in particular?

I feel along the dead man's arm; it is bent slightly at the elbow, as if he could have reached a tiny bit farther, or did and retreated. I feel behind the smooth surface of the paw and find a coin that must have rolled there when Twersky was confronted, assaulted. But next to the first coin, I discover something unusual, a number of coins, thin cylinder atop thin cylinder, painstakingly stacked in a tiny leaning tower. Coins are strewn randomly across the rest of the private office, but they are arranged neatly here.

I crawl around the body that will soon be replaced by a chalk outline. I want to examine the coins that have—by accident or on purpose—withstood the whirlwind in the rest of the office.

Placing my palms flat on the rug, I sweep slowly in from the corners so as not to disturb the coins' placement. Perhaps they form a pattern. Beside the single coin and the tower of coins, I find a third, shorter pile. There are fourteen coins in all, one and then ten and then three. What their origin or denomination is I don't know, though Twersky would have. And if he was writing a message in the midst of his death throes, his chosen implement might be the coin. Also, he wouldn't have been able to get to his desk and pick up a pen while literally expiring on the floor. Just in case I am wrong, I lift the coins and clutch them in my palm in the order in which they were laid out, but I am certain that it is the numbers that matter.

One. Ten. Three. The first letter of the Hebrew alphabet is aleph, the tenth yud, and the third gimel. They spell nothing.

One. Ten. Three. It isn't a phone number, though perhaps it is half of a phone number. 011 is the code for an international operator. What might three represent? It doesn't make a difference. If I know a country, that hardly limits the possibilities. What would I do, call France? Besides, Jacob Twersky was an exacting man. 1103 is not the same thing as 011.

One. Ten. Three. What about an address? I could probably get a clerk in the Interior Ministry to track it down. There can't be thousands of 1103s in Israel.

But Twersky told Abdullah it was "easy." He knew the answer to the riddle of Strange Fire immediately. Unless 1103 is as significant as 10 Downing Street or 1600 Pennsylvania Avenue, he would not have laughed.

The late Jacob Twersky knew three subjects as well as he knew his name, three domains he could scan more swiftly than a computer search engine. They represent the three portions of his brutally abbreviated life. There are coins themselves, the city of Jerusalem, and Jewish sacred texts.

Strange Fire probably does not involve Twersky's professional career. That's too arcane. He would not have denigrated his secret lore by laughing and deeming it "easy." Tentatively eliminating numismatics, this leaves Twersky's latter two areas of expertise, the city his passion, the texts his inheritance. Most likely it is the former, but an address is not a great deal of help. So what if there was a famous fire at a 1103 street address? I've already learned from Noam Abravanel that Strange Fire is destined to occur in the tunnel excavated less than a kilometer from the Cardo.

I think about police codes for different crimes or a reference to municipal statutes, but draw blanks. I wonder if some treaty enacted at U.N. Session 1103 relates to nuclear disarmament, but I can't think of anything and neither is there any reason Twersky should have had such knowledge.

What about Talmud? What if the key to the mystery is in that third, mystical/religious realm? Twersky last attended yeshiva decades ago, yet the precocious memorizer of tractates would never forget a lesson. Remembering one, he might even laugh. For all I really know, he might have taken it seriously. As ostensibly secular a pig-eater as myself, the coin dealer wore tzitzis, God help him. It is even possible that he maintained the faith of his forefathers in that lonely house that his biological father, the rabbi who mourned his theological death, never entered. I imagine a secret altar to an ungiving God.

When I first arrived in the Holy Land, I took a course in Judaism conducted by a scrawny-chinned rabbi-in-training hired by the immigration authority, but most of the wisdom Reb Shashlik—that's what we called him—imparted to his class of Russian immigrants pertained to the laws of Shabbes and Kashrus. As long as we refrained from turning on lights on Friday night and eating pork, we had mastered the essentials. As for text, zip. The only Jewish numbers that come to me are forty days and forty nights or twelve tribes. One ten three is meaningless.

But I have sources. I stand over Jacob's body and am sitting at Jacob's desk, a last violation of privacy or a last imposition on friendship, about to use Jacob's telephone to make a call to a friend at the university, when a buzzer rings.

I hear footsteps and curse the fact that I have forgotten to shut the door to the office. Anyone glancing in this direction from the cracked display case would immediately notice the coin dealer's body. If I try to intercept that view, I will draw attention to it.

The buzzer rings again. Either the first person has left or a second person has entered.

The buzzer rings again. Either a third person has entered or one of the first two has left.

I move quickly, take four swift steps, leave the office, and pull the door closed behind me. "Hello?"

"Hello," a Yiddish accent replies.

There is only one person in the room. "Was someone here with you?"

"No, I mean yes, a man poked his head in for a second." I smell shoe leather, old clothes, half-digested brisket, and cherry soda, an Orthodox Jew. I feel his gaze. He is suspicious, then curious. "Where's Yakov?"

"He's . . . unavailable. He asked me to tend the store for a while. May I help you?"

"I'm Katz. We had an appointment."

"Yes, he mentioned that."

"I'll just wait in his office."

I stand my ground and improvise. "I'm sorry," I say, "I don't know who you are."

"I told you, I'm Katz. Besides, I don't know who you are, either."

"Were you looking for the third century coins?" I don't have the faintest idea what I am saying, but it sounds right.

"No."

"Well, that must have been someone else." And then, pretending that everything in this abnormal situation is absolutely normal, I pick up the phone at the counter and dial—not my friend at the university, but a number that the unaccountable customer has placed in my mind. It's funny how the brain works. Instead of calling a secular academic from my own world, the smell of brisket has led to me to call a kibbutz.

"Beis Machpelah," the receptionist answers.

"Der . . ." I don't want to give away too much to the genuine customer who walks around the room, humming ostentatiously. People often hum or tap their feet around me, as if they feel some need to signify their presence. "Moshe, please," I request.

"Who is speaking?" the operator asks.

"Nathan Kazakov," I say, aware that Katz is listening. If he is a customer, then it doesn't make a difference, and if he is following me, then he already knows my name. What about the second man who entered and left? I still clutch the roll of fourteen coins in my right palm.

"A minute, please." the operator says.

"Can you tell him I was here? Katz. He'll know what it's about."

"Sure." A lot of good it would do.

Luckily he leaves before Der Alter picks up the line. "Where are you?"

"Back in Jerusalem."

"We didn't know if you made it."

"I made it," I say, too aware that Jacob Twersky has not. "And yourself?"

"A flesh wound."

"All wounds are flesh wounds."

"No, there are wounds to the soul, too, but you did not call to discuss incorporeal things. You have a question."

"Yes."

"Ask."

"One. Ten. Three. What do those numbers mean . . . to a Jew?"

"You are a Jew, Mr. Kazakov."

"To a knowledgeable Jew. Do they have any special significance?"

He thinks and then replies, "They could refer to a *parsha* from the Torah."

I feel the same tingling I did in the cave. "What *parsha* would that be?"

He knows this without looking it up. It's easy. "One, the first book of the Bible, Genesis. Ten, Noah. The third verse would probably be the generations after the flood. Noah lived three hundred and fifty years once he landed at Ararat. Verse one: He begat Shem, Ham, and Yefet. Verse two: And Yefet begat Gomer and Magog, Madia, Yavan and Tuval, Meshekh and Tiras. Finally, verse three: And Gomer begat Ashkenaz, Rifat, and Togarma."

"That's it?" I feel a huge disappointment.

"You can look it up." Moshe X is terse. Though enjoying showing off, he wants to get off the phone. Whether he knows that I disbelieve in his Bible and his uranium or whether he has found out that I am an abomination or whether whatever he wanted from me at the Dead Sea has ceased to matter, he is disgusted. I am a Jonah, a jinx, who hardly knows that I am a Jew.

"Well . . ."

"Are you sure that you have the numbers in the correct order?"

I face the closed door to the room in which Jacob Twersky lies dead on the floor, his hands outstretched to write his last message in the coins that were as essential to him as language. But I am reading in Braille, a universal language, like English, from left to right, One Ten Three, and Twersky was writing in Hebrew, from right to left, Three Ten One. The answer is inside my clenched fist, which contains coins that might have been three-dimensional letters. Trembling, I say, "The third book is Leviticus, right?"

"Yes."

"And chapter ten, verse one?"

"Look it up, bright boy. It's Strange Fire."

# CHAPTER 20

A hand lands on my burnt shoulder as I leave J. Twersky, Numismatics, and the pain flares up.

I spin around and slam my fist full of coins into the blur of a face in front of me with all the rage that has been building in me. I am tired of people popping up and dragging me to one place after another, tired of cryptic tidings that baffle more than they enlighten, tired of death and just plain tired. "This is for Jacob." I feel like screaming. "For Jacob and Rafi and endangered Gabriel, for Ezekiel whom I forced to abandon his moral stature, for Dmitri whom I abandoned."

Damn, it's Dmitri; I try to pull my punch as I revolve, but the momentum is too great, and my fist connects with his bearded chin.

Coins burst out of my fingers like a flock of pigeons from a shattered coop. They fly all over the Cardo, between a display of backpacks and under a rack of magazines outside the bookstore, into the fountain for good luck.

The doctor reels backward and stumbles into one of the Roman columns that had lain buried under the city for two thousand years.

I hear a crack, but nothing more. The column stands, and so does the doctor. My hand hurts like hell.

Rubbing his cheek, he says, "Not bad for a poet."

Pathetically, I apologize. "I'm sorry."

"Sorry that you have an unaccountably potent right hand?" He hasn't noticed the coins.

"Sorry that I used it."

"Never mind. I shouldn't have surprised you."

"That's no excuse."

"I said never mind. I'll just eat liquids for a week. Lose some weight."

I can't help but grin at his attitude. Suddenly I'm not tired anymore. "Here." I extend my hand in peace.

He grasps it and I nearly faint.

Goldie growls when she perceives my pain. "Down, girl," I command. "It's all right."

"Let's take a look at that hand."

This time I extend it like a wounded paw.

He takes the hand with a gentleness that I didn't know he had in him, holding the smaller limb like a bird and massaging the different sections, murmuring professionally, "Tell me if it hurts."

"No, no, ow."

"It's swelling already. I'd say you have two, possibly three broken knuckles. Shall we return to the hospital?"

"No."

"How did I guess you'd say that? For the most accident-prone patient I've ever had, you have an extreme reluctance to treatment."

"I have to find a bookstore." Of course, there's a store within spitting distance, but I'm so crazed and my hand aches so much that it doesn't occur to me.

Dmitri thinks about insisting, realizes the futility, and offers a compromise. "First a hospital, then a bookstore."

I don't have much choice with a hand that feels like a pecan after an encounter with a nutcracker. We set off and Dmitri asks, "What do you have such an intense craving to read?"

I am about to tell him when I grow suspicious again. Dr. Dmitri is the person who entered Jacob Twersky's shop after the genuine customer, Katz, but how do I know that he didn't enter it before as well? Before Twersky was murdered. "How did you find me?"

"I listened to your messages."

"You—"

"I told you to call me, and you didn't, so I spoke to your mother again. She told me about the messages, told me how to access them from my phone—"

"She doesn't know a thing about technology."

"You'd be surprised what that woman knows, Nathan. But that's another story. I called back, listened in, recognized Abdullah's voice, paid him a visit, got this address."

"Why did you leave as soon as you entered?"

"What is this, a cross-examination?"

"Why did you leave as soon as you entered?"

"You really want to know?"

"Yes."

"Because my controller from the Chinese secret service called me with an emergency delivery of missile fuel. Why do you think? Because I was hungry."

"Hungry?"

"I had a sandwich at the deli around the corner. Roast beef, if you've got to know. Mustard and mayonnaise. Hold the lettuce. Or can't you smell it?"

Everything about this man makes me laugh. For a second I forget where I am and what I'm doing and that my hand is broken, my foot burnt, my shoulder sun-poisoned, my ear obliterated, and my eyes . . . well, they're ancient history. "Okay. But afterward—"

"I know. I know. We have to go somewhere."

Off to the hospital for the last time. Dmitri pulls rank at the emergency entrance and we return to the cubicle back on the fourth floor that I occupied so comfortably a few days ago. Home, sweet home. The doctor takes care of his bruised chin and injects me with as much painkiller as a fountain pen contains ink. "Enough," I say.

"Not really, but I suppose it will have to do."

"Okay. Now to—"

"Are you—"

"I'm sure."

"Daddy!" a familiar voice calls from down the hall. It's good to know that some things never change.

"Daddy!"

I think about my former neighbor, the ancient Daddy-seeking Sonny. He can probably see, and the rest of his senses are probably all right, too. When judgment goes first, it's a blessing. If I didn't know what I couldn't do, I wouldn't mind. If I could scramble time and bring Akiva, Jonathan, David, and Platoon Sergeant Herzberg back from Lebanon along with the more dispersed recently deceased, Rafi and Twersky, and even Chester Llewellyn, I'd forfeit sanity in a second. Jeez, there are a lot of them. I know as many dead people as I do living, but Sonny only knows one. "Daddy!" he calls again.

"Poor sap," I mutter, yet something in Room 404's expression is different than his previous ramblings. I know intonation as well as most people know color. The dying old man isn't calling into the void anymore.

"Eh," an impossibly older voice replies.

"Who's that?" I ask the doctor.

"Who's who?"

"Eh," I imitate the voice he must hear, but before Dmitri can reply, I know. Unless, like Room 404, I, too, am losing my mental faculties. It can't be true.

"It's his father," Dmitri says, thinking nothing of it.

And I nearly break down. Whatever 404 lacks in the way of ambulatory, circulatory, and respiratory systems, and whatever my abundance of creative, intellectual, auditory, and olfactory capacities, he still has the one thing I'll never have, a father.

Fuck.

Filled with codeine for which Dmitri writes a prescription on the spot, I let him splint my hand and wrap it in an Ace bandage that reminds me of tefillin, which reminds me of tzitzis, all the ritual apparatus of a faith that emerged from a single book written by or delivered to the only people who could read it thousands of years ago. "Back to the Old City," I say. "We've got to find a Bible."

Dmitri puts a hand on my elbow worriedly.

"No, I haven't found religion, although perhaps religion has found me. Twersky, the coin dealer, he left a message for me . . . before he died. . . ."

The doctor's grip stiffens.

I admit, "Back there, yes. I found him strangled."

"You're sure?" he asks, and answers his own question. "Yes, you're sure." The doctor has witnessed—and tended—the wounds each stage of my search has left on my body, but he still doesn't know what I am searching for besides the elusive Strange Fire. After the wild goose chase for Simon's private reading material, I sent him home, and wouldn't blame him for thinking that the whole plot is my delusion.

Yes, I filled him in on the general background, but I withheld the details. Now I have no choice. I tell him that Noam told me that Strange Fire will occur in the tunnel under the Western Wall and that Twersky's final clue will reveal what Strange Fire is.

"Why did he tell you?"

"Because he was a friend."

"Not Twersky. Abravanel. Him, I met. He wasn't a friend."

"No."

"So why did he tell you?"

"Because I'm a bastard."

"Hmm." He thinks, and asks one more question. "Is he alive?"

"I'm a bastard, not a killer."

"Good, let's find a Bible."

We could return to the small bookshop next to Twersky's, but I want to keep as far away from the Cardo as possible. By now, the body might have been discovered. By now, Katz might have told the police about a blind man who shouldn't have been there. By now, the half of the city that isn't looking for Gabriel might be looking for me.

Dmitri commandeers an ambulance, which drives us back to the Jaffa Gate. Fine. It's the only form of transportation I haven't taken besides the P.M.'s jet. We enter the Armenian Quarter and walk past restaurants broiling rows of kebab for the lunch hour and tile manufactories that smell of ceramic dust and the Church of St. James from which orisons slip out the open door along with a scent that paralyzes me with foreboding.

"Nathan?"

"Let's go in."

"But—"

"They'll have a Bible," I justify my irrational desire, already halfway up the rounded stone steps.

Inside is cool, and the particular scent that compelled me is stronger and mixed with other scents, those of dripping wax tapers and elderly Greek women who remind me of my mother.

The priests' chant from an apse in front of the church rises to a higher pitch, then higher still. Organ music flows down from a loft above our heads. Goldie leads me up the central aisle, and Dmitri follows a pace behind. The scent floats in the crepuscular air, stronger now, then weaker, coming in waves. The priest must be swinging a censor filled with a burning substance half spice, half citrus. I nearly swoon onto a nearby bench, and Dmitri sits next to me.

"Read," I command.

He takes a Bible from a shelf built into the bench in front of us and flips pages. During our walk, I had described the coins Jacob Twersky built into a message while dying, so Dmitri knows where to look for Three Ten One. "Book three, Leviticus," he recites.

"The Jews are in the Sinai after escaping from Egypt." I set the scene, not sure how I know this. Yet so far my knowledge is far from esoteric.

"Chapter ten," he whispers. " 'And Nadab and Abihu, the sons of Aaron—' "

"The high priest," I say, as the priest of the church takes a lectern and reads something in a language I don't understand, either Greek or Latin, though he is Russian Orthodox. I can tell from the great black tent shape that looms higher than any normal human being; he wears robes and a miter.

Before Dmitri continues, I think back to a day a quarter of a century ago, when I was bouncing a ball on the street several blocks from the communal flat where mother and I lived at the time. There was a church on the street that had been converted into a "youth center." It was open to all good Soviet children who wished to learn the Marxist/Leninist catechism, yet I had never entered the structure, superstitiously afraid of the dome that remained from its previous incarnation and more so of the cemetery attached to the church. Its mossy tombs were starting to break apart from ailanthus trees that grew between their stones, and local childhood legend had it that ghosts escaped through the cracks. The ball took an unexpectedly high bounce and flew over the rusted wrought-iron fence that surrounded the graveyard.

I could see the pink rubber sphere in a pile of dead leaves heaped beside a tombstone by the not-very-careful caretaker, a short, wizened gnome who frightened all of the neighborhood children when he left the premises to buy vodka. I found a stick and reached through the fence, rustling the leaves, poking the ball toward freedom.

A rake slapped down on my wrist, imprinting seven tiny marks that remain even today, and pressed my hand into the mulch. I looked through the wrought-iron bars of the fence and up into the gleaming eyes of the caretaker.

Before I could scream, another figure appeared, in a black outfit similar to the one that the priest in the Armenian church in Jerusalem wears. An apparition out of the cemetery, he scared me more than the caretaker, but he spoke in a kindly voice and said, "Leave him alone, Artemyi. It's just a boy."

"Boys," the caretaker hissed. "Nasty boys."

I must have been seven, and churches must have still been outlawed by communist edicts, but perhaps Glasnost had already lessened the force of the edicts, or perhaps my savior was a renegade priest in a renegade church, risking as much as I would risk years later when I read poetry in the back rooms of the Arbat. He said, "What are you doing here, my son?"

"Playing ball," I answered truthfully.

"But this is holy ground. You shouldn't play ball on holy ground."

"It was a mistake, Father. I meant to play here, on the street." My wrist ached under the pinions of the rake.

"Would you like to come in here, my son?" he asked.

I should have said yes, but I hadn't yet learned how to lie. Again, I answered as honestly as I could. "I can't, Father."

"Why not, my son?"

"Because I'm Jewish." I hardly knew what that meant other than that I couldn't enter a church, even if it pretended to be a youth center, but Mother had inculcated certain lessons in me, and that one stuck.

"A Jew," he said, thought, and ordered the caretaker, "Cut off his wrist."

The rake rose, I pulled my arm free, the rake fell, and I ran.

Dmitri continues, " ' . . . the sons of Aaron, took each of them his censor . . .' "

A chill goes up my spine.

" ' . . . and put fire therein, and laid incense thereon . . .' You know this, don't you?"

"No, I swear it," I croak. "Keep going."

" ' . . . and laid incense thereon, and offered Strange Fire before the Lord, which He had not commanded them.' "

"Yes?"

"That's it. Verse one. That's all there is, but there's a note at the bottom."

"What does it say?"

Dmitri reads the commentary silently and summarizes its contents. It identifies Aaron and Aaron's sons and various Temple rituals, which, apparently, did not include Strange Fire. Nadab and Abihu's Strange Fire may have been their own private worship and it may have been as mundane as alcohol. Perhaps Aaron's sons were having a party. And what were the consequences? "Verse two," I whisper, dreading and expecting exactly what I receive.

Dmitri reads, " 'And there came forth fire from before the Lord, and devoured them, and they died before the Lord.' "

That's it. Gabriel ben Levi, the son of the priest—substitute Prime Minister—was afraid of being smitten on behalf of the divine imperative. He, not I, was, of course, the target of Rubinstein's gun, while the settler himself was merely the pistol finger of the Lord.

But who is the Lord who pressed Rubinstein's button, pulled Rubinstein's trigger? Obviously, it's Der Alter, Moshe X, the lunatic American rabbi who thinks it is his personal mission to redeem the Holy Land. How this mission became a vendetta against Gabriel ben Levi, I don't know, and frankly don't care, though it probably has to do with an archaeological find, perhaps at the cave by the Dead Sea. Why people do what they do has always been less important to me than what they do, and Der Alter is obviously intending to try again, this time more effectively, at the tunnel. He brought me to the Dead Sea with that bullshit story about uranium to determine what I knew and send me off in an entirely wrong direction. He was tense on the telephone, because it became clear that through luck, pluck, or intuition I was back on track and closing in. Perhaps it was that same intuition that led me to call the master of Strange Fire himself to inquire about Strange Fire.

I can see—almost literally—why Gabriel chose this passage to reveal his anxiety. Like a rabbi or a former rabbinical student turned coin dealer, an archaeologist dedicated to unearthing the stones of the Bible would know that Bible as well as he knew its stones. The name Strange Fire was a cry for help, but why didn't Gabriel simply tell his father and throw himself into the protective cocoon of Shin Bet? I mull this over as the Orthodox priest descends from his platform and leads a procession of acolytes down the aisle.

That's when I understand that Gabriel is frightened of more than one rabbi. Despite his thundering oratory, Moshe X proved incompetent in his first choice of an assassin and not much better in our encounter with the Yemenite at the Dead Sea. Yet someone managed to slice off an Arab boy's head without leaving a drop of blood and cut off the air to a very determined coin dealer's brain. That final someone has to be Cyril Klein, who, with the help of Noam Abravanel, would have intercepted any attempt at communication from son to father. Again, the motive is unclear, but this alliance between secular-British and religious-Brooklyn Jews means that Gabriel can't trust anyone on the Israeli side of the green line. That's why he sought out Gita Mamoun. An Arab was the only refuge the son of the Israeli Prime Minister had.

Correction: an Arab and a blind, half-deaf, half-crippled, failed poet.

Gabriel can trust me because, well, who wouldn't? This whole drama is what Ms. Mamoun tried to reveal in Lerner's Boucherie when she taunted me by asking, "Is your rabbi good?" She understood that I had to discover the answer to the mystery for myself or I wouldn't believe it, either.

Now that I know what the play is about and, thanks to Noam, where the stage is set, I am desperate to find out when the curtain is due to rise. I decide to head for the tunnel, but before that, I ask Dmitri to read further in chapter ten of Leviticus. I want to know what happens next.

After killing his own high priest's sons with only a comma's delay, God tells Moses to inform the bereaved father, " 'I will be sanctified . . . I will be glorified.' " What a guy! What a story!

"Glorified and sanctified may His great Name be," go the words of the Kaddish, which Aaron presumably recited three times a day for the next eleven months. I wonder if the prayer for the dead has its origins in this passage. God tells Aaron the priest and, by extrapolation, the people: I kill your loved ones, and you proclaim my glory. I kill you, and those who loved you proclaim my glory. You don't stand a chance.

Gabriel ben Levi, however, stands a chance of avoiding this horribly human form of Strange Fire. I've heard enough, and had enough of the Jewish God. I reach out and shut the book resting in Dmitri's lap. Tempted for a moment to let my fingers linger, I don't. Instead, I stand and follow the priest and the cadre of singing acolytes of a merciful God out into the street.

# CHAPTER 21

The young IDF guard at the entry to the tunnel off the plaza in front of the Western Wall doesn't even remove my ID from the plastic sheath inside my wallet. Instead, he appears more concerned with my blindness than with any security precautions. "Are you sure you wish to go here, sir?"

"No," I snort, answering more honestly than the question requires. In fact, I am quite sure that I do not *wish* to go here. "But I will." From the second I left the Armenian church, I knew that this was the destination that has been pulling me across Israel since a bullet nearly killed me in Tel Aviv. Each step northward, back into the Jewish Quarter, each step along the winding Ha Shalshelet market as crowded with natives, tourists, and pilgrims as the number four bus was with commuters, each step toward the Wall has brought me closer to the heart of the mystery. I am as volitionless as an iron filing drawn to a magnet.

"Please wait just a minute, sir," the guard says, and retreats to a phone box next to the Wall itself.

Beyond him, the crows of God are praying to their Lord, "Glorified and sanctified be His name," while a guide is making the usual suggestion that his group write letters to God and tuck them into the cracks of the Wall. As the story goes, an anonymous Israeli soldier placed the first letter in a crack shortly after the Old City was liberated, and the custom took hold. Nowadays, every crevice in the wall is jammed with communications from supplicants to their respective deities. From a distance, the white dots give it a Pointillist image. Pointless, if you ask me. I wonder whose job it is to winnow those cracks to make room for new prayers and pleas. Does that person read the letters?

"This way, please." The deferential guard leads Dmitri, Goldie, and me through an alcove where yet another minyan has gathered. I hear a rattle of keys on a chain by his belt. He unlocks a gate and we enter an anteroom that must have served as a miniature archaeological museum for visitors until the entire installation was shut down because of the protests from Arabs who feared the literal undermining of the Dome of the Rock. I run my hands over glass cases similar to those in Jacob Twersky's shop. They probably have some coins, too, along with the usual shards of pottery and a coroded dagger or primitive atom bomb and sepia photographs chronicling the tunnel's discovery and excavation.

"The lights are on." The guard speaks to Dmitri while staring at me. I can tell by the direction. "Is there anything else you'll need?"

"Luck," I answer.

"I . . . I didn't mean . . ." He doesn't finish the sentence. Staring is a social taboo people are often able to violate with impunity with a B.P., but if you point it out they stammer and lie.

Dmitri and I stand together at a large opening from which a faint breeze whistles upward. Wind currents are curious in tunnels. They have no ostensible source, yet find their way in—like water seeping through rocks—and then out. I step forward and think that two men and a dog should only be so fortunate.

We descend a long sloping ramp lit by humming fluorescents set into the new construction, but once we touch ancient grade level, the earth turns rough, and bare incandescent bulbs hang from the ceiling directly above our heads. I guess that this was designed to lend a frisson of the past to those present-day tourists who were expected to flock to this "attraction" until it was shut down for good.

At this point we are several meters beneath Jerusalem, probably at the spot where the Jewish Quarter meets the Moslem Quarter, moving westward with the Wall above, which is not, as most people think, the actual wall of the Holy Temple, but rather the enclosure within which the more finely wrought house of worship was erected and destroyed.

"I don't like this," Dmitri says.

"Neither does Goldie," I reply. Usually she can hardly wait to move forward, cross the next street, sniff the next hydrant. Now her leash is slack. If I let her go and shout, "Run," she'll immediately turn back.

"Good girl." Dmitri bends to pet her soft head. "Smart girl. Smarter than your master, aren't you?"

"Look, we're just investigating. We still don't know when Strange Fire is going to happen. Until then, it's better to have the lay of the land. Besides, if you don't like it, you can go home." I tug Goldie's leash and keep walking.

I say this, but the truth is I don't like the situation, either. I distrust the place and the ease of our entry. Also, I don't think we are alone. One-eared, I still have the hearing of ten men, and detect human sounds ahead. How far ahead, I can't tell, because sounds, like winds, carry oddly in tubes. I focus on these details to avoid thinking about where I am, but my level of anxiety is mounting. I've avoided tunnels since Lebanon.

I touch the wall. The recentness of its excavation is evident and palpably unlike the dust-thickened caverns underneath Tel Arnon. Small comfort. I am, no matter how benignly I try to frame it, buried.

"Okay," Dmitri says. "In for a centimeter, in for a kilometer."

I am grateful for his loyalty and for his weighty, friendly presence.

We continue forward, coming across thick timbers that support the walls at apparently random intervals. Once, there is an anomalous curve in the path, but Goldie angles me rightward just as Dmitri starts to suggest the same. Instead, he comments, "This should lead under the Wall."

"That's what the Arabs fear," I say, and explain some of the politics that affect the tunnel. Visible usurpations of property are bad enough; the invisible brings forth all sorts of atavistic suspicions. I know.

Then the path turns left and again we trek parallel to the Wall.

"Wait," Dmitri says, and we stop.

"Yes?"

"Do you hear something?"

I've heard it with increasing clarity for ten minutes. "Voices."

"Whose?"

"I don't know."

"How far ahead?"

"Not far."

"Should we turn around?"

Obviously we *should* turn around, but I won't. I can't. Why? I tell myself again that I don't care about motives, that actions are all that matters, that I am behaving well, perhaps for the first time since I alit on holy soil, certainly since I gave up poetizing, which, if it wasn't a necessarily worthy activity, wasn't baneful, either.

Innumerable childhood memories have come unbidden to me this week, and though I recognized places and events, I didn't recognize the memories' protagonist. Or perhaps I didn't recognize the man that boy has become. I've lived the last half dozen years in, yes, blind certainty that life is a Darwinian struggle in which I am determined to be the fittest. This doesn't make me a particularly pleasant person, and I wouldn't have it any other way, because reality is a stronger principal than imagination. Yet this week I have acted against self-interest. 'Tis a far, far better thing, et cetera. That provides its own satisfaction. Why?

Initially, it was the least self-interested of emotions that must have led me on: love. Not mature love, but adolescent infatuation. How ludicrous. If I expect a grateful Gabriel ben Levi to leap into my arms and cradle and cuddle me forever, I deserve to be crushed.

I think of soldiers, not the olive-drab IDF forces who hold the line against rock-throwing teenagers, but Roman legions or the crimson-clad creators of the British Empire or the coonskin-capped American patriots who brought down that empire. I think of spies and astronauts and Arctic explorers. Maybe it bespeaks the frivolousness of my nature that I think of the vicious whirlpool of Strange Fire in such romantically adventurous terms, but I can't help it. Horrible to say, but I am having fun. It makes me small and young, and almost able to see.

And then there is the other motive, the one that can never be discounted as a foundation for actions noble and base; I'm curious. "Let's see who's there."

Way before we arrive at the juncture where the tunnel intersects several lesser tunnels in a kind of underground plaza, I know who will be waiting for us. Rather, I know the larger group this smaller group must be drawn from. If the tunnel is the set and the cast of characters has expanded with each act, the time has come to block them out before the show. But why now? How did I happen to wander into the theater at the curtain? It couldn't be mere luck, good or ill, and I am still too much of a realist to ascribe my random timing to a Samarran date with destiny. Unless this is a rehearsal—it must be, because Gabriel, the hero, is still in the wings—it's as if the assembled players have been gathered on the dimly lit stage forever, frozen, just waiting for the audience. Me?

My feet drag as I continue to walk with the pace of a prisoner on the path to judgment on my own personal—or maybe, since, like Christ, Jerusalem has risen in the last two thousand years, the original—Via Dolorosa.

Station One Ten Three. All aboard for Strange Fire.

The ground turns dusty here, approaching the crossroads, and the wind more brisk. The lights strung from cabling attached to the roof of the tunnel flicker. Goldie barks. The voices cease.

We take another twenty steps into the arena. Noam Abravanel, who didn't have time to change clothes, stands out, stinking of last night's fear-generated sweat and Dregs's beer-drenched atmosphere, but beside him stands Serena Jacobi, so redolent of perfume it practically defines her shape. The usual phalanx of flacks and gofers fill in the background. I swivel from left to right, trying to make out the odorless presence of Cyril Klein, the villain.

Serena welcomes me. "Nathan, you look . . . awful."

"I'm sure that you look splendid, Serena."

"Actually not. This place is filthy and it's ruining my clothes." I hear static as she rubs her hands down her hips.

"That's what dry cleaners are for."

"We've been waiting for you."

"Apparently."

"But we are waiting for one more person, and then we can begin."

Dmitri speaks with his usual brusqueness. "Begin what?"

"Dr. Tatarsky." Serena knows his name. "We didn't expect you to accompany Nathan, but of course you are welcome, too."

"Begin what?" he repeats.

"The killing," she says calmly.

Here's Simon, underground. I certainly can't see him and haven't been able to see anything, not a shape, not a color, not a blur, since we entered this subterranean nightmare, and I didn't notice his subtle eau de cologne at first, but of course the Prime Minister must be present, too—this is a command performance and he's the commander-in-chief—yet he hasn't said a word and doesn't now as several members of his private security force march forward and neatly tie my and Dmitri's hands behind our backs and arrange gags under our chins so they can silence us on a moment's notice.

"May I ask a few questions?"

"Anything you wish," Serena replies. She is the perfect hostess. A blind foreigner who overheard us without understanding Hebrew would have thought he was at a tea party. I feel like throwing up.

"My right hand is broken and it hurts. Would you mind tying it in front?"

Eli Khadoury, Klein's alter ego, murmurs urgently, deeming this concession unwise.

Simon breaks his silence. "I don't think that Nathan will do anyone any harm. Retie him more comfortably. Also his friend. There is no reason to inflict any unnecessary pain."

Even though I didn't write these words, they are used accurately. Politicians learn to avoid imprecision, unless of course they prefer vagueness in a given situation, and then they might as well be hummingbirds. This situation, however, does not require delicacy. I ask, "What pain is it necessary to inflict, Simon?"

"I assume it will be momentary."

Simon's reluctance to divulge what is going to happen is a faint signal of humanity from a man who disappeared into his own image years ago. I am already prepared to hear, but I am determined to make him say it so that *he* can hear it, too. "What will be momentary, Simon?"

"Don't answer," a whisper pierces the space. Klein is beside the exit.

"Simon, I don't know what they told you, but these people are planning to kill Gabriel. That's what all of this is about. Gabriel, your son," I speak as fast as I can, fearing the gag. "Gabriel was the one that Rubinstein was trying to shoot. That's why Klein was so eager to find him. Gabriel's in danger if I'm . . . killed." I choke out the horrible word that Serena said as smoothly as, "Aperitif?" and go on and on, repeating the name Gabriel like a mantra, until I exhaust myself, and there is stillness. Ignorantly, I think that the worst is over.

But I can't see the response to my last-minute peroration.

Sadly, Dr. Tatarsky, whose last name I didn't use until this evening, whose real first name I didn't use until I had already dragged him into the quicksand, takes it upon himself to convey the bad news. It's a skill doctors learn in medical school. "He knows that, Nathan."

"What?" I am still too stupid to recognize the final truth as it stares into my blank eyes.

"We don't work independently," Noam says curtly.

"You just follow orders," Dmitri declares.

Noam steps forward and punches him in the face.

Dmitri spits weakly, and a tiny object clinks on the floor—a tooth. He turns in my direction. "Your punch was better."

From under my restraints, I wiggle my bandaged right hand. "When you punch, you have to be willing to hurt yourself. That's Noam's problem. He's only willing to hurt others."

The executive assistant lunges at me, but Klein swoops out of the corner like a hawk and restrains him.

Yet Klein isn't the primary decision maker here. He, too, follows orders, and I still can't reconcile myself to the ultimate fact that Simon himself has given those orders. "Tell me. There's no reason you shouldn't tell me. Tell me, goddamn you."

Simon leaves the safety of his entourage and steps forward until he is standing close enough for me to feel his breath. Usually scented, it is rank with intestinal ferment. This gives me hope. Perhaps there is an element of uncertainty to his determination, a last residue of decency that can make him change his mind.

"I'll tell him," Serena says.

"I want Simon to tell me."

"What *you* want," Klein interrupts, "is irrelevant." He and Serena are the human armor the P.M. wears to protect himself from having to confront himself.

"It started with the election," Serena explains calmly.

"The election?" I repeat dumbly.

"You've heard of it," Noam sneers.

They are a team within the team that I was once a part of. But though I was trusted with words and trusted with ideas, I wasn't trusted with strategy. Deluded about my position, I have been on the outside of a magic circle within the inner circle. I recall hush-hush meetings to which I wasn't invited, private conversations that halted the moment I walked into the room. I thought it was just that they hated me, were making dinner arrangements that excluded me, and I didn't give it a second thought. I had my own world.

"The polls were bad. The polls don't lie."

"As opposed to the pols."

"Play with words while you can, Nathan. That's always been your problem."

"And his virtue," Simon admits.

"Thank you," I say.

"I'll miss you," he replies.

"We had more important things in mind," Serena continues. "If something didn't happen, we were going to lose. We examined previous elections, especially '96 when Netanyahu beat Peres by a single percentage point. Peres was a political dud who shouldn't have stood a chance, but the reason he came so close was because of Rabin's assassination earlier that year. The sympathy vote. We needed that vote. At first we considered staging an assassination attempt on Simon, but unless we could find a willing martyr who understood that his mission was to fail . . ."

"And people smart enough to understand strategy are seldom stupid enough to sacrifice themselves for it."

"Right. We needed a genuine believer."

"Whom Mr. Klein conveniently found at Beis Machpelah," I supply the rest as I recall the blur of energy in Tel Aviv. The would-be assassin under the Hasidic overcoat probably felt the exact same passion as the boy who stalked me in Lebanon. Back home, we took great pride in the dramatic extravagance of the Russian soul, but everyone in this part of the world is clearly insane. "Rubinstein, whom Mr. Klein himself enabled to slip through Mr. Klein's own security net. I wondered how he got into the pressroom."

"Yes. But we still couldn't be positive that the attempt would fail. So we decided on an actual assassination. As Peres, not quite sufficiently to win the election, reaped the benefit of Rabin's death, so Simon would reap the benefit of—"

"Gabriel's."

"Remember, the right wing was voting for Simon no matter what. But if the incumbent's son was killed by a settler, there would be such an outpouring of sympathy that even left-wingers would vote for Simon, too, or enough of them to effect the result."

"So you told the rabbi that Gabriel had made some discovery, was violating some ancient cemetery, or something like that."

"Something like that. It doesn't make a difference."

"And you told Gabriel that his father was in danger and that he had to appear at the press conference in Tel Aviv."

"Something like that."

Still missing the main point, I follow the sequence of events as coldly as chess moves. "Unfortunately, Rubinstein failed anyway."

"There's the irony. If we could have known that, we would have set him on Simon after all. An ear is a small thing to lose."

"For an election."

"For an election," Serena repeats blissfully.

"You were ready to kill an innocent man for an election. In fact, you did kill an innocent man, Rubinstein in the ambulance."

"Coronary occlusion," Noam says. "Convenient but true."

I thought I was cynical, but these people had me beat from the start. I turn away from the spot where Serena and Klein are practically licking their lips over the elegance of the scheme that went awry. Compared to them, I'm a poet.

If not for Rubinstein's bad aim, it would have worked perfectly. After all, everything in Israel comes down to fathers and sons. Abraham and Isaac, David and Absalom. Ben-Gurion as the father of his country. Not accidentally, the only woman we've ever had as a leader looked more like George Washington than Marilyn Monroe. I can imagine the padonna, Simon, cradling his dying son. I can imagine the speeches that I would have written for the rest of the campaign, after an appropriate mourning period. I'd have had half of Israel grieving with the Prime Minister. They'd have staggered sobbing into the ballot booths with one name on their mind, the same name of the martyr and his father: ben Levi.

And then a more awful thought occurs to me. Why didn't they invite me to participate? Wouldn't I, after a token wrestling match with my conscience, have joined the jolly murder brigade? Were they able to tell that I didn't have it in me, that I was weak or—worse—moral in a manner that I would have laughed at two weeks ago?

"For an election," I repeat with as much disgust as I can bring to the word that is the grail of everyone in this horizontal coffin. Directly above us sits the most spiritual spot in the monotheistic world and here we are. "You . . ." I aim the empty machine gun sockets of my eyes directly at Simon. "You were going to kill your own flesh and blood for an election."

"No," he says quietly.

"No?" I repeat incredulously.

"I was going to do it for the country. This is a critical moment in Israel's history. Weiner would make an untenable peace with the Arabs. The entire nation would suffer." His voice rises with every false justification, until, probably tearing on cue for imaginary cameras, he concludes, "I had to do it."

"Simon, do me a last favor."

"What?" His voice is so somber, so sincere, so round and soft, he sounds like a parish priest.

"Spare me the bullshit. Don't spare me, but don't give me that crap. I spent years writing it, and I know what it means. It means crap." I relapse into vulgarity. No other words will do. "You're a fucking killer, a parricide, for your own personal, individual, uniquely selfish . . ." I am losing my own words, and end ineloquently, redundantly. "Self."

"Think of it that way if you must. That's why we didn't invite you," he answers my earlier, unspoken question. "Because you don't believe in anything, Nathan. But we all make sacrifices."

Even now he has the gall to tell me that I am inferior to him because I wouldn't help him murder his son. And still, still, all I think about are the practical effects of the plot. I take sadistic pleasure in pointing out, "But your sacrifice didn't work. Your pawn hit the wrong guy."

"Actually"—Serena takes the floor in her roll as pollster—"we got a nice bounce immediately after you were wounded, and for a day or two we thought the plan worked after all, but the momentum started to slow almost immediately."

"The speechwriter wasn't the son. I didn't hold the sympathy vote."

"Unfortunately."

"So, pack it up. Strange Fire's over."

"You still don't understand, Nathan." Simon is determined to convince this most difficult audience. "It was at that point that Strange Fire began. Cyril, tell him."

Klein hesitates, then starts. "Somehow, Gabriel found out, or guessed what really happened in Tel Aviv. He gave it the name Strange Fire, told that to Moshe X, who told it to you, which gave us a much better idea."

"Us?"

"Me," he acknowledges modestly.

"You're a fucking maniac."

"No, I'm a fucking genius. Gabriel didn't understand what his little biblical reference meant. For him, it was just a clever, intellectual clue to draw attention to his predicament. The son of the leader in danger. But if you know your Torah you know that the real center of the story is the violation of the sanctuary that brings down the wrath of God. Therein lies Plan B. You see, or rather you don't," he taunts me, "that while you came into the tunnel from that end, witnessed by hundreds of people, we came in from the other end, unseen."

I think of the relentless drilling sounds Abdullah heard under his café.

"And"—Klein just has to gloat—"we have a bomb, which will explode in approximately fifteen minutes, blowing up several of the holiest sites in Islam. Of course, the Arabs have been insinuating that this was going to happen for years, and there may be a short war, which will perforce unite the country under one banner."

"And you plan to blame it on me."

"No, that's the real genius. We plan to blame it on Gabriel."

"Why?"

"Because ben Levi the younger is a liberal. The left won't be able to touch this, because it will have been caused by one of their own."

"There's only one problem, genius."

"What's that?"

"He's not here."

"Wait a minute," he says, and I swear I see the gleam in his eye. "Gag him."

Despite my gloomy surroundings, I might as well be in the desert. I smell salt and sand and a flower I can't identify. I smell the dung of a herd of Bedouin goats. I hear the overlapping footsteps of two people who have slept—together?—on the earth under the sky. I smell Gabriel ben Levi and Gita Mamoun and try to warn them, but the gag across my mouth holds tight.

"At last," Noam Abravanel says as the last actors enter the grotto.

Three security men click the safeties off their guns.

"What?" Gabriel says.

Simon walks across the opening and embraces his son. I hear his hand pat Gabriel's shoulder.

Serena Jacobi's fingernails click impatiently.

Simon steps back to behold the son he hasn't seen since he sentenced him to death.

I struggle to speak.

Simon must nod in my direction, because a thick hand belonging to one of the guards unknots my gag. Mouth freed, however, I say nothing. I have lost track of when the plan about to conclude here began and can't imagine how it will end, but I continue to occupy individual moments without reference to their predecessors or successors.

Gita Mamoun asks, "May I leave?"

Serena says, "A deal is a deal."

A deal? I spiral down the repercussions of this small exchange. The two women have hardly said more than half a dozen words, but they reveal a world of complicity. I can imagine the days after Rubinstein's bullet, when everyone was searching for Gabriel ben Levi while I mended in the Smolinsky Wing of Hadassah Hospital. Distrusting anyone connected with the government, Gabriel, through Rafi, sought and thought he found refuge in a hotel suite that was really a snake pit. But he was smart enough to distrust his penthouse haven, and he approached me when I was released. Everyone in this grotto besides Gabriel and me and Dmitri knows that.

But if Simon hopes to win an election over his son's corpse, what does Gita Mamoun want?

And who made the first overture? Mamoun or Jacobi, it doesn't make a difference. I picture them sipping vodka martinis in the lobby of the King David Hotel, the two most sophisticated women in Jerusalem designing a plan for their mutual betterment no matter the cost.

Silently, I marvel at the extent of the conspiracy, the intricacy of its parts, and the willingness of its participants to sacrifice on its behalf. Simon anted his son and Gita Mamoun checked with her beloved nephew. They were just bodies on the table, dead soldiers tossed into battle to serve their respective masters. Even Noam had sacrificed himself by taking my drugs, enduring my torture, and lying.

Rather, he told me what he wanted me to know, the location of Strange Fire. He could have told me without the torture, but that would have been too easy. I might have become suspicious. But it was all easy. Jacob Twersky knew the origin and real meaning of Strange Fire, and that's exactly why they allowed me go to him. And if the coin dealer hadn't been able to reveal enough to set me in motion, the plotters would have had some alternative way of informing me ready to go. For all I know, Klein was clever enough to erect the little stacks of coins after he killed Twersky. He would have enjoyed that.

I've been tracked from the moment I first left Hadassah Hospital. When Gabriel ben Levi approached me in his Hasidic costume, they knew that I was the key to his capture if I was manipulated properly. Moshe X and the settlers were called in from one side, the Yemenite from the other, pawns all. Perhaps the German tourist who drove me from the Dead Sea was really Shin Bet, perhaps the soldier on the number four bus was planted for my sake, or perhaps the driver. They kept me alive and teased me forward with tidbit after tidbit of information, because I was the one who had to betray Gabriel, because I was the only one he really trusted, because I had nearly been killed. They told me everything but the hour, because that was the nastiest trick of all. There was no divine clock; there was a human clock, me.

I thought I was the smartest person in Israel when I was really the stupidest.

Gita Mamoun kept Gabriel ready until I gave the inadvertent signal by entering into the plaza. "We were watching you from a house overlooking the Wall," she admits. "Only when you entered the tunnel did Gabriel believe that it was safe to enter." Then everyone else converged. The bomb had been waiting, and Simon was never more than ten minutes from readiness. I, the speechwriter and fuse, am speechless.

Dmitri, whose gag must have been removed at the same time as mine, comments, "*Et tu,* Mamoun." I am glad that he can summon wit in the situation.

"I don't believe that we've been properly introduced. Dr. Tatarsky?"

"You presume correctly. But Nathan has told me all about you."

"As I learned that you were involved. I hear that you are an excellent surgeon. Too bad."

"Why?"

"Because your medical skills will soon be much in demand . . . when . . ."

"When the War begins," Serena finishes her coplotter's sentence.

"That's why we're here. Mr. Klein, did you bring . . ." She omits the end of the sentence, an Arabic locution that allows for interpretation.

"Of course," he says heartily, and signals to one of his thugs. I hear an unlatching and feel a wave of nauseating coolness infiltrate the chamber as a trunk is opened and a sacklike object hits the floor. The container is a refrigerated Igloo meant to carry a half dozen six-packs to the beach, but it holds the missing body of Rafi. When Gabriel is found together with an Arab at the site of the explosion, everyone will have someone to blame, and the war they all want will begin.

"You're—" Dmitri starts.

"Please don't say 'crazy,' " Gita Mamoun cuts him off.

Serena Jacobi continues, as if they are two halves of the same personality, "It's so clichéd, and besides, you're not a psychiatrist."

Dmitri must remember what I told him that Zev Schechter told me, and asks Gita Mamoun, "Is it money?"

"Of course, tremendous sums will be made. The armaments alone will mean billions of profits. But money is only part of it."

"Please, then, enlighten me," Dmitri requests in his thickest Russian accent.

He is playing for time and they know it, but can't resist. Like most criminals, this obscene gang takes so much pleasure in their plans that they have to tell someone. Of course, that someone must never have the opportunity to tell anyone else. Ms. Mamoun describes the future she envisions with a clairvoyant trill. "And even more money will come with the rebuilding of a Palestine that stretches from the Jordan to the sea."

At last it dawns on me. Besides being a mercenary, she is a patriot. All of them, settlers, terrorists, politicians, journalists, have been driven mad by living in this sun-boiled sliver of land that all of them believe God has given to them alone.

And so, the only sane one in the crypt, I find my voice. "You expect to win?" Israel has a vast superiority over Palestine and the Arab nations in terms of tanks and planes. We also have the pilots and commandos who know how to use those weapons, and backing it all up, we have my specialty, moral propaganda. Israel, the only democracy in the Middle East. Israel, the noble; Israel, the good. I could write the script right now. Israel, the homeland of the Jews. Israel, redemption of the Holocaust. We have everything, and they have rocks.

Still, Gita Mamoun is ready to fight. The depth of hatred from this most liberal of Arabs astonishes me.

Klein speaks freely now that we are discussing strategy rather than ideology. "Of course, contrary to Ms. Mamoun's hopes, we will win, but this may be the last moment the Arabs can put up a decent fight. Dissent between the left and right, between the religious and the secular, between hawks and doves, has weakened Israel within. Likewise, we've squandered our moral capital without. The United States is fed up with us. Europe won't come to our rescue, except for Germany, which has no choice and no army. Unlike '67, we cannot expect help from the rest of the world. We'll have to win this ourselves, and the cost will be grave."

So, Mamoun's lunacy has a meager rationale, but why, then, if we are bound to grow stronger and the territories' temporary boundaries more permanent, would anyone on the green side of the line help her? In fact, Klein is more than helping; he's writing the Arabs' battle plans. "I don't understand."

"Of course you don't," he gloats. The man hasn't had so much fun since the summer he spent as a double agent in Damascus. Gita Mamoun suffers over her idealism and makes an evil accommodation on behalf of a presumed greater good, but Klein loves the accommodation itself, the pageant and the ruin, the blood and the flames. "Only if the war to come entails pain will it produce the desired results. Another six-day wonder would secure the region temporarily, but there would be even more refugees, which would re-create the scenario that has proved so debilitating for the last half century. Only a truly devastating war, one which they almost win, one with casualties, will secure the future. Only if our backs are to the sea can we use the weapons we have."

"Nukes," Dmitri says.

Klein ignores him and contemplates a forest of mushroom clouds with bliss. That's the Strange Fire he adores. In a way, Moshe X is right. There is uranium in Israel; it isn't to be found in a cave, but on a missile base with this devil just waiting to press the button. "Only then can we obliterate them entirely. It is a risk that both sides are willing to take, because this is the blink in time—a blink that you won't see, not . . ." he adds with malicious gratuity, "that you could have anyway, when a final victory can be attained by either side. Only then can we arrive at the final goal."

"An election?" I say dully, still way behind the curve.

"Not an election," Simon speaks up. He has listened to all the explanations and justifications like a zombie. "A title."

Stuck in silly, literary vocabulary, I can only think of *Pomegranate Blossoms*.

It takes Serena to complete the picture. "After Rubinstein failed and I met with Gita, we saw the real possibilities—thanks to Cyril. As far as she is concerned, war is her people's last chance for sovereignty. Of course, she's wrong, and we'll kill her."

Goldie, perceiving the tone of ominous threat, growls and crouches.

Gita Mamoun laughs at the dog's protectiveness and says, "And if she's wrong, we will certainly return the favor."

"But for us, it's Israel's last chance for a truly, ultimately, eternally unified Holy Land, not under elections. Democracy is a frail system that allows people like Weiner to mess up the works. No, we need to return to the days of glory. We need to return to the Bible, whose ways we have abandoned. We need—"

I can see the end coming, the end of logic and the end of my life and life as I know it, and am stunned. So is Dmitri. Both of us are silent. Gabriel says one word, "Father."

"He may be your father." Serena barely conceals her jealously. "But after the war to end all wars, he will be—"

I announce the horrifying truth. "King Simon."

Klein says, "Set the timer."

# CHAPTER 22

"Timer" is the last distinct word I hear. A buzzing in my good ear and filtering through the bandage over my bad ear grows so intense that I feel like I am standing amid a swarm of bees. Instinctively, I cringe, and feel Cyril Klein exhale with pleasure. Heat, not smoke, emerges from his nostrils and fills the vault.

My skin prickles and my throat muscles tauten. I am burning.

My sight long gone, my hearing recently departed, my faculty for smell dwindling, I am senseless. Bereft.

I am suffocating in an oven with a timer that has started counting down to my demise. I may already be dead, except for the brute anatomical instinct that keeps animals breathing until they stop.

And yet the tableau surrounding me and Dmitri and Gabriel and a headless Arab boy remains vivid. The two women anchor the portrait like pillars, while between them stand Cyril Klein, Noam Abravanel, and the presumptive King of the Jews, Simon ben Levi.

Four paths diverge from this central gathering place, two of which end in the open in opposite quarters of Jerusalem, the other two of which . . . don't.

I flash back to the dead-ends of Tel Arnon, and return in a blink to the moment. In a few moments, the only ones left on this underground altar will be the sacrifices to the God of War.

But someone has to remove our handcuffs first, because the offerings can't be bound.

Khadoury, Klein's henchman, lifts a creaking timber and says, "Will this do?"

Klein considers and says, "Yes."

Of course—they'll kill us first and remove the handcuffs later. We'll be found under tons of rubble, three with skulls staved in by the medieval buildings that tumbled into the ancient chasm where the Old City met the Temple, another decapitated by a stray blade of glass that thought it was a guillotine.

But Khadoury pauses. Perhaps his boss wants us to beg, like the cripples and cancer patients who send their letters to God via Western Wall express. Still, I won't give Klein the satisfaction, and neither, apparently, will Dmitri, the doctor resigned to death, nor Gabriel, who has spent his entire short life in search of dead cities.

Gita Mamoun backs off and Serena ushers Simon into the mouth of one of the tunnels. The king doesn't need to see the consequences of his ascension, but he lingers nonetheless. Maybe he's curious.

As for me, curiosity is finally beside the point. I don't care why this is happening, don't care who is doing it. For a moment, I don't even particularly care that I am about to die, yet it bothers me that I haven't accomplished my goal. If Strange Fire was a genuine secret I uncovered, I might have made my peace with the poisoned fruits of forbidden knowledge. But the notion that all my enterprise, all my intelligence—how I admired myself despite all evidence to the contrary—is predestined to serve Cyril Klein's purposes is galling. I try to remember how I started; it wasn't merely an intellectual puzzle or an adventurous game. For once in this life, I wanted to do good in the world. I intended to save the beautiful archaeologist. I guess I hoped to save myself, too. It's been years since I wanted to live, but I want to now, to spite them.

I also want to live to quit my job and write one more volume of bad poetry, drink too much and wake up in a stranger's bed, eat my mother's gruesomely overcooked chicken. I want to live to feed Goldie and bump into mailboxes. It isn't much, but that's what I want.

Goldie! They haven't cuffed Goldie's lovely, unclipped paws or muzzled her ferocious German mouth. Unlike Serena Jacobi and Gita Mamoun, my bitch was bred to be gentle, but like them, she will do anything for those she loves. If provoked, she will attack.

The lights blink. I can tell. I am a connoisseur of darkness. I know the nuances and variations of black as well as most people do the difference between bud and Kelly green or blushing pink and crimson. Actually, I can distinguish between shades of black better than between green and red. I know the texture and the flavor of obscurity.

"Hurry."

Tick, tick, tick. I have all the time in the world. The bomb is set to detonate in ten minutes, but ten minutes from now is the infinitely distant future.

Gita Mamoun has started backing away. Simon is lost in his own fog, half science fiction, half biblical prophecy, and Klein is a stone. Of all the people in the vault, one is vulnerable.

Summoning my wits, I call out, "Noam."

"Here," he answers like a schoolboy at his desk. Noam must have been a good student. He learned multiplication tables and murder with equal facility. He has his goals, too, namely my office and a pat on the head from Cyril Klein. He has mastered the present with an eye to the future, but I will crucify him on the past.

"You know you really had me fooled last night, Noam. Say, did you tell Cyril what you did for the cause? Cyril, did Noam tell you about our night together?"

As I link word to word, I realize that I am composing the most important speech of my life, but unlike my other speeches on sewage and foreign trade, I have to deliver this one without the benefit of Simon's powerful voice, so I pull out every oratorical stop. Commencing with the intimate vernacular to establish a connection with my audience, I shift to a rhetorical mode. It is a device I've used before. You set the agenda by putting the questions that you intend to answer inside your listeners' heads.

"That Noam." I laugh heartily, just telling stories. "He took a big one straight up the ass, and then, get this, he tried to fake us out. It must have been hard, because he had to pretend that he didn't enjoy the experience. But if he was assigned to squeal about this tunnel under duress, we had to believe his distress. Otherwise, I think he could have hung tough forever. . . ."

I deliberately use words like "hard" and "hung" because they evoke rough sex, and I must plant that seed firmly before I can water it.

"You know why it was hard for him to pretend he was being tortured? Because he really liked it."

I feel Noam tensing.

"Oh, yeah."

"Shut up," he snaps.

"Oh, yeah, he really enjoyed it. In fact, he begged for more. 'Give it to me,' he begged. You should have heard those modest little gasps and yelps when . . ."—it was time to get explicit—"when Ezekiel's cock slipped in between those tight little cheeks."

"I said, shut up, Kazakov. You're a dead man."

"I may die, but I guess I can rest content knowing that Dregs has one more customer."

"What's that supposed to mean?"

I was glad to respond. It's always good to get an audience involved. "Ezekiel told me he thought he had seen you in there before, but you were always too shy to go into the basement. He felt he was doing a good deed, helping you out of the closet."

"You're lying."

"Uh-huh, uh-huh, uh-huh." I imitate the sounds of sex and thrust my pelvis forward farther with each higher-pitched, "Uh huh."

"Liar."

"Uh-huh."

"Liar!"

"Uh-huh."

We are working together now, in counterpoint, thrust and release, thrust and release, echoing the pattern of sex itself, which makes the dialogue more passionate.

"Enough!" Cyril Klein hits the brakes.

Tick. Tick. Tick.

"As long as you don't mind, I sure don't," I say calmly, while Noam continues to stew. "And I'm sure Simon doesn't. Do you, Simon?"

"Khadoury," Klein calls to the man with the timber.

I have to get Simon to speak, yet he stands without his usual strong presence. Could they have drugged him, or is he blinded, blinded, blinded by his vision of the catastrophe he is about to create and the grandeur of the throne he aims to occupy? "Simon. Simon! Or should I say Your Lordship?"

Tick. Tick. Tick.

"I don't care," Simon says.

Good enough.

"He doesn't care, Noam. He's a liberal politician on certain issues. He let me work for him and he'll let you work, too. You can be yourself and bring your boyfriends to the office and get his autograph: 'To my favorite homo.' "

"Shut up," Noam says, and comes near. I feel his breath.

" 'To my best laddie. To my slip-sliding pretty boy.' "

"Khadoury. Now."

"Oh, come on, Noam, it's not shameful. I got used to it, and so will you."

He spits in my face.

The liquid dripping down my cheek gives me ammunition. "It's not the same stuff that you licked up last night, is it, Noam?" I keep taunting, bracing myself for the attack. If I bend low without cause, Khadoury will be on me in a flash, but if I have a reason to bend low, I have a chance to shoot high.

A chance, one chance, like the one chance Gita Mamoun has to win a homeland or the one chance Simon ben Levi has to gain a kingdom. If Noam laughs and says, "I don't speak to dead men," it's over.

"Move over," he says to Khadoury.

"Go," I say with as much nonchalance as I can muster. "Get out of here. I'll see you in the gay hell, you . . ."—I have one ultimate word in reserve—"faggot."

In the space of a millisecond, three things occur. Noam comes at me, foot raised to kick me in the balls. I crouch and twist askew to take the blow on my thigh, which is still pretty painful, and then two bodies shoot upright.

Goldie lunges while I propel myself as high as possible, arms raised like the basketball players on the Hadassah court. Hey, you make do with your "disabilities." My cuffed hands hit the low ceiling and scrape against the jagged rock until they find and grip a length of conduit pipe and yank as hard as they can. I fall to the ground, holding the pipe and the wires within. Glass shatters beside me. The vault is in darkness.

Here's Simon, about to die. "What's going on?" he cries, my man the P.M., the most powerful if not most intelligent person in the Mid-east, utterly ignorant of what he has wrought and will receive.

Simon's lost. He doesn't know it yet, and I may not live to savor it, but the second the lights went out, I won. Some of my captors may escape, not all. In the dark, no one knows the way out. If my body and Gabriel's, Rafi's, and Dmitri's are found together with a few of Simon's bodyguards, his explanation for Strange Fire won't wash. Worse yet, neither Simon nor Serena nor the rest of the inner circle can see, either.

In the land of the blind, Nathan Kazakov is king. With one eye, I'd be God.

Noam screams, and a shot rings out, hits flesh, sprays as it exits. I feel droplets, an underground rain, blood. An object hits the ground with two distinct sounds, *cuh . . . chunk*, a timber, dropped by Eli Khadoury, who stood between myself and Cyril Klein. Okay.

Frantic voices collide against the walls. The place is a jigsaw of sound, one piece fitting into the next, footsteps, shouts, names, tick, tick, tick.

The first gunshot sets off a fusillade as the secret service, trained to respond, like Goldie, does so. I feel one bullet, two, clip my sides, tear through the flesh, lower left belly, upper left shoulder. They are taught to aim for the torso. Other bullets ping against the ancient walls and rebound. An agent yelps like a dog.

Goldie leaves Noam moaning on the ground and leaps for another enemy, any enemy in a circle of enemies.

"Get him out of here," someone yells, although no one knows where *he*, Simon, is.

He is on the floor . . . tick, tick, tick, five minutes maximum, and Serena is next to him, their scents coalescing as if they are making love.

"Get up," she says as she sits down, ready to meet the end with the man she adores. Serena is the first to understand that Strange Fire has fizzled, irreparably. She always could read the writing on the wall.

Time stops yet the clock ticks and I contemplate the lovers cooing amid the frenzy of their former sublunaries fleeing in any direction they can. Simon and Serena are an island of peace surrounded by storm. More shots ring out, random and idiotic unless they come from Cyril Klein's pistol, in which case they are calculated and lethal. Someone curses as he trips over the headless body of Rafi. But Simon and Serena sit, backs curved into the base of the tunnel. It's over and they both know it. Simon says, "Hey, did I ever tell you the one about the ex-politician and the bees?"

"No," Serena sighs.

In that second, I envy her. Reluctantly, I also give her credit. I used to think of Ms. Jacobi as the consummate career girl in high heels, devoted to advancement above all, a whore by any other name, smelling as sour. But Simon wasn't merely the means to Serena's end; he was the end. I wouldn't have believed it, but Serena is in love. Arab and Israeli aspirations may be crashing down, and it doesn't make a difference to her because the pollster has won the pol she desired. As Prime Minister, Simon had to return to his wife in the government mansion every night, but as King he could have made Serena his consort and delivered his famous punch line to the masses: "Screw them."

Now neither Serena nor Simon has to worry about such minor considerations as public perceptions. Love triumphs, but the lovers lose. The war is over. There is no reason to escape. This is their bunker, and they are happy.

Of course, such happiness is bound to be short-lived, but if the poet can see a world in a grain of sand and eternity in an hour, then Serena has done better than Blake and gained eternity while the grains of sand trickle through an electronic glass. Tick, tick, tick.

Not more than three minutes left, but I am mesmerized by the scene in front of me.

"Screw them," Dmitri huffs.

It is the voice of sanity. "Right," I say.

Doomed by darkness, Serena and Simon ben Levi's only reprieve from fate will be death. But if the would-be igniters of Strange Fire are resigned to immolation on their self-constructed pyre, I'm not ready to join them. I have work to do. The new Prime Minister will require my services. First I'll have to write the press release describing the tragic accident that occurred as Simon was visiting his son's latest archaeological discovery—Israel prefers martyrs to villains. But what was dynamite doing beneath Mount Moriah? Obviously—it was for excavation. I'll have to answer questions from the fourth estate, but that will be easy. They will repeat whatever I say. Have pen, will travel.

"Hurry!"

But first I have one more task underground. I have to find Gabriel amid the chaos. Noam lies howling, Goldie barks, and soldiers bounce off the walls like pinballs.

Another gunshot echoes from one of the tunnels. Klein. He'll be the first out, and prefers to be the last, too, leaving all witnesses behind. Then, before the tremors subside, before the commission that will be appointed to study the "incident" issues its report, he'll be halfway to Brazil.

Another gunshot, in a different register, replies. Gita Mamoun must have been carrying a weapon under her capacious robes. Does she shoot Klein, or does he shoot her, or are they shooting together, escaping arm in arm, another love match—love is all around me—making sure that they are the sole survivors?

Both of the shots come from the tunnel that Dmitri and I took in from the Wailing Wall. That leaves three alternatives, two of which lead farther into the labyrinth that will be sealed off in minutes. Tick. Tick. Tick.

And then I hear Gabriel. Most of the soldiers have gone in the direction that the first bolting soldier took at random, so there is less noise in the cavern, but Noam and several of the baffled and wounded abandoned on the battlefield remain. Still, the soft-spoken archaeologist's voice carries farther in its emotional urgency than the cries of physical agony. Utterly calm, he says the worst thing he possibly could, the one word I can't bear, as bad as "faggot" for Noam. I'll give you a hint. They start with the same two letters.

From across the crypt, I hear the ghostly cry of Gabriel ben Levi calling, "Father."

Worst of all, he calls out with love. Whatever Simon's selfish and malevolent intentions, Gabriel forgives him, and has to let him know. Where does this loyalty come from? Is it merely a matter of blood and loins or is it a function of the power of Simon's oratory or is it the result of his hypnotic stare, and is my inability to perceive that stare the reason why I am the only one who is immune?

Simon shouts, "Get out of here."

"No," Gabriel sobs, and crawls in our direction.

"Dammit, go!" commands the man accustomed to immediate obedience. Whether, having failed to slaughter his son, he has repented and wishes to save Gabriel, or whether he just wants to huddle with his evil muse in these precious few moments, I don't know, but, for the last time, he gives an order which, for the last—or perhaps the first—time is refused.

"Father," Gabriel moans.

Desperately, I want to scream, "Screw them all." But if Gabriel wants to die, he'll have to kill himself later. I grab him under the arm.

Following me, Dmitri takes hold of Gabriel's other arm, and together we propel him toward the intersection of three tunnels—avoiding the fourth, from which more gunshots burst. One of the three is the way Simon and company entered. That is the one that leads to an exit in the Arab Quarter.

I try to make out the residual smell of dust left over from their arrival, but the disorder has ruined any clues.

"Goldie," I call, wondering if I sound as plaintive as Gabriel did when calling his father.

The shepherd trots over to me.

"Which way, girl?"

Tick, tick, tick.

She noses toward the passage the soldiers have taken and then starts hesitantly in another direction.

"Okay," I say. "Let's rock."

I am on the right, Gabriel in the center, and Dmitri lagging on the left. The two of them carom off the walls every few steps, but I am like a bat in a cave. Call it night vision, I can sense the turns and take them smoothly. I have to, because, more clearly than the route, I can see the future. In several dozen seconds, the bomb will detonate and take down the cavern and, through spreading shock waves, most of the tunnel. Our only hope is that the charge was calibrated to produce the minimum necessary damage, but if Cyril Klein set the bomb, that hope is faint. "Run," I cry, and run as fast as Goldie's pitter-pattering paws.

We must travel several blocks. I begin to think I feel a breeze, but don't stop to make sure, when we hear a muffled boom behind us.

So much for the King of the Jews. He might as well aspire to be a Pharaoh in a pyramid.

Gabriel gasps and turns. He jerks free of me and Dmitri and starts back, but almost immediately loses his balance as the ground shakes and a section of wall gives way. We grab him and, a second later, are moving again, as smoke and hot air roll up behind us like a wave. We are either at the end of the line or not, but we continue to run, all of us tripping, stumbling, crashing into each other, suffocating on the fumes.

We hurdle struts that topple like tenpins as reverberations carry through walls and weak points collapse. Boulders and stones that might come from the hidden foundation of the Wailing Wall tumble in our path, and God knows what pandemonium there is above among the tourist stands, kiosks, and dwellings of the city.

I hit a wall, reach left, reach right, find nothing, am just about to surrender when Dmitri sighs, "Thank God."

"What?"

"Look! I mean, here!" He lifts my fingers off the craggy surface and places them inches away, on an encrusted iron rung set into the shale. More importantly, he has seen my hand easily enough to touch it unerringly. Some sort of light is filtering down.

"You first."

"Him first."

"Father," Gabriel sobs.

"Shut up," I say, and place Gabriel's hand on the rung. "Climb, you wimp."

He climbs until his feet are about even with my head, and then he pushes open a trapdoor that sucks a cloud of smoke up into the sunlight that pours down in its place. Even I can tell the difference between gray and black.

"Now you," Dmitri says.

I put my good foot onto the first rung and my cuffed hands above my head. A drop of blood thinned with sweat drips from my midsection.

"I'm right behind you." The doctor coughs and holds my waist. His hands are strong and he stands firmly on legs like tree trunks. Above us, a cluster of teenage boys and tourists and women on their way to market —the usual Jerusalem stewpot—gabs and gapes at the unexpected voyagers emerging from an unexpected rift in the surface of the earth. As soon as I join them, the greatest adventure of my life will be over, but I don't want to return to the tediousness of the office, and as for poetry, I'd rather burn the remaining copies of *Pomegranate Blossoms* than think about them one more time. Like Serena, I want something less dramatic yet more satisfying. Common as it is, I want love. I let my body sag into Dmitri's grip. Contentedly wordless, I pivot on the bottom rung, place my aching hand on his bristly neck, and face my savior. "One question, Doc?"

Smart as well as good and, to my fingers, which tease an endearing bit of hardened cheese out from his beard, beautiful, he knows the question before it is out of my mouth and says, "Don't."

"Why?"

I shouldn't ask that, because I have always claimed and always believed that I don't care why things are the way they are; I only care what they are, but I am so needy and—maybe, at last, halfway through my life, mature—so willing to be needy that I can't stop myself. "Why?" I repeat. "Or rather, why not?" I plead, though it is obvious: because of orientation, actuality, and character, because I am a faggot, because I am ugly, because I am bitter. Who in his right mind would want to hook up with me?

"To begin with, I'm much older than you."

Of course, that isn't the real answer. I shake my head. He owes me the truth.

"Besides, I met a woman."

"Met," he says, not "have," as if his "meeting" has been recent. But the only person he has met during the last week has been me. When did he find the time to date? We spent every available free moment together, searching out Strange Fire in the hospital, on the streets, underground, and at Rehov Rambam.

Noooo.

I start laughing so hard I nearly slip off the ladder, because I have always thought that that chicken soup has special powers.

"What's so funny?"

"Do I know the woman?"

"You might say that."

Jesus Christ! It all comes together. I've been blind not only to the external physical, but to the interior invisible world. That's why I couldn't understand Gabriel's filial or Serena's erotic devotion to Simon, and that's why I couldn't perceive the swirl of currents on Rehov Rambam. We, all of us, even mothers, have emotions, and some of them are reciprocated, some of the time. And me, what have I yearned for for even longer than I've lacked eyesight? Is it possible that at this stage in my life I have lost a lover and gained a father? Well, I've also lost an ear, wounded a foot, burnt a shoulder, broken a hand, and taken at least two bullets, so what's a heart anyway?

Alone, I climb up the ladder and stumble outside, into the dark day.

| | |
|---|---|
| Siri Hustvedt | *The Blindfold* |
| Hester Kaplan | *The Edge of Marriage* |
| Starling Lawrence | *Legacies* |
| Don Lee | *Yellow* |
| Bernard MacLaverty | *Cal* |
| | *Grace Notes* |
| Lisa Michaels | *Grand Ambition* |
| Lydia Minatoya | *The Strangeness of Beauty* |
| John Nichols | *The Wizard of Loneliness* |
| Roy Parvin | *In the Snow Forest* |
| Jean Rhys | *Good Morning, Midnight* |
| | *Wide Sargasso Sea* |
| Israel Rosenfield | *Freud's* Megalomania |
| Josh Russell | *Yellow Jack* |
| Kerri Sakamoto | *The Electrical Field* |
| Mary Lee Settle | *I, Roger Williams* |
| Marisa Silver | *Babe in Paradise* |
| Josef Skvorecky | *Dvorak in Love* |
| Gustaf Sobin | *The Fly-Truffler* |
| Frank Soos | *Unified Field Theory* |
| Jean Christopher Spaugh | *Something Blue* |
| Barry Unsworth | *Losing Nelson* |
| | *Morality Play* |
| | *Sacred Hunger* |
| David Foster Wallace | *Girl with Curious Hair* |
| Brad Watson | *Last Days of the Dog-Men* |
| Rafi Zabor | *The Bear Comes Home* |